All the Stars in Heaven

All the Stars in Heaven

a novel

Michele Paige Holmes

Covenant Communications, Inc.

Cover image: Boston's Skyline at Night © Lorraine Kourafas. Courtesy of iStockphoto.com

Cover design copyrighted 2009 by Covenant Communications, Inc.

Published by Covenant Communications, Inc.
American Fork, Utah

Printed in Canada
First Printing: June 2009

15 14 13 12 11 10 09   10 9 8 7 6 5 4 3 2 1

ISBN-13 978-1-59811-621-2
ISBN-10 1-59811-621-5

To all those who have found the strength to change
and the courage to stay strong.

Acknowledgments

Shortly after *Counting Stars* was accepted for publication, I eagerly began work on this manuscript, assuring my family that the process would most certainly be shorter this time around. Unfortunately I was wrong, and this story, like the last, was a long, involved process of many rewrites. My wonderful family stood by me once again, though some of them—the younger ones—were more than a little upset to discover I wasn't done with this writing business yet.

But you already wrote a book, Mom. Why would you want to write another one?

Admittedly, there were days I wondered that myself! It was during those discouraging times that my husband and children were at their most supportive. My many thanks to my daughter Carissa for being my "teenage" reader. Her honest opinion got me back on track more than a few times. And my husband turned out to be a well of ideas when it came to the suspense elements of this novel. I thank them both, along with the rest of our patient family, for hanging in there with me on this one.

As the story morphed through its various rewrite stages, several talented writers and friends were there to help me pull it together. I am grateful for their time and continued willingness to share their expertise. Jeff, Jennifer, James, and Josi—thanks for your not-so-subtle ways of letting me know which parts of the manuscript needed major work. Lynda and Stephanni, I so appreciate your input and the years we had together in our critique group. Annette, Heather, and LuAnn, thank you so much for always being just an email away, and for always being ready and willing to read—and reread—those troubled chapters. Once again, I wouldn't have a book without your generosity and talents.

Research for *All The Stars in Heaven* involved learning about and becoming very familiar with a place I'd never visited before. I am grateful to my stepfather, Jack Hansen, for his enthusiasm for this project and his help in putting me in touch with Jane A. Callahan, archivist for Harvard University Art and Museums. I thank Ms. Callahan for her help in answering my many questions about the Harvard campus and the Fogg Art Museum.

My appreciation also runs deep for those at Covenant who've been so patient and worked alongside me to get this story in print. From my first drafts and first editor, Angela Eschler, to the final copy and a new editor, Noelle Perner, I've felt so fortunate to enjoy a good working relationship with those involved in the sometimes painful process of editing. Thank you for your ideas, input, and understanding.

Finally, I feel enormous gratitude for the readers of *Counting Stars*, those many of you who took the time to let me know how much you enjoyed the story. I appreciate your feedback and personal stories. I loved hearing that you related to Jane and were, at times, moved to tears as you read. Though Jay's story is very different, I hope you enjoy it as well, and I'd love to hear from you again.

Prologue

December 1986

"Hurry up, Sarah." Grant Morgan lifted the collar of his overcoat as wind whipped through the cemetery, causing the twenty-eight-degree temperature to feel even colder. Frowning, he looked down at the little girl standing three feet in front of him with her thin sweater, short dress, and bare legs. The child wasn't shivering, wasn't moving at all, despite his attempts to get her going and this over with.

He looked around uneasily, wondering if the feeling that he was being watched was ever going to leave. He tried to shrug the worry away but, like the cold, it seemed to have seeped through his coat, through the pores of his skin, into his soul.

Another gust of near-arctic air swirled past them, stirring up the late-fallen leaves at their feet. The wind ruffled the back of the child's dress, and Grant detected the slightest movement from her—an involuntary shiver as the cold danced around her legs.

So, she is human, he observed, feeling both relief and regret at this hint of vulnerability. He'd hated that in the few hours they'd been together he'd seen nothing of the lively toddler he'd once known and no sign she remembered him from before the divorce—no possibility of any connection between this sullen girl and himself. But he also realized that a child who displayed such little emotion would be that much easier to deal with.

A corner of the Astroturf lifted in the stiff wind, revealing the cavernous hole in the ground beneath the casket. Grant watched as Sarah leaned forward, then looked back at him, her blue eyes wide with fear and . . . questions.

"I said, hurry up." He gave her a none-too-gentle push that sent her stumbling forward, her scuffed Mary Janes barely stopping at the edge of the grave. Knees shaking, she continued to clutch a single flower in her hands as she caught her balance. Her small fists were stacked over the slender stem, between two protruding thorns of the blood-red rose. She straightened with natural grace and then stood there with remarkable stillness for a child of only five years.

"Please get her out." Sarah's voice, though tiny, was calm and surprisingly full of authority for someone so small. "Roses are her favorite."

"I know," Grant snapped.

"She'll wake up when she smells this one."

Grant felt a stirring of pity. A very dangerous feeling—for both of them. Stepping forward, he plucked the rose from Sarah's hands.

"Ow!" she gasped.

"No flower is going to wake her up," Grant said as he tossed the rose on top of the casket. "Let's go." He looked down at Sarah and saw the shock on her face. She held her hands open, drops of blood welling on each, where the thorns had pricked her skin. A matching pair of tears gathered in her eyes.

He turned away and walked toward the car, feeling those hurt and betrayed eyes on him the whole time. *Other eyes might be watching too,* he reminded himself as he retrieved his keys from his pocket, opened the door, and climbed inside. A quick glance out the window told him Sarah still hadn't moved.

He started the engine, put the car in gear, and rolled down the passenger window to call to her. She didn't come after him, and he watched with growing concern as Sarah turned away from the car and threw herself across the casket, her tiny fingers trying to pry it open.

"Mommy! Mommy! Wake up, Mommy."

"Sarah," he barked. "Stop this nonsense and get in the car."

Tears tumbled down her face as she looked at him, the imploring in her eyes reaching out across the twenty feet between them to sear his heart. The pity swelled. He fought it, taking his foot off the brake to let the car idle forward.

Sarah turned back to the casket. More anguished cries came from her throat. Grant pressed his lips into a thin line as the car nudged nearer the cemetery gates. The door to the caretaker's shed was ajar, and Grant wondered if the man—or someone else—was inside watching him.

I can't just leave her.

His glance strayed to the rearview mirror as he turned the dial on the stereo, pretending to be searching for a station, pretending that he didn't care about his daughter.

The car rolled halfway through the open gate. Grant's foot edged toward the brake. He was going to have to go back and get her. He'd be swift, stern. He'd spank her and show anger. But anyone watching would still know he cared enough not to leave her behind. Anyone watching would realize they'd found his new weak link. His hand went to the gear shift as Sarah began running toward the car. Relief washed over him.

Pasting an irritated, impatient look on his face, he put the window up and waited for her.

A second later he cringed as she slipped on the gravel and fell face-first onto the road. His hand automatically gripped the door handle, but—remembering the open door of the caretaker's shed—an inner restraint stopped him before he could get out and go after her. Returning his fist to his lap, he clenched his teeth and silently counted the seconds it took Sarah to get off the ground and begin walking again.

When his nerves had just about worn thin, she reached the car then spent several seconds fumbling with the handle before her little hands found enough strength to pull the heavy door open. Again, Grant resisted the urge to lean across the seat and help. But when she climbed inside and he took in her bedraggled appearance, he wavered, reaching into his suit pocket for a hanky so she could wipe away some of the bloodied gravel embedded in her knees. He tossed the white cloth at her.

"Clean yourself up," he said gruffly.

Without looking at him, she snatched the hanky and swiped it across her face. Tugging at her thin, too-short dress, she managed to cover one of her knees. Then she realized blood was also dripping from her chin, and she pressed the handkerchief to the wound. Staying well on her side of the seat, she turned away from him and looked out the window.

The car started forward, and from the corner of his eye Grant studied Sarah's reflection in the glass. Fresh tears rolled down her cheeks, though she didn't make so much as a whimper. Her hair was in need of a good brushing, and it hung long and wispy halfway down her back. He thought perhaps tomorrow he would take her to get it cut short; it would certainly be easier to care for. But then he thought of Rachel and reconsidered. Sarah's golden hair, when washed and brushed, would no doubt be as beautiful as her mother's had been. It was comforting to know there was something in her to remind him of Rachel.

Sarah shifted on the seat, tugged her dress down again, then removed the handkerchief from her chin and placed it carefully across a four-inch tear down the front of her dress. She wiped a dirty hand across her cheeks,

drying the last of her tears, and turned to her father with a positively muti-
nous expression.

Grant nearly smiled. "Yes?"

"I'm hungry, and I want my kitty."

"I'll feed you shortly, but there will be no kittens at my house."

"My kitty . . . isn't real." Her eyes were hopeful.

"Hmm."

"I can't sleep without her."

"Too bad." Grant stopped at a light and caught the driver in the car
beside them looking at him.

Unnerved once more, Grant eased the car into the intersection when
the light turned green. The car in the other lane moved ahead and turned
three streets later. Grant headed toward the Boston University Bridge, thick
now with rush hour traffic leaving the city.

"Kitty is at Mommy's house," Sarah said.

Grant heard the desperation in her voice. "We can't ever go back there,"
he said with a note of finality.

"Why not?" Sarah demanded. "That's where I live."

"Not anymore it isn't."

"I don't want to live with you," she said.

"Yeah? Well, I don't particularly want to live with you either," Grant
lied. He'd wanted nothing more for the past two years than to have his wife
and daughter back in his life. Every time he and Rachel had tried to patch
things up, their differences became more apparent, but he'd never stopped
loving her.

And now she was dead.

"Then take me home." Sarah's voice was quiet now.

He glanced across the seat and saw her blue eyes filling with tears again.
He suddenly felt helpless. "Listen, Sarah. We can't go back there because
the police won't let us. They have to look at everything in the house and see
if they can find out why Mommy died. How about you tell me what your
kitten looked like, and we'll see if we can find you another one."

"No." Sarah shook her head and turned away from him. Her shoulders
lifted up and down in a dramatic sigh.

Grant thought he saw her lip quiver again, but she remained silent. His
daughter had his wife's coloring and features, but she wasn't schooled in how
to use her looks to her advantage. *And she never will be,* he vowed. Sarah
need never know how beautiful she was. He would keep her away from
men. He'd raise her to be strong and sensible.

What am I thinking? The safest, most practical thing would be to ship her off to a secure boarding school—as far away from him as possible. As he drove, he mulled this over—the pros heavily outweighing the cons—and made up his mind to do just that. For the remainder of the drive he studiously ignored her, focusing instead on his recent job change to the small police department in Summerfield. It was his chance to start over. To keep things honest, simple.

Pulling into the driveway, he cut the engine and looked over at Sarah. Her eyes were closed, and she was curled up in a ball on the seat. Grant got out of the car, made a point of slamming his door, and walked to the box at the curb to retrieve his mail. He shuffled through the envelopes as he came back up the drive, then rapped his knuckles against the car window. Sarah didn't stir.

So much for not being able to sleep without Kitty.

He stuck the mail in his coat pocket, opened the door, and carefully lifted Sarah in his arms. She stirred for a second, turning her face into his chest.

He froze, a sudden déjà vu overtaking his senses. She weighed next to nothing and still had that same little-girl smell he remembered. It seemed just yesterday he'd cradled her like this when she was a baby.

Setting his lips in a stern line, he walked toward the house, his eyes darting habitually to survey his surroundings. He opened the front door, kicked it shut behind him, and carried her to the couch. He placed a pillow beneath her head and covered her with a blanket, tucking her slender arms underneath.

Stepping back, he watched as her tiny chest rose in a shuddering breath. Her lips puckered for a brief moment, and Grant wondered if she was having a bad dream. Something much more than pity stirred deep inside him, causing his throat to constrict. Leaning forward, he placed a gentle kiss on her forehead.

"It'll be all right, Sarah," he whispered, praying it would because he suddenly knew he couldn't send her away—just as he knew he already loved his little girl even more than he had once loved her mother.

Part One
Falling Hard

Chapter One

September 2005

"Pick any one you want," Archer encouraged, nodding toward the stage, where the women of the Harvard Ballet Troupe were rehearsing. "There's Brenda, the tall blond in the middle, or Katy, the one with—"

"Is that why you asked me to meet you here?" Jay interrupted. "I *don't* want, so just forget it." He slouched lower in his seat.

"You must be blind." Archer waved a hand in front of Jay's face. "I'm offering you the best of Harvard right here—beautiful, talented women, and you won't even consider it."

Jay looked at his watch, then fished his motorcycle keys from his pocket. "I'm going to the library. I'll leave the bike for you and Trish." He bent over, reaching for his backpack.

"No way." Archer grabbed the pack and set it down a few seats away, out of Jay's reach. "You've hit the year mark. You've got to snap out of this. Besides, I promised Trish we'd double to Homecoming in the Yard, so you'd better pick a girl today. Otherwise all the good ones will be taken."

Jay scowled. "You shouldn't have promised Trish anything. The last thing I want to do is spend the evening riding a mechanical bull or eating pie with a bunch of freshmen. Anyway, I'm sure she'd rather have a night alone with you." The music for the ballet started, and he leaned his head back, brushing his hair off his collar. He'd been letting it grow since June— when he'd attended Jane's graduation. Turning into a typical suit hadn't been enough to win her, and as far as he was concerned, there wasn't any other woman worth impressing.

It wasn't that he hadn't tried to find someone. In an odd sort of way, seeing Jane with her husband had encouraged him to find a woman he cared for as much, someone he could build a life with. But the half dozen or so dates he'd had over the summer had completely turned him off. He hadn't found anyone who could scratch the surface of Jane's compassionate and caring nature. And he certainly didn't think he'd find someone here today—in Harvard's famed ballet troupe.

Archer elbowed him. "You're not even watching the rehearsal. I mean, come on, check out their legs. Do you have any idea how flexible ballet dancers are? You should see—"

"No thanks," Jay said, cutting him off.

"You're missing out on life," Archer said. "If I'd have known what a stuffy old law student you are . . ." He turned his attention back to the stage.

Jay glanced at his backpack a few seats away and decided it wasn't worth a scene or struggle to try and get it. Instead of going to the library, he'd close his eyes and indulge in a nap. The lights were low, the music soothing. His body relaxed and his eyelids grew heavy as the melody lulled him into a peaceful, much-needed rest.

Archer elbowed Jay again. "Sit up and at least pretend you've been watching,"

Jay opened his eyes, glanced at his watch, and saw that twenty minutes had passed and the dancers were taking a break. Trish waved as she left the stage and headed down the aisle toward them, followed by a gaggle of tutued dancers.

Jay groaned.

"Hey, Arch," Trish called a minute later, bending over the row of seats in front of them. She leaned close, giving Archer a juicy kiss.

"Hi, Archibald," a girl behind her said.

Jay fought back a grin as he caught his roommate's scowl. Archer hated this slander of his name—who wouldn't? But it came with the territory. Archer's dad—a comics enthusiast—had named him after his favorite character, Archie. But when Archer was three years old, he'd developed his own enthusiasm—for the movie and stories of Robin Hood. Since then he'd been telling everyone he was an archer, and the name had stuck—though the brunette standing beside Trish obviously thought Archi*bald* a bit more appropriate. *Poor guy,* Jay thought. Archer *was* getting a little thin on top.

"Jay, I'd like you to meet Candice. And this is . . ." Archer looked to Trish for help.

"Melanie," Trish supplied, winking at Jay. "She's a political science major. You two might have a lot to talk about."

"Oh?" Melanie asked, raising thin eyebrows.

"Jay's a third-year law student," Trish said.

"Ooh," the girls chorused.

"I'm planning to work for the government," Jay said. "You know, a simple life of public service. Hopefully it'll be enough to pay off my thousands of dollars in student loans." *Gotcha,* he thought, noting several crestfallen faces. Archer's was one of them.

Nice, he mouthed to Jay.

Jay shrugged and shot him an innocent *what'd-I-do* look.

"We've only got a few minutes for break," Trish said as the other dancers filed past her toward the exit. "Wanna come with me to get a drink, Archer?" She ran her tongue over her lips seductively.

Jay looked away, disgusted. He and Jane never would have behaved like that. No sooner had the thought come than he remembered the day, so many years ago now—so why couldn't he forget it?—when he'd taken Jane's face in his hands and kissed her in the hall at work. She'd been fired from her internship because of that kiss, and he'd almost lost his spot in the rehab program. But at the time, that one kiss had seemed worth the risk. Jay looked at Archer and Trish as they walked away, considering for the first time that maybe they really were in love.

Rising from his seat, Jay leaned over and grabbed his backpack. He put one strap over his shoulder as the piano started playing again—though this time it wasn't the ballet accompaniment he heard. Shrugging the strap onto his other shoulder, Jay looked toward the stage and saw that it was still empty.

The music continued as Jay made his way toward the aisle. The melody was haunting, unfamiliar . . . beautiful. Strangely moved by the notes, Jay hesitated at the end of the row, then removed his pack and sat down to listen. His classes were over for the day, and there really wasn't any rush to get to the library. If only Archer had brought him to a concert rehearsal instead of ballet practice, Jay probably wouldn't have balked at staying. Music had always been and continued to be the one sure love of his life. And he would have bet money that the person on the other side of the piano felt the same way.

Jay closed his eyes, feeling the emotion as the piece hit a crescendo, then grew soft once more. He listened intently, noting the key change a few moments later as the music built again in fervor. He leaned into the aisle, trying to catch a glimpse of the pianist, but the instrument was angled such that he couldn't see who was behind it. He imagined the person must be bent over the piano, as he couldn't see the top of anyone's head.

"You're still here," Archer said, coming up behind him.

"Shh." Jay held a finger to his lips and nodded toward the front of the auditorium.

"What?" Archer asked, stepping over Jay to get to the seat next to him. "Are you deep in thought, contemplating who you want to take to Homecoming?"

Jay didn't reply but listened as the music trailed off into a few last, lingering notes. He heard the foot pedal release, and he stood. "I want to meet the pianist."

"Tell me you're not going to ask *her* out," Archer said.

So it's a woman. Jay felt the stir of curiosity. "Behind that piano is a very passionate female."

Archer shrugged. "Suit yourself then, but I don't think Trish will want to double with her."

"I didn't say *date,*" Jay whispered. "I said *meet.*" Though as nervous as he suddenly felt, he might as well have been going on a date. He made his way down the aisle, trying to think of a good pickup line. Reaching the piano, he leaned over it, looking at the top of a blond head.

"Do you take requests?"

The woman looked up, and Jay could see he'd startled her. She held a pencil in her hand, and Jay glanced at the clipboard resting on the keys. Notes sprawled across staff paper that Jay could tell had been erased many times.

"I wondered if you wrote it," he said. "It was beautiful—you play beautifully."

"Thank you." Her voice was quiet. Behind oversized glasses, her blue eyes darted around nervously.

"My name is Jay." He held out his hand as his eyes quickly scanned the name typed at the top of the paper—*Sarah Morgan.* "I play the—" Someone tapped him on the shoulder. Thinking it was Archer, Jay turned around as the woman gasped.

A fist met his left eye, and he staggered backward. A second blow followed the first, and this time Jay went down, blackness overtaking him.

Chapter Two

Jay lay back on the sofa, a frozen burrito pressed to his face. The rolled, unyielding tortilla was a poor choice for a compress, and he supposed a steak or bag of frozen peas would have worked better. Too bad steak didn't figure into his budget, and he couldn't stand frozen vegetables. It was one of the strange carryovers from childhood. His father, never quite having grasped the concept of the refrigerator, had stopped by Pike Place Market nearly every evening on the way home from work. Fresh fruit and vegetables had supplemented their otherwise unhealthy diet of pizza, macaroni and cheese, and the like. To this day, Jay found he couldn't eat any type of produce frozen or from a can.

The apartment door banged open, and he cracked an eyelid. One of his roommates, Charlie, staggered in, an armload of books weighing him down. He tossed them on the coffee table and glanced over at Jay.

"Man, what'd you do to your face?"

Archer looked up from one of two computers cluttering the narrow living room. "His choice in women hasn't improved, that's what."

"A *woman* did *that?*" Charlie asked, bending closer for a better look.

"Hardly," Jay said, irritated.

"He picked another *un*-available female," Archer explained. "And her boyfriend objected."

"No kidding." Charlie walked toward the kitchen. "Must've been some woman. Hope she was worth it. Looks painful."

"It is," Jay grumbled, closing his eyes and adjusting the burrito to another spot on his face, feeling frustrated again that both the pianist and the guy with the fist had taken off by the time he'd come to.

"I'd say your chances for a date this Friday are nil," Archer said. "I might've gotten one of Trish's friends to go with you, but that was before your face looked like a bloated fish and you told them you're planning to be a pauper all your life."

Jay didn't bother responding. He could only feel relieved he hadn't been cornered into wasting money on a date he didn't care about. Unfortunately, Archer wasn't ready to let it go. He rose from his chair and stood by Jay.

"Why do you want to be an attorney anyway?"

Jay shrugged and found even that painful. Whoever had hit him had done a thorough job.

Archer persisted. "I mean, law school is a ton of work. You never get to go out and have any fun. So I figure you've got to want the car and the house, the—"

"I want to help people," Jay said.

"Yeah, whatever." Archer walked to the end of the eight-foot-long, seventies-era, orange plush couch and sat down. "Tell the truth . . . You want to be the guy on television—the one who will help you get a million bucks when someone chips a little paint off your car."

Jay gave a disgusted grunt. That wasn't what he wanted at all, but he figured Archer was too shallow to catch on. Jay knew exactly the type of clients he hoped he'd have. Teens and twenty-somethings mostly, people who'd ended up on the wrong side of the law, not necessarily because they were bad but because of the circumstances in their lives.

From his own experience he knew that the courts were full of kids with druggie parents or parents in jail or any number of other things that led kids to commit crimes. They needed legal representation. They needed someone to believe in them and help them get on a better track. Jay supposed that much of how he imagined helping was really the work of a counselor or therapist, but people in trouble needed lawyers too. He would be a part of a team that gave people a second chance—much like he'd been given.

Archer thumped Jay's foot. "You're not still thinking about that piano player?"

"No," Jay said, repositioning the rapidly thawing burrito.

"Then what?" Archer asked. "You've got that faraway look . . . No!" He smacked his forehead with his palm. "Tell me you're not still thinking of that girl in Seattle." Without giving Jay a chance to deny it, Archer rose from the couch and went into the bedroom.

A few minutes later he was back—the strong scent of cologne announcing his presence before Jay had opened his eyes to see who was in the room.

Archer popped a disc into the CD player. "I'm going to Trish's. She's cooking me dinner, then we're going to rent a movie. During the movie she'll give me a back rub . . ." A look of bliss crossed Archer's face. "I'm getting fed and loved, while you're here with a black eye—all because you can't get over the woman who dumped you oh . . . a *year* ago. Think about that tonight while you listen to this, and maybe next time old Arch offers to fix you up, you'll try harder." He grabbed his jacket from the back of a chair and headed toward the front door as the first strains of Maroon Five's "She Will Be Loved" came through the speakers.

"Archer," Jay yelled. He tried to sit up but moved too quickly. A searing pain shot through his head. "Turn it off." The CD *Songs About Jane* that he'd once listened to almost nonstop was the one he now—for obvious reasons—couldn't stand.

"See ya," Archer said with a wave of his hand.

Jay managed to get to a sitting position with both feet on the floor. "I'll kill you if you don't come back and turn that off."

Their other roommate, Mike, walked out of the kitchen, a sandwich in his hand. "If he kills you, Arch, can I have that half carton of rocky road you left in the freezer?"

"What's going on?" Charlie asked, coming into the room.

"Jay's making idle threats," Archer said. "And don't you dare touch my ice cream, Mike."

Charlie frowned in the direction of the blaring speakers. "Mrs. Larson is gonna be on our case again if you don't turn that thing down. You know how stuff carries through the floor."

"The old bag isn't home right now," Archer said. "So don't touch the volume. It's for Jay's own good." He opened the door and stepped out into the hall.

Jay hucked the burrito at the power button on the stereo and missed.

* * *

Sarah sat cross-legged on her bed, arms wrapped around her, stomach in knots. She stared at the clock on the wall, a black plastic cat clock she hated. The slanted eyes watched her knowingly, and the tail that counted seconds switched methodically back and forth, drumming the words *trou-ble, trou-ble, you're in trou-ble* into her head. She didn't need any reminders. After the incident at rehearsal, a confrontation with her father was inevitable.

At exactly five-fifteen her door opened. She didn't bother looking up, but tried instead to swallow the lump of fear that had formed in her throat.

"Who is he?" her father demanded.

"No one, Dad."

"Look at me, Sarah."

She obeyed, tilting her face up to look at her father. He filled the door-frame, his dark police uniform bespeaking authority and sharply contrasting with her pink walls. He hadn't taken his belt off yet, and the gun she despised hung at his hip. The badge on his shirt—the one proclaiming he was chief, the best of the best here in little Summerfield—caught the light from her floor lamp.

"I've never seen him before today, and after what Carl did, I'm sure I never will again." The thought made her sad.

"You should be grateful Carl was there."

"*Grateful?*" Sarah said, then instantly wished she could recall the word. Her father took a step into the room.

Knowing the harm was already done, she plunged on. "Why does Carl have to tail me on campus? I can understand why you asked him to keep an eye on me when I'm working, but—"

"I *always* know what you're doing, Sarah." Her father came closer, towering over the bed. "You know it's for your protection."

Protection from what? she wanted to scream. Carl scared her more than anything. She felt her fingers digging into her sides.

"I hear of theft, rapes, even abductions. Besides, do you know what the percentages are for drug use on university campuses?" Grant sat down on the end of the bed. He lowered his voice. "I don't want you to end up like your mother. I want to keep my little girl safe."

Sarah looked over at him. "I *won't* end up like Mom. If you would only trust me." She chanced a look into his eyes for any sign of softening. "I want to have a life," she added quietly.

He gave her a hurt look. "You have one. You have a home, a father who takes care of you, a good job in law enforcement, and you're getting a fine education."

"And I appreciate those things," Sarah said. *Except for the job.* "But no other girl my age has a bodyguard like I do." *Not that I know any other girls.* She'd spent kindergarten through twelfth grade attending a parochial school several miles from her home, so she'd never had a chance to interact with the neighborhood children. Her father had made sure of that, keeping her indoors when she wasn't at school, and telling anyone who had seen her and ventured by that she was too ill to play outside or have other children over.

At school, friendships were not easily formed either, as the rules were strict and the curriculum rigorous. Her elementary, middle, and high school years melted together in a blur of lined-up girls, all dressed in matching plaid, knee socks, and polished black shoes. There had been little chance for talking between classes, and no opportunity at all while sitting at their individual desks in orderly rows.

During recess, jump ropes turned, and balls and secrets were passed back and forth, but somehow Sarah missed out on that too, having been labeled "that quiet, shy girl" from a very young age. Ironically, she was not that quiet but had a voice that could carry across the chapel, as Miss Amelia had discovered the year Sarah was in the fourth grade and finally old enough to participate in the school choir.

Remembering that day and the weeks, months, and years that followed with Miss Amelia as her music teacher, Sarah felt happiness and gratitude. Friends would have been nice, but music was a fine substitute and had given her life some purpose.

But now she was restless again. In the years since high school, she'd observed everyone her age moving out and on with their lives. Everyone but her. She looked up at her father again.

"I'm not your little girl anymore. I'm almost twenty-four. I ought to be out on my own. If you're worried, there's campus housing with chaperones or—"

"Impossible." Grant's stern tone returned. "We've had this discussion before, and if you continue to bring it up, I may change my mind about school altogether. Your tuition is expensive enough. We don't need to waste money on a dorm room when you can commute from home." He rose from the bed, his hand going to the holster at his hip. "Most young ladies don't have a police chief for a father. They don't understand what's going on in the world like I do. I don't expect you to understand it either, but I need you to respect my wishes and remember what happened to your mother."

If only I could. More than anything Sarah wished she could remember her mother—and understand what had possessed her to marry such a man.

Instead Sarah uttered a meek, "Yes, Dad." She was desperate to move out, desperate to leave this bleak house and her controlling father, but she wouldn't do that at the expense of her education. She'd waited five long years after high school before her father allowed her to attend the university and pursue the career she wanted. Now that she was finally there, she would continue to wait, to bide her time and somehow endure her situation for a few more years. Though *a few more years* seemed like eternity when she thought about it.

"All right then. No more of this nonsense." Her father turned and walked away. Reaching the doorway, he paused and looked back. "You're certain you don't know the man who came up to you today?"

"I don't," she answered truthfully.

"Keep it that way." The door clicked shut behind her, and Sarah let out the breath she'd been holding. She lay back on the bed, her eyes closed.

I don't know him. I won't ever know him. But I do know his name—Jay—and he thinks I play beautifully.

Chapter Three

Jay stepped outside, leaving behind Langdell and three tedious hours in the law library. Squinting against the afternoon sun, he started down the steps, then paused a moment, adjusting his backpack and appreciating the scenery. The crisp October air had set the trees to changing, and the historic campus looked every bit as enchanting and inspiring as he'd always imagined it. Students hurried down paths, the ivy-covered buildings beckoning them to enter and learn. It was one of those surreal moments where he almost felt the need to pinch himself. Even with his first two years behind him, he was still in awe that he was really here—Harvard.

He'd always wished he could've sat in on the admissions review when his application was discussed. He was certain it hadn't received an automatic stamp of approval. Straight A's, an LSAT score of 179, and well-done essay aside, Jay knew he didn't fit the typical Harvard Law student profile. But someone had shown compassion, and the foolish mistakes of his youth had been forgiven. When it came time for his interview, the only questions that had come up about his criminal past had been those directed toward how he might use his experience on the wrong side of the law to be a better attorney. That was exactly his plan, and he'd been thrilled someone higher up actually seemed to grasp it.

So here he was—six years and a long way since he'd seen the inside of a lockdown rehab facility. And he was grateful. A smile on his lips, Jay headed toward Widener Library and its wealth of books. The weekend stretched before him, and in between work and studying, he wanted something he could relax with. A good biography seemed just the thing.

* * *

Sarah reached a hand under her glasses and rubbed her aching eyes. She was tired enough that even the hard library table looked inviting, and she was sorely tempted to lay her head down for a few minutes' rest. Only a month into the semester, she could tell that five hours of sleep a night wasn't enough. If only she didn't have to work so late. If only her father understood how much her education meant to her. If only . . .

She redirected her focus to the text in front of her, *The Polish Music Journal,* Volume 5, Number 1, Summer 2002. If she could gather at least some of her research this afternoon, she could begin writing her paper at home this weekend—when she wasn't allowed to go anywhere.

"You done yet?" Carl tossed a recent copy of *Auto Trader* aside, raised his hands above his head, stretching, and stood.

"Not even close," Sarah said, trying to keep her attention focused on the page in front of her. She glanced at the car magazine. *Thinking of stealing a car again, Carl?* Why her father thought he could trust his nephew was beyond her.

"Too bad." Carl reached across the table and flipped her book shut. "Let's go."

She looked up at him, eyes pleading. "I can't. I don't have nearly enough information."

"So?" He shrugged. "Take the books with you. You got a card, don't you?"

"Yes, but—"

"No buts. I want to eat. If we go now, you can fix me a steak before your dad gets home."

Sarah continued to stare at him, the pleading in her eyes replaced by something between fear and anger. "If I flunk out of Harvard, Dad will be upset about all the money he spent." Her voice belied any emotion. "And if I don't spend enough time in the library . . ."

Carl bent over, his face nearing hers. "Take—the—books—*with*—you." He spoke loudly enough that three girls sitting at the next table looked at him.

"They're periodicals," Sarah whispered. Her face heated with humiliation.

Carl shrugged. "I don't care what they—"

"Reference books," she said. "They can't be checked out."

Understanding dawned on his face. "You want me to sneak 'em?" He held open his acid-wash jean jacket, revealing a particularly obnoxious t-shirt of a woman with excessive cleavage. "I could put them in here." He reached for a book.

"No!" Sarah answered louder than she should have. She pushed the book out of Carl's reach. "If you want to help, then take these two—" She lifted two other open periodicals and handed them to him. "And go copy these pages for me."

He looked skeptical. "What're you going to do while I'm gone?"

"Finish my notes from this article." Sarah had already opened the journal again and was moving her finger down the page, studying the melodies she'd been comparing.

Carl stayed put, face disgruntled as he watched her for another minute. Then his stomach growled and, as if reminded of his hunger, he grabbed Sarah's wallet from her backpack on the table and stalked off in search of the nearest copy machine.

She sighed with relief and continued working.

* * *

Jay stared through the space in the bookshelf, undecided. It seemed a little too fortuitous that he'd run into the mysterious pianist again—not quite two weeks after their first, *brief,* encounter. His face no longer felt tender, but the melody she'd played still echoed through his mind. He watched her now as she toyed with a strand of hair that had escaped the braid trailing down her back. She was bent over, deep in study, and Jay's curiosity grew. Surely the punches he'd taken last time earned him the right to talk to her—or at least the right to an explanation.

After a few seconds, he made an impulse decision and hurried down the row of books, following the guy she'd given the periodicals to, until he'd reached the three-person line at the copier. Judging by the volumes each person held in his hands, Jay decided he would have at least a few minutes to talk to Sarah before her boyfriend—*the guy who hit me?*—returned. Jay hurried toward her, then slowed as he came to the table.

"Hi again." He slid into the chair across from her.

She raised her head, blue eyes widening as she took in his face.

"I see you remember me." Jay touched his finger to below his eye. "I've still got the shadow of the bruises your boyfriend gave me." He was pretty certain the black circles under his eyes had more to do with the lack of sleep than anything else—between late nights playing at the club, his internship, and his heavy class load, he'd pulled a couple of all-nighters already this semester. But he didn't tell her that. "Nearly broke my nose too."

"I am *so* sorry." She held a hand to her mouth.

"Really?" Jay raised an eyebrow. She sounded genuinely distressed. "Do me one favor then. I'm considering a thesis on what women are attracted to in men, and so far I'm not doing too well in my research. Everything I try goes all wrong." He touched his face again. "Case in point. Anyway, tell me what you see in that guy." Jay nodded in the direction her friend had walked.

"*See* in him?" she asked, clearly appalled. "The less I see him, the better." At Jay's confused look, her lips formed a tentative smile. "Carl is my cousin."

Jay returned her smile as he leaned forward. "A bit protective, isn't he?"

Sarah nodded. "It's my dad—his idea, I mean. It's my first time attending a big university, and he worries a lot."

"You're a freshman?" Jay asked. He would've guessed she was a few years older, but maybe it was the old-fashioned glasses and way she wore her hair.

"Yes, but I'm starting kind of late." She looked over her shoulder, her nervousness apparent. "You should probably go. I'd hate to see you get another black eye."

"Ouch." Jay put a hand over his heart and frowned. "You think I'm *that* weak, huh? Guess I'd better add a weight-lifting course next semester. Don't worry, though. Your cousin had unfair advantage last time. Trust me, it won't happen again."

Sarah bit her lip as she continued to look around.

"What's your major?" Jay persisted, emboldened by his interest.

"Bachelor of arts," she answered, offering no details.

"Emphasis in music, I hope?" he asked. "You're very talented."

"Thank you." The hint of a smile returned.

It changed her whole face, and Jay was pleased she could accept a real compliment. So many of the women he'd dated played ridiculous conversation games.

She looked over her shoulder again. "I'm actually sort of a double major. It's a five-year program, and when I'm done, along with my bachelor's from Harvard, I'll have a master's of music from New England Conservatory."

Jay whistled. "That's more like it. What are you studying right now?"

She glanced down. "Oh, it's nothing—just for a paper. You wouldn't be interested."

"Try me," Jay said. He caught her gaze and held it.

She didn't move for several seconds, then blinked rapidly, turning aside and adjusting her glasses. "It's an article about Chopin and Maria Sqymanowska. Their music was quite similar, leading the author to believe they must have known each other." She kept her eyes averted.

"Go on," he encouraged, far more intrigued by her than the article.

"There isn't any proof they ever even met, but if you compare their compositions . . ." She slid the book closer to him. "It's quite fascinating to note the similarities."

Jay glanced at the pages and soon saw what she had discovered. The two compositions *were* alike. He traced his finger along the bar line for a couple of measures, internally playing the melody. His gaze returned to Sarah.

A blush crept up her face. "I'm boring you." She started to pull the journal away, but he reached out, his fingers brushing hers.

"You're not," he insisted. That she was so interested in music was only a bonus, as far as he was concerned. "I'm a musician too. I think it's great you get to study what you love. For me it's a hobby I have to squeeze in whenever." *How long has it been,* he wondered idly, *since I've had a meaningful conversation with a woman?* "Tell me more about your research," he coaxed.

She hesitated, then spoke fast, sounding flustered. "It's about musicians of the 1800s and the influences that helped shape their compositions. I'm focusing on Chopin and the pieces he wrote for dances."

"And you play for the ballet . . ." Jay studied her. "Is Chopin your favorite composer?"

"One of them." She seemed surprised at his question.

"I'm a Mozart man myself," Jay said, showing her the biography he'd selected earlier. "Though I must confess my tastes vary greatly and I appreciate good, hard, classic rock."

"I actually don't follow rock that much—at all," Sarah confessed.

"At *all?*" His curiosity was growing by the minute, though she was—so far, anyway—the complete opposite of every girl he'd taken out in the last year. Maybe that was why he liked her. "I'd be happy to introduce you to some of the greats. You could consider it a well-rounding of your musical education." He gave her a hopeful smile.

She ignored his invitation and twisted in her seat to look around again. The lines of worry returned. "Please. You really should go."

"Okay." Jay held up his hands. "I'll go. But only because I want you to finish the notes for your paper." He stood and walked around to her side of the table.

She tilted her head up, meeting his gaze once more. Behind her glasses, her eyes were a clear, unreadable blue.

"I'd love to hear you play again. Do you think that's possible?"

"I don't know." Her voice was unsure, but the corners of her mouth tilted upwards.

"Okay then," he said, grinning. "That's the first positive step in my research, because 'I don't know' definitely supersedes plain old 'no.' I'll look forward to seeing you again and hope for a 'maybe' next time. See you around, Sarah." He gave a casual wave and forced himself to leave the table, disappearing in the stacks.

When he'd walked along a few aisles, Jay turned around. He waited a couple of minutes and watched as Carl, *the cousin,* returned and Sarah gathered her things.

It didn't take much to convince Jay that cousin status wasn't what Carl had in mind. *What is he? A third cousin once removed or something?* Jay wondered as Carl put his arm around Sarah's shoulders. She shrugged it off and hurried ahead of him. The predatory look that crossed Carl's face made Jay's stomach churn. Before Jay realized what he was doing, he'd started following. They were heading to the elevator. Realizing he couldn't get on with them, Jay hurried to the stairs and ran down to the main floor. He waited there, standing inconspicuously—he hoped—behind a rotating book rack.

A couple of minutes later he saw them again and once more followed at a distance. They left the building, and Jay started after them, but stopped abruptly as the alarm went off. He'd forgotten all about his book. Whirling around, he headed to the checkout desk, hoping that neither Sarah nor her creepy cousin had seen him.

Chapter Four

Sarah waited for the bus to leave and any passengers to disperse before stepping out of the alley where Carl had left her and beginning the walk to the park, her three-inch stilettos clicking a steady rhythm. The shoes were miserable, slanting her foot at an absurd angle and forcing her toes into an impossibly narrow point. She hated heels, but at least, after nearly two years and who knew how many setups, she'd mastered walking in them—almost. In this neighborhood, the cracked, uneven sidewalks were treacherous. And there was nothing like falling facedown on the cement to blow one's cover. She stepped cautiously as she covered the longest two blocks of her life.

She reached the rundown park, the broken concrete walkway taking her past the ancient brick bathrooms, known as "the office," where numerous drug deals were rumored to go down. She'd seen more than a few herself. Peeling metal doors hung loose on their hinges, and only one of the dim overhead lights flickered on in the early dusk. A man left the bathroom, rolling down his sleeve as he walked. Sarah looked away. It wasn't her job to get involved there, though she still didn't understand why the Summerfield Police Department didn't go after those guys as well. It seemed to her that if there were fewer buyers in the picture, the sellers would start hurting too.

Making her way across the matted, patchy grass, Sarah headed for the bench where her own deal was to take place. Relieved to find it empty, she sat, tugging her skirt as low as it would go—still a good five inches above her knees—and took a compact from her oversized purse. Opening it, she looked in the mirror, checking the application of her fire-red lipstick.

"Hi, gorgeous."

Sarah jumped at the unexpected voice and the face behind her in the mirror. The compact fell to the ground, shattering.

"Seven years' bad luck," Carl whispered in her ear. Standing, he walked around the bench, kicking the pieces of glass out of the way.

"What are you doing?" Sarah whispered fiercely. "You're not supposed to be anywhere near me."

Carl shrugged and sat on the bench beside her. "Why not? Seems pretty natural that a hot-looking chick like yourself would attract some attention."

"Dad will kill us both if we blow this. What if Preece sees you and takes off?"

"Don't worry so much, sweetheart," Carl drawled. He leaned close to kiss her on the cheek, but Sarah turned her face away. He chuckled. "I just wanted you to know that I'm here and you're safe."

"I'll feel safer if you leave."

"Suit yourself. Remember—I'm watching." He gave her bare knee a squeeze then stood and continued down the path.

Unnerved, Sarah shivered, rubbing her arms. The night was chilly, and she dreaded the coming winter. *Why can't more deals go down indoors?* She frowned at the absurd thought. *Why can't there just be less deals, less drugs, less criminals?* She sighed as she took the latest issue of *People* from her bag, pretending to read, as if she cared about—or even recognized—any of the celebrities in the articles.

The minutes ticked by slowly. She glanced at her watch. Two minutes late, then four, then six. *Great.* Nothing put her father in a worse mood than when she came home empty-handed. Rules were, she had to wait a full thirty minutes past the meeting time, so she refocused her attention on the magazine, reading about movies she'd never see, studying fashions her father would never let her wear. He insisted, for safety reasons of course—it was *always* about safety—that she dress as plainly as possible during her normal life so as not to draw attention to herself.

As if her life were anything close to normal.

"It would be a nightmare," he'd said on more than one occasion, "if someone you met working undercover recognized you in real life."

Not likely. Sarah thought of her outdated wardrobe—mostly pants she'd become too tall for in high school, and plain, collared shirts, many of them pink because her father had some absurd idea that's what girls should wear. And her 1980s-style oversized glasses, her lack of makeup, and her straight, long blond hair were a far cry from the cat's-eye glasses, dark hair, and overly made-up face of the woman she pretended to be tonight. She sighed inwardly, hating both images and longing for the day when she could be who she wanted.

It was too dark to even pretend to read now, so she closed the magazine and stuck it in her purse. She shifted positions on the bench and leaned her head back, looking up through leafless branches to the night sky. A lone star shone in the distance, and Sarah couldn't help the slight smile that formed on her lips.

The first star of the evening. A wishing star.

Someone long ago—her mother, she liked to think—had told her that myth, and she still believed it, if only a little.

"Star light, star bright," she whispered. "First star I see tonight. I wish . . ." What *did* she wish? That Preece wouldn't show, and she wouldn't have to live through the terror of meeting with him again? Yes, except that would mean disappointing and angering her father. Maybe she should wish that Preece wouldn't come, but his elusive boss, Eddie Martin, would, so her father could shut down Martin's operation once and for all. Maybe then she could get a different job, something safe, something she wanted to do.

As if in answer to her half-wish, a man approached the bench and sat down beside her.

Without looking over she knew that it wasn't Preece. This guy was shorter and stockier than the tall, lean, twenty-something man she'd bought from before. Disappointment, quickly followed by fear, knotted her stomach. Heart pounding, she rummaged through her purse as she went through the mental steps of what she needed to do next.

Another minute passed before she turned to the stranger. *A replacement? Martin himself?* She couldn't be certain. He didn't fit the profile of the typical person she bought from. He looked older, with plenty of wrinkles and a nearly bald head, and if he was a pusher she'd bet he wasn't a user. His face and arms were unmarked, and his steel gray eyes were clear.

She pulled an unopened package of cigarettes from her purse and gave him the password. "Got a light?"

He hesitated, and she held her breath while he took in her appearance, from her black, frizzy wig and overdone makeup to her too-tight clothing and awful shoes.

"I got more 'n that," he finally said, giving her a lopsided grin.

Sarah felt her skin crawl, but she forced herself to return his smile. "Let's see."

She scooted closer. He glanced at the walkway, then reached into his jacket, extracting a tiny package wrapped in brown paper. He held it out to her.

Pouting, she took it. "That's *all?*" She unwrapped the paper and held the plastic bag up, examining the contents.

"Put that away." He slapped his hand over hers. "There might be cops around."

"Really?" Sarah's eyes widened, and she gave him what she hoped was a look of shocked innocence. "I've never had no trouble in this park before."

"I bet," he said sarcastically. "You got the money?"

"You got the rest?" she shot back. "We had an agreement, and this"—she looked down at the bag—"ain't nothing but a sample."

"Agreement," he scoffed. His gray eyes stared at her. "That's all, babe, but it's pure. Best you can get around here." He held his jacket open, patting the empty pockets.

Sarah hesitated, rolling the bag around in the palm of her hand. It wasn't much. Her father wasn't interested in busting small-time dealers. He wanted her to catch the professionals, those with ties to bulk supplies of ephedrine. Still, if she backed down now, she might get herself in trouble. She sensed the new guy testing her.

"All right," she said at last. "It better be good. I gotta share with my man." Reaching a practiced hand down the front of her shirt she removed just one of four rolls of bills secured with a rubber band. "Count it if you'd like." She slapped the cash into his hand.

He unrolled the rubber band and thumbed through the bills. "Been a pleasure," he murmured, shoving the money in his pocket. He gave her a once-over as he stood. "Maybe I'll be seeing you again. Tell your old man I said hi."

Sarah watched as he disappeared in the same direction Carl had gone. Fingers trembling, as they always did as soon as a job was finished, she dropped the bag full of meth crystals into her purse. A sense of foreboding washed over her as she predicted her father's fury. Even if the replacement could be linked back to Martin, she hadn't bought enough to do any good. For an arrest and charges to hold over into real jail time, a seller had to either be within three blocks of a school zone or have substantially more than a few hits in his possession. The measly bag she'd bought today wasn't sufficient evidence for that kind of conviction.

It will be okay, she told herself as she gathered her things and stood. But she knew it wouldn't. No matter what she did, it was never enough to win her father's approval.

And she was tired of trying.

* * *

Grant started in on her as soon as she walked through the door. "Where have you been? I waited over an hour."

"Carl never came to get me. I had to walk." Sarah limped over to the couch, sat down, and began unbuckling the straps of the offensive heels. Her fingers moved slowly, as if that might somehow delay the inevitable.

"So you walked *home?*" Grant's eyes bulged with anger. "Tell me you're smart enough to remember we meet at the rear entrance of the warehouse after a job."

"Home was closer," Sarah said, gingerly probing a newly formed blister.

"Well, where is it?" The old sofa sank beneath her father's weight.

Sarah braced herself to stay upright. "Preece never came."

"What do you mean? And look at me when you're talking."

She turned to her father. "It was a new guy, and this is all he had." She took the bag from her purse. "I pushed for more—"

"You bought from the *wrong* guy?" Her father's voice rose. "Of all the stupid—"

"He was the only one who came," Sarah insisted, cringing at the verbal tirade she knew was coming. Though her father never physically harmed her, he was often angry, and the lashings he gave with his tongue left their own scars. "He knew the code, so I figured he was the replacement. I tried to get more, but he didn't have it. Of course I didn't give him all the money . . ." Her voice trailed off as she pulled the remaining wads of bills from her shirt, holding them out as a desperate peace offering.

Her father grabbed the money and threw it aside. A few bills came loose, and Sarah watched as they fluttered to the carpet. Grant's eyes narrowed as he took the bag and examined it, muttering a string of expletives under his breath.

"Where's Carl?" he demanded, looking up suddenly.

"I told you I don't know," Sarah said. "He talked to me before the job, but—"

"At the *park?*"

"Yes." Sarah rose from the couch. Kicking her shoes aside, she edged toward the hall. "He sat next to me for a minute—so I'd feel *safe.*" She wasn't entirely successful at keeping the sarcasm from her voice. "Then he forgot to pick me up afterward. I waited for him by the convenience store, but he never came, so I finally walked home."

Several unreadable expressions crossed her father's face.

Sarah knew better than to ask what was wrong. Her dad was always on edge when she had a job. If things went wrong—as they had tonight—that edge could get scary. If he was going to blame Carl for her failure with Preece . . . so much the better.

Her father stood and began pacing. "Tell me about this new contact."

"I've never seen him before." Sarah was surprised at the worry on her father's face. "He was older than the typical dealers. Kind of stocky. Thin hair." She wrapped her arms around herself, chilled as she remembered the hard look in his eyes. "Was it Martin?"

"No." Her father shook his head. "What else? Did he say anything unusual?"

"He told me it was pure—the best I could get around here. And I said that was good, because I had to share with my man . . ." Her forehead wrinkled. "And then I think—he said to tell my old man 'hi.'"

Alarm flashed in her father's eyes for the briefest second. "Your room," he ordered, pointing down the hall. "The rest of the weekend. Not even church on Sunday."

"But I'm supposed to sing . . ." The feeble protest died on her lips.

"Do you know—" A heavy sigh escaped his lips as he ran his fingers through his hair. "*You* were set up tonight, Sarah. Don't be so foolish as to worry about something paltry like choir."

"But, Dad." Her voice caught. Singing wasn't paltry. Music was her life, and church was the one place she felt comfortable around others, felt a measure of peace.

Her father grasped her shoulders. "Didn't you hear a word I just said? You're lucky to be here, to be alive." He pulled her close in a fierce hug.

Sarah stiffened in his arms, wishing he'd let her go. Physical displays of affection were a rarity in their home, and this one, following so quickly on the heels of her father's anger, seemed especially strange. She pulled back from his embrace.

"Dad, I want to quit. I know you think it's good for me to see firsthand how awful drugs—and the people who use and sell them—are, but I've seen enough. It's great you've dedicated your life to the war against drugs, but I don't want to dedicate *my* life to it. It scares me." She paused, looking into his eyes. "And I think it scares you too. Haven't we both paid enough for Mother's mistake?"

Her father stepped back. He looked at Sarah for several seconds, as if seeing her for the first time in a long time. "It wasn't her mistake."

Sarah frowned. He'd spoken so quietly she wasn't sure she'd heard him correctly. "What did you say?"

He looked away. "Nothing—I don't know. I just don't know anymore."

She wanted to grasp his shoulders as he'd grasped hers a moment ago and tell him that he *did* know, that she'd waited for years for him to tell her the whole story of what had happened to her mother. But something in his countenance kept Sarah silent. Unable to stop herself, she felt her frustrations dissipating, replaced by guilt that she'd failed him and sympathy for the man who'd lost his wife so long ago.

"Go get cleaned up. We can talk about this later."

But we never do, she thought. He would shut her out again. How she wished she understood her father. It was like he was two people, and she never knew if Dr. Jekyll or Mr. Hyde was going to come home from work. She'd never quite figured out what it was that would set him off and when it would happen.

Instead of following his order, she hesitated, sorrowful as she looked at him, seeing only a broken, lonely man. A man who'd never recovered from his loss and had dedicated his life to fighting the evil that had claimed his wife.

At last Sarah turned away and walked slowly down the hall. Going into the bathroom, she closed and locked the door and made sure the light was off. Grabbing an extra towel from the vanity, she reached up to the window and worked the towel into the corners until no light came through. Satisfied it was dark enough, she stepped in the shower and pulled the heavy curtain. Only then, in almost complete darkness, did she begin removing the distasteful clothes.

Her father had said they were *always* watching, and she wasn't taking any chances.

Chapter Five

"Do you have a death wish? Or do you want to go back to jail?" Grant asked, blocking the way to the kitchen, getting in Carl's face.

Carl moved around him, dropping his keys on the counter. "I'm sorry I forgot to pick up the princess," he muttered, unapologetic. "I met this woman at the park, and we got busy."

"I'm not talking about Sarah walking a couple of miles alone, in the dark—*unprotected.*" Grant grabbed Carl's jacket and shoved him against the wall. "Though that'd be bad enough. But you *sat* with her at the park."

His nephew pushed back, but Grant was ready and caught him in the gut with a solid punch. "So you left her after that, while you were 'getting busy' with some woman?"

"The guy—wasn't—coming." Doubled over, Carl clutched his stomach. "I waited forever, and then this *woman . . .*" He tried to stand, then staggered across the linoleum, rolling his eyes and head at the same time.

"You're drunk," Grant said. He grabbed Carl's arm and hauled him into the kitchen, shoving him into a chair. He made a cup of instant coffee while he watched Carl—slumped across the table—from the corner of his eye.

A few minutes later Grant set the steaming cup in front of him. "Drink this." When Carl didn't raise his head, Grant lifted it for him, pulling back on his hair.

"Ouch!" Carl rubbed his head.

Grant nodded toward the coffee. "Drink it."

Carl picked up the mug, took a sip and spit it out, making a face as he stuck the tip of his tongue between his lips.

"Hot?" Grant asked.

Carl glared at him.

"Get drunk again while you're supposed to be watching my daughter, and you'll wake up in jail—or worse."

"Don't threaten me, old man."

"I'm not the one threatening." Grant leaned over the table, his face close to Carl's. "One of Rossi's men happened to be watching tonight—checking up on me. Then Preece never showed up. Guess where he is now?"

Carl closed his eyes and leaned his head against the wall. "I dunno."

"Fished out of the river about an hour ago. He never met with Sarah." Grant watched Carl's face as he digested this information. "One of Rossi's men did. I know because she described him to me—that was about half an hour before he called me personally. I don't *like* personal phone calls."

"What do you want me to do about it?" Carl asked, sitting up straight in his chair.

Grant knew his nephew was wide awake now. He could see the criminal glint lighting his eyes. "You're no match for them. Not in a million years."

Carl scoffed. "That's what you think. You have no idea what I'm capable of."

"Tonight you proved you're *in*capable of protecting my daughter."

"She's all right, ain't she?" Carl asked.

"No thanks to you," Grant snapped. "You're supposed to protect her, not put her in more danger. Now Rossi suspects she wasn't alone. He thinks I haven't kept my end of the deal."

Carl picked up the mug and took a careful sip. "So what? Pay him off or something."

"As if any amount of money I could ever give him would matter." Grant drummed his fingers on the table. "But *something* is exactly what he wants."

"What's that?" Carl asked, suddenly wary.

"Not you," Grant said, a malicious smile forming on his lips. "Not yet, anyway. I might have convinced him that you're some druggie who's been harassing Sarah in the park. But if he sees you there again . . ." He left the statement and its implications hanging in the air. "And, of course, he requires further proof of my loyalty. He wants Martin off the street—*now.*"

Carl leaned back in his chair, relief evident on his face. "What do you want me to do?"

* * *

Sarah put a CD in her player and turned up the volume. A few seconds later the soothing strains of Bach's *Orchestral Suite No. 2* drowned out the sounds of her father and Carl fighting.

Pulling her desk chair over to the window, she sat down, hugging her knees to her chest to ward off the cold draft seeping through the poorly sealed panes. So many things in their house needed repairing, but her father didn't seem to care about fixing them—even when she'd offered to help. A few years ago she'd stopped offering and instead spent her energy dreaming of and planning for the day when she could leave.

Tilting her head back, she peered through the barred glass out to the night sky. A handful of stars sprinkled across it, adding their light to the lone star she'd seen earlier. Sarah thought of the endless constellations hidden from view by the city lights. An entire universe was out there, but she could only glimpse the tiniest portion of it. Her life was much the same. Though she'd finally been allowed out of the house, had stepped on the hallowed grounds of Harvard, she was only allowed to peek at all that was offered there. Just as the lights blocked the stars she loved from her view, her father and Carl were keeping her from the opportunities she craved. The cultural world she longed for lay at her fingertips, but she wasn't allowed to touch.

A particularly bright star seemed to wink at her, and Sarah thought about crossing her room to the shelf where her astronomy book lay. With a bit of research, she could probably figure out which star it was or which constellation it belonged to. But she was too cold to move, and her thoughts drifted back to campus, this time to the library instead of the concert hall. A wistful smile touched her lips as she thought of Jay and the conversation they'd had. Was it possible he *really* wanted to hear her play again?

The telltale floorboards in the hall squeaked loudly, and Sarah stiffened, knowing her father was coming to check on her. It wouldn't matter if Jay did want to see her again. A friend was yet another thing she could not have.

Easing herself from the chair, she tiptoed across the room and climbed into bed. She rolled to her side, eyes closed in pretend sleep, as she'd been doing since she was a little girl.

She heard the door open and sensed her father's presence. His footsteps were heavy across her carpet, and he stood over her.

"Thank goodness you're safe." He bent and brushed her skin with a light kiss.

Sarah forced herself to lay still, though part of her longed to sit up and hug him.

When she heard the click of her door shutting, she opened her eyes, blinking back unexpected tears. Her father had both hugged and kissed her *and* spoken of her mother all in the same night. Yearning swept through her, and Sarah struggled to cope with a tide of emotion.

Somehow, in the past few hours, the barrier holding all of her hurt and emptiness in place had cracked. And though she tried her best to patch it up, a lifetime of sorrowful memories began to leak through.

In the wee hours of the morning, she finally gave up and gave into exhaustion, knowing in her heart that, sooner or later, a flood was inevitable.

Chapter Six

Detective Brandt of the Summerfield, Massachusetts, Police Department stopped in front of his colleague's desk. "Ned's bringing in a DUI."

"Good for him." Kirk Anderson glanced at the clock on the far side of the room. It was nearly seven A.M. One hour left until he could go home and crawl into bed—with his wife maybe, if she could be persuaded to leave her projects until later and climb under the covers with him for a little while, since the boys would be at school.

He looked up at Mitchell Brandt, still lingering in front of his desk. "One more nut off the road before the school buses start rolling."

Brandt nodded slowly as a corner of his mouth lifted. "Yeah. And fortunately this guy had just finished his grocery shopping."

"What? Did he bring donuts?" Kirk's voice was laced with sarcasm as he looked pointedly at the paunch hanging over Brandt's belt. "Listen, I've got a report to finish." He returned his attention to the paperwork in front of him. "So unless it's something important—"

Brandt leaned forward, placing his palms on the desk. "Not donuts. He had a carton of *milk*."

Kirk's head snapped up. "Not *Eddie*," he breathed.

"Yep. And he'd been shopping at the meth lab. He's moved from quarts to half gallons. Had fifteen bags jammed in one carton. We've finally caught the Milk Man."

"Meth Martin," Kirk said, excitement in his voice, though he still couldn't quite believe the news. They'd been after this guy a long time. Kirk rose from his desk. "Where is he?"

"Having his photo taken and nails done as we speak," Brandt said. "I already told Ned you'd want to be in on the questioning."

"Absolutely." Kirk pulled a ring of keys from his pocket and unlocked his bottom file drawer. "We'll have to get him sober first, or whatever he says won't hold up in court."

"A strong pot's already brewing." Brandt watched as Kirk flipped through his files. "What's all that? I've already pulled Eddie's folder."

Kirk took a manila envelope from his drawer. "My own copies," he explained. "A few too many things have gone missing around here since I started, and I'm not taking chances with something as important as this. I've got enlargements of the photos and transcript from the tape that kid turned in last June."

Brandt pushed off the desk. "This guy's going down."

"And if we do it right, so is his supplier." Envelope held tight, Kirk walked toward the hall, thoughts of going home on time having fled with the possibility that one of Massachusetts's most well-known meth traffickers would soon be behind bars.

* * *

Christa Anderson looked at her watch as she heard her husband walk through the front door. It was 9:10, an hour later than expected. "I was getting worried about you. Rough night?" she called from the kitchen as she poured him a glass of juice.

"Not too bad." Kirk came into the room. He removed his holster and gun, checked that the safety was on, then reached to put them on top of the kitchen cupboard. He sat down and picked up the juice Christa had set out. He took a drink and leaned forward, elbows on the table, a faraway look on his face.

Christa slid into the seat beside him. "Want to talk about it?" She moved his glass aside. Taking one of his hands in her two, she shivered and began rubbing his fingers. "You're freezing. Is it that cold out already?"

Kirk turned to her. "Getting there. You're still my Southern California girl, I see." He smiled, then leaned forward to give her a kiss. "How was your night?"

"Fine. I let the boys watch a half hour of *Winnie the Pooh,* and they both went to bed without complaint."

Kirk's eyebrows rose. "How come we don't have those kind of nights when I'm home?"

"Because you're the one who gets them all wild." Christa gave him a knowing smile. "What about your night?"

The faraway look returned. "Nothing much—a minor traffic accident on main, an eighty-five-year-old woman locked herself out of her house when she took out the trash, and Ned brought in Eddie Martin this morning."

It took a moment for the name to register.

"Eddie Martin?" Excitement lit Christa's face. "Isn't that the guy—"

"Yep." Kirk nodded. "He's the big one. If we shut him down, there'll be a lot less meth finding its way to the streets. Better yet, if he leads us to his supplier . . . that may well impact the other operations in this area."

"That's fantastic." Christa squeezed Kirk's hand. "You've been after him for months."

"Yeah. Ned got him on a DUI inside a school zone—automatic two years. And besides being high, Eddie had a milk carton stuffed with meth in his car. *Fifteen* bags of it—all neatly packaged and ready to sell. We called Chief Morgan, and he came right down. I don't think I've ever seen him so excited."

"And you haven't even been here a full year." Christa beamed. "*This* is the difference you knew you could make."

"Well, I wasn't the one who caught him," Kirk reminded her.

"But you're the one who has testimony from the kid he sold to. You've compiled all the evidence."

"Me and half the department. But you're right. This is big. It gives me hope that we'll be able to keep Summerfield the nice, peaceful community it is."

"Of course you will." Christa squeezed his hand once more, then pushed back her chair and stood. "How about some breakfast to celebrate?"

"I'm not really hungry, so . . ." Kirk reached out, wrapping his arm around Christa's waist, pulling her onto his lap. "How about we go back to bed?"

Christa shook her head. "Sorry. My visiting teachers are coming in twenty minutes, I have to cut Sister Nelson's hair at ten-thirty, and it's my turn for preschool carpool."

Kirk scowled. "So you're telling me that visiting teaching, Sister Nelson's hair, and a bunch of screaming three-year-olds are more important than me?"

"Hmm." Christa pretended to consider. "Yep. Pretty much." She gave Kirk a quick kiss on the forehead and jumped off his lap. "Kind of how interrogating Eddie Martin was more important than coming home on time this morning? Because if you'd asked me to come back to bed oh, say, an hour ago . . ."

"I was at work," Kirk protested. "You're not playing fair."

"I'm not playing at all." Christa giggled and moved out of his reach before he could grab her again. "Sorry."

Kirk gave her a pitiful look. "I didn't even get to talk to Eddie."

"How come?" She pulled the dish drainer from beneath the sink and set it on the counter.

"Chief wanted to make sure Eddie was good and sober and understood all his rights before we started. There have been too many problems—too many mistakes—so this time Chief Morgan is being extra careful. When we do get Eddie in that courtroom, there isn't going to be any loophole his attorney can find to get him off."

Christa put the plug in the sink and started the water. She turned around to face Kirk. "Well then, I'm sorry you didn't get to grill the suspect."

"Sorry? You ought to feel guilty," Kirk said. "I could've stayed, you know. Instead, I came home to spend time with my lovely wife."

"*And* so you could get some sleep and go in early this afternoon when Eddie *will* be talking." Christa folded her arms as she gave her husband a knowing look. "Now who's guilty?"

"Man." Kirk raised his hands in the air and rose from the table. "What is it with you hairdressers? You've got the scoop on everyone. I ought to bring Eddie over to sit in your chair this afternoon. He'd probably confess everything."

Christa laughed. "I doubt it. Now go shower so you can get some rest before the boys come home. Today the tall tale characters—including Paul Bunyan—are visiting kindergarten. Jeffrey was beside himself with excitement. He'll want to tell you all about it."

Kirk left the kitchen, and Christa turned back to the sink and squirted some dish soap under the stream of water. Looking at the oatmeal-crusted bowls, she grimaced, missing the dishwasher they'd had in their condo in California. Though, she reminded herself as she pulled on her gloves, there was plenty to be said for the quaint home they'd found in Cambridge.

Instead of the fifty-minute commute Kirk had before, it was now a short twelve-minute drive to the police station in Summerfield. And here the boys had a yard to run and play in. Lack of a dishwasher aside, everything else about the home was perfect. Everything about Cambridge was too, as far as Christa was concerned, and she could honestly say she was glad they had moved across the country.

Here the pace seemed slower, more peaceful—still a bit of small-town America. Part of that, she knew, depended on keeping the drug problem at bay. She hated to think that Cambridge or Summerfield could someday be as bad as Pasadena had become.

Christa turned off the faucet, plunged her hands into the soapy water, and began scrubbing the bowls. Aside from needing the sink clean so she could wash hair, she simply hated having the kitchen dirty when her clients came. Someday she hoped to have a little salon in the basement. Kirk had been working on it, but between his schedule and a tight budget, things were going slowly. *Maybe Kirk will get a raise or promotion when Eddie Martin is behind bars for good.* The thought cheered her.

Christa knew how seriously Kirk took his job and how hard he was working trying to get a handle on the meth problem. She also knew that Chief Morgan was aware of that too—at least in part. The chief's obsession with getting drugs off the street was the reason Kirk had been hired last spring. His experience on the narcotics team in a big precinct in LA had made him an immediate favorite with the chief, who, rumor had it, had never gotten over his own wife's overdose years earlier.

The phone rang, jarring Christa from her thoughts. Tugging off her gloves, she grabbed it from the counter.

"Hello?"

"Is Detective Anderson in?"

He just got home, she wanted to say. Instead she replied politely, "He's in the shower. May I take a message?"

"This is Chief Morgan. It's important."

"Just a minute. I'll get him." Scowling at the phone and the chief's typical gruffness, Christa went to the bedroom and banged on the bathroom door.

She heard the water shut off, and she called to Kirk. He opened the door, a towel wrapped around his waist.

"It's Chief Morgan," Christa whispered, holding out the phone.

Kirk took it. "Maybe Eddie's talking." He held the phone up to his ear. "Hey, Chief."

A few seconds later, Kirk's head bent slightly and an incredulous look crossed his face. "He's *what?*" He continued to listen. Christa stepped back and sat on the bed while she waited.

"Thanks for calling," Kirk said finally. "I'll be down later. Bye."

"What?" Christa asked, trying to read the expression on Kirk's face as he ended the call.

"It's Eddie—he had a heart attack. He's dead."

Chapter Seven

Sarah clasped her books to her chest and pressed her lips together to keep from smiling as she read the single word written on the index card.

Maybe?

Quickly she slipped onto the bench and put her music on the stand, covering the card. Her cheeks warmed as she peeked over the top of the piano, stealing a surreptitious glance around the auditorium.

It was vacant except for Carl, slouched in his usual seat in back, and the dancers taking their places on stage. Jay wasn't here. She felt both relief and disappointment. She didn't need to worry about Carl punching him again, but she wouldn't see him today either—would she? *I'll look forward to seeing you again and hope for a maybe . . .* Had he really meant it? She'd nearly convinced herself he hadn't, certain she'd done everything wrong during those few minutes at the library. Rambling on and on about her paper, never asking Jay a single question about himself . . .

With a sigh, Sarah opened her music to the beginning of the ballet. A guy like that couldn't possibly be interested in her, so it was best to forget the whole thing. It was best for a lot of reasons, not the least of which was her need to focus on her education so she could get *away* from the men in her life.

Sliding her music aside, she glanced at the index card once more. It was probably something else entirely—or if it was from Jay, it was likely a joke. She knew what the reflection in the bathroom mirror showed her each day. And no guy could really be interested in her.

Picking up the note card, she ripped it in pieces, then dropped them in her backpack, watching as they filtered down around her folders.

"Attention," the ballet director called, her French accent echoing through the auditorium. Sarah's head went up, and she watched for her cue to begin playing. For the next thirty minutes she focused her thoughts on the music and rehearsal. It required all her concentration, her eyes constantly moving from the notes to Madame Trenchard and her signals. Stop. Start. The last measure again. Slower. Faster. Stop. Once more from the beginning.

At last Madame Trenchard called a break, and the dancers hurried offstage to their water bottles.

Sarah stretched her fingers and reached for her own water. A single piece of note card rested on the lid, the corner piece of the letter M. She flicked it away, unscrewed the lid, and took a long drink, feeling upset all over again.

Trying very hard to forget about it—to forget about Jay—she opened her folder and selected her favorite piece of her own composition. It was lighter than the one she'd played the afternoon Jay had listened. Placing the sheet on the piano, she began to play, quietly at first, then louder, filling the auditorium with a lyrical melody that helped her imagine happiness, freedom, magical summer days, nights under starry skies. It was the only song she'd ever written in G major—the only piece she'd ever written in *any* major key—and she felt uplifted every time she played it. Today she felt her soul stir with hope as she read the notes and her fingers moved across the keyboard. No one was going to keep her from her goals. Someday she was going to be free.

Bent over the piano, absorbed in her music, Sarah didn't realize the break had passed and the dancers were reassembling until she heard clapping. She looked up as she completed the finale—a trill of staccato notes dancing up the highest keys—and found Madame Trenchard staring down at her.

"You wish to write for the ballet?" she asked in her heavy French accent.

Sarah shook her head. "Oh, no. I only—"

"I want it for the second half. Melissa and Chelsea will come up with the choreography. You'll need to get the music to the conductor right away, so he can separate it into parts for the orchestra." Madame Trenchard turned back to the stage. "Places."

Sarah tried to explain. "I was practicing. I never meant—"

"You never meant your talent to be shared?" Madame Trenchard looked over her shoulder disapprovingly. "It is a shame to hide such a gift."

But I have to, Sarah thought. "Yes, Madame," she murmured instead, shocked at the compliment and turn of events.

"Places for Act Three," the director called, resuming her usual no-nonsense demeanor.

The remainder of practice passed in a blur, and Sarah had trouble keeping up, as her thoughts were elsewhere—worried about her father's reaction if he found out one of her pieces was to be played in public. She'd have to make sure her name was left off the program. For safety reasons, her father never wanted anyone to know she was the police chief's daughter.

As the dancers dispersed, she gathered her books quickly, knowing Carl was impatient to leave. He had no use for music or dance—or anything remotely cultural. She bent over, stuffing everything into her backpack.

"Sarah?"

Looking up, she saw one of the dancers standing next to the piano. The woman held a note card in her outstretched hand.

"Jay asked me to give this to you."

"Thanks." Sarah took the card and read the three words written there.

Impressive. Thank you.

"He was here?"

"Backstage the whole time."

Sarah bit her lip to keep from smiling.

The dancer was giving her a peculiar look. "He said to tell you he'll be at the library again this Friday—in the afternoon around one o'clock."

From the corner of her eye, Sarah saw Carl pacing by the exit.

"Thanks," she managed to get out before the woman walked away. Sarah stuffed the index card deep inside her pack and started up the aisle toward Carl. She hoped he wouldn't notice she was flustered. She wished she could figure out why she was, why her heart was suddenly racing, why she suddenly couldn't wait to be home and in her room, alone with her thoughts.

And why, even more than that, she couldn't wait for Friday afternoon.

* * *

1:06.

Sarah forced her eyes away from her watch and back to the book in front of her. She made herself read a page and a half before her eyes strayed again. 1:09. Her gaze kept wandering to the watch. 1:11. 1:12. *He's not coming.* She felt the sting of tears and, appalled, wiped her eyes.

What did you expect? That a man would actually be interested in you? That he's some knight in shining armor who would save you from a life you despise?

Sarah shut her book and reached for her backpack. She unzipped it and put the text inside, then grabbed a tissue from a pocket. Telling herself that she was acting ridiculous, she scrunched the tissue in her fist and dabbed at one eye and then the other. She took a deep, steadying breath, pushed her chair out, and stood. Turning, she came face-to-face with Jay.

Like last time he was casual, smiling. "Leaving so soon?"

"I—I thought you weren't coming."

He looked repentant. "Sorry. My class just ended. I hurried over as fast as I could."

"Class?" she asked stupidly.

"Over at Langdell, and my professor wanted to talk to me for a minute afterward."

Her brow wrinkled. "Langdell? Isn't that . . . Are you in law school?"

"Yeah." He grinned sheepishly and shrugged. "Kind of surprising they let a guy like me in, huh?"

"No—not at all. I just . . . My father always says . . . Um, let's just say I haven't met a lot of lawyers I like."

Jay laughed out loud, then, catching the angry look of a passing librarian, coughed into his fist. He took a step closer to Sarah, lowering his voice to a whisper. "Know what I like about you?"

She shook her head.

"Most women I've met on campus get all starry-eyed when they learn I'm a law student. I can almost always see the social aspirations on their faces and the dollar signs in their eyes. But you looked absolutely *horrified*."

"I'm sorry. I didn't mean to offend you." Sarah pushed her glasses farther up on her nose.

"Don't apologize. It was a refreshing change," Jay said. "In fact, why don't you share your reasons for your less-than-favorable opinion of the legal profession with me over a sandwich. I'll treat you to a late lunch."

"Oh, no." Sarah took her backpack from the table. "I don't think that's a good idea."

"Why not?" Jay asked. He looked in the direction of the copier. "Is your bodyguard lurking nearby?"

"No. Carl won't be on campus until three. That's usually when I meet him. Normally I've got private sessions from one until three, but we can miss two a semester, so I—cancelled today."

"You're free, and you forgot to tell the cousin." Jay snapped his fingers and smiled. "Too bad." He reached for her backpack and took it from her. "Come on. We're *definitely* going somewhere. You don't have to eat if you don't want to, but we're not going to let two hours go to waste. Let's at least get out of the no-talking zone."

Vacillating between sheer joy and complete panic, Sarah followed Jay toward the elevator. In her wildest dreams, she hadn't imagined he would ask her out to lunch. Rather, she'd fervently hoped for another five minutes in the library and the ability—*this* time around—to make coherent conversation.

She bit her lip. "We're not going anywhere far, are we?"

"We'll stay on campus. I know a great place," Jay assured her. "Somewhere I'm pretty certain your cousin would never venture."

"Okay," Sarah agreed, deciding to take the risk. She stepped onto the elevator with him.

Jay pressed the button for the main floor. "So you have a private two-hour piano lesson every Friday?"

She shook her head. "It's actually every Wednesday and Friday, and very little of the two hours is spent at the piano."

"You play another instrument too," Jay guessed. "Guitar?" he asked sounding hopeful.

"No. Though I've always wanted to. I—"

"Don't tell me," Jay said. "I'll figure it out." He looked her over as if sizing her up. "I know. Flute."

"Wrong."

"Harpsichord."

Sarah held up three fingers. "Three strikes. I think that means you're out."

"Little League. I get at least five balls," Jay insisted. "French horn, oboe, cello, violin."

"Sorry." She smiled. "Give up?"

"Not yet." He caught her eye. "Maybe never."

She looked away.

"Piccolo, recorder, trombone . . . *drums.*"

She heard herself laugh and was as surprised at the sound as he seemed to be. "I sing," she finally admitted.

He reached out, lightly touching her hand just as the elevator stopped. "You mean to tell me you've got a voice to match your piano skills?"

She shrugged. "A few people have told me it's nice."

The doors slid open, and they stepped out onto the main floor.

Jay turned to Sarah, hand over his heart and a huge grin on his face. "I think," he said solemnly, "that this could be serious."

Chapter Eight

Sarah followed Jay up the steps of the Fogg Art Museum. "You're right," she said, walking past as he held the door open. "Carl would never set foot in here."

Jay looked at her sideways. "I had a hunch . . ." He stepped into the lobby. "Ever been to the museum before?"

She shook her head. "No. Truthfully, I didn't even know what this building was. I've walked past it a few times, but I pretty much just attend my classes. Going to the library is a treat."

"If you enjoy the library, then you'll love this place. I like to come here and wander around when I need some quiet to think. If you have your ID, admission is free."

Sarah took a plain, brown wallet from her backpack. They showed their Harvard IDs to the student at the front desk, and Jay grabbed a map of the museum. He knew where everything was, but he thought he could give Sarah a better idea of her choices if she had a visual of the building.

They stopped at the entrance to the Italian Renaissance courtyard. Sarah stepped inside, her low heels clicking on the travertine floor. Jay watched as her eyes scanned the columns and statues, then traveled upward to the arches lining the second floor. Her skirt swished around her ankles as she turned in a slow circle, head tilted back as if she were trying to take in the entire three-story courtyard at once.

"Wow."

Jay grinned. "I notice something new every time I come here."

"I had no idea Harvard had a collection like this," Sarah said.

"I'm guessing from your reaction that we're not going to have time to go out to lunch *and* see the museum. But if you get hungry, I have a fine BLT on toasted wheat bread right here." He patted his backpack. "I'm happy to share. We could sit outside and eat first, or, if you'd rather, we can go straight to the galleries. The voice levels allowed there are slightly better than at the library."

"Hmm." Sarah looked at his backpack. "The sandwich is tempting, but I think I'll opt for viewing the art first. I may not get another chance to come to the museum, and I'd like to see what they have."

Jay worked to hide his frown. *Why can't she come back whenever she wants?* "What kind of art do you like? They've got a lot of variety."

"I don't really know," she confessed. "I've never been to an art museum before."

"*Never?* Don't schools around here do field trips?" Jay asked. "You'd think with Boston being so close . . ."

"They do them," Sarah said. "I was never allowed to go. My dad's a bit—"

"Overprotective?" Jay finished with her.

"Yes." She gave him a wry smile. "Guess you figured that out already."

Jay thought *overprotective* seemed a bit of an understatement. "What would your dad do if he knew you were here with me?"

She looked toward the entrance. "You don't want to know. Maybe this isn't such a good idea."

Jay took her arm and led her toward the galleries. "It's a *great* idea. Art, like music, provides some of the best life has to offer." *Something I'm guessing you've had far too little of.*

Sarah resisted for just a second before allowing him to pull her a few steps farther into the museum.

"I'll tell you some of my favorites, then you can choose what you'd like to see first." Reluctantly he let his hand drop from her arm so he could open the map. "The Impressionist collection on the second floor is amazing. That's always a good place to start. And right now, until the end of the month, there's a fantastic photography exhibit." Jay pointed to another room on the map. "I also really like the American collection. They've got some great paintings of the Founding Fathers."

"Let's go there first," Sarah said. "I love U.S. history."

Me too. Score. "Tell me you've been able to visit all of *those* sites in Boston," Jay said. "That was one of the first things I did after I moved here. Boston Harbor, the Freedom Trail—" Seeing Sarah shaking her head, he broke off.

"Boston is a big, dangerous city," she said in a deep, serious voice. "It's no place for a young lady."

"Not even when she's with her parents?" He wanted to understand this family she'd come from—so different from the way he'd been raised by a father who barely required check-ins.

"Par-*ent,* as in singular," Sarah said. "My mother died when I was five."

"I'm sorry." Jay looked at Sarah's face for any sign of sadness and saw only resignation. "My mom is dead, too, but she and my dad split when I was little, so Dad raised me by himself. I guess single parents can tend to be paranoid about things." He really didn't know what that would be like, but he suddenly wanted nothing more than to steer the conversation away from the topic of parents—namely Sarah's.

They walked in silence the rest of the way toward the staircase. When they passed the navy-clad guards standing at its base, Sarah turned to Jay with a questioning look on her face.

"They help you find things," Jay whispered as they started up the stairs. "And beat you up if you try to steal stuff."

"I hope you don't speak from experience."

"Well there was that one time . . ." Jay joked. "No. Of course not. I have too much respect for artists, musicians—anyone who creates—to ever want to steal from them. I can't even burn copies of CDs anymore without feeling guilty. It's terrible."

"Appalling," Sarah agreed. "You *used* to copy CDs?"

"All the time in high school. Didn't everyone?"

"No. I had the entire London Philharmonic collection—what else would I possibly want?"

"You're serious, aren't you?" Jay asked as they reached the top of the staircase.

"I'm always serious," Sarah said.

"Maybe that's something we should work on." He held his hand out, gesturing her ahead of him into the gallery.

Once there they spent several quiet minutes wandering around the room, looking at the paintings, drawings, and sculptures. Because Jay had been here many times before, he found himself studying Sarah more than the art. He felt a strange contentment when she lingered at some of his favorites, and he bit back a teasing comment when he noticed her blush as she hurried by the nudes. When they came to Gilbert Stuart's works—his favorites—he spoke up.

"I love these paintings. I can't count the number of times I've come here to look at them."

"They're magnificent," Sarah said as she gazed up at portrait of Jefferson.

"They were great leaders—not perfect men—but the way they achieved independence and set up our government is amazing." After a minute, Jay followed her to stand in front of a painting of George Washington. "Sometimes I wonder what our world would be like today if more of our leaders now were like them."

"Different," Sarah said. "I sometimes worry that all those who were noble and brave lived long ago."

Jay wanted to ask her why she felt that way, but she'd already turned away and was walking toward the next painting—another one of his favorites, *Mrs. Israel Thorndike.*

"Beautiful, isn't she?" Jay asked after a moment when Sarah hadn't moved on. He meant the picture, but looking at Sarah's profile, it struck him that she was beautiful too. Not in an eye-catching or obvious way, but in a very subtle, *real* way when he took notice. Her hair, braided again, hung long and blond, halfway down her back, and behind her large glasses he'd glimpsed very pretty eyes. But it was her profile that he noticed now. Her features were delicate and her skin flawless. He found himself wondering if it was as soft as it looked and what it would feel like to brush his fingers against her cheek.

"Who is she?" Sarah asked.

"Other than Israel's wife, I don't know." Jay forced his attention back to the painting. "But Israel Thorndike was a revolutionary war hero, a wealthy merchant, a successful politician, *and* the one responsible for acquiring four thousand of the best American history volumes in the Harvard library."

Sarah raised her eyebrows and turned to Jay. "How many have you read?"

He smiled. "Several. Though there are quite a few that can't be checked out—fragile, you know."

Sarah folded her arms and looked at him thoughtfully. "What I know is that you're turning out to be different than I thought you'd be. You're a musician, you enjoy art and reading about Mozart, and you have a passion for U.S. history."

"Guilty," Jay pled. "You're making it painfully obvious why I also don't have many dates."

"*That,* I wouldn't guess," Sarah said. Shyly, with a blush that started in her cheeks and worked its way down to her neck, she looked him over. "I can also see that you'd hold your own against my cousin in a fair fight."

Her remark was so frank and unexpected that Jay laughed out loud. "I'm glad you noticed."

He waited, hoping for maybe another observation or compliment, but Sarah had turned away, reverting to her quiet self.

He touched her elbow gently. "Come on. I think we have time to look at the photography exhibit. Unless you want to eat now."

She followed him into the hall. "You really don't date much?" she blurted when they were outside the gallery.

"Almost never. Guess I'm too busy reading history books," he teased.

She looked down at the floor. "I never go out either—*never.*"

Thanks to your obsessive dad, Jay could have added, but he didn't want to start down that path again. "Maybe we should both try it more often, with each other of course. I'm enjoying this."

"Me too." She spoke so quietly he almost missed it.

"So . . . do we eat or stroll some more?" he asked, still trying to cajole her out of her serious mood.

Sarah looked up at him. "I don't think I'd better do either. I'd love to stay, but if Carl comes to pick me up early, and I'm not there . . ."

"Say no more." The last thing Jay wanted to do was turn her over to her cousin, but he could tell she was starting to worry, and he didn't want that either. "One more quick stop, then we'll go." He led her downstairs to the gift shop where he made his way to the packages of small prints. It took less than a minute to find what he wanted, and he took it to the cash register. Sarah lingered by the books.

Jay paid for his purchase and met her by the door. He walked her to the museum entrance. "I'm not going to go outside with you—on the off chance that we'd run into Carl on the way to the library."

Unmistakable relief crossed Sarah's face. "Thank you for understanding. And thank you for bringing me here. It was—"

"A date." Jay grinned. "Now you can't say *never.*"

She looked down at the floor again.

"Sarah?" He stepped closer and held the bag from the gift shop in her line of vision. "These are for you, so you can remember your first trip to the museum and our first official date."

"I can't—"

"If your father asks, tell him you got them free on campus—it's the truth." He pressed the sack into her hands. "And whether or not he asks, enjoy them." Jay noticed her fingers shook slightly as she opened the bag and removed the package of Gilbert Stuart prints. She stared down at George Washington for several seconds.

"I—I don't know what to say," she stammered.

"Say I can meet you at the library again sometime."

She finally looked up at him. "I'd love to, Jay, but if my father found out . . ."

"He doesn't want you to have friends?"

"He wants me to do well in school—wants to see that it's worth what he's paying."

"A good education is about more than acing tests and writing papers." Jay didn't want to argue with her, but he was having a hard time understanding how her father wouldn't want his daughter to enjoy all that Harvard had to offer. "It's about experiencing new things—*all kinds of things*—music, art, drama, politics. There's so much more than classes."

"I know." She turned away. "Good-bye, and thank you again." She walked across the foyer and out the door. He watched her until she'd gone down the steps and disappeared from view. Jay stuffed his now-empty hands in his pockets and walked toward the gallery that held the American exhibit. He needed to look at those paintings again and feel of the greatness of those men. Somehow they'd discovered a way to liberate the colonies and found a nation.

Surely then, he could find a way to liberate a girl and build a friendship.

Chapter Nine

"Point and shoot," Grant ordered.

From the corner of her eye, Sarah could see her father's lips moving. Though the earmuffs muted the sound, she'd heard these same instructions so often that she was even in sync with the timing of his words.

With her feet planted the standard eighteen inches apart, she attempted to hold her hands steady as she took aim and fired the 9mm Glock at the target seventy-five feet away.

"No—*no!*" Grant shouted. "You're still listing to the right." He shook his head as he scolded her. He grabbed the chain pulley and drew the target closer so she could see her mistake.

Bracing herself for a rebuke, Sarah lowered the earmuffs to her neck.

"It may not seem like much right now," her father continued. "But you can't afford that kind of error."

Sarah lowered the gun and put one hand on her hip. The other arm hung at her side, the pistol hanging from her fingers. Both shoulders were tired and sore from the repeated practice, and her back was starting to ache. She wasn't sure why her father was obsessing about this so much today, but she couldn't care less if she hit her own target or the one beside it. Looking up she said, "I never carry a gun anyway, so who is it you think I'm going to shoot?"

"Anyone who threatens you," he said in a low, menacing voice. Stepping close, he took the gun from her hand. "And from now on you *will* have a weapon with you. After that stunt Carl pulled at the park, we have to change things up a bit. He isn't going to be following close enough to do you any good if something goes wrong. And if that should happen, you don't want to find yourself in a position like this." He pointed the gun at her chest.

Sarah drew in her breath sharply as she looked down at the barrel touching the fabric of her shirt.

Her father lowered the gun, then reached for her hand and put the pistol in her palm as he turned her toward the targets.

"Got it?"

She nodded, still waiting for her shock to subside. *He pointed a loaded gun at me!* With shaking fingers, she covered her ears and raised her arms once more, this time trying hard to focus her line of vision on the cardboard mannequin at the end of her lane. She took aim and pulled the trigger, hardly flinching at the recoil. She'd grown up around guns, and as much as she hated them, she was also used to handling them.

Grant pulled on the chain and stepped forward to see how she'd done. She lowered the earmuffs to her neck again.

"Better," he grumbled. "But not your best. You're not focused today. If school is going to interfere with your job—"

"It isn't school," Sarah cut in.

"Then what?" Grant pointed out her latest shot on the target—high and to the right—then released the pulley.

"I don't want to do this anymore. I don't want to work on the drug task force. I tried telling you the other night. I hate it. The dealers scare me, and—"

"And it helps pay the bills," Grant said. "I'm spending a fortune on your tuition. If we're going to make ends meet, you've got to work, Sarah."

"I'll find another job," she insisted. "Mrs. Strouse has been after me for months to give her girls private singing lessons. I could teach piano, too."

"Piano," Grant scoffed. "You think that will make a dent in thirty-five thousand dollars a year? The only reason you're able to go to college is because of your job. Do you have any idea the kind of strings I had to pull to get you this position?"

"I wish you hadn't. But I'll work two jobs to make up the difference." Sarah hated that she sounded as desperate as she felt. "I can find something on campus. I'll work in one of the cafeterias or be a janitor—*anything* would be better than spending my nights buying drugs."

Grant sighed heavily. "It's not possible, Sarah. You can't quit—no matter how much either of us might wish you could."

"Then fire me—on the grounds that I'm a lousy shot today." She gave her dad a half smile, hoping to ease the tension building between them. She knew she'd pushed about as far as she dared. But hadn't he crossed the line too—a few minutes ago, pointing a gun at her like that? "Fire me and hire someone else who's as passionate about fighting crime as you are. It would be better for everyone."

"You're irreplaceable."

Against her will, she felt her heart warm with the unexpected and rare compliment. But then she realized what he was doing. *You always try to turn things around, Dad.* "I can see that people might not be lining up for the job, but surely you can find someone."

"No." Grant shook his head. "You don't understand. There simply isn't anyone else who can do exactly what you do."

* * *

Sarah stretched plastic wrap over the bowl of spaghetti and stuck it in the near-empty fridge. A six-pack of beer and the usual condiments lined the shelves of the door. The interior shelves, however, were bare except for a half gallon of milk, a couple of apples, and the leftover spaghetti. Sarah frowned. There was no way she could conjure tomorrow's dinner out of that, and the pantry was just as empty. They'd starve soon if she didn't remind her father it was time to go shopping again. She should have told him earlier, so they could have stopped by the store on the way home from the shooting range. But his mood hadn't exactly been stellar, and she'd been too upset to think about groceries. She dreaded telling him now, dreaded the argument that was sure to come up for the hundredth time.

"Grocery shopping is a woman's work. I shouldn't have to be bothered with it," he'd say.

"I'll do the shopping, Dad. I can ride the bus and—"

"No daughter of mine is going to set foot on a bus. Do you have any idea the kind of people who ride public transportation?"

"People who don't own cars?" she'd dared to say to him once when she was about seventeen and hadn't yet given up hope of getting a driver's license someday. He'd nearly slapped her for her impertinence, and he hadn't let her eat a bite of the dinner she'd made that night.

Hopefully this time he'd complain about the lack of food as usual and then decide it was safe to let her do the shopping—with Carl in tow, of course. *Ugh. More time with Carl.* Maybe starving was the better option. If she thought her father wouldn't yell at her when there was nothing for dinner the following evening, she might have chanced it.

Returning to the table, she grabbed the salad—hardly touched—and carried it over to the sink. It seemed that neither she nor her father had been very hungry tonight. Her stomach was still in knots over the incident at the shooting range. What her father was upset about remained a mystery. Sarah supposed she ought to be concerned that he hadn't been eating well for the past couple of weeks, but right now she was too angry with him—and too hurt and scared by his ultimatum that she couldn't quit the undercover job—to be concerned with his health.

Trying to shake the feeling of uneasiness, Sarah glanced over her shoulder as she turned on the faucet. Through the space between the overhead cupboards and the counter, she saw her father dozing in his chair. If she were very lucky, he'd stay asleep the rest of the night.

She dumped the salad in the garbage then returned to the table to collect the plates and silverware. Trying to make as little noise as possible, she placed the silverware carefully in the sink. The paper plates she tossed in the trash. They'd never had a set of real dishes. Instead, her father bought paper products by the case at the local Costco every six months. She poured the rest of her milk down the drain and threw the cup away—their cups were all disposable too. She supposed the tradition had started back when her dad was on his own, then continued as he'd tried to juggle work with single parenting. And since she was on kitchen duty every night, she wasn't about to complain about it.

With the kitchen clean, she switched off the light and headed down the short hall. Grocery shopping could wait until tomorrow. A night free from her father and Carl wasn't to be wasted.

"Where you going, Sarah?"

She squeezed her eyes shut. *Just three—more—steps to my room.* "I've got a test to study for," she called over her shoulder.

"Not tonight, you don't. You're working."

"What?" Sarah turned around to face her father, shock and dismay clearly visible on her face. "It's Thursday. I never work on Thursdays." The stern look on her father's face told her it was hopeless to argue. "Is this some kind of punishment because I told you how much I want to quit?"

"I'm trying to make things easier," he said, nodding to a bag near the front door. "I thought a different beat and disguise might make working more—bearable."

Sarah forced herself to walk to the door and retrieve the bag. Under scrutiny of her father's gaze, she pulled out a pair of worn, grungy jeans. Her brow wrinkled in confusion while her nose wrinkled in distaste.

Her father leaned forward in his chair. "Take the rest of it out."

She pulled a large black sweatshirt from the bag, followed by a pair of battered sneakers. A puke green knit cap finished the ensemble.

"Well?" Grant asked.

"They're . . . different." *Disgusting.*

"That's the point. It's different from anything you've ever worn before. There's also a box of hair dye at the bottom of the bag. I want you to use that too, and put your hair in two braids. It'll be a better disguise than that rat's nest of a wig you've been wearing."

"I've never colored my hair before. I thought you said I had to leave it natural."

"It'll be back to natural soon enough—the dye is just temporary. Now hurry. Carl will be here in forty minutes. He'll drop you off five blocks from your job. You'll carry a Glock with you—that's why the sweatshirt is extra large."

The knots in her stomach multiplied. He was serious about her carrying a gun.

"Hurry up. Go." Grant shooed her down the hall with a wave of his hand.

Reluctantly Sarah went into the bathroom and shut the door. She sat on the edge of the tub as she read the instructions for the hair dye, wondering if the red would really wash out. She stood up and looked in the mirror, pulled the rubber band free from her ponytail, and shook out her hair. *What I really need is a new hairstyle,* she thought glumly. But her father always insisted on long and plain. He said anything else might attract unwanted attention.

Sighing, she donned the disposable gloves, mixed the solution, and squirted the foul-smelling liquid all over her head. When it was rubbed in as much as possible, she picked up the bag of clothes and went to her room. Glancing at her cat clock, she noted how many minutes she had to wait until she could rinse her hair.

Taking a folder from her backpack, she pulled out the prints Jay had bought and sat on her bed and shuffled through them, remembering each moment at the museum when she'd stood in front of the real paintings. When she came to *Mrs. Israel Thorndike,* she paused a little longer, remembering how she'd been aware of Jay looking at her instead of the painting. And she'd known, if she had only turned her head, what kind of look she would have caught in his eyes. It baffled her.

Perhaps the idea of taking her out had started on a bet—or a joke between him and the dancers he knew. But if so, something had changed last Friday. *She* would bet now that he was serious when he said he wanted to see her again.

But why?

She wished she knew, wished there was some way to find out. Because when Jay looked at her, it didn't creep her out, which was the way she felt around Carl—like prey being tracked by a predator. Being around Jay was nice, comfortable. Not the comfortable she felt around Reverend Daniels and the Ladies' Aid women who were always so kind to her, but a more interesting kind of comfortable—*friendly*.

A wistful smile touched her lips as she placed the prints back in the folder. With some effort, she forced thoughts of Jay and friendship to the far corner of her mind and hurried to get ready.

Grimacing, she pulled the jeans and sneakers from the bag. No doubt these things had come from some secondhand store. She tried not to think about someone else's skin touching the fabric, another person's *feet* wearing the shoes. She took a can of Lysol from her shelf and sprayed the pants, shirt, and shoes inside and out. When she finished, she was coughing, and her nose burned with the antiseptic smell.

Kills ninety-nine percent of germs, she told herself as she dressed quickly, saving the shirt until after she'd rinsed and braided her hair. But she was already counting the hours until she could shower tonight.

Thirty-eight minutes after her father had sent her to get ready, she emerged in full costume. Over the years she'd also learned not to be late.

"I'm ready," she announced as she walked into the living room. Her father was in the chair where she'd left him.

"You look good," he said. "You'll fit right in with the crowd."

"What crowd?" Sarah asked warily.

"College students mostly. It's a much safer beat than you've had. These rave parties are becoming popular—and a real concern. We've got to get a handle on them before they grow too much. You feel better in that getup?"

She nodded. Aside from being grossed out about who the outfit's previous owners might have been, she did feel better. Gone were the plunging neckline, too-short skirt, and dreaded heels. She didn't miss the itchy wig either, though her hair felt like straw and she was worried the dye wouldn't wash out as easily as the box promised. "It's better. Thanks."

He nodded and cleared his throat. "Come here so I can tell you what's up with this group. There's been an infusion of drugs around the university lately. We think a new dealer is moving in and—"

"Cambridge?" Sarah said bleakly. "You want me to work near the university? Isn't that out of your jurisdiction?"

"Yes and no. There are several cities working together on this. The more we cooperate with each other, the better chance we have of getting the stuff off the street. But you'll still be in Summerfield. There are a couple of clubs . . ."

Sarah focused as her father explained her assignment and showed her the pictures of the contacts. Only after her gun was secured beneath her sweatshirt, the cash was stuffed in the front pocket of her jeans, and she'd climbed into Carl's old truck did she finally allow her mind to wander again.

Ignoring Carl's suggestion that she scoot closer, she leaned her head against the passenger window, welcoming the cold that both kept her awake and renewed her sense of longing for escape. Feeling as trapped as if she were behind bars, Sarah pressed her fingers to the glass, wishing she were on the other side. The night was dark and cloudy, and she felt gloom descending. Letting the cold seal off her emotions, she prepared to do the job she hated.

Chapter Ten

With several grocery bags in each hand, Jay kicked the door shut behind him and headed for the compact galley kitchen in their apartment. Entering the narrow space, he saw Trish sitting on the far counter beside the sink, her arms wrapped around Archer, who stood in front of her. Eyes closed, she murmured something unintelligible as she leaned forward, covering his lips with hers.

Doing his best to ignore the two of them, Jay set the bags on the floor and opened the fridge. He began shuffling things around—mostly moldy and green—making room for the food he'd bought.

"Do you mind?" Archer asked, pulling away from Trish long enough to send Jay a look of annoyance. "We're trying to have a moment of privacy here."

"Sure. I'll just let my milk curdle while you two go at it." Jay tossed a container of take-out Chinese toward the trash and continued putting his food away.

"*Excellent*—you bought milk." Mike sauntered into the kitchen, pajamas pants flapping, though it was well past noon. "Did ya get some cereal to go with it?" He grabbed the carton from Jay, popped it open, and began to chug.

"Hey," Jay said. "That's not—"

"Cookies! Even better." Mike wiped his mouth with the back of his hand, then reached down, snagging a package of Double Stuf Oreos from one of the bags.

Jay took both from him. "*My* milk. *My* cookies."

"But we're roomies. We're supposed to share."

"I share all the time," Jay said. "Tell me what you've contributed to this kitchen lately—besides dirty dishes."

Mike scratched his head, causing his case of bed head to worsen. "I ordered pizza in September."

"It's almost Halloween," Jay reminded him.

"Trish and I are having a moment here," Archer snapped. He stepped away from Trish and walked toward them. "Take your Oreos and your argument elsewhere. I was here first."

"This is the kitchen, Arch." Both Jay and Mike spoke at the same time.

"You can't expect us to stay out of here," Jay finished.

"It's all right." Trish came up behind Archer and put her arms around him. "I've got to get home to study anyhow. Come over at seven, okay?"

"Okay." Archer looked sullen as he turned to give her a quick kiss.

"And you two should come to the Halloween party at our sorority," Trish said to Jay and Mike. "It's next Friday—the twenty-eighth. Everyone's invited. But you have to come in costume."

Archer hauled Trish up against his side. "We're going as Robin Hood and Maid Marian. I'm taking the bow out of storage." His free arm drew back as he shot an imaginary arrow.

Jay raised his eyebrows. "Original. Who'd have guessed?"

"What kind of food did you say there would be?" Mike leaned over, peering into one of the open grocery bags.

Jay nudged it out of his reach. "Find your own breakfast."

"Well, I gotta go. Bye, Arch." Trish left the kitchen, waggling her fingers at him.

"See ya," Archer said.

"Later," Mike mumbled.

"Good luck with your test tomorrow," Jay called.

As soon as the door closed behind Trish, Archer turned to Jay with a scowl. "What test?"

"Economics." Jay set a block of cheese in the fridge door, wondering as he did if it would still be there tomorrow. "She's really worried about it."

"How come she told you instead of me?"

Jay shrugged. "Maybe because I ask her about stuff like that. If you'd give her a chance to do something else with her lips once in a while . . ."

Archer grinned, his good humor suddenly restored. "Why would I want to do that?" He stuck his hands in his pockets. "Come to think of it, why would I want to hear about some stupid econ test? No. I've got things right."

"Speaking of things that *aren't* right—there's a bunch of rotting food in here that belongs to you guys. You gonna clean it out sometime soon?"

"It's not mine," Mike said, raising his hands as he backed away from the fridge. "I haven't bought groceries in weeks."

"No kidding," Jay muttered. "Arch? Any of this stuff yours?"

Archer stepped closer to the fridge, bending over to peer inside. "Yeah, probably. But I don't need it. Trish feeds me almost every night."

"Sounds like a pretty sweet deal," Mike said. "She have any available roommates?"

"None you'd want to look at." Archer grimaced and gave an exaggerated shudder.

Figuring it would take more energy to coax someone else into cleaning the refrigerator than it would to do the job himself, Jay pulled the trash can closer and started dumping things in it. The crisper yielded two black bananas, a small bunch of grapes that used to be green but were now growing some kind of fungus, and a shriveled-up apple that resembled a shrunken head.

The shelves were worse. Jay held his breath as he threw away two slices of hard, stiff pizza—likely from the box that Mike had ordered a month ago—a bowl of hairy raviolis, and a reeking package of mystery meat, still in the white paper wrap from the butcher. As the latter dropped into the trash with a resounding thud, Archer sprang forward.

"Hey, whatcha doing? That's my moose." He reached into the can, pulling the package from the garbage.

"Whoa." Mike grabbed a dishtowel from the counter and covered his face.

"Your *moose?*" Jay closed the refrigerator and stood in front of it. No way that thing was going back in there.

"Yeah. I shot it with my bow." Oblivious to the odor, Archer stroked the package tenderly. "For high school graduation my dad took me hunting in Alaska. I shot this giant moose. It was sweet."

"Arch, you're in your second year of college. You've had that meat—"

"It was in the freezer until recently, and it's aging," Archer said defensively. "This is the last package. I've been saving it for a special occasion."

"That occasion's now," Jay said, holding up the trash can. "Give it up before someone gets hurt."

"Really. I'm about to pass out from the smell." Still holding the towel over his face, Mike edged toward the door.

"I'll take it to Trish's tonight and have her fix it." Archer moved toward the fridge.

Jay stood his ground, folding both arms across his chest. "If the smell doesn't get her, the first bite will kill you both. Throw it away."

Archer looked down at the package in his hands. Mike left the kitchen as Trish returned.

"Arch, my car won't start. Can you come jump it for me? Eew." She pinched her nose. "What's that awful smell?"

"Told you," Jay said.

"It's my moose," Archer said, looking hurt. He glanced at Trish. "I thought you got a new battery."

"I was going to, but they said the old one was fine. Maybe you could come with me this time. I don't know anything about cars, and—"

"Ah, Trish. Not now. You know I've got a ton of homework."

Since when? Jay wondered. He'd hardly seen Archer crack a book in the last few weeks. For a journalism major, he seemed to have an extreme lack of required reading and writing. "Did they check the alternator?" Jay asked. Being careful to keep his position in front of the fridge, he began gathering the empty grocery bags from the floor.

Trish shook her head. "What's that?"

"A lot of times the battery will run down quickly if the alternator is going bad. Come on, Arch. Let's take a look at it." Jay shoved the bags in an overflowing drawer and turned toward the door. Archer stood still, continuing to stare at the package in his hands.

"Think you could cook up this meat, Trish?"

No, Jay mouthed to her, shaking his head.

"I—uh. I could try," Trish said without enthusiasm. "But not unless I can get home." She walked into the kitchen, took a bag from the drawer, and held it open in front of Archer.

He dropped the package of moose meat inside. "Great. Seven, then?"

Trish nodded and looked away. Her eyes were beginning to water.

When Archer went to the sink to wash his hands, she sent a pleading glance in Jay's direction. "Will you come look at my car?"

"Sure." Jay followed her to the door, waiting for Archer. "Aren't you coming? You know more about cars than I do."

Archer hesitated, then finally trotted along behind. The three left the apartment and went down the stairs to the street. Archer pulled his keys out of his pocket and went to get his car from the back parking lot.

Trish was parked in front of their house, and she already had her hood up and the jumper cables on the front seat.

"How will I know if it's the alternator?" she asked.

"The battery will continue to die because it isn't getting charged. Once we get your car started, you should take the alternator in and have it tested.

When's the last time you had your car in for any kind of service?" Jay opened the passenger door and took out the cables.

"Ummm—never." Trish looked dismally at the 1996 Oldsmobile. "The only reason I have it at all is because my grandma can't drive anymore, so she gave it to me. I have no idea what service or repairs it may have had in the past."

Archer pulled his bug in front of Trish's car. Jay handed the cables to him as he got out.

"What're you giving them to me for?" Archer asked. "I don't want to get all greasy."

Jay shrugged. "Just thought you'd want to be the one to help your damsel in distress."

Grumbling, Archer clamped the cables on Trish's battery. Stretching the cords as far as they would go, he opened the passenger door of his bug and leaned inside. He popped the back panel out and leaned in, trying to reach the battery, but it was too far away. He backed out of the car and tossed the cables at Jay. "Hold these."

"Sure." Jay watched with amusement as Archer maneuvered the bug closer.

When it was sideways and only inches from Trish's car, Archer climbed in the back seat again and wrestled the alligator clips onto the battery.

"Give it a minute, then try the Olds," he ordered Trish as he got out, checking the front of his shirt for grease.

Obediently she climbed into her car. Jay turned toward the house.

"Where you going?" Archer demanded.

"To fix myself something to eat before I have to leave for work. I only came out here so you would."

Trish stuck her head out the window. "Now?"

"I said in a minute," Archer yelled.

"Give her a break," Jay said. "She gives *you* enough," he added quietly.

"Stay out of it," Archer said. "Like you'd know anything anyway. It's not as if you've got a girl. Try it now," he called to Trish.

Jay listened as she turned the key and tried the engine once, twice, three times.

"It's still clicking—won't even turn over," Trish said.

"Great," Archer mumbled, rubbing the back of his neck like the whole thing pained him.

"Does your insurance have towing service?" Jay asked.

"I don't know." Trish bit her lip and looked from one man to the other before retreating back into her car.

"Sometimes she doesn't know anything," Archer muttered under his breath.

Jay shot him a look. Archer unfastened the cables, slammed the passenger door, hopped in the bug, and drove off to park the car.

Jay walked over to Trish's window. "He'll be back in a second. And he'll help you with whatever you need."

"I know." Trish sighed. "I wish he wouldn't act so irritated about it though."

Jay looked over his shoulder. "Yeah. Patience and helpfulness aren't exactly his virtues, are they?"

Trish giggled. "No. And I'm not sure what is."

Then why are you going out with him? Jay wanted to ask. "Come on." He opened her door.

She got out. "How come you don't have a girlfriend, Jay? Arch says you're weird, but—"

Jay laughed. "He does, huh?"

Trish winced. "Sorry. I shouldn't have said that. I'm forever opening my mouth without thinking."

"No worries," Jay assured her. "Coming from Arch, that's a compliment."

"Well, I think you're great." Trish waited for him to close the door and walk beside her back to the apartment. "And I really don't get why you won't go out with any of the girls in the ballet company. A lot of them are very nice—and smart, like you are."

"It never seems to work," Jay said, thinking of Jane.

Trish looked at him sideways. "What about that piano girl—Sarah? You like her, don't you?"

Jay shrugged. "I do, but it's hard getting to know her."

"Don't give up," Trish encouraged. "Ask her to the Halloween party."

Jay shook his head. "She'd never be able to come—not without her cousin anyway."

"Invite him, too. There will be enough girls there without dates that I'm sure we could keep him occupied—while you get to know Sarah better, if you know what I mean." She flashed Jay a smile usually reserved for Archer.

"That's not what I meant." He stepped ahead of Trish and held the front door open for her. She stopped before walking through.

"It isn't, is it? You're not interested in finding a free bedroom. You'd rather have some free time to find out who her favorite composer is and what classes she's taking." Trish looked wistful as she spoke. "How'd you get to be so nice, Jay?"

"I wasn't always," he assured her. "And hopefully Archer won't always be the way he is now. He'll wake up and realize what it's all about."

"I hope you're right." She tilted her head back and looked up, gracing him with another pretty smile. "Because I really love him."

"I know." For a second Jay felt that old familiar pang of loneliness.

He wasn't interested in Trish, but he did wonder what it would be like to have someone say that about him. His parents had never said those words that he could recall, nor had any of the string of girls he'd dated in high school and college. And of course, Jane hadn't felt that way toward him, no matter how strong his feelings for her.

Even with Trish and Archer, Jay could see that one was giving way more than the other. *Is it always that way in a relationship? What are the odds a guy can actually fall in love with a girl, have her feel the same, and have a good life together?* Given the divorce rate in America, it seemed chances were pretty slim. With things stacked against him from the onset, he wasn't sure it was worth the effort. Though being alone all the time wasn't all that great either.

"Archer's a lucky guy," Jay said as he followed Trish into the building. Behind them, the door closed slowly before he could notice Archer, a short distance away, his arms folded and a scowl on his face as he watched the couple disappear inside the house.

Chapter Eleven

Sarah set her books on top of the piano and slid onto the bench. No index cards were waiting for her on the stand, she noted with keen, though silent, disappointment. Apparently Jay had believed her at the museum when she'd told him they couldn't see each other.

It's for the best, she told herself. *Feels lousy, but it's for the best.*

With an inaudible sigh, she set out her music, hoping she'd be awake enough to play it. Her new schedule was making school and playing for the ballet difficult. She just had to make it through the next few weeks until they started rehearsing with a full orchestra and wouldn't need her anymore.

As she arranged the pages, one of the dancers approached the piano.

"Hi Sarah, I'm Trish." Her brow furrowed. "Did you color you hair?"

Sarah's hand went to her braid, now strawberry blond thanks to the *temporary* hair dye, as she fumbled for an explanation. "I was experimenting."

"Oh. Looks good." Trish nodded. "Well, anyway, there's a big costume party this Friday. Jay'd like you to come."

Sarah's heart gave a funny little leap. "He knows I can't."

"Sure you can," Trish said, frowning at her. "At Boston Costume on Broadway you'll find outfits reserved for you *and* your cousin. They're paid for and everything. All you have to do is convince him to come with you. Once you get to the party, we'll—" She glanced toward the stage and the dozens of dancers warming up. "Take care of the rest. I promise you'll get to be alone with Jay."

"I can't go," Sarah said again, though her mind was already whirring through possible ways to explain such an event to her father.

Trish sat on the bench, forcing Sarah to scoot over. "Listen, Jay's a really good guy. Any girl would be lucky to have him. And don't tell me you aren't interested. I can tell you are. So give him a chance."

If only I could, Sarah thought. "I can't go," she said again, more forcefully this time. "Please tell him no for me."

* * *

Jay parked his motorcycle along the curb and took off his helmet. Glancing at his watch, he saw he had about seven minutes until Trish would be out of rehearsal. He'd offered to give her a ride because Archer was staying late to work on an article, and her car still wasn't running—and because he was eager to hear if she'd convinced Sarah to come to the party.

The sounds of the marching band drifted toward him from the stadium. Posters were plastered all over campus, advertising the game with Princeton. He'd only been to a couple of football games in his two years at Harvard—law school plus an internship and a night job didn't leave a lot of time for leisure activities. But Jay felt a sudden desire to go to the game, to grasp every last minute of his college experience that he could. All too soon it would be over, and he was fairly certain life would take him far from the charmed world of Cambridge. The northeast was beautiful, and he'd loved living here, but Seattle was calling him home with increasing persistence. Come June, he knew that's where he was headed.

But for now he was here and wanted to savor the experience. For a brief minute, Jay allowed himself to fantasize about going to the game and taking Sarah. Since it was a night game it would probably be cold, but he'd buy one of those crimson blankets he'd wanted for a while. He'd wrap it around the two of them as they stood, cheering the team. He doubted she'd ever been to a game, and it was something every student ought to experience at least once. They'd share a hot chocolate. The overhead lights would shine down on the field and the top of her blond head. He'd coax a smile from her before the night was over.

The image seemed so real that for a second he imagined Sarah coming down the sidewalk toward him. Jay blinked and saw that it *was* her. And she was alone. She held her books clutched to her chest, and her head was cast downward. It was a pathetic picture, and Jay felt a surge of sympathy. Something was really messed up in her life, and he wished he could fix it.

He waited until she was almost in front of him. "Hey, stranger."

She looked up, a brief smile lighting her face before the old worry was back. She glanced toward the street.

"Lose your cousin?" Jay asked hopefully.

She shook her head. "He went to get the car. It'll just take him a minute."

"Too bad." Jay set his helmet on the seat and stepped up on the sidewalk.

Sarah's arms tightened around her books. Her eyes were worried, but she didn't leave.

"I'll be quick," Jay said. "I had a great time with you at the museum. I'd really like to see you again, and there's this party—"

"Trish told me," Sarah broke in. "I can't, Jay. My father would never let me go. And if by some miracle he did, Carl would have to come too, and he'd watch me like a hawk."

"I think we've got the Carl problem solved—for the party, anyway. Go ahead and bring him. Trish has promised me he'll be *plenty* distracted." He glanced toward the rehearsal hall and saw the dancers starting to trickle out.

"It's not just that. If I defy my father, he'll be even more strict. He's already looking for a reason to pull me out of school."

"I *want* to understand this," Jay said. "But you're an adult. You don't have to follow your father's wishes when they're ridiculous. Unless, of course, that's an excuse. I've been around long enough to know the games women play. I really hope that's not what this is."

"It's not," Sarah said, looking hurt. "I wish—I haven't been able to stop thinking about our hour at the museum—or about you."

"Thinking will only get you so far." Jay gave her a wan smile.

"But that's as far as I can go. It would be a mistake for us to try to see—Jay!" Her mouth opened in a scream as she grabbed his hand, yanking him away from the bike. Behind them tires squealed, and an engine roared.

Sarah held on, pulling him across the sidewalk with more force than he'd have guessed her to have. Surprised, he stumbled forward, bumping into her as she tripped and fell back toward the grass. Her hand flailed in the air as she tried to catch herself, causing her books and papers to fly everywhere. Jay reached for her and missed. She hit the grass, her head snapping back sharply. His own fall continued, and he barely avoided landing on top of her, only just catching himself when his knee hit the ground beside her leg.

"Watch out!" a girl next to them shouted a warning. "He's going to jump the curb."

Jay twisted to follow the sound and saw a truck, less than ten feet away, barreling straight for them. There was no time to move, but instinctively he crouched over Sarah, hoping to somehow shield her with his body. Her eyes fluttered open, and she was gasping like she'd had the breath knocked out of her when she fell.

Jay squeezed his eyes shut, tensing for the moment they'd be hit. A deafening crash sounded behind them. The awful screeching of metal grinding on metal filled the air. Sparks flew up from the street. Glass shattered, spraying across the sidewalk and the people on it. What felt like rocks pelted his back. He lowered his face closer to Sarah's and cupped his hands over her head, trying to protect her from the flying debris.

An engine revved and tires squealed again. *We're not hit,* Jay realized. Miraculously the truck had missed them. He looked up and saw the twisted remains of his bike less than two feet away. The truck was backing up.

"Come on." He reached for Sarah's hands as he got to his knees. "We need to move before that lunatic comes back for a second pass."

"So—sorry." She looked around, dazed.

"This isn't your fault." He pulled her to her feet as she held her head and tried keeping her glasses, broken on one side, on her face. "Sarah, are you okay? Is your head—"

"I'm fine—can't believe he'd do something like this." She took one wobbly step before Jay put his arm around her.

"Who would? What are you talking about?" he asked.

"Is she okay?" another student asked, looking as concerned as he felt.

"I think so," Jay said. "But she hit her head when she fell." He looked around and saw a few other people getting up from the ground and staggering away in stunned silence.

"The truck's coming back!" someone yelled. Jay glanced behind him and saw that it was. Wrapping his arm tighter around Sarah, he started to run with the others toward the closest building, Lowell House. Reaching the doors, he gently pushed her inside. "You'll be safe in here," he called over the head of another student, hurrying to get in the building.

Jay turned away from Lowell and ran a few steps back, scanning the lawn for anyone else who might have been hurt. The truck neared the sidewalk and went barreling past, toward the end of the street.

With adrenalin pumping and without stopping to think what he was doing, Jay sprinted after it. A sharp pain stabbed his foot, and he looked down to see a piece of his side mirror embedded in his shoe.

He yanked it out, ignored the pain, and kept running after the truck. "Someone get his license," he called to the bewildered students standing around in various states of shock.

A couple of students responded to his plea and joined the chase, running alongside him. One woman pulled out her cell phone.

"He's turning down Plympton," a guy called. Jay sprinted toward the corner, straining to make out the letters on the back plate. But the truck was too fast, and by the time Jay reached the corner, it was too far away.

Anger surged through him as he stood there another second, then finally turned around.

"You all right?" the man who'd run with him asked.

Jay nodded. He didn't trust himself to speak. Sarah's words after the crash finally registered, and he had a hunch about who was behind the wheel of that truck. If he was correct . . . It was one thing for the guy to punch him in the name of watching out for his cousin, but nearly running them down was another thing entirely. The nutcase belonged in jail.

Realizing he'd left Sarah without really making sure she was okay, he started to jog again. It only took him a minute to get back to Lowell, but he couldn't find her inside. He went outside and saw that her things were gone from the lawn. Walking up and down the curb, he called her name and asked the other students if they'd seen a girl with broken glasses. Only one woman recalled seeing Sarah gathering her books and walking back toward the main campus.

Frustrated, Jay returned to the wreck of his bike. Angrily, he kicked a piece of tail pipe aside as he worried about Sarah.

If her cousin would do something like this out in public, what would happen when Sarah was alone with him?

Chapter Twelve

"Jay!" Trish stepped over the glass on the sidewalk and made her way to his side.

He looked up from the mangled remains of his motorcycle.

"You're bleeding." She pointed to his head.

Jay pressed his fingers to his temple and winced as he touched something sharp. He pulled his hand away and saw that it was covered with wet, sticky blood. For the first time he felt the trickle down the side of his face.

"What is it?" he asked Trish.

She moved closer, and he bent his head so she could see. "It looks like—" She reached up, fingertips carefully removing a piece of glass. "A mirror maybe?"

Jay glanced at the quarter-inch piece she held. "Yeah." He touched his head again but couldn't tell how bad the cut was. He tried to recall how long it had been since his last tetanus shot. "Stitches you think?"

"I can't tell. But use this." Trish pulled the scarf from her hair and held it out to him.

"No—I'm fine," Jay reassured her. "I'd ruin your—"

"Shh." She leaned closer, pressing the cloth to his head with shaking fingers. "Hold it tight there until we can get something better."

"Thanks." Jay felt ridiculous holding a woman's scarf to his forehead.

"What happened?" Trish asked. "I heard the crash on my way out here."

"Some idiot ran over my bike—and almost me—on purpose. He got away before I could get the license, but I'm pretty sure I know who can give it to me."

It took a second for Trish to understand. "You think it was Sarah's cousin?"

"One and the same."

A campus police officer arrived on a bicycle and came over to get Jay's information. He looked down at the wrecked motorcycle. "Wow. You okay?"

"I wasn't on it at the time," Jay assured him.

"Good thing," the officer said. He took out a notepad and pen.

"He thinks he knows who did it," Trish piped up. "And the guy's a creep. He should—"

"I didn't get a license plate, so there's no point in making accusations." On the other side of the officer, Jay shook his head.

"But—" Trish protested.

"What I really need is to do is get this cut taken care of and call my insurance company." Jay looked around for his backpack and spotted it, still intact, on the sidewalk a few feet away.

"Can you describe the vehicle that hit your bike?" the officer asked.

"It was an old truck—Ford, I think," Jay said. "The way the guy was swerving, he might have been drunk."

"But no license?"

"Nah. The guy was too fast. Though maybe somebody else caught it."

Jay groaned as an ambulance roared up the street. He looked around to see if anyone else was injured and spotted two girls sitting together on the curb about twenty feet away. "Hey, I think you should go see if they're all right," he said to the officer. "Some of the pieces flew pretty far, and one of those girls might be hurt."

"Fill this out," the officer said, handing him a small clipboard. "And don't leave yet."

"No worries. My mode of transportation has been slightly altered." Jay attempted a lighthearted remark, but looking at the wreck all he could think of was Sarah. He scrawled his information across the form as a sense of urgency filled him. He needed to know she was okay.

"You're still bleeding." Trish leaned up on her tiptoes, wiping the drops of blood that had escaped the scarf and trickled down the side of his face.

Jay grabbed her hand, annoyed with the attention when Sarah was likely hurt as well or in continued danger. "I'm fine."

Trish looked up at him, her honey-colored eyes brimming with tears. "I know, but a second earlier, a foot closer, and you'd have been"—she gulped but was unable to stop the tide of emotion—*"killed."* She brought her hands to her face.

Trying to set his annoyance and worry aside, Jay pulled her close with his free hand. He held her as she cried. "I'm fine," he reiterated. "It's a scratch. Nothing serious." He patted her back awkwardly.

Down the street the officer was talking with other students. One of the two girls Jay had seen sitting on the curb was being attended to by a paramedic. Jay glanced the other direction and saw several people milling around, but no sign of Sarah.

Where did you go so fast? Are you okay? He didn't want to think about her getting in the truck with that maniac.

The officer returned. He took the clipboard from Jay. "You didn't write a time down," he said as his eyes scanned the paper.

"Sorry," Jay said. "It was—" He glanced at his watch. "About seven minutes ago. It happened so fast. One second we were talking, the next the truck was practically on top of us."

"It jumped the curb?"

"Yeah. See the tire marks?" Jay tried to move toward the sidewalk, but Trish was still clinging to him.

"You say the driver might have been intoxicated. Any chance he'd blacked out? Did you get a look at him at all?"

"No," Jay said. "But he was awake enough to know what he was doing. After he hit the bike, he backed up and came in for another pass, but the second time he swerved close by and then went on down the street."

"And this young lady was with you?" The officer looked at Trish, who was quickly going into meltdown mode.

"Uh, no," Jay said. "She's just upset." *About this, and what else?* he wondered. It didn't seem normal for a girl to go on like this over her boyfriend's roommate's near-death experience.

The officer made some additional notes, and Trish continued to cry all over Jay's shirt while he stood there worrying about Sarah. It seemed to take forever before Jay was free of them both and could finally collect his backpack and call his insurance company. After that the paramedics insisted on checking him, and it took another ten minutes to get both his head and foot looked at and bandaged. Fortunately the cut on his foot wasn't too bad, but it looked like he'd be heading to the medical center to get a tetanus shot and stitches for his head. He'd do that as soon as his bike had been hauled away. And by then . . . well, Sarah was already long gone. The best he could do was hope she was okay—and worry.

Once the paramedics left, he walked over to Trish, who was sitting on the sidewalk near his bike.

"You okay now?" He hoped he wasn't going to inspire a new flood with that question.

"Yeah." She gave him a shaky smile. "Girls always feel better after they cry."

"That's because all their angst transfers to the guys they're with." He thought suddenly of Jane and all the crying she'd done—both happy and sad—last September during the day and a half they'd spent together in Washington, D.C. "I feel awful right now," Jay said. "Didn't know you had so much water in you. I'd hate to see you at a funeral, Trish."

"Sorry." She looked down at the ground, nudging a leaf with the toe of her shoe. "It's been a rough week."

"You and Arch?" Jay guessed.

She nodded. "You're pretty perceptive for a guy."

"For a guy." Jay smiled. "Don't give up on him yet. Arch's been moping around the apartment the last couple of days. I figured something might be out of sorts with you two."

"He has?" Trish looked up, a hopeful smile lighting her face.

"Yep. He's been a real crab. So kiss and make up already," Jay teased.

"Wish we could." Trish sighed. "But I did a terrible thing."

"Let me guess." Jay stroked his chin. "Did you suggest he might make his own dinner?"

"Worse," Trish said.

Jay raised his eyebrows. "Come on. Spill it."

"I threw away his moose steak and lied about it."

"You did?" Jay held his hand out for a high-five as he laughed out loud.

Trish slapped his hand.

"Heck. Arch ought to be thanking you. You probably saved both your lives by not eating that thing."

"That's what I thought. You should have seen it—completely green. And the *smell*."

"You actually *opened* the package?" Jay asked.

Trish nodded. "I was going to try to cook it, but it was soooo bad. I bought a steak from the store instead and told Archer it was the moose. I should have known he'd be able to tell the difference since he's hunted and eaten so many different animals."

Jay nodded in agreement. "I can see where you got in trouble there."

"The worst part is that Archer was out working on my car all afternoon. He was trying to do something nice for me, and I threw away his moose. Oh, Jay. He was *so* furious with me."

"This *is* bad," Jay agreed. "But if anyone can soften Archer's heart, it's you. I know he misses you, and I bet if you planned a nice evening for just the two of you, all would be forgiven. Oh, and you might have to go hunting with him."

Trish rolled her eyes. "I was afraid of that." But her smile was back. "Thanks, Jay. For letting me cry about everything, and for listening. You're a great friend." She stood up, leaned in, and gave him a hug.

"Anytime," Jay said.

"And this is for you." Trish pulled some papers from her bag. "I found these on the ground over by that tree. I thought maybe they belonged to Sarah. There's an address on the back." She placed the papers in Jay's hand and turned to go. "See ya."

Jay turned the papers—a choral arrangement—over and looked at the gold sticker on the back.

> *Summerfield Community Church*
> *359 W. Mallory Avenue*
> *Summerfield, MA* 98110

"Thanks," he called to Trish.

She turned and waved.

Pulling his eyes from the paper to his wrecked motorcycle, Jay thought again of the close call with the truck. Sarah had likely saved his life. But what of hers? He kicked at a bent tire and stared at the scattered scraps of metal—evidence that something in Sarah's life was very, very wrong.

Chapter Thirteen

Anger fueling her courage, Sarah marched up the steps of the Summerfield Police Station. She pushed open the first set of glass doors, then the second, and went straight to the front desk. Chief's daughter or not, she couldn't just go back to her father's office. Though with the storm that had been building inside her the past few hours, she had no doubt she could have easily jumped over the counter and started running for it before anyone caught her.

Common sense prevailed. "I need to speak to Chief Morgan, please." She forced her voice to remain calm as she addressed the woman at the front counter. She was new—or at least new since Sarah had last been in to see her dad at work. That didn't surprise her. The turnover rate for those working under her father was high. *Wish I had the luxury of leaving too.*

"Name?" the woman asked.

"Sarah Morgan. I'm his daughter. It's urgent," she added.

The woman picked up the phone, and Sarah went to the door, expecting to be buzzed back immediately. Her father didn't like her coming to the station—something to do with a few employees who had hard feelings about the "good" position she'd been given—and he always whisked her into his office and out of sight as quickly as possible.

This time was no different. The buzzer sounded; she pushed the door open and walked through, heading down the short hall. Her father's door wasn't open, but she didn't bother knocking, and instead went right inside, starting in with her complaint before he could lecture her about being there.

"Carl tried to kill me on campus this afternoon." She stepped aside so the door could close behind her. "He drove straight at me with his truck, ran over the curb, over a student's motorcycle, and onto the sidewalk. He was within two feet of hitting me. He's *dangerous,* and I won't have him following me around anymore." *There. I said it.*

Her father's face was surprisingly calm, though she detected anger boiling beneath the surface.

"Sarah, I'd like you to meet Detective Anderson. He joined our department earlier this year." Grant Morgan swiveled toward the far side of the room and the before-unnoticed detective.

Sarah swallowed back her mortification as she slowly turned to follow her father's gaze to the man rising from his chair. "Nice to meet you, Detective," she somehow managed to say.

"Pleasure," he said, nodding at her. "Looks like you two need to talk, so I'll come back later, Chief."

Sarah backed away from the door as Detective Anderson left the room. She closed her eyes, unable to fully grasp how incredibly angry her father was going to be. *Well, I'm angry too.* Swallowing the lump in her throat, she turned back to her father.

"I'm sorry. I had no idea someone else was in here with you. But everything I said about Carl is true. He's snapped or something. What he did today is inexcusable. What if he had hit someone?"

"Haven't I taught you to knock on a door when it is closed?" her father asked in a deceptively quiet voice.

"Yes, but—"

"How many times have I told you I don't like you coming here?"

"A lot, but this was an emergency. Haven't you heard anything I've said?" For the first time that she could remember, her voice was louder than her father's. "Carl tried to *kill* me. He almost ran me over. Look at my glasses." She thrust the broken frames toward him. "And my elbow. I cut it when I fell. And I've got a huge bump on the back of my head. He—"

"I'm sure you're overreacting," Grant interrupted.

"He almost *hit me with his truck!*" She threw her hands up in exasperation. "Don't I mean anything to you?"

"No," Grant answered quickly, then pressed his lips together as if he were biting back an additional remark.

Sarah took a step back, feeling a physical pain in her chest as she tried to digest the hurt his one word caused.

Her father clenched and unclenched his jaw a couple of times before speaking again. "Right now you mean inconvenience and expense. This very minute you're costing me valuable time and money. I was in the middle of an important briefing with Detective Anderson, and now we'll have to start over."

"I'm sorry," Sarah whispered. Tears burned the back of her eyes, and she prayed they wouldn't fall. Crying only angered her father more.

"Later, you'll mean my dinner is ready and my clothes are ironed. And lest you think that's harsh," Grant continued. "I'll remind you that I mean a roof over your head and food in your belly, and that expensive education you want so badly."

Sarah couldn't believe what she was hearing. His words burned in her chest—worse than the fall that had stolen her breath this afternoon. She tried to edge toward the door without staggering, tried to mask the pain her father's callous words brought. She'd guessed their relationship wasn't what other fathers and daughters shared, but she'd never known she was only tolerated. There had been times throughout the years—the other night even—when she honestly would have said she thought her father loved her.

But no more.

Wordlessly she backed out of the office and walked down the hall, through the door to the lobby, and left the station. Somehow she cleared both sets of glass doors and was halfway down the steps outside before the first tear fell. She brushed it away and walked faster. She had to get to the house, to her piano. Her fingers flexed with unexpressed emotion. They would cry for her. They would pound out her frustrations, fears, sorrow. Already the notes of a new composition filtered through her mind. She grasped onto them, onto the vision of the piano beneath her fingertips, notes ringing out as fast as she could play them. This melody would not be happy, light, or carefree, but a dark piece in A-sharp minor, as full of sour notes as her life was.

The leaves crunched, unnoticed, beneath her feet. Near-bare trees shaded her way in the already-cool afternoon. The few neighbors who watched her walk by in her trance thought nothing of it—she'd been the chief's recluse daughter for so long. The children out playing gave her wide berth as they rode their bicycles down the street.

Sarah turned up the drive to her house, the only one on the street not sporting Halloween decorations. There was no paper skeleton hanging from the door, no carved pumpkins on the porch, no autumn centerpiece on the table when she unlocked the door and went inside.

Her book bag fell from her hands, and the shoes slid from her feet as she collapsed on the bench in front of the old piano. Closing her eyes, she took a deep breath and let her fingers rest on the keys. One note to start. Followed by a low chord. A series of chords. A seventh. Her right hand joined in the solemn march that slowly built in fervor and anger. Minutes ticked past on the clock in the kitchen. Violent music filled the house; she was pounding on the keys now, abusing the instrument as she almost never did.

Finally the notes softened. They were sad. Worse than the funeral march she'd played for old Mrs. Newell last month. She tried to make them happier, tried to force her fingers to keys she knew would sound more harmonious. They wouldn't go. Her right hand never went an octave above middle C. High notes were too unbearable right now—there were none in her life. And her own small attempt to grasp at one—to have a friend-ship—had plunged her to the lowest point she'd ever been.

Twenty minutes passed before the notes trickled to a stop and she felt calm enough to free her fingers from the ivory keys. Sarah went to the bathroom to wash her hands and was surprised at the red-rimmed eyes of the girl staring back at her from the mirror. She brought her hands to her cheeks and found them damp. Her throat was sore with the tears she'd held back, but it seemed they'd somehow escaped anyway. Grabbing a washcloth from the counter, she ran it under the cold water and pressed it to her face. She couldn't let her father know.

She would wash her face. She would fix his dinner. She would iron his shirts.

And soon, very soon, she would find a way to leave.

Chapter Fourteen

Feeling extraordinarily grumpy, Jay trudged up the walk, into the house, and up the stairs to his apartment. After seeing his bike towed away for scrap metal, he'd gone to a nearby health clinic for stitches and a tetanus shot. By then he was late for work and not feeling too hot, so for the first time ever, he'd called in sick. An unexpected night off might have been great, except for the fact that his head was killing him and he couldn't stop worrying about Sarah.

Jay put his hand on the doorknob and was about to turn it when the door flew inward, yanking him with it.

"Stay away from her," Archer said, shoving Jay back out into the hall.

"Don't—touch—me," Jay warned, eyes narrowing. He straightened and took a step toward Archer. "It's been a bad day, and I have no idea what you're even talking about." He pushed past him into the living room.

"Trish," Archer said, grabbing Jay's backpack as he walked by.

"Hey! What do you think—"

Archer pulled Trish's soiled scarf from the mesh pocket on the side of the pack. He waved it in front of Jay's face. "*This* is what I'm talking about. I saw you two today. You were all over her."

Jay groaned as he flopped back on the couch. "We're not in high school, Arch."

"Stealing a guy's girl is plenty immature."

"I'm *not* stealing her," Jay said. He held both hands up. "Really. I told her I'd give her a lift today *because* I wanted to find out if Sarah agreed to go to the party. I got Trish to ask her for me."

"Oh." Some of Archer's anger seemed to dissipate. "Then how come you had your arm around her? And the other day after we'd been looking at her car, you two were all cozy in the doorway."

"I haven't been cozy with a woman in a long time," Jay said, somewhat depressed by the reminder. "We were talking about *you* that day—I was trying to convince Trish that you weren't always such a jerk."

Archer scowled. "She didn't need to be convinced of anything until you started hanging around her so much."

"I'm not," Jay said. "Today she was bawling her eyes out 'cause she thinks you two are on the verge of breaking up."

"We are," Arch said. He dropped the backpack on the floor and sat down on the opposite end of the couch.

"Because of a stupid package of meat?" Jay asked.

"It wasn't stupid."

"No. Just rancid." Jay rolled his eyes. "Trish loves you—she didn't feel right about feeding you deadly food. Get over it, or break up with her so she can have a chance with someone else."

Archer turned toward him, anger flashing in his eyes again. "You *are* after her. I knew it."

"That's not what I meant." Jay rose from the sofa, dismissing him and the whole ridiculous conversation. "I'm going to bed. Don't bother me unless the house is on fire."

"Don't worry," Archer mumbled. "I won't bother you then, either."

Chapter Fifteen

"Daddy's home!" Jeffrey galloped across the kitchen, his cowboy boots leaving scuffs on the old cream-colored linoleum Christa hated so much. But instead of scolding their oldest son, she shared his enthusiasm.

"Yippee," she shouted, scooping up James, their three-and-a-half-year-old, and running toward the front door. "Daddy's home, and he's bringing pizza, and it's his turn to give baths and tuck-ins." *Cause for celebration, indeed.* This evening she'd finally have time to finish sewing their costumes for the Halloween party this Friday. And the boys wouldn't be right beside her, unwinding the thread, stepping on the foot pedal when she wasn't ready, or using her good scissors to cut paper—or each other's hair.

Jeffrey took his place by the front door, lasso ready. James wiggled out of her grasp and straightened his cowboy hat. The front door opened, and Kirk walked in, weariness and worry plainly written on his face.

"Gotcha!" Jeffrey shouted as the rope he'd tossed looped its way over Kirk's outstretched hand. Jeffrey tried to pull the rope tight, but he'd knotted it wrong, and the loop came undone. He stumbled back into the shoe basket beside the door.

James laughed. "Did it wrong. You did it wrong."

"Don't tease your brother," Christa scolded.

Momentarily abandoning the cowboy act, Jeffrey reverted to his favorite ninja stance and kicked his foot up, sending a boot—spurs and all—sailing toward James's head.

Kirk reached down and caught the boot easily before another bruise could be added to the trio James currently sported. Kirk looked at his oldest son. "Do you need to go to your room, Jeffrey?"

"No," Jeffrey huffed. He grabbed for his boot.

Kirk held it out of reach. "Apologize."

"He laughed at me," Jeffrey said. "How come he doesn't have to 'pologize?"

"He will." Kirk closed the door behind him and knelt down. He set the boot on the carpet and reached his hands out to both of his sons. James came eagerly. Jeffrey folded his arms across his chest and scowled, though he allowed his dad to pull him close.

Christa felt a rush of tenderness as she looked down on her boys—all three of them.

"You boys are very lucky," Kirk began, "to have each other to play with. I always wanted a brother—"

"But you just got sisters," Jeffrey finished, coming out of his tantrum. "And now you have to share a room with Mommy."

"Poor Daddy," James said.

"Poor, poor Daddy." Christa rolled her eyes.

Kirk winked at her. "Mommy's different. She smells good."

"Did your sisters stink?" Jeffrey asked, curiosity lighting his eyes as he looked intently at his father.

Kirk nodded. "Dreadfully. They each had these little bottles of pink perfume called *Loves Baby Soft*. And they put it on everything."

"Like what?" Jeffrey wrinkled his nose.

"What?" James asked, not to be left out. He scrunched his face up, trying to imitate his brother.

"My pillow," Kirk said. "My clothes. Even my—" He lowered his voice to a whisper and pulled the boys close. "Once they put it on my *underwear*."

Jeffrey gasped as his hands went automatically to the seat of his pants.

"Underwear." James giggled.

"Pizza?" Christa reminded them.

A look of panic flashed across Kirk's face. He gave Christa an apologetic smile as he rose from the floor. "I forgot."

"I called you an hour ago," she said, trying not to sound irritated. Since Eddie Martin's death two weeks ago, she knew things at the station had been stressful. It seemed like all of Kirk's hard work over the past six months was unraveling before his eyes. The supplier he'd been close to finding remained as elusive as ever, and all of Eddie's files were frozen, pending further investigation into his death. She knew Kirk didn't need extra stress at home, but the boys needed their dad, and she needed her husband.

"But it's no problem," she forced herself to say. "Why don't you play with the boys for a while, and I'll run out and grab one."

"Sure." Kirk didn't look very enthused as the boys each grabbed one of his hands.

"Come on, Dad. You be Cowboy Dan. I'm Johnny Silver." Jeffrey stopped to reach down and grab his boot. He held it up high, clinking the spurs.

"I'm Applejack," James said.

"No. That's cereal," Jeffrey said. "You're Flapjack."

"Which is a pancake." A reluctant smile tugged at the corner of Kirk's mouth. "Either way, you're something yummy to eat! Mmm." He growled as he picked up James and threw him over his shoulder. "Who needs pizza when we've got an apple flapjack?"

"Dad-dy," James giggled.

"Flapjack is a *cowboy.*" Jeffrey jumped up, trying to free his brother, and landed, stomping his boot across his dad's toe.

Kirk winced. "Have they been watching *Howdy Town*? I thought we hid—"

"Grandma sent another one!" Jeffrey exclaimed. "'Cause I told her on the phone that we lost the first one."

"Another one," James echoed.

"Remind me to thank Grandma," Kirk said without sincerity as he helped James slide to the floor.

"We got stars in the package too." Jeffrey stuck out his chest, showing off the shiny metal badge pinned to his homemade cowboy vest.

"Me too," James said.

"We're sheriffs like you," Jeffrey said. "Now we just need guns. But Mom still says no."

"Mom is right," Kirk agreed. "Guns are dangerous. They're not something you ever play with." He disentangled himself from the boys and went to the bedroom to safely store his own weapon.

Christa started to follow him, to retrieve her purse and shoes. "Boys, you can each have half of a Go-Gurt from the Ziploc bag in the freezer. Eat it at the table, though."

"Yippee—Go-Gurt!" Jeffrey galloped across the room on his imaginary horse. James tried to follow, but his boots were even bigger than Jeffrey's, and he tripped on the carpet twice. Christa reached over and picked him up the second time, tousling his hair. "Careful there, pardner."

He shrugged off her affection and followed his brother to the kitchen. Christa decided she'd use the few free minutes to talk to Kirk. She went to their room and sat beside him on the bed.

"Are you still up for Dad duty tonight so I can finish the costumes?"

He turned to her. "I am. I haven't forgotten. And I remembered the pizza until the last minute. Sorry."

"It's okay. I'll go get one. Maybe I can strike up a conversation with the cashier to help fill my quota for adult conversation today. I've had about all I can take of talking ponies and roundups. Jeffrey lassoed the vacuum when I had it open to empty the canister. Dirt and hair and everything else—all over the floor. Those boys wear me out."

"I'll bet." Kirk put his arm around her, pulled her close, and kissed the top of her head. "You're a good mom. Our boys are lucky."

"You're a good dad, too."

"I try." Kirk sighed. "Today I witnessed some of the worst parenting I've ever seen."

"Oh?" Christa went to the closet and grabbed the closest pair of sneakers. "You get called out on a domestic case?"

Kirk shook his head. "That's the sad thing. It wasn't a case at all. Happened right in the office."

"*What* happened?" Christa returned to the bed and began untying the laces.

"Chief Morgan's daughter came to the station—first time I've seen her." Kirk removed his holster and set it aside. "Chief and I were meeting in his office, going over the evidence for the Rossi trial, and his daughter came in all upset."

Christa finished tying her first shoe and moved on to the second. "And . . ." she prompted.

"It sounded really serious, so I got up quickly, left my folders and everything on the floor, and went out so they could have some privacy. A couple of minutes later she left, looking worse than when she came in."

"How does that make him a bad father?" Christa asked.

"It doesn't—didn't," Kirk clarified. "To be honest, I didn't think anything of it. I imagine a lot of girls get upset with their dads. The chief called me back in his office, we wrapped up our meeting, and I packed up my stuff to come home. As I was driving, I thought I'd replay the tape of our meeting, so I could go over the list of things the defense attorney is likely to bring up." Kirk paused, a serious look on his face. "I rewound the tape—but not far enough—and discovered I'd left it on when his daughter was there. It recorded their conversation."

"You didn't listen to it, did you?" Christa asked, clearly appalled.

"I didn't plan to," Kirk said, "but it was already running, and I couldn't quite believe what the chief said. So I replayed it and listened again."

"*Twice?* You played it on purpose a second time? Kirk, I'm—"

"I'd like you to listen to it," Kirk said quietly.

"Isn't that wrong? A breach of privacy or—"

"Just listen," Kirk urged. "And tell me if I've misunderstood or something." He pulled the tape recorder from his pocket and hit *play*.

Christa frowned as she sat on the edge of the bed and listened to Chief Morgan's daughter describe almost being hit by a car—on purpose, it sounded like. Christa gasped at the chief's cruel response. She felt her mouth open with shock at the cold description he gave of the role his daughter played in his life.

"I can't believe that," she said, outrage in her voice. She looked up at Kirk. "It's—it's awful. No wonder you had to listen twice. Of all the heartless—"

"I know," Kirk said. "And the thing that really bothers me is that she was reporting a crime. It sounds like she's in danger, and he's just blowing her off."

"And breaking her heart," Christa added, feeling a pang of sympathy for the young woman she'd never met.

"I've heard a lot of weird rumors about the chief since I started," Kirk said. "And I've observed some unusual behavior myself—some days he's really on top of things, and I feel we're making progress. Other times it almost seems he's thwarting our best efforts. But I really don't know what to make of this—or what I should do."

"What *can* you do?" Christa asked. "I mean, could he fire you for taping him like that?"

Kirk shrugged. "I don't know. And I'm not planning to find out, though the officer in me feels like I ought to do something to help his daughter. She reported a crime—sought help and protection—and she got neither. I think maybe I'll call the campus police and see if anything is being done from that end. It's really worrying me."

"I can see that." Christa scooted closer, wrapping her arm around her husband. "It's your superman syndrome rearing its head again." She leaned against his shoulder, thinking of all the times Kirk went above and beyond to help those in need—be they family, ward members, coworkers, or complete strangers. At times she wondered if she'd just married an exceptionally good guy, or if he secretly harbored a desire to save the world, one person at a time.

"Maybe you're right," Kirk agreed. "But this time I can't help but feel that Chief Morgan's daughter is one person who could really use a hero."

Chapter Sixteen

Kirk left the courtroom and walked down the hall of the Middlesex County courthouse. He stopped to get a drink from the closest fountain, and his phone started ringing just as the cool water reached his lips. Stepping back, he pulled his cell out and saw that it was Christa. He exhaled, feeling a little of the stress leave his body.

"Hi, sweetheart. I'm just leaving now—running a few minutes late—but I haven't forgotten I need to stop at the store. Knee-high pantyhose for your costume and a carton of ice cream for the babysitter and the boys," he said, reciting the instructions she'd given him earlier.

"Never mind stopping." Christa sighed into the phone. "Challise just called. She has strep. We're out of luck for a babysitter for the party tonight."

"What about her little sister?"

"That's who she caught strep from," Christa said. "And I've already tried the other two girls in the ward that I trust. They're both going to the Halloween dance at their school. So unless you can pull a babysitter out of your back pocket . . ."

Kirk frowned. "You want me to ask Detective Brandt?"

Christa snorted. "Hardly. I hate to think what the boys would learn—and eat—if they spent an hour in his company. I guess we're sunk." She paused. "How was your day? How'd the trial go?"

It was Kirk's turn to sigh. "'Not guilty' on four out of the five trafficking charges. Minimum sentence on the last." He rubbed the back of his neck. "Not the verdict I was hoping for."

"Not guilty—how can that be?" Christa asked, her astonishment carrying through the phone lines. "You guys had photos and witnesses and—"

"His attorney knew all the loopholes. Made sure the photos were inadmissible and did a great job discrediting the witnesses. I should have known something was up when he wasn't even interested in the plea."

Kirk looked down the hall where Steve Nicholsine, of the Holt and Nicholsine law firm, was just leaving the courtroom. For a split second he looked at Kirk, and their eyes met, challenging each other. *You got him off this time,* Kirk thought. *But we're not finished with this. Sooner or later, he's gonna screw up again.*

Nicholsine broke their gaze and walked in the opposite direction.

"Kirk?" Christa asked. "Did you hear what I said?"

"Um. Yeah," he answered absently. "We should take the boys to that corn maze tonight?"

"*Tomorrow,*" Christa said. "What I suggested is that you pick up a movie on your way home. I would've liked to go out, but I guess renting a DVD will have to do."

"Okay." Kirk resisted the urge to turn around and watch the attorney until he left the building.

"Why don't you get some really romantic chick flick?" Christa said.

"Sure." *Bet he drives a BMW or something—funded by the criminal wealth of his clientele.*

"Maybe a period piece set in England."

"Okay."

"Now I *know* you're not listening," Christa accused, but there was concern in her voice. "Kirk, are you okay?"

"Fine." He realized he was still standing in the same spot and staring at the courtroom door. "Just distracted. Sorry. We can get whatever you want." He started walking down the hall and forced his attention back to Christa and the weekend with his family.

"No thanks," Christa said. "You'd be a million miles away for sure. On second thought, I think you'd better just come home. I'll put the boys to bed early and we'll talk."

"I don't want to talk about it, but maybe we could think of something else to get my mind off work . . . I'll get ice cream for us instead, all right?"

"With nuts?"

"Loads of them." He smiled. "And some quadruple-bypass chocolate flavor."

"I'll get the boys in their pajamas right now."

"See you in about twenty minutes," Kirk said. He left the building and walked to his car, trying to forget about the case and the reality that J.D.

Rossi was not going to be behind bars for long—if at all. Not only had he gotten off easy, but the Summerfield PD had missed another opportunity to get closer to busting up the local meth market.

First Eddie's death, and now this. For the moment, the police had nowhere else to turn.

If we could just get to their distributor, Kirk thought. Chances were Eddie Martin and J.D. Rossi had the same supplier, and given the increasing volume of meth on the streets, it was likely an East Coast source. Chances were also good that if things continued as they were, the Boston/Cambridge area was soon going to rival some of the West Coast cities for methamphetamine use. It was a chilling thought.

Kirk climbed in his cruiser and started the engine. He drove up Thorndike Street, watching pedestrians out of the corner of his eye. He doubted he'd see Nicholsine again—probably a good thing, as he wasn't feeling too charitable toward the man.

How do people like that sleep at night? Kirk wondered. *Don't they have any conscience? Don't they worry that the guys they get off may harm someone else, or sell drugs to their own kids?*

"Too many crooked lawyers," he mumbled. "And more on the way," he noted, seeing a group of law clerk interns walking down the sidewalk.

Recognizing one of them, Kirk's mood took an upward swing, and he pulled over to the curb. Rolling down his window, he called to the man walking ahead of the others. "Hey, Jay. Need a ride?"

Jay looked over and lifted a hand in recognition. "Depends on if you're offering the front or back seat."

"Today it's the front, though after you pass the bar . . ." Kirk grinned.

Jay laughed and walked toward the car. "Which one's got you angry now?"

"Nicholsine," Kirk said. "But interns like you give me hope for the profession. Get in. I'll give you a lift. Is your motorcycle nearby?"

"Not exactly." Jay pulled the sedan door open and climbed in the passenger seat. "It's kind of out of commission right now."

"Must make it difficult to take the ladies out on Friday night." Kirk pulled away from the curb as Jay fastened his seat belt.

"It would," Jay said, "if that were an issue."

"Still not dating, huh? I could introduce you . . ." Kirk let the offer hang in the air. He'd been impressed with Jay since meeting him last June when they worked on a case together. That had led to an invitation to a barbeque that Kirk and Christa hosted for the young single adults in their stake. A few of the women there that night had asked about Jay. But, so far, he'd shown no interest in seeing any of them again or attending the other LDS singles' activities Kirk and Christa had invited him to.

"No thanks," Jay said.

Oh well, Kirk thought. *No harm in trying.* "So how's the third year so far?" he asked. "You haven't come by the house for a while."

"It's busy," Jay said. "In fact I'm thinking of quitting my job at the club. I enjoy playing there, and it pays the rent, but I really need the time to study."

"I guess the internship looks a little better than night club performer on a résumé," Kirk said.

"Just a little," Jay agreed. "If I quit, it'll probably mean an additional student loan next semester, but I want to finish strong, and right now there just isn't enough time to do everything."

"Hate to tell you this," Kirk said. "But it doesn't get any better. After school, other stuff fills in the time you thought you were going to have." He signaled and changed lanes. "Drop you off at your apartment?"

"Yeah. I really appreciate this," Jay said. "How are Christa and your boys?"

"The boys are so wild you'd think they're already on the sugar high from Halloween, and Christa's not too happy right now. We were supposed to go to a costume party tonight, but our sitter canceled at the last minute."

"I'll do it. I can watch the boys for you."

Kirk shook his head. "Are you kidding? You just got through telling me how much you have on your plate and how little time you have."

"True. But tonight's a bit different. There's a big Halloween party, and my roommate's girlfriend is really pressuring me to come. I was going to if I got a date—"

"But you didn't," Kirk guessed.

"I tried. Honestly," Jay said. "I asked a girl, took the night off . . . But it didn't work out, and now I'm the charity case for my roommate's girl-friend—which, of course, doesn't make my roommate all that happy. It's not a good situation."

"Must be bad if you want to hang out with a couple of monkeys all night."

Jay shrugged. "Jeffrey and James are great. And when they go to bed I can study."

Kirk looked at him sideways. "You sure?"

"Yes," Jay said. "In fact, don't even take me home. That way I can avoid the whole party issue."

"Okay. It's your Friday. If you want to spend it on the floor with a couple of kids climbing all over you . . ."

"Sounds like the best Friday night I'll have had in quite a while," Jay said.

Kirk could tell he meant it. "You know, you're not the typical college student."

"Yeah, I'm a lot older."

"I'm not talking about age, and your difference is *good,*" Kirk assured him.

* * *

"Well, what do you think?" Christa asked Jay as she hobbled into the living room, leaning heavily on a cane.

"You look really—*old,*" Jay said. *Really awful. I didn't say that, did I?* He shoved his hands into his pockets and tried not to stare at Christa's ugly house dress or the nylons pooling at her ankles. Looking at her gray-streaked hair and wrinkled face wasn't any better. He racked his brain for a better comment.

Christa laughed at his obvious dismay. "That bad, huh? I'll take it as a good sign."

"You look like Great-Grandma," Jeffrey said.

James's brow wrinkled, and his mouth puckered like he was getting ready to cry. "Grandma?"

"No, silly. Mommy." Christa abandoned the cane and walked lithely toward the couch. She sat between the boys so they could get a closer look at her. "Mommy's dressing up, the same way you're going to dress up for trick-or-treating."

"You don't look like a cowboy," Jeffrey said. "You don't even got a hat. And you're using that stick wrong." He jumped up from the couch and grabbed the cane, straddling it. "You got to sit on it like this." He galloped around the room. "Then people know you're riding a horse."

Christa laughed again. "I'll remember that." She reached out to tickle him as he came closer to the couch. "You two better get into the kitchen and eat your ice cream before it melts."

"You hear that, Arrow?" Jeffrey asked his imaginary horse. "We get ice cream." He swung his leg over the cane and handed it to his mother.

"Be good tonight," Christa said, grabbing his arm and pulling him close. "Be Jay's helper, and don't tease your brother."

"Don't tease," James echoed.

"That's right." Christa gave him a hug before he ran after Jeffrey.

Kirk appeared in the doorway. If Jay had thought Christa's costume strange, he was even more bewildered by Kirk's attire—a loose Hawaiian shirt made from the same gaudy fabric of Christa's house dress, a pair of Bermuda shorts, argyle socks with geriatric-looking white tennis shoes, a broken straw hat, a half-inflated pool ring around his middle, and a walker with some type of mini surfboard wired on top.

"You're quite the pair," Jay said. "Is this party at the old folks' home or something?" He said it jokingly then wished he hadn't as he realized the idea wasn't that far-fetched. In the five or so months he'd known Kirk and Christa, he'd discovered they were very involved in their church—always serving someone or hosting activities. Kirk wasn't kidding about all his time being filled up.

"No," Kirk said. "Though maybe we'll swing by if it turns out the party isn't that great."

"It's a costume party with a twist," Christa explained. "Mormons are big on discovering their ancestors, so as a sort of tie-in, everyone was supposed to dress up in something that has to do with their heritage."

"And yours would be . . . old people?" Jay asked.

"No—oo," Christa said, rolling her eyes. "C'mon Mr. Law Student. You're smart. Think harder."

Jay scratched his head. "I'm not *that* smart, I guess."

"You are," Kirk assured him. "Think about what state we're from."

"California," Jay said. "You're retired snowbirds?"

Kirk shook his head and started humming a Beach Boys song, but Jay still didn't get it.

Christa finally took pity. "I'm 'The Little Old Lady from Pasadena.'"

"*Oh-h,*" Jay said. "That's clever—and funny." He turned to Kirk. "Who or what are you?"

"I'm a beach*ed* boy," Kirk explained. "You know, like the band, except old and all washed up."

Jay laughed. "That's great. Did you think of that, Christa?"

She nodded. "Neither Kirk or I have the pioneer ancestry many people in our church claim. We're first-generation converts from a state considered to be radical, so I decided to have some fun with it."

"How long did it take to get your skin to look like that?" Jay asked. He stepped closer, inspecting their wrinkles. "Because you look pretty authentic."

"An hour or so. Just some tricks that I learned in beauty school," Christa said.

"It's a very useful profession," Kirk pointed out. "If I ever need to go undercover, she can dye my hair, alter my face—pretty much whatever I need. I keep trying to persuade the chief to let Christa set up shop at the station. You wouldn't believe the stuff people spill while getting their hair cut."

"I'll keep that in mind," Jay said, his fingers brushing the hair curling at the base of his neck. Christa had been after him to let her cut it since July.

"How about taking our picture?" Kirk asked. He pulled a digital camera from his shirt pocket.

"Sure." Jay took the camera and held it up as Kirk and Christa moved close together. Kirk turned to her, leaned over, and planted a kiss on her cheek as Jay snapped the photo.

"Hey. You're going to mess up my wrinkles," she complained.

"So that's how it's gonna be when we're older," Kirk said. "No affection. Guess I'd better enjoy it while I have it." He gave Christa a playful swat on the backside. "Get moving, old woman."

"Watch your hands, you lecherous old man." Christa waved her cane at him.

Kirk took the camera from Jay. "Thanks."

"Have a great time," Jay said.

"Thanks so much," Christa called over her shoulder as Kirk nudged her toward the porch with his walker.

Jay closed the door behind them, listening as the walker and cane clunked down the steps. Christa's giggles and Kirk's laughter carried through the window.

Must be nice, Jay thought, picturing Jane for the first time in a while. *Is her life like this? Does her husband tease her the way Kirk teases Christa? Does she have a cozy little house, toys strewn about in every room?* He picked up a board book about a train, *Thomas the Tank Engine.* A matching toy was sticking out from beneath one of the couch cushions. *Does Jane snuggle up with her daughter every night and read to her before snuggling up with her husband?*

Surprised at the fresh hurt the thoughts dredged up, Jay found himself suddenly eager for the boys' company. He shrugged out of his suit coat and laid it across the back of the sofa. Then he removed his tie and rolled up his sleeves just as Jeffrey and James came galloping into the room.

"Good ice cream?" Jay asked, noting the rings of chocolate around their mouths.

"Grrreat," Jeffrey shouted. "Hey, where'd my horse go?"

Jay squatted down in front of them. "Your mom needed it, pardner. But no worries. I've got something better."

James stuck his thumb in his mouth and hung back behind his brother.

"You got a *real* horse?" Jeffrey's eyes lit up.

"As real as your imagination." Jay dropped to all fours. "This horse moves all by himself." He crawled away from the boys. "But he's *wild,* and you'll have to catch him if you want a ride."

Chapter Seventeen

Jay collapsed on the sofa and leaned his head against the wall. *Ouch.* Lifting a hand, he rubbed his fingers over the back of his scalp. *If I go bald there first, I'll know why.* The boys had found his hair a perfect "mane," pulling it more than a few times during the hour they played horse and cowboys on the floor.

Glancing at the knees of his pants, Jay hoped he hadn't ruined one of his two suits. He probably should have gone home to change, though it had been nice to be free of the Trish-and-Archer drama for a whole evening. Thinking of the party he was avoiding and remembering the boys' laughter as they played brought a smile to his face. He was surprised at how much fun he'd had.

A little of his earlier melancholy crept back. Not for the first time he wondered what it would have been like to have a brother. *What would it be like to have boys of my own? Girls, too. A real family like Kirk and Christa's. Like Jane's.*

Knowing this was a train of thought that would lead him nowhere, Jay opened his briefcase and prepared to tackle the stack of Medicare fraud cases he'd been handed today—more exciting work for the intern.

Jay read through the first two files and was contemplating taking Christa up on her offer to finish off the ice cream when his cell phone rang. He pulled it from his bag and glanced at the screen. It was Trish, and there was no way he was going to answer. *And she has no idea where I am,* he thought with satisfaction. Maybe, if he were very lucky, Archer and Trish would patch things up tonight.

A minute later his phone beeped, letting him know he had a text. Annoyed, Jay hit the key to retrieve it.

Where R U. Sarah came. Call me. T

"No way." Jay read the message again, then went to his call log and found Trish's number. If it was a trick, he'd be plenty irritated, but if it wasn't . . . His heartbeat quickened as he waited for Trish to pick up.

"Where are you?" she demanded when his call went through. "Why aren't you here?"

"I'm working late," Jay said. "Last I heard, there was no RSVP required, and since I didn't have a date—"

"You've got one now," Trish said. "Sarah's here, and her cousin didn't come. She asked for you."

"Are you serious?" After their last encounter, he could hardly believe it.

"I told her you're chronically late, and she'd be better off dating someone like Archer."

"Trish," Jay warned.

"Do you need a ride? 'Cause I'll come get you," she said. "The Olds is working again."

Jay shoved his papers aside and rose from the couch. "I can't leave. I'm sort of—babysitting."

Trish made a choking sound. *"Babysitting?"*

"It's the truth," Jay said.

Trish sighed into the phone. "I know. You're just that kind of guy—the kind that does things like clean out the fridge, help friends with their homework, and babysit."

"That's me. Mr. Domestic." Jay rolled his eyes.

"Give me an address, and I'll bring Sarah to you," Trish said. "I'm sure you're the only reason she came. I can tell she isn't having any fun by herself."

"Isn't anyone talking to her?" Jay tried but couldn't imagine Sarah chatting with the girls at the sorority house.

"She's not exactly a social butterfly, and that *costume,* Jay. You could've chosen something a little more—well, next time you need to pick something out for a girl, let me help."

Jay frowned. *What's wrong with a medieval gown?* he wondered. The woman at the store had assured him they rented a lot of dresses like that. And he hadn't been able to resist getting a knight's costume for himself. Which of course left Sarah's cousin to be the dragon.

"Address?" Trish asked again.

"It's not far." Jay crossed the room and stepped outside on the porch. He read the house numbers to Trish and gave her directions.

"See you in a few," she said and disconnected the call.

"Yeah," Jay mumbled. He leaned against the porch rail. *I can't believe Sarah's coming here.* Running his fingers through his hair—hair that no doubt looked wild from his time spent acting like a horse—he went back inside.

Some date I turned out to be. He'd gone from a knight in shining armor to a little kid's horse. Jay started gathering up the toys from the living room floor.

Nothing like going all-out to impress.

* * *

Worried about the late hour, Sarah clenched her hands within the confines of her choir robe. If she wasn't back at the church in forty minutes . . . she pushed the thought from her mind and glanced at Trish—in the middle of a phone conversation while she drove. Instead of feeling nervous, Sarah was in awe, wondering how it would be to drive with such confidence and to have a cell phone and friends who called her. Though from the sound of it, this wasn't a particularly nice call.

"I'll be back when and if I'm good and ready," Trish said, her voice rising. "It's not my fault you chose to show up an hour late—and with some other girl hanging all over you. And I don't want to hear excuses, Arch."

Sarah flashed another concerned glance Trish's way. *I guess other people have problems too.*

"It's none of your business where I am," Trish said. "And no, I'm not alone. No. I'm not with Jay—*yet.*" Trish snapped the phone shut. "Oooh," she fumed. "That man is driving me crazy, and not in a good way."

"I'm sorry," Sarah said. "I hope I haven't caused a problem."

"Of course not." Trish waved a hand in the air. "Archer and I had problems long before tonight. I wish . . ." She smiled wistfully. "I wish we'd get over them and get back to how things were when we first started going out."

"I hope . . . that happens," Sarah said. She had no clue about dating or relationships, and she didn't know anything about Trish's boyfriend. *Is he like Jay? Is he kind and interesting and funny at all the right times? Does he listen when you talk and hold the door open and buy prints of paintings you like?* She hoped, for Trish's sake, that Archer was that kind of guy. And she hoped, for her own sake, that tonight Jay wouldn't be quite so nice. It would make what she had to say to him easier.

She'd come to the party to apologize for wrecking his motorcycle—and to explain why she couldn't see him again. She couldn't risk any more Carl incidents, couldn't risk Jay getting hurt, or her losing her opportunities at Harvard, her future freedom.

"Here we are." Trish stopped the car in front of a small, craftsman-style bungalow a few blocks from campus. "Looks like Jay is waiting for you."

"Thanks again," Sarah said. She unbuckled her seat belt and opened the door.

"I think I'll go back to the party," Trish said. "But if you need a ride home later, have Jay call me."

"I've already arranged for a taxi. Thanks, anyway." Sarah closed the door and walked around the front of the car. She lifted her choir robe and touched her satin slipper to the sidewalk. She kept her gaze down for the first three steps, then, against her will, felt her eyes pulled to the man standing on the porch.

Jay leaned against the post, watching her come up the walk. A cobweb-covered light illuminated his best features—slightly messy dark hair, fine cheekbones, a trim physique. He was dressed differently than she'd seen him before, in navy slacks and a white button-down shirt. But his sleeves were rolled up to the elbows, and the top button was undone. She got the feeling that if he'd worn a tie earlier, it had long since been abandoned. Still, Sarah felt she was glimpsing the business professional—the attorney in him—for the first time.

It seemed he'd gone from college student to all grown up. She could imagine this was his house, that he'd just come home from a long day at the office and was waiting for her to do the same. The carved jack-o'-lanterns on the steps belonged to their children. *What an imagination,* she chided herself, but continued to drink it all in, knowing that for months—probably even years—she'd call up this quaint image and hold on to it.

Jay came down the steps toward her. "Hello, Sarah."

He seemed about to take her hand, then changed his mind, his arm brushing hers as he stepped aside to let her pass. She hesitated on the porch, and he held the door open for her.

Stop it already, Sarah scolded her escalating heartbeat. She crossed the threshold into the living room. The brief fantasy she'd indulged in continued as she took in the cozy room—comfy-looking sofa; family pictures; antique, upright piano. *Some lucky woman lives here.*

"Whose house is this?" she asked.

"Friends of mine—Kirk and Christa Anderson. They had a party to go to, and their babysitter canceled at the last minute, so I offered to watch their two boys." Jay pointed to the pictures above the sofa. "Jeffrey and James, also known as Thing One and Thing Two."

"*Cat in the Hat,* right? I remember that book," Sarah said.

"Some *Things* stay with you more than others," Jay said. "Pun intended." His eyes met hers.

She looked away. "My dad got it for me—he thought since I liked cats I would enjoy the story."

"Did you?" Jay asked.

She shook her head. "No. The *Things* drove me crazy. I liked the fish, though."

Jay frowned. "I don't remember the fish. Guess I'll have to check the book out at the library for a review."

"The fish obeyed the rules," Sarah said. "It tried to keep the Cat and Thing One and Thing Two from destroying the house."

"Ah," Jay said. "You were a rule-abiding child who liked to keep the peace."

She tilted her head to the side, considering. "I guess that describes me. Why do I suddenly feel as if I'm on the witness stand?" She folded her arms, waiting for an answer.

"You are," Jay said in mock seriousness. "And as the prosecuting attorney, it's my job to get inside your psyche and mess it up so you can't answer straight."

Sarah played along. "Exactly what am I accused of?"

"Failure to notify me you were accepting my invitation to the party tonight. And failure to wear the great costume I selected for you."

"What about failure to bring my cousin? Is that a charge, too?"

Jay grinned. "No. Case dismissed based on the plea agreement. *No cousin* far outweighs *no notice* and *no costume.*"

"I couldn't get to the shop," Sarah said. "And I didn't intend to stay long at the party." She attempted to steer their conversation to the reason for her visit. "About the other day, I need to explain—"

"Why don't you sit down?" Jay nodded toward the couch. "Can I get you some water or something?"

"Um—sure."

"Be right back," he called as he left the room.

She walked over to the sofa, intending to use the break to gather her thoughts that seemed to have scattered in Jay's presence. *So far, so good. He thinks I'm a boring fish. Shouldn't be too hard to convince him we can't even be friends.* She sat down, turning to look at the pictures on the wall behind her. There were several photos of a couple on their wedding day, and even more pictures of the little boys Jay had pointed out. An aching emptiness swept through her. This home felt so different from hers. And she knew—after less than five minutes inside—what that difference was.

She focused on the woman in the photos. *This mother will never abandon her children. She wouldn't dream of killing herself the way my mother did.* Sarah's eyes shifted to the man in the picture. He looked vaguely familiar, and she wondered if he had anything to do with the university. His smile seemed to reach his eyes, and Sarah couldn't imagine him being unkind to his darling boys.

At that moment, the smallest of the two toddled into the room, rubbing his eyes with his fists. He took one look at Sarah, walked over, and climbed on her lap.

"H—hello," she said. Uncertain what to do, she looked down at the head nestled against her chest. She'd never held a child before.

"I see we have company." Jay returned with their water. "I'm afraid your choices are a Ninja Turtle mug or a sippy cup. Apparently glass is at a premium around here." He set the cups on a side table and held his hands out. "James."

"He just came to me," Sarah said.

"Can't say that I blame him," Jay said. "I'd snuggle with you too, given the opportunity."

Sarah tried to ignore Jay's comment but felt a blush heating her face. She didn't dare entertain the images his suggestion called to mind. Keeping her head down, she adjusted James's leg, clad in fuzzy, blue footsie pajamas, so that it wasn't pulling up her choir robe. "He's cute."

"Mmm-hmm. And he's also supposed to be in bed. Sir James?" Jay squatted down in front of him.

"You forgot"—James yawned—"my story."

"You mean the one about the talking train that I read *three* times?"

James stuck his thumb in his mouth.

Jay stood and reached for him. "Come on. Your parents won't let me come over and play anymore if they come home and find you up." He took James from Sarah. "Be right back."

James pulled his thumb from his mouth long enough to say, "I didn't get my drink."

"Yes, you did," Jay said.

"You didn't sing the good-night song."

"I don't know the good-night song." Jay walked toward the hall.

"But I can't sleep without the good-night song." James began kicking his legs. "I can't sleep!"

Sarah watched helplessly as some distant, long-buried memory tugged at her heart. Once *she* had been the little girl pleading that she couldn't sleep without that something special. "Wait." She rose from the couch. "I'll sing to him."

Jay stopped mid-stride. He turned around slowly. "You will?"

She nodded, feeling awkward and foolish for volunteering. But the hopeful look in the little boy's eyes gave her courage. She walked over to him. Brushing the bangs from his forehead, she said, "I don't know your good-night song, but I'll sing you a lullaby."

She followed Jay to the bedroom, waiting while he tucked James in. When his covers were pulled up and Jay had stepped aside, she sat on the bed, humming the first few measures of "Brahms' Lullaby."

"Do you know this one?" she asked.

Thumb back in his mouth, James shook his head.

"That's okay. I'll sing and you join in if you want to." She picked up where she'd left off with the melody. James scooted closer and put his hand on hers, looking up with trusting, innocent eyes. A longing she hadn't even known existed stirred somewhere deep inside. Receiving a child's affection was an entirely new, delightful experience. She softened her voice and sang until James's eyes drooped with sleep.

Sitting on the floor beside them, Jay hummed along through the last notes. Sarah tucked James's slender arm beneath the quilt. She dared to look at Jay and found him staring at her, a tender expression on his face. Emotion seemed to flow between them, and her senses went from content to reeling in a matter of seconds. This was different—far beyond the spark of attraction she knew they'd felt for each other, more than those moments in the library and museum when they'd discovered similar interests. Her heart beat wildly as they stared at one another, neither quite able to pull away from the unseen force holding them.

She finally expelled the breath she didn't realize she'd been holding. This was new and dangerous and . . . she could hardly bear to think of giving it up.

"Thank you." Jay rose from the floor and held his hand out to her. "Sarah, that was—"

"He's not too bad for a Thing." She cut Jay off and got up without taking his hand, afraid just one touch or word from him would cause her to lose her resolve.

"Yeah."

She heard disappointment in his voice. He left the room, and she followed. Wiping suddenly sweaty palms on her choir robe, she tried to convince herself that she was more grateful than sad the moment between them had passed. Glancing at her watch, she sat on the sofa. Time was ever the precious commodity. She took the cup Jay had offered earlier, hoping the cool water would quench her thirst *and* clear her head.

"Cheers," Jay said, tapping his cup against the turtle head of her mug. He sat on the couch—not too close to her, but not exactly on the opposite end, either. His arm extended casually across the back.

Focused once more on her purpose for coming, Sarah looked at him and wondered why he continued to be so nice. Because of her, his motorcycle was wrecked. Her stomach turned, thinking about the accident, thinking of what a close call it had been for both of them—but especially Jay. *I almost got you killed.*

She took another sip of water, then set her cup back on the table. "I wasn't going to come tonight, but I needed to tell you I'm sorry about your motorcycle. And I wanted to make sure you're okay."

Jay held out his arms. "No broken bones or anything. It's *you* I've been worried about."

"I'm perfectly fine," she lied.

"What about your glasses?" Jay asked. "How are you managing without them?"

"Quite well." She patted the pocket of her robe. "Though I've taped them together and keep them with me just in case."

"Tape? You're not getting new ones?" Jay leaned forward, concern on his face.

"I am," Sarah said. "I looked up an optometrist and took the bus by myself and—" She broke off, cringing inwardly. *He must think I'm a complete idiot.* She pulled a fat envelope from her other pocket and handed it to him. "Here. I know this won't be enough to fix your motorcycle, but I thought it might help."

Jay's brow wrinkled. "What's this?"

"It's what I've saved up," Sarah explained. "It might cover the deductible to fix your bike. Or at the least, it could pay your bus fare for the rest of the semester . . ." Her eyes met his. "I'm so sorry I ruined your motorcycle."

"*You* ruined it?"

"Well, if you hadn't been talking to me . . ."

"If I hadn't been talking to you, I likely wouldn't be talking to you now." He gave her a lopsided grin. "I seem to recall it was you who pulled me out of the way of the truck. So take whatever this is back, and absolve yourself of any guilt."

"Is that more attorney speak?" She returned the faintest of smiles.

"Nope." Jay reached for her hand and placed the envelope in it. "It's concerned friend lingo—concerned friend who hasn't stopped thinking about you, by the way."

But you have to. Reluctantly, she pulled her hand away. She broke their gaze and looked toward the front door. "I need to go."

"You just got here," Jay said.

"I've got to get back before my father comes to pick me up at the church." She held out her arms, the wide sleeves of her robe billowing. "He thinks I'm at choir practice." She tried handing Jay the envelope again. "I really wish you'd take this. It would help with the whole absolving guilt thing."

"I really wish *you'd* let me take you out to dinner," Jay said, ignoring her outstretched hand. "How often do you have choir practice? I think I see some possibilities here."

"Oh, no." Concern filled Sarah's eyes, and she stood. "I can't, Jay. Please. You've got to understand. What happened with Carl the other day—it's only the beginning. If we keep seeing each other . . ."

Jay stood, moving closer to her. "Your cousin ought to be locked up for what he did. He could have killed someone. Attempted homicide isn't anything to joke about."

"I'm not joking." Still clutching the envelope, she folded her arms. "For reasons you can't understand, I have to be by myself. *Especially* at school. I need to be alone. If I continue to disobey my father, then he's going to pull me out of Harvard. I won't be able to finish my degree. And that will mean I'll be stuck like this forever." She looked down at her robe. "Sneaking out in a choir robe for a few minutes' freedom."

"It doesn't have to be that way."

"You don't understand." She lifted tear-filled eyes. "Harvard is expensive, and my father is paying for it. Getting an education is my only chance . . . at freedom. When I'm done I hope to be able to teach, to support myself, so I don't have to depend on my father."

A long moment passed between them. She could tell he was trying to hide his disappointment and holding back something he wanted to say. Finally he shoved his hands into his pockets and stepped aside, clearing the path to the door.

"How are you getting home?"

"Trish gave me this address earlier. I called a cab before we left." She pushed back the sleeve of her robe to look at her watch. "It should be here any minute." *My first bus ride, my first time riding in a friend's car, and my first cab ride—all in the same week. And all because I met you.*

"Okay, then. Guess I—won't be seeing you around." Jay's voice sounded regretful. "But if you change your mind . . ."

"I won't." She pulled the door open and stepped outside. "Thanks, Jay, for trying to be my friend. I'll never forget it."

"Neither will I," Jay said to himself as he watched her walk down the drive and step into the waiting cab.

Chapter Eighteen

Jay climbed in to the passenger seat of Kirk and Christa's Jetta. "Thanks for giving me a ride. I appreciate it."

"No problem," Kirk said, grinning. "We always take the babysitters home. It'd be bad form to expect you to walk—bad enough you won't let us pay you. I'm *sure* you earned it."

"Nah." Jay shut the door. "Your boys are great. We had a good time."

"Dinner then," Kirk said. "How about Sunday? I'll see if Christa will make her famous chicken and dumplings."

"Who else is coming?" Jay asked warily. He knew Christa had a few women in mind for him.

"No one. Unless you want to bring a date, that is." Kirk turned around in his seat and backed out of the driveway.

Jay leaned against the headrest. "Nope. No dates for me." He reviewed the depressing end to his very short evening with Sarah. *Archer's right. I really know how to pick them.* Jay looked over at Kirk. "I probably should tell you though—in case James does—I did have a female visitor at your house tonight."

"You did?" Kirk asked, obviously surprised. "What, was it an early trick-or-treater or something?" He put the car in gear and drove down the street.

"I'm not quite that desperate," Jay said. "Actually she was supposed to be my date for that party tonight."

Kirk's face fell. "I thought that didn't work out. I never would've had you stay if I'd known—"

"It *didn't* work out," Jay said. "Sarah came over to tell me that she can't see me anymore. She's got this freak cousin who almost ran us over last week because I was talking to her, and her dad has some serious control issues. But she's got to do what he asks because he pays her tuition."

"What'd you say her name is?" Kirk asked. He brought the car to a stop at an intersection and looked over at Jay.

"Sarah," Jay said. "She's this amazing musician. Sarah—"

"Morgan?" Kirk finished for him. They stared at each other for a long second.

"How did you—" Jay began, then stopped as Kirk flipped a U-turn and headed back toward his house.

"I can't believe this," Kirk said.

"Believe what?" Jay asked. "Do you know Sarah?"

"I know her father," Kirk said. "Chief Morgan. My boss. He *does* have some major control issues. Though the other day . . ."

"What?" Jay prompted.

"The other day Sarah came in to report an accident." Kirk glanced at Jay. "Probably the one you were telling me about. She told her dad that someone named Carl tried to run her over. The chief didn't care at all. She seemed pretty shaken up about it, and he blew her off."

"We can't be talking about the same woman," Jay said. "This girl has a dad who is so overprotective he watches her every move."

"Maybe, maybe not," Kirk said. "But I've got a gut feeling about this, and there's something I want you to listen to in case I'm right." He paused, sending a solemn look Jay's direction. "And if I am, I think this girl needs help."

Chapter Nineteen

Sunlight streamed through the stained-glass window behind the choir loft, warming Sarah's back. She wished it could warm her heart as she listened to the sermon on honesty. But guilt, cold and accusing, filled her. Normally she was honest to a fault. Her earliest childhood memory—one that, until last night, she hadn't thought about in years—had taught her that lesson well.

The night of her mother's funeral, she'd expected her father, a stranger then—*even stranger now*—to take her back to the Boston apartment she shared with her mother. She knew if she could just get home, get back to her room, and especially the nine-week-old kitten, Snowflake, that she'd received for her birthday, everything would be okay.

But her father had not taken her home. She'd started to tell him about Snowflake, then decided she'd lie instead, certain that if her father thought her kitten was only a stuffed animal, he would let her get it. And then, when he saw the real Snowflake, he couldn't help but love her too.

Only things hadn't worked out that way. Her father believed her and also believed that a stuffed animal was easily replaced. He'd tried, for quite a long time, to make it up to her. She owned more stuffed cats than anyone ought to—ever. And she hated them all because they reminded her of the real kitten she'd lost. The one she'd left behind. Many, many nights as a little girl she'd lain awake, wondering and worrying about her pet. To this day she was haunted by the thought of what might have happened to it.

But that experience taught her to be honest. Always. And she was. Or she had been until recently, until she met Jay. *That's over,* she reminded herself. *And a good thing, too.*

Friday night she'd come close to being caught. Her father's car had been parked in the church lot when she arrived in the taxi. Fortunately, he'd been inside, and she'd come in the west entrance, near the women's restrooms.

"Where have you been?" her father's voice had echoed through the deserted chapel. "Why isn't anyone else here?"

"They've all gone home. I was in the bathroom." *First lie.* "Practice ended early." *The truth.* "Only soloists stayed an extra hour for rehearsal and to get fitted for our new robes." *Second lie.* "Mrs. Miller would have given me a ride home, but you always tell me not to go with anyone."

Sarah's acting skills must have been better than she thought—that or the dim light of the church had kept her face in shadows and saved her. Either way, her father hadn't said another word about it all Saturday, and this morning she'd been allowed to go to church as usual. But now that she knew the topic of today's sermon, she was starting to wonder if her father had known she was lying after all.

Could he see her face from his seat in back? She placed a hand against her cheek, warm with shame, no doubt. *I don't* want *to be a liar.*

Why not? You're already a thief.

Am not, she argued with her conscience, though the thick envelope still in her robe pocket said otherwise. *It's not as if I took the money from his wallet,* Sarah thought. A part of her knew that what she'd done—keeping a dollar or two here or there from the money he gave her for groceries, buying only a milk at lunch all through junior high and high school so she could keep her lunch money, sneaking a five-dollar bill from the envelopes that held Carl's pay—was just as wrong.

"Honesty in *all* our doings is equally important," Reverend Daniels continued.

Sara glanced to either side of her. She had the uneasy feeling she was being watched, like there were at least a half dozen pairs of eyes—along with her father's from the back pew— staring right at her.

"In the book of Leviticus, the Lord tells us plainly, 'Ye shall not steal, neither deal falsely, neither lie one to another.'"

Sarah closed her eyes as another wave of guilt assailed her. The money at her side felt as if it were burning a hole through her robe, into her skin. *I'm not honest at all. I should give every penny back to my father. He's spending a fortune sending me to Harvard. But how would I ever explain $798? And what money would I have to take with me when I go? He's never going to let me leave. I'll have to run, and I'll need this.*

She shifted uneasily in her seat as the answers to the dilemma that was her life continued to elude her. Finally deciding she couldn't risk giving the money back, she vowed she wouldn't take any more. *And I won't lie, either. No lies. No Jay. No friends.*

No hope.

But as she rose with the choir for the closing hymn, she caught a glimpse of hope sitting at the back of the chapel.

* * *

Archer leaned forward, squirming on the hard, wooden pew. "I'm numb," he whispered, rubbing his backside. "And it's hot in here. Why don't they let in some fresh air?" He looked longingly at the tall windows lining both sides of the chapel.

Trish shot him a disapproving glare.

Jay looked away from them and back at Sarah, who was standing in the front row of the choir.

"I can barely breathe." Archer tugged at his shirt collar.

"Shh," Jay and Trish both said together.

Trish brought a finger to her lips and frowned. "Quit being such a baby," she scolded.

"This tie is *choking* me," Archer whispered and continued to fidget.

"We're almost done," Jay said. "The choir is about to sing." He leaned forward in his seat, eager to hear the music.

"I don't care if the president's going to speak," Archer mumbled, then closed his mouth as the elderly woman sitting on the pew across from them stared reproachfully.

In one fluid motion the choir stepped forward in the loft. The organ belted out a prelude, and gospel music filled the overflowing chapel.

Wow. I ought to come to church more often. Jay wished again they hadn't been late this morning and missed the earlier musical numbers.

"No wonder this place is packed," Trish whispered after the first verse of the stirring song.

Jay nodded. The sermon had bordered on the dry side, but the music was fabulous. It seemed to tangibly lift the atmosphere in the room.

"Can we go now?" Archer asked before the choir had closed their mouths on the last note.

Trish shook her head. "Look—Sarah's doing a solo."

Jay kept his gaze riveted to the front of the room where Sarah stood alone. The others in the choir returned to their seats, leaving her standing there, looking every bit an angel in her white robe. Today her hair was down—the first time he'd seen it that way—and it framed her face in liquid gold.

She wore her mended glasses, and Jay wondered if she'd noticed him yet. If so, she might be upset to see him here. But after hearing the taped conversation with her father, he'd had to come make sure she was okay. He understood why she'd been in such a hurry to leave that night, and he realized the risk she'd taken to come at all. He'd spent half the night imagining what her father would do if he found out, the other half wracking his brain for a way to help.

With a serene expression on her face, Sarah lifted her head and sang. Jay sat spellbound, and even Archer's fidgeting stopped as her lofty soprano cast across the crowded room, reaching all the way to the back.

The congregation fell silent. Babies and toddlers snuggled quietly on their mothers' laps as Sarah's voice hushed them like the lullaby she'd sung for James. A peaceful calm descended over the crowd. Jay glanced over at Trish and saw tears glistening in her eyes. Archer had stopped fidgeting with his tie and put his arm around Trish and pulled her close. *The power of music,* Jay thought as he noticed Trish take Archer's free hand in both of hers.

One problem solved. Turning his head slightly, he glanced at the congregation again, wondering if Sarah's father was here.

The song came to a close, and Trish kept hold of Archer's hand, keeping him from clapping. Everyone bowed their heads, and the reverend offered prayer.

"At last," Archer said, when the lengthy prayer was through. He practically ripped off his tie as he rose with the rest of the congregation.

"Sit," Trish ordered. "We can't leave yet. We've got to check on Sarah."

"She just sang, didn't she? She's fine." Archer stepped into the aisle. He looked eagerly toward the open doors and the crowd spilling out of them.

"We don't know that," Trish argued. "I'll make my way up front and talk to her—to make sure nothing bad happened because of the other night."

"Nothing happened to her voice," Archer said. "And who could tell with her face? Might as well be wearing a ski mask for all you can see of her behind those ugly glasses."

Trish extended her leg and kicked his shin. "You're so mean."

"Knock it off, you two," Jay ordered. *So much for making up.* He wondered again if it had been wise to bring them—though since Archer had the car, technically he and Trish had brought Jay.

He glanced around the chapel, looking for anyone who might be Sarah's dad. Not seeing any older men waiting to leave, he returned his attention to Sarah. She had picked up two music stands and was carrying them to an open door at the back of the loft.

"Look. She's lifting stuff," Archer said. "The old man obviously didn't hurt her. Let's go."

"Give me a couple of minutes. She's coming this way." Trish watched as Sarah headed for the stairs leading to the chapel floor. Another member of the choir stopped her before she could reach them.

Trish pushed past Archer and stepped into the aisle. "You two stay here. I'll see if I can talk to her for a minute." She headed toward the front.

"If you want a ride . . ." Archer threatened in a loud whisper.

"If you want dinner tonight . . ." she countered with a backward glance.

Archer muttered something under his breath and walked to the back of the chapel to hover by the doors. Jay stayed in his seat, watching the room empty, wishing he could go with Trish. But they'd agreed ahead of time that it was probably best if, initially, he didn't try talking to Sarah. He hadn't come to get her in more trouble.

The chapel was almost empty when Sarah finally made it out of the loft.

"Sarah, do you have a minute?" The reverend's voice echoed through the hall. He met her at the bottom of the stairs before Trish could get there.

"Not really," Sarah said. "My father is waiting in the car."

"Of course." The reverend's lips turned down slightly. He matched her pace as she walked toward the exit. Sarah didn't look up as they passed Trish.

Jay grabbed a Bible from the back of the pew in front of him. He opened it, pretending to read, while he strained to hear the conversation. Archer continued to sulk by the doors.

"I wanted to let you know that your scholarship has been renewed through the next semester," Reverend Daniels told Sarah. "And I was hoping you wouldn't mind writing another letter to the Ladies' Aid to thank them. I personally know that Gladys Beecher spent forty-six hours on a quilt to sell at the bazaar, just so she could contribute to your college fund."

"College fund?" Sarah looked bewildered. Her pace slowed. "What are you talking about?"

What is *he talking about?* Jay wondered. *I thought her father was paying for Harvard.*

Sarah shook her head. "You must be mistaken. My father is paying—for everything." Her voice faltered as if she were suddenly unsure.

The reverend looked even more confused than Sarah did. He raised his hand, pushing the spectacles further up the bridge of his nose. "Your father, while a very fine man, is in no position to pay for that kind of education. But it's nothing to be ashamed of."

"I'm not ashamed—just confused." Sarah's voice sounded shaky. She stopped walking and placed her hand on Reverend Daniels' sleeve. "Please tell me what you're talking about. I—I really don't know."

"But you do," he insisted. The lines on his face deepened. "You wrote that lovely thank-you letter last summer."

"I didn't," Sarah insisted. She continued to clutch his arm. "I never wrote a letter. I've never heard of this. My father told me—"

"Told you *what*?" A tall, heavyset man brushed by Archer and entered the chapel. "What's wrong now, Sarah? What's taking so long?"

Her father. Jay tensed in his seat as he stared at the older man with thinning hair and a stern face. Jay hadn't been sure what to expect when he came this morning, but a scene like this had never entered his mind. He glanced at Archer, who no longer looked bored.

Trish lingered a few pews behind Sarah and the reverend.

"Good to see you, Grant," Reverend Daniels said. "There seems to be some mix-up with Sarah's scholarship." He hesitated, looking at her apologetically. "She claims she knows nothing about it."

Jay noticed the subtle change on her father's face. A false mask of concern seemed to cover his previous irritation.

"I'm afraid there are a lot of things Sarah doesn't know anymore," Grant said, his voice gentler than it had been a moment before. "She's starting to develop the same problems her mother had at this age."

"What are you talking about?" Sarah said. "You never told me the church was paying for school. You *lied* to me, made me work that awful job—"

"That's enough," her father said sternly. "Good day, Reverend." He took Sarah's arm and steered her toward the doors.

She resisted, trying to pull away from him.

Jay stood and moved to the edge of the pew.

"Mr. Morgan." Reverend Daniels took a hesitant step forward as if he wasn't certain whether or not he should interfere. "Something seems terribly wrong here. I'm—I'm sure we can clear this up if you'll both come into my office for a few minutes."

"That won't be necessary," Grant said. "I need to take Sarah home and get her medication." He towed her a few more steps toward the door.

"I don't take any medicine. There's nothing wrong with me." Sarah looked back at the reverend, pleading.

Jay stepped into the aisle beside Archer, blocking the exit.

"Excuse me," Trish said. She hurried around the reverend to face Sarah and her father. "My friends and I were actually waiting here, hoping to get an interview with Miss Morgan. *Archer*," she said, beckoning him with her finger. "Now is good."

Archer looked startled for half a second but recovered quickly. He strode forward. "I'm Archer Harris, from *The Harvard Crimson*."

Jay moved to Sarah's other side, sending her an encouraging smile while Archer dug through his wallet for his Harvard press pass.

"Now is not a good time," Grant said, hardly glancing at the credential in Archer's outstretched hand.

"But Miss Morgan's composition was recently selected to accompany the Harvard Ballet Troupe in an upcoming concert," Trish said. "And we'd heard her singing was even more phenomenal, so we came to find out." She looked at Sarah. "We'd like to do a piece in the Arts section of the paper."

"As you can see, that won't be possible," Grant said. "In fact, it's questionable whether Sarah will even be able to continue her schooling."

"Grant," Reverend Daniels reprimanded gently. "Sarah has *so much* to offer, and these young people mean no harm."

"The show would be incomplete without Miss Morgan's music," Trish said.

"Then it will have to be incomplete." Still holding her arm, Grant took a step toward the exit.

"I'd like to do the interview." Sarah's voice was calm again.

"I said, *no!*" Grant shouted. "I don't want you in the paper. I don't even want you on that campus anymore." He turned his fury on the reverend. "She wouldn't be there, wouldn't be in this kind of danger, if not for you and those meddlesome old biddies."

Sarah wrenched her arm free, and Jay stepped between her and her father. "Mr. Morgan, you have no right—"

"Who are you?" Grant demanded.

"I can't believe you lied to me." Sarah stumbled up the aisle out of her father's reach. Her eyes shone with unshed tears.

Grant made a move toward her, but Jay and the reverend blocked his way.

"She's a good girl," Reverend Daniels said. "And she's doing as the Good Lord has asked by developing her talents."

"The Good Lord also said that children are to obey their parents," Grant reminded him.

"She isn't a child anymore." The reverend's voice was soothing. "Let her do the interview. No harm is going to come of it. It's time Sarah was recognized for her abilities. It may even be that she can earn a scholarship on her own."

"She doesn't need a scholarship; she needs protection."

"From what?" Sarah demanded. "The one person I want protection from, you force me to be with." Her voice broke. "Should I have to stay home the rest of my life, so you can make sure I'm safe?" She swiped at a tear trailing down her cheek. "I can't live like this anymore."

"We'll discuss this at home," Grant said. "Let's go."

Sarah shook her head.

Archer's hands clenched into fists at his sides.

Don't do it, Jay thought. *This will go from bad to worse if someone starts throwing punches.*

As if she'd read his mind, Trish spoke up. "You'd better go," she said to Sarah's father. "Or I'll call the police." She held up her cell phone.

Grant swung his gaze on her, eyes narrowed to slits. A wicked smile curved his lips. "I *am* the police."

"But you aren't the law." All eyes turned to Jay. He looked directly at Sarah's father. "I'm here as Sarah's legal representative. We both know she's well beyond the age of independence. And—" He plunged on, praying he was correct. "She has no physical or mental history that requires medication. You have no right to detain her further, Mr. Morgan."

Chapter Twenty

Reverend Daniels returned to his office, a tray balanced in his hands. Placing it on a side table, he turned to Sarah, who was sitting in one of two chairs in front of his desk.

"Drink this," he suggested gently, pressing a cup of chamomile tea into her hands. "It will help calm you."

"Thank you." Sarah brought the cup to her mouth and took a small sip.

"I must say your timing was fortuitous," Reverend Daniels said to Jay, who was seated beside Sarah. He handed him a cup and saucer that matched Sarah's, then walked around the desk, sinking into the old, weathered chair behind it.

"I did feel somewhat inspired to come this morning," Jay said, giving the reverend a wry smile. He turned to Sarah. "And *definitely* inspired now. Hearing you sing made all the drama worth it."

"Perhaps you'll join us again?" the reverend asked. "Sarah blesses us with a solo the last Sunday of each month. And our choir sings each week."

"I'd like that," Jay said. "If it's all right with Sarah."

She was taking another drink of tea and looked at him over the brim of her cup. "Yes."

"In the meantime," the reverend continued, "we've got to see what we can do for you, young lady." He swiveled his chair around to face Sarah. "I doubt your father was serious when he told you not to bother coming home. However, after this morning's display, I don't think that's the best place for you to be. Are you prepared to go out on your own?"

Sarah waited a minute before answering. "I don't know," she admitted, her shoulders sagging.

"There are campus organizations that can help," Jay offered. "And I can think of several places you can stay temporarily until we find you an apartment. You can apply for financial aid, and I'll help you file a restraining order."

"I can't do that, Jay." The hand holding the teacup trembled. "He's my father."

"I'm not talking about your dad. I'm talking about your cousin." Jay faced the reverend again. "Her cousin nearly ran us over last week—and it was no accident."

"Did you tell your father about this?" Reverend Daniels asked Sarah.

"I tried." She placed the saucer and teacup on her lap. "It didn't go well. I don't think he believed me."

A bit of an understatement, Jay thought. But he couldn't exactly tell Sarah that he—and a couple of other people—had been privy to that conversation with her father. Instead, he tried to fill in the details Sarah was avoiding. "Her father has assigned his nephew as Sarah's bodyguard. He follows her everywhere, threatening her if she doesn't do what he wants, threatening anyone else who gets too close to her."

"Is this true?" Reverend Daniels asked.

"Yes." She leaned back in her chair and closed her eyes. "Between my father and Carl, I have someone with me nearly every minute of the day. I'm only allowed to go to school if Carl is with me, and then it's only to my classes and occasionally the library. I'm never allowed to go anywhere else or do anything—unless I'm working for my father."

Reverend Daniels pulled a notepad and pencil from his desk. "I don't quite understand. You attend church as your health permits, and I've never seen your father or this cousin attend choir rehearsal with you."

"One of them usually waits in the car outside. And my health *always* permits me to come to church." Sarah glanced at Jay, then down at her lap. "I'm hardly ever sick. Those times my father told you otherwise, he was lying. Whenever he's displeased with me, he takes away the privilege of singing in the choir. And he's been threatening to cut off my tuition since the semester began."

"Tuition he doesn't pay," the reverend mused.

Sarah ran her finger around the rim of her teacup. "The ladies must think I'm so ungrateful."

"Not at all," Reverend Daniels assured her. "On the contrary, they're most impressed with the time you continue to dedicate to our little choir. Without your talents, I'm afraid our Sunday services would be somewhat less—inspiring." He cast a wry grin in Jay's direction.

"Thank you," Sarah murmured. She lifted her face to the reverend's. "Please tell them for me—please explain."

"Perhaps. When the time is right." Reverend Daniels leaned back in his chair, a hand to his mouth. "Your father is a well-respected member of the community, and I think it would be wise to proceed with care. Fortunately, we were the only ones left in the chapel this morning." He glanced at Jay. "I am very grateful to the Ladies' Aid, and may the Lord bless them for all they do, but my, how their tongues can wag sometimes."

Jay chuckled. "So," he said, attempting to summarize the plan that had been forming in his mind. "I'll help Sarah find a place to stay for the near future. You'll talk with her father later this week, and we'll go from there."

"What about my books and clothes and everything I need for school?" Sarah asked. "I can't get by without my music or lecture notes or—"

"I'll take care of that," Jay said. "You concentrate on keeping up with school so the Ladies' Aid feels like they're getting their money's worth."

"How are you—"

"I don't want you to worry about it," he said. "I'm going to pay a visit to your father, and I'm fairly certain he won't have a problem letting me bring your things to you."

"Are you *crazy?*" Sarah asked. Her knees shook, and the teacup clinked against the saucer on her lap. She picked up both, put them on the table, and turned to Jay. "Carl will most likely be at my house too. Have you forgotten he beat you up once already?"

The reverend's eyebrows rose at this.

"It was an unfair fight," Jay assured him. "And besides, there won't be anyone punching anyone else. There's a much better way to handle things."

"Really?" Sarah sounded skeptical. She looked at him, waiting for an explanation.

He wasn't going to give it.

"Diplomacy," he said simply, rising from his chair. He held his hand out for Sarah. "And a simple economic principle called supply and demand."

Chapter Twenty-One

At exactly 5:15, Kirk rang the bell at Chief Morgan's house. "Hi, Chief," Kirk said as the door opened. "May I come in for a minute? I know it's Sunday, but there's something that's been bugging me all weekend."

"Talk to me on Monday." The chief started to close the door.

"I brought you a loaf of my wife's fresh-baked bread. Payment for your time . . ." He held up the still-warm loaf.

Chief Morgan paused, but his expression didn't change. For a minute Kirk was certain the door was going to slam on him, even if the bread—or his hand—was in the way.

But the chief surprised him.

"Make it quick." He moved aside, ushering Kirk in.

Kirk handed the bread to him as soon as they were inside. "It's about the Rossi case."

"What about it?" Chief Morgan asked.

"Mind if I sit down?" Kirk didn't wait for an answer but sat on the couch, where he could see down the hall and hopefully catch a glimpse of Carl. His truck was parked out front, so chances were, he was around.

Chief Morgan closed the front door, walked to the kitchen bar, and placed the bread on the counter. He returned and sat in his chair.

"Rossi got off—or almost, anyway," Kirk said. "I bet he appeals the charge that stuck."

"I'm sure he will. So?"

"So it's wrong." Kirk leaned forward, elbows on his knees as he spoke. "Doesn't it upset you that we're getting nowhere with these guys? We know they're the ones introducing meth at the high school. We've linked Rossi to the rave parties breaking out all over student housing. And we both know it only takes once—one hit and we've got a whole new group of users. It's going to keep spreading exponentially. Soon Summerfield will rival some of the worst meth pockets in LA and the northwest."

"We're doing our jobs," the chief said. "I can't control attorneys or juries. You caught the guy. You did what you could. Case closed."

Kirk couldn't believe what he was hearing. "But it isn't closed. And you can bet—because Rossi got off so easy—that it will be business as usual, maybe even more than usual."

"So you catch him again and bring him in. Maybe it goes better next time."

"*Maybe?*" Kirk said, incredulous. "I want to do better than that, and we both know that's going to take more than catching him making a deposit at the bank." He spoke emphatically. "We need a team to watch his distributors twenty-four-seven. This isn't some operation filtering up from Mexico. It all points to a local supplier, and if we can find—"

Chief Morgan chuckled. "Oh, to be so young and thirsty for blood. What'd you do in that big precinct in LA, Anderson?"

"We followed leads, found pushers who'd talk—same things we're doing here."

The chief nodded. "Exactly."

"And it wasn't enough," Kirk said. "You want this area to be like LA? There's no way our small force will be able to deal with anything like that. But I think we still have a fighting chance if we jump on it now. Reassign Brandt and Simmons temporarily. Get everyone together, focused on this— even if just for the next six months."

The chief's frown deepened, and Kirk knew he wasn't enjoying being told how to do his job. *Careful,* he reminded himself. *You're not here to vent your frustrations.* Upsetting the chief more wasn't going to help Jay's cause.

"Since you seem to know so much, I'm surprised you aren't following the news more." The chief pushed out of his chair and ambled down the hall. He disappeared into a bedroom for a minute or two, then came back, a newspaper in his hand. He returned to his chair, tossing the paper on the coffee table in front of Kirk. "Read that," he said, pointing to an underlined passage.

Kirk picked up the paper, the September 24th issue of the *Berkshire Eagle.* "John W. Selwin's acquittal on drug-dealing charges yesterday in Berkshire Superior Court suggests that the District Attorney's office will be hard-pressed to get any convictions of those collected in the drug sting last year in Great Barrington." He paused. "Yes, but—"

"Keep reading."

"Jurors may have bought the defense's argument that entrapment was used by a member of the county's drug task force. In the end, the Great Barrington sting and prosecution has accomplished nothing.'"

"I rest my case," Chief Morgan said.

Kirk set the paper down. "I *had* heard about that," he said defensively. "I think it's an opportunity to learn from their mistakes. I *know* we could make something like that work here."

"You're a big-city boy with big-city ideas, Anderson. And while I appreciate your ambition, it's not why I hired you. I hired you to do exactly what you did in LA. Eventually we'll catch a big fish in the net too. We got Eddie Martin, didn't we?"

The doorbell rang. Chief Morgan leaned forward and eased himself out of his chair, signaling the end of their conversation. "Grand Central Station today," he muttered under his breath. He walked the two steps to the door and yanked it open.

Kirk watched as his expression darkened.

"What do you want?" Chief Morgan practically growled.

"A minute of your time. It's about your daughter, Mr. Morgan."

Kirk recognized Jay's calm, practiced, attorney voice. He looked up, feigning interest.

The chief hesitated. "Get in line," he said, but he stepped aside for Jay.

"Thanks," Jay said, coming into the room. "I'll be brief."

"I don't have time for anything else. As you can see"—Chief Morgan nodded toward Kirk—"one of my officers and I were having a meeting."

Jay looked over at Kirk. "Sorry to interrupt." He returned his gaze to Sarah's father. "If I could get Sarah's things, I'll be out of your way."

The chief's face mottled with anger. "If she wants them, she can get them herself."

"I'm afraid not," Jay said. "Reverend Daniels was concerned about our earlier conversation. Sarah is with a counselor right now."

"She doesn't—" Chief Morgan broke off. He turned to Kirk. "Detective, we're done."

Looking disappointed, Kirk got up from the couch and walked to the door. "See you tomorrow, Chief. Thanks for listening to my concerns." He closed the door behind him.

"Sarah needs a father who will listen to her," Jay continued. "One who will protect her instead of forcing her to be with someone she's afraid of."

"What are you talking about?" Grant demanded.

Jay pulled an envelope from his pocket.

"Last Monday Carl Morgan came within two feet of running over your daughter with his truck. Those are pictures of the 'accident.'"

Grant opened the envelope and pulled out the first photograph, Jay's wrecked motorcycle.

Jay leaned closer, pointing to the lawn directly behind the bike. "Sarah was right there," he said. "It was a *very* close call."

"Was anyone hurt?" Grant asked, sounding shaken.

Jay was pleased to see the older man's fingers tremble as he shuffled through the pictures. Standing this close to Sarah's father, he found himself less intimidated than he'd been upon first meeting him. Grant Morgan *was* tall—a couple of inches above Jay's six feet. But his breadth was more about being overweight than having muscle, and the deep creases running across his forehead and on either side of his eyes made him look older, worn out.

"Was anyone hurt?" Grant repeated.

"Five stitches," Jay said, pushing the hair back from his forehead so Grant could see the sutures. "A few other students had minor injuries. A couple of girls were pretty shaken."

"Whose motorcycle?" Grant asked, returning to the first picture.

"Mine."

Grant shoved the photos back in the envelope and held it out to Jay.

"Keep them," Jay said. "I have copies. I figured you might want to use them for a discussion with your nephew." He glanced around the room. "He's here, isn't he?"

Grant didn't answer. "What is it you want, Mr.—"

"Kendrich," Jay answered. "Jay. And I *need* three things. First, Sarah's clothing and school books. I need those today. Right now." He paused, prepared for Grant to protest. Surprisingly, he didn't.

"Second, you need to arrange your life such that Sarah never has to be around her cousin again—*ever*. And third, I want a promise from you that *if* Sarah should ever decide to return to your home, she'll be able to live a normal life, go to school by herself, to church, to the mall—and participate in any other activity appropriate for a twenty-three-year-old woman."

Grant's brow furrowed. "And if I don't wish to meet your terms?"

"I might decide to press charges. After all, I'm out a motorcycle now, and the doctor's bill wasn't cheap."

"None of these pictures"—Grant slapped the envelope against the palm of his free hand—"are of my nephew or his truck."

"True enough," Jay agreed. "But the campus police took statements from a half dozen witnesses, including detailed descriptions of the vehicle."

And as we speak, Kirk is taking snapshots of your nephew's fender. "We both know that attempted manslaughter is a serious charge."

"I don't *like* being threatened or blackmailed," Grant said, his eyes narrowing.

"This is neither," Jay insisted. "Just a simple case of supply and demand. I'm assuming you want your daughter back in your life. I'm telling you what you need to do to make that a possibility." He placed his hand on the doorknob. "If you think the price is too high . . ."

Jay waited, feeling the tension mount as he listened to the seconds tick by on his wristwatch. He could see that Sarah's father was furious with him—no doubt he rarely found himself in a position of being told what to do. But there were other emotions filtering across the older man's face—concern, grief . . . *fear?* Jay found himself more intrigued than worried.

"Where will she be staying?" Grant finally asked. "With *you?*"

"No," Jay said. "I hardly know your daughter, Mr. Morgan, and I've no plans to take advantage of her at this difficult time."

"At *any* time."

"That too," Jay said.

"I don't want her to be alone," Grant said. "It's imperative—" he broke off, his fisted hand shaking at Jay.

Jay sensed his frustration went far beyond Sarah's decision to leave.

"Please," Grant said. "Don't leave her alone. Walk her to her classes. Make sure she locks the door to wherever it is she's staying. And don't let her use public transportation."

"Sarah's quite capable of getting around on her own."

"She's very capable," Grant agreed, surprising Jay yet again. "But that doesn't make her invincible. It's not enough to protect her. And Sarah *does* need protection." He turned away from Jay. The gruffness left his voice. "You have no idea what you've done."

"What *I've*—" Jay began.

"If you care for my daughter at all, you'll see that she is back here as soon as possible. It's the only way to keep her safe." Grant started down the hallway. "Give me ten minutes."

* * *

Grant watched as Jay climbed into the waiting car—the same unfamiliar Volkswagen that had been at the church this morning. He'd had a bad feeling about it then and knew he should have listened to his gut and gone right in, taken Sarah, and brought her home. But no—he'd gone soft. She was singing a solo, and he hated to deprive her—or himself—of those moments she seemed happiest. Now his poor judgment might deprive them of much more than that.

Carl came up behind him. "So Sarah's got herself a new babysitter." Sniffing the air appreciatively, he turned toward the kitchen. Spotting the bread, he walked over to the counter.

"You wrecked his motorcycle," Grant said.

"Yep." Carl opened the bag and ripped a big hunk from the fresh loaf Kirk had brought.

"Leave that alone." Grant closed the front door. "Now that Sarah's gone, what do you think we're going to eat? Are *you* going to do the cooking?"

"Want me to get her back?" Carl mumbled between bites.

"It's not that simple." Grant crossed the room, tossed the pictures on the counter, and pushed the bread out of Carl's reach. "Did you think you'd get away with a stunt like that?"

Looking at the photo of the crushed motorcycle, Carl smirked. "I figured you'd take care of it. You always have before."

"Not in Cambridge, I haven't. I can't. And attempted manslaughter is a bit more serious than grand theft auto and armed robbery."

Carl shrugged. "You'll fix it." He leaned across the counter, reaching again for the bread.

Grant slammed his fist down beside Carl's hand. "*No. You* will."

Carl didn't seem the least bit fazed. "You want me to run him over next time? 'Cause I didn't have to stop before."

"What I want," Grant said, "is for you to do your job. I pay you enough that you don't have the luxury of making stupid mistakes. First you talk to her in the park and now this."

"Hey." Carl pointed a finger at Grant. "I put my life on the line for your daughter every day." His tone matched Grant's angry one. "Why do you think I went after that guy? I leave her for two minutes, I come back, and she's not alone. I did what you told me to. Act first, take care of the mess later."

A vein pulsed at Grant's temples. "If you'd done what I told you, she wouldn't have been alone—*even for two minutes.*"

"It ain't so easy trailing around after her all day," Carl argued. "Those classes she takes are so boring I think I'm gonna slit my throat. And I can't get in all of them anyway—just the ones in the big rooms." He went to the fridge, grabbed a beer, and brought it to the table. "Sitting outside picking my nose all day isn't fun." He popped the can open. "And that ballet thing she plays for is the worst. So I left a minute or two early 'cause I was losing my mind."

"I pay you handsomely to lose your mind," Grant reminded him. "You got a better offer? Feel free to leave." He gestured toward the door. "I'll find someone else to be her bodyguard."

Carl laughed. "Yeah, right. You gonna hire the loser that was just here? I took him out with two punches a month ago."

Grant's eyes narrowed. "What do you mean?"

"He's the one who tried talking to her while she was at the piano."

"He's not an attorney?" Grant walked into the kitchen and sat in one of the chairs while he digested this information.

"I don't know what he is," Carl said. "You always told me that wasn't my business. Only thing I got to remember is that no one gets close to Sarah. He got close. I hit him. He got close again. I took it a little more serious this time."

Grant's elbows rested on the table, and he put his head in his hands. *My nephew is an idiot. But . . . he does protect Sarah. Now she's out there alone with . . .* He stood suddenly, grabbed his keys from the tray on the counter, and headed toward the front door. He walked outside, taking purposeful steps toward his cruiser parked on the street.

Who are you, Mr. Kendrich? And what are you playing at? Grant could hardly wait to get to the computer in his office. He climbed in his car and started the engine, eager to understand who the enemy was so he could figure out how best to dispose of him.

Chapter Twenty-Two

"He wouldn't give it to you?" Sarah sounded disappointed as she looked at Kirk and Jay—empty-handed—walking through Kirk and Christa's front door.

"O ye of little faith," Kirk said, grinning. "On the contrary, everything went like clockwork. The chief and I had a nice chat while I scoped out the place. Then I left, waiting outside for a while—listening in on the conversation, mind you—lest my unarmed friend required assistance."

"Which I did not," Jay said. "Though your father thinks *you* do." He pulled a Ziploc bag from his pocket and tossed it to Sarah. "There's your pepper spray. Your dad insisted you're to keep it with you all the time. I got the feeling he would have preferred you carry a gun—and that you use it on me."

Sarah held the bag away from her as if there were a poisonous spider inside. "Did he also tell you I'm not to ride the bus or subway, and that I absolutely *cannot* walk anywhere alone?"

"Something along those lines, yes." Jay crossed the room and reached for her hand. He pulled her from the couch. "But your suitcase and backpack are in Archer's car. He'll drop them by later after we work out where you're going to stay. You have everything you need for school tomorrow—without Carl."

"Oh, he'll be there," Sarah said. "You can bet I'll pay for this little twenty-four-hour furlough."

"Pay how?" Kirk asked. He shrugged out of his jacket and hung it on the rack beside the door.

"It doesn't matter." Sarah stuck the pepper spray in her skirt pocket.

"We're not going to let anything happen," Jay assured her. "And I'm not so sure Carl *will* be there. Right now I get the feeling your dad is having a bit of a wake-up call where your cousin is concerned."

She continued to look skeptical. "My father wouldn't have given in so easily if he didn't have something in mind. And chances are, that something has to do with Carl."

"Try not to think about him," Jay said. "Tonight—right now—you're free. We're going to do everything we need to do to keep it that way."

Kirk rubbed his hands together and sniffed the air appreciatively. "Christa's making her famous chicken and dumplings."

"Made," Christa called from the kitchen doorway. "Kirk, if you'll get the boys from their room, we'll eat now."

"Hey, where *are* the wild things?" Jay looked around the living room, noticing for the first time that it was free of the toys usually strewn about.

"After church they have to play quietly in their room—puzzles, blocks, things like that."

"And that *works?*" Jay asked, doubtful.

"Well, we're trying anyway," Kirk said. "You guys go ahead. I'll get the boys washed up, and we'll be right there."

Jay stepped aside so Sarah could go ahead of him into the kitchen.

She walked past, looking apprehensive. Jay felt his own worries. It had been a long day for all of them—but especially for Sarah. After visiting her home and speaking with her father, he had a better feeling for what she'd come from, and he knew this must be a huge change.

She just needs some time, he told himself, and hoped he was right.

* * *

Sarah waited on the porch while Jay talked to Kirk inside for a moment. Part of her wished they would share more of what had happened when they met with her father. Another part didn't want to know what had transpired at all. Regardless of how her father had acted and what words had been exchanged, he had to be furious with her. That he would send Carl out to find her and fetch her home tomorrow—away from school forever—was a certain consequence.

"Christa said you can borrow this." Jay held up a white sweater as he stepped outside. "It's getting chilly." He helped Sarah into the sweater, and they started down the walk.

"Where are we going?"

"Well, since you're certain you don't want to stay with Kirk and Christa—"

"I can't," Sarah insisted. "If my father found out, he'd be furious, and Kirk could lose his job. I don't want to cause them any more trouble."

"You haven't caused anyone trouble," Jay said. He looked at her sideways. "But I do have a plan B. If you're feeling brave, we can discuss it at my four-guys-three-of-whom-don't-ever-clean apartment."

"You're the one who cleans?" she asked hopefully.

Jay nodded. "How'd you guess? No—don't tell me. Is it because I read history books for fun and attend the occasional ballet rehearsal?"

She smiled. "No. I'm pretty sure I read somewhere that guys who ride motorcycles are cleaner than those who drive cars."

"What about guys who walk?" Jay asked.

Her smile fled. "I'm so sorry about your bike."

"No, *I'm* sorry, for bringing it up again." Jay flashed her an apologetic smile. "Believe me. I'd much rather be walking with you than riding my motorcycle alone."

They continued in silence for a few minutes, brittle leaves crunching beneath their feet as the sky transitioned from violet to deep blue. Street lamps flickered on above them, and Sarah realized how very tired she was.

"Dollar for your thoughts," Jay said.

She raised an eyebrow. "Wow. Inflation."

"Your thoughts are worth more than the average penny," Jay said. "I'd offer more, but I'm a little shy right now. Your singing was so phenomenal, I just kind of spilled my wallet into the collection plate."

"You didn't have to do that."

"I wanted to," Jay said.

"You don't have to do this, either—help me, I mean."

"You realize," Jay said, "that I have my own ulterior motives. Like the possibility of taking you on a real date this Saturday."

"If I'm still around Saturday," Sarah said, seriously doubting she would be. "I really don't think my dad is going to let this go."

"Which is why you should stay with Kirk," Jay said. "He's got the ability to protect you."

Sarah shook her head.

"Well then," Jay said with a sigh, "I guess we'll have to be extra careful. We'll make sure you're with someone all the time so Carl can't get to you—if he's so inclined. Unfortunately I've got a killer week at school, and I work almost every night this week."

"Oh," she said, feeling disappointed. Though she really didn't think she'd make it a whole week away from home, it would have been nice to spend what time she did have with Jay.

His arm brushed against hers, and goose bumps sprang up that had nothing to do with being cold or scared.

"But there are a lot of other people who will be happy to be your friend and help too. As for where you can stay—" Jay held up his index finger. "Choice number one—Trish's apartment. Number two—with Mrs. Larson, my landlady. And door number three—my personal favorite—on Tiger. That's what we call our couch. It's orange plush, and my roommate, Mike, striped it with electrical tape. It's the ugliest thing you've ever seen, but decent to sit on and long enough to sleep two of you end-to-end."

"And it's located in the guys-who-don't-ever-clean facility?"

"Pretty much."

"Pretty much, no thanks then."

Jay shrugged. "Can't blame a guy for trying."

"Tell me about Mrs. Larson."

"She's great—to me anyway," Jay said. "My roommates aren't too fond of her, but then, they're all thoughtless slobs. I've carried her groceries in a few times, and now"—he held up one hand, fingers crossed—"we're friends for life."

"I don't know," Sarah said. The reality of sleeping somewhere other than the house she'd lived in for the past eighteen years was starting to sink in. "Letting me stay there seems like kind of a big favor compared with carrying in groceries."

"Lots of groceries," Jay said. "She eats a ton. But seriously, she'll love the company. When I asked her about it this afternoon, she was practically giddy. I wouldn't be surprised to find that she's put her favorite afghan on the spare bed and set the table with her best china in honor of a house guest."

"Oh, no," Sarah said, feeling more agitated by the minute. "I don't want to use her best china or anything else. You don't think she'll expect me to eat with her, do you?"

"It'd be nice if you did. Like I said, she's always eager for company."

Sarah stopped walking and turned to Jay. "I've never lived away from home. I don't think I can do this."

"What?" Jay asked. "Sneak around in a choir robe for a few minutes' freedom the rest of your life? This is your *chance,* Sarah. Maybe it's a little sooner than you expected, but take it. There's nothing to be afraid of—except going home."

"There's everything to be afraid of."

"Like what?" Jay prodded.

"Like eating a meal on special china with a woman I don't know. I barely made it through dinner tonight at the Andersons'. And I'm sure I wouldn't have if Jeffrey and James hadn't been there, playing monsters and cannonballs with their drumsticks and dumplings, keeping everyone's attention off me."

"*I* wasn't watching the boys," Jay said.

Sarah brought a hand to her forehead, rubbing her temple. "Then you know what I'm talking about. If I embarrassed you tonight, please forgive me."

"*Embarrassed* wasn't exactly what I felt sitting next to you," Jay said. "If you're looking for an E word, maybe *excited, exhilarated,* or *ecstatic* would be a better fit."

"Oh yes," she said sarcastically. "It was *exciting* when I didn't pass the gravy boat right away because I didn't know what it was."

"No one noticed if it took you a second to find the gravy boat." Jay's brow wrinkled in confusion. "I'm not sure what dinner has to do with you thinking you should go back home."

"Everything," Sarah said. "I'm not ready for this. Do you realize that tonight was the first time I've ever eaten on a set of real dishes?" She waited a second, watching Jay's expression as this sank in. "We've used paper plates and bowls and cups my whole life. And at my house, no one ever talks at dinner—half the time my dad doesn't even look at me. It was very stressful trying to have a conversation tonight. And I know that probably seems silly, but it's the truth. It's how I feel—how I am."

"You did great," Jay said.

It didn't seem that way to me. Sarah toyed with a strand of hair that fell over her right shoulder. "How can I live in an apartment with a bunch of girls like Trish who drive and date and curl their hair and wear makeup and—"

"Whoa," Jay said. "You're getting way ahead of yourself. You don't have to live with Trish. We'll find somewhere less—social, where you'll feel more comfortable. And as for eating on real dishes and other stuff you've never done before, well, don't sweat it. It's all small stuff."

"Small, *important* stuff," Sarah countered.

"No." Jay stepped forward, closer to her. He took both of her hands in his.

This isn't small. Sarah forced her hands to stay where they were, though her first impulse was to snatch them away and run down the street.

"The big, important stuff you've already got covered. You're nice—genuine. And if I could pick one quality I'd like a girl to have, that's it."

Jay rambled on, oblivious to her distress. "I can't believe you'd worry about managing silverware when your fingers . . ." He paused, lifting their linked hands in the air. He looked at them reverently. "Your fingers create a masterpiece each time they touch the piano keys. And your voice . . ." His eyes found hers.

Sarah felt her face grow warm and knew she was blushing.

"Today when you sang, you quieted that entire chapel," Jay said. "It was the most amazing thing I've ever heard—aside from Hendrix playing the *Star-Spangled Banner,* maybe." Jay grinned. "But my point is, *no one* is going to know that you're not an old pro at regular things like the family dinner."

"*I'll* know," Sarah said, but she felt his words boosting her confidence the slightest bit. "You'll know."

"I'll never tell," he said. "And to prove my loyalty, when we go to dinner on Saturday, I'll tell you things about my past that will make your family seem like *The Cosby Show.*"

"I doubt it." Sarah frowned. "And I've only seen that show a few times. My dad was pretty restrictive with TV, and I've never been to a movie, either." She sighed. "This is what I mean. I don't see how any of this can work. I'm too different."

"Different is great." Jay chuckled. "I knew a girl once who was so into movies that she compared everything in her life to one. Half the time I couldn't figure out what she was talking about." He released one of Sarah's hands but kept the other, and they started walking again. "I'll take you to a movie. Better yet, I'll pick out some of my favorites, and we can spend evenings sitting on Tiger, eating popcorn, and watching them. It'll be great—the perfect opportunity to indoctrinate you with action films before you can be influenced by the world of chick flicks."

Sarah nodded, unsure what he was talking about but unable to squelch the burst of happiness she felt inside because he continued to hold her hand and talk like they would keep spending time together. Like she was any normal girl he might date. Like any minute now she wasn't going to be whisked away, thrust back into solitary confinement.

She glanced over her shoulder, feeling uneasy once more. She'd never been away from her father for an entire day like this. It was strange, and she couldn't quite believe it was real yet. But no truck came roaring up the street; no police cruiser followed them. And her hand, nestled in Jay's warm one, grew warm as well.

Gradually the quiet beauty of the evening began to wrap itself around her heart. The sugar maples lining the street blazed red, yellow, and orange.

The air was crisp and infused with the faint scent of smoke curling from nearby chimneys. Sarah studied each home as they walked, fascinated by the glimpses of reality each portrayed. Inside those houses were normal people doing things like eating dinner together, talking, watching television.

Across the street a father and son played basketball in their driveway. On the next block, a woman pushed a baby stroller. Looking up, Sarah found the first few stars proclaiming that twilight was nearly over. Soon the black of night would fill the sky, and somewhere out across the universe, billions of stars would glitter in the darkness. A whole galaxy of constellations sparkled, unseen, above them. *Someday I want to be where I can see them all.* Jay squeezed her hand as if to say, *You can. You will.*

"I will." She moved her lips, whispering the words, as if that would somehow make them true. But in the back of her mind, doubts about her abilities, and worries about her father and Carl, continued to nag. She struggled to subdue her negative thoughts.

Somehow Jay seemed to notice. He stopped walking as they turned the corner and the Charles River came into view. He let go of her hand and put his arm around her waist, pulling her close.

She stiffened at first, then forced herself to relax, almost resting her head against his shoulder. *Another first.* She was surprised how comfortable it felt. There were seldom hugs in her home, nor expressions of affection, physical or otherwise. Jay's hand at her waist, his arm across her back, his shoulder beside hers—it all felt *so* good.

They stared out at the water, peaceful and calm.

"You know," Jay said, "it was pretty miserable when Washington and his men rowed across the Delaware on Christmas night, 1776. The river was partially frozen, and they had to use their oars to break up chunks of ice."

She knew this story well. "Many had nothing more than rags to wrap around their hands and feet to protect them from the bitter cold."

"That trip took courage and faith," Jay said.

"Probably a little bit of insanity too," she concluded.

He shook his head. "Not insanity so much, but desperation. The tide of war was not in their favor, and the outlook was bleak. They had to take a risk."

Sarah sighed. She could guess where he was going with this.

"Freedom was a long, difficult process," Jay said. "Years."

"I know." She blinked, the sudden burning behind her eyes catching her by surprise.

"And worth it," Jay finished.

His arm tightened around Sarah's waist, and a warm rush of gratitude filled her. Who would have imagined a month ago, a week ago—*yesterday*—that she would be standing here beside this amazing man, this ally—a friend?

A lone boat rowed near the shore, caught in a ray of moonlight shining on the water. The simple beauty of the peaceful scene—and the events of the day—finally overwhelmed her. Emotions she'd kept in check began spilling down her cheeks.

Jay turned to her again and used his thumb to brush a tear from her face. He took her hand and held it high in the air with his own.

"To victory."

Taking courage, Sarah raised her other hand.

"To freedom."

Chapter Twenty-Three

Grant plunked the manila folder on the kitchen table and took a seat opposite Carl. "Pizza again?" He scowled at the open box and shoved it aside.

Carl took a bite that encompassed half his slice. "What'd you find?"

"He's no attorney, just a student. And worse, he's got a record."

"Everyone's got a record. Who cares?" Carl picked up his beer and tilted his head back, chugging.

"*I* care when it concerns my daughter." Grant popped open a can and took a long drink. "I *especially* care because he did time for possession, use, and distribution."

Carl leaned forward, laughing, choking, spewing liquid from his nose. "This is good."

Grant ignored him, reclining in his chair, a thoughtful look on his face. "It seems that Mr. Kendrich had a little cocaine problem a few years back. Got so bad that he did some jail time. He straightened up and has been clean ever since—*supposedly.*"

"Supposedly?" Carl stuffed the rest of the slice in his mouth, then wiped his face with the back of his hand. "What you got in mind, Chief?" He leaned forward, elbows on the table.

Grant flipped open the folder, turned it around, and pushed it toward Carl. "This is going to take at least a month to set up, and you're going to have to be very careful."

"A month?" Carl frowned. "I'm telling you, there's easier ways to get rid of this guy. And isn't Rossi going to get suspicious if Sarah's not doing her job for a month?"

Anxiety flashed briefly in Grant's eyes. "Let me worry about Rossi. And you're going to do this *my* way. Thanks to your stunt with the truck, anything sloppy will lead the authorities right to our door." Grant poised his finger on a map inside the folder. "But if we play things right, Mr. Kendrich will be out of the picture, and Sarah will have learned a valuable lesson."

Chapter Twenty-Four

Jay bounded down the stairs, two at a time, backpack jostling against his side. He had an early class, but he wanted to stop in and see Sarah before heading to campus. She had walked with him the past two mornings, but today Trish and Archer were going to be her escorts. Though Jay still thought her dad's worry was excessive, it did make him a little uneasy. And it never hurt to be careful.

At the bottom of the stairwell, he stopped and knocked on the door on the ground floor. A fall wreath hung at the top, and white lace curtains covered the glass behind it. He could tell the kitchen light was on.

"Come in, Jay," Mrs. Larson said as she pulled open the door. "Sarah didn't tell me you were joining us for breakfast."

"I'm not," Jay said, though the smells coming from inside the apartment were enough to make him reconsider. "I've got a class to get to. I wanted to say hi to Sarah before I go."

"Hi yourself," she said, appearing in the doorway beside Mrs. Larson.

She was wearing an old-fashioned apron over her clothes and had her hair piled on her head in a messy bun. A few strands had escaped on either side and hung down in front, framing her face. He resisted the urge to lean forward and tuck them behind her ears. Instead, he commented on the new glasses she'd picked up yesterday afternoon.

"Those frames look great on you." They really did, accentuating her eyes and no longer hiding the rest of her face.

"Thank you." She held a muffin out to him. "Blueberry. Fresh from the oven."

"I wasn't stopping by for food, but since you insist . . . thanks." His fingers brushed hers as he took the muffin.

She smiled and looked down at the floor as her cheeks turned pink.

I love that about you, Jay thought. *Love that my touch affects you as much as yours affects me. And I love that you can't hide it.*

"Well, if you're certain you can't stay." Though smiling, Mrs. Larson leaned heavily on the door, as if she wished to close it.

Jay was certain she did. She was ever the conservationist, continually lecturing her tenants about their excessive use of electricity. She didn't believe in air-conditioning and rationed heat like they were living in the era of the Great Depression. *Windows open at night in summer, rags in the windows and beneath the doors in winter,* she always told them.

He held his hand up in farewell as he stepped back. "See you later. Have a great day."

"Bye," Sarah said.

Did I detect wistfulness in her voice?

Mrs. Larson closed the door. He headed off to class, feeling inordinately happy as he took a bite of muffin and walked the tree-lined streets.

Sarah seemed to be adjusting well. Thus far, her creepy cousin hadn't shown up to bother her, and Jay had spent as much time with her as possible the past three days. Each day she opened up a little more. Considering the environment she'd come from, she was adjusting very well. Jay knew that much of that had to do with where she was staying, and he had hope that her current living arrangement would last beyond the week.

Trish, on the other hand, was certain she could pull strings to get Sarah in her sorority and was still vying for her to apply. Jay didn't think that was such a great idea, but he kept his mouth shut, knowing how important it was for Sarah to start making her own decisions. In the meantime, Mrs. Larson was far less intimidating than Trish and her apartment full of giddy females. As he had hoped, Mrs. Larson had taken Sarah under her wing and appeared to be thoroughly enjoying having someone to fuss over. And while Sarah had been guarded her entire life, to her recollection she'd never had anyone mother her the way Mrs. Larson did.

"Mrs. Larson brought me a glass of warm milk last night," she'd told Jay at lunch yesterday.

"Maybe that's her before-bed tradition," Jay suggested. "I warned you she can be a little eccentric."

Sarah shook her head. "It wasn't before bed. It was the middle of the night. I was having a nightmare, and she came in and woke me up. Then she heated the milk for me and sat on the edge of my bed and told me about her daughter."

"I didn't know she had a daughter," Jay said.

"She doesn't," Sarah said sadly. She set her uneaten apple on top of her bag. "Her name was Katie, and she died when she was ten—polio."

"I knew Mrs. Larson had been married, but, wow."

"Katie was her only child. They wanted to have more but never could."

"How sad," Jay said.

"It is," Sarah agreed. "That house she lives in—and all the apartments it's divided into now—was the one she and her husband bought shortly after they were married. They wanted to fill it with children."

"No wonder she gets so upset when Archer fills it with women and loud music and stinky meat."

"Stinky meat?" Sarah's nose wrinkled as if she were imagining the smell.

"Long story," Jay said. "Ask Trish sometime."

"Okay."

Jay wasn't sure if Sarah would ever ask Trish, but she was talking to him a little more each day. She'd confided in him how terrified she was that day he'd taken her to the museum, how she'd worried she wouldn't be able to carry on a conversation with anyone for that long.

Now she was learning they could talk a lot longer than an hour.

And on Saturday, we'll see how we do for a full day. Jay polished off the muffin and walked toward Langdell. He needed to work hard for the next couple of days because Saturday he had big plans involving Sarah and Boston. She'd never been to the city except to attend her class at the conservatory. He got excited thinking of all the things she would be experiencing for the first time.

Vaults of possibility were opening for both of them, and he had a feeling that they were just scratching the surface.

Chapter Twenty-Five

Jay handed Sarah an electronic pass card as they walked over to the turnstiles. "Your first gift of the day. This is a student pass, and it's good for the rest of the semester. You swipe it like this." He inserted his own card.

She did the same, then used her hip to push through the stile, grinning at him when she'd gone through.

He took her hand as they made their way toward the train. "The T runs until 12:45 A.M. You can catch it about every fifteen minutes during the week. It's a little slower on weekends."

Sarah stood up on her toes trying to see over the people in front of her. "This is so exciting."

Jay laughed. "That's it. I've got to take you to Disneyland someday."

Her eyes widened. "That would be *great*. I still remember when a girl in my sixth-grade class did her 'What I Did Last Summer' report on their family vacation to Disney World. It was hard to imagine that such a place really existed."

"It does." He gave her hand a squeeze as the crowd surged forward. "Come on. The monorail awaits."

Jay enjoyed the ride into Boston more than ever before. He enjoyed watching Sarah watch everything and everyone else. There were plenty of seats at first, but after a few stops in the city, it was standing room only.

"Will we have to stand on the way home?" she asked, sounding worried.

"Depends," Jay said. "At least we're safe this time—unless some little old ladies get on. Then we should probably let them have our seats."

Sarah looked repulsed as she studied the straps hanging overhead.

"What's wrong?" Jay asked.

"I'm thinking of how many different hands have probably touched those."

Jay chuckled to himself, then noticed *her* hands, folded prim and proper on her lap. When they turned a corner, she leaned but didn't touch the side bar or place her hand on the seat for support. He remembered the unusual way she'd gone through the turnstile at the station.

"Uh-oh. I'm dating a germ-o-phobe."

She nodded solemnly. "Afraid so."

"I'm impressed that you let *me* hold your hand."

"That's different," Sarah said, looking away.

"Well, that's a relief." Jay chuckled. "But you're going to have to touch stuff today. Why don't we stop at the store and buy a bottle of hand sanitizer?"

"You want me to carry around a can of Lysol?" She looked appalled. "I'm weird enough already. I wish I had my gloves, but they weren't in the suitcase my dad gave you."

"We'll buy new ones. You'll need them soon enough anyway," Jay said. "And I didn't mean a can of Lysol. Haven't you seen those little bottles of sanitizer? Everyone carries them around now. If you're that freaked out about germs—" He glanced at the hanging loops. "Come on. This is our stop." He stood, then took Sarah's hand, pulling her up so she wouldn't have to touch the bar.

The train slowed; the doors folded open. Jay tugged Sarah along through the stream of people coming and going. He headed for the stairs. "Race you."

"Why?"

"Because it's fun and there's so much I want to show you today. And that was before I put buying sanitizer and gloves on the list. Ready. Set." He set his foot on the bottom stair. "Go."

He bounded up the steps, Sarah one stair behind him the whole way. He reached the top and held his hands up in a show of victory. She stopped on the last stair and bent over, breathless.

"Better add eating something good too, if you expect me to run around like this all day."

"Eating is definitely part of the plan," Jay said. "But first, it's time you went whale watching."

* * *

Sarah leaned against the rail, watching the Boston shoreline grow in size as their boat drew closer. She'd just spent the two most amazing hours of her life out on the ocean, feeling the crisp, salty sea air blow in her face, glimpsing one of God's most awesome creations, while standing beside the nicest person she'd ever known.

The boat docked, and she followed Jay toward shore, staggering down the ramp.

"Careful. You've got a case of sea legs." He took her arm as they walked.

"Thank you, Jay. That was incredible. I can't believe we actually saw one." She took a deep breath, inhaling the salty air.

"Its tail, anyway," Jay said.

"Well, yes," Sarah said. "I guess that's what we get for being on the wrong end of the boat."

"That's what I get for watching you instead of the water," Jay said.

Sarah looked at him sideways. "Do you *enjoy* making me blush so much?"

"Every time," he admitted. "Red becomes you."

"I feel like I'm going to be white soon if we don't eat. Do you want to see what I look like when I pass out?"

"Not particularly. Think of all the germs here at the wharf. That will keep you upright a little longer."

"Funny," Sarah said, not laughing. They reached the dock and Jay let go of her arm. "How do you feel about seafood?"

She shrugged. "You mean beyond your basic fish sticks?"

"Answered that question. Give me two more blocks, and I'll feed you the best meal you've ever tasted."

"I don't know about that," Sarah said. "Mrs. Larson makes a fabulous chicken pot pie." Thinking of it made her stomach grumble. From her pocket she pulled the miniature bottle of sanitizer that Jay had bought. "Want some?"

"Sure." Jay held out his hands. "Aren't you glad we stood on the deck and leaned over the rail?"

"Very." She squirted sanitizer on her own hands, rubbed them together, then dangled them at her sides so they would dry.

Sarah walked beside Jay along the wharf—faster than she would have liked—though she was hungry. There was so much to see, smell, hear. *Taste.* They passed a street vendor with steam and a delicious aroma coming from his cart. Sarah cast a longing look at him before forcing herself to face forward again.

Beside her, Jay laughed. "*Many* women would be mortified to let their dates know they're hungry."

"Why?" Sarah looked at him, baffled.

"I don't really know. Other than it's some weird female thing. I don't think guys are supposed to know that women have physical needs like we do."

"Oh."

"You're not blushing."

"I'm not embarrassed. Just starving."

"Good. Because we're here." Jay stepped aside so Sarah could walk in front of him down a narrow dock.

She looked at the compact, worn, wooden building at the end of it. Glancing down, she tried to tell if it was floating or attached to the land.

Jay reached in front of her to open a creaky door. She stepped inside a dark-paneled, dimly-lit room. The odor of fish nearly knocked her backward.

"We'll eat outside. Don't worry."

"I *am* worried."

"Trust me," Jay said.

The hostess came, asked where they wanted to be seated, and took them up a winding staircase to a narrow deck outside. Jay seemed to already know what he wanted, and Sarah urged him to order for her as well.

Bringing her hands to her mouth, she blew on them. The view was gorgeous, and she didn't think she could stand the smell inside, but the breeze outside was a little chilly.

"Would you like a coffee or hot chocolate?" Jay asked Sarah as the hostess/waitress pulled out a notepad.

"Hot chocolate."

"Two please," Jay said. "With extra whipped cream."

The waitress left, and Jay scooted his chair close to Sarah's. "Give me your hands."

She was only too happy to comply. He took them in his and began rubbing.

Sarah felt warmer almost instantly—his touch had a way of doing that. "Do you come here a lot?"

"At the end of every semester—usually to celebrate making it through finals. I discovered this place my first year. And though I've tried other seafood restaurants . . . Well, you'll see."

Their waitress returned and set two steaming mugs on their table.

"Thanks," Jay said. He unwrapped his silverware and used his spoon to take a bite of the whipped cream piled on top, then lifted the mug to his lips and took a drink. "*Very* hot. Careful."

Sarah wrapped her hands around the mug. "I think I'll just hold mine." But her stomach growled again, and hunger won out. She ate the melting cream, then spooned some of the hot liquid into her mouth. Her eyes closed in bliss. "Mmm. This is great."

"Tell me you've had hot cocoa before," Jay said.

"I have. Not often, though. Christmas mostly." She wrapped her hands around her mug again. "I know you don't mean to," she began, choosing her words with care, "but you make me feel bad when you act shocked I haven't heard of or seen or experienced a lot of things before."

Jay set down his cup. "I'm sorry. That wasn't my intention."

"I know." Feeling bad she'd even brought it up when he'd been so very kind to her, she reached out tentatively, her fingertips barely brushing his arm. "Believe me, I *wish* I'd experienced everything that the other ninety-nine percent of the American population has. Half the time I feel like I'm from another planet, but I can't change the past."

"It's the future I'm concerned with." Jay pulled her hand closer and placed his on top. "It's a privilege to be the one to take you out to seafood for the first time, to have been at your side when you saw your first whale."

"First boat ride, too," Sarah reminded him.

"I want to take you to the movies, bowling, dancing, to the zoo. There are a thousand things I can't wait for you to try. And experiencing them with you is like living them myself for the first time. I feel like a kid at Christmas."

"Halloween was only a few days ago," Sarah joked.

"Yes. And because I had to work, you didn't go trick-or-treating. Next year we'll borrow Jeffrey and James if we have to, but you're going. Everyone has to have that experience at least once."

"Do I have to throw up afterward like Jeffrey did?"

"Only if you choose to stuff your face with four pounds of candy in less than half an hour. And speaking of stuffing our faces . . ." Jay looked down through the rail where they could see their waitress carrying a tray up the stairs. He looked back at Sarah. "I promise not to be upset if you're sick later. This is one time it's worth getting stuffed."

Chapter Twenty-Six

Sarah groaned as they walked back down the dock to the street. "I just *might* throw up."

She'd never felt so full in her life. She'd also never eaten such good food.

They'd shared a platter that included boiled lobster and clams steamed with seaweed. *Seaweed . . . who'd have thought?* Fresh corn on the cob and baked potatoes had rounded out the meal. And, of course, she couldn't forget the half pound of melted butter she'd likely gone through, dipping the lobster and clams.

"Shall I roll you down the street?" Jay asked.

"It would probably work." Sarah held her hands over her stomach.

"Actually, I've got a better idea. We could rent bikes for the rest of the afternoon." He glanced at his watch. "But first I thought we could go see Paul Revere's house while we're in this part of town—though I feel a little bad each time I go there."

Sarah gave him a puzzled look. "Why?"

"He wasn't really the one who sounded the cry, 'The redcoats are coming.' It was actually a Dr. Samuel Prescott. Paul Revere and the other man he was with, William Dawes, were arrested before they could warn the rebels."

"Are all law students this knowledgeable? Or were you a history major or something?"

"I got my undergrad in history," Jay said. "That's a large part of the reason I came to Harvard—being the oldest university in America and all. Am I boring you?"

"No. And now I won't be quite so intimidated by your vast knowledge."

"Hey, you're the one who wrote a paper comparing early nineteenth-century composers. Talk about intimidating and over my head."

Sarah turned to him. "So I *was* boring you that day."

Jay stopped at the curb. "No. I was fascinated—really," he added when she continued to look doubtful. "I could tell you had a musical gift the first time I heard you play. And when you spoke so passionately about the pieces you were studying . . ." Jay paused, then reached out, tucking a stray hair behind her ear. "I imagined what it would be like if you were to feel so passionately about something else—or *someone* else."

Sarah brought her hand to the spot on her face Jay's fingers had touched. Her skin tingled, and the sensation was quickly spreading throughout the rest of her body. "I don't know if that's possible."

"I believe it is," Jay assured her. "And how lucky I'll be if I'm the one you discover it with."

Mesmerized by his words, Sarah stood rooted to the spot, staring at him. She didn't care if they saw Paul Revere's house or rode the subway again or did anything else this afternoon. The warmth flowing through her at this moment made the entire day better than anything she'd ever imagined. Again she found herself in awe that someone like Jay would value her company, her friendship. *Maybe even my affection?*

It was possible she'd be around long enough to find out. She'd made it nearly a week without a glimpse of Carl or a word from her father. It seemed too good to be true, and the only explanation she could think of was that her father was so angry that he really *didn't* want to see her ever again. Could she bear it if that was the price for her freedom?

Moments like this one with Jay made the answer seem simple. But other times, when she was alone, she felt doubtful, and guilty she'd left. She was all her father had, though he didn't seem to return the sentiment.

"You have beautiful eyes," Jay said, interrupting her thoughts.

"They're the same color as yours."

"But blond hair goes better with blue." He gave a low chuckle.

"What?" Sarah asked. She reached behind her, touching the braid hanging down her back. "My hair is probably a mess from the boat ride, the wind."

"Sort of." Jay grinned. "But I like it that way. It's softer—it looks pretty hanging around your face like that."

"What are you laughing about then?" Sarah asked.

Jay took her hand and tucked it in his arm, then turned them both toward Hanover Street. "A girl I liked—who didn't necessarily like me back—once told me she hoped I'd meet someone like the character from the movie *Legally Blond.*"

"Legally what?"

"Blond," Jay said. "It's a movie set at Harvard. Anyway. When Jane—this girl I liked—told me that, I couldn't imagine that I'd ever be interested in anyone else, especially a blond. I was wrong." He looked meaningfully at Sarah.

"This Jane wasn't a blond, then?" Sarah said. A tightness was forming in her stomach, threatening to overtake the previous tingling warmth.

"Brunette. And brown eyes too. Another good combination," Jay said. "Not that stuff like that should matter so much. But I guess all of us guys are somewhat susceptible to that sort of thing—physical attraction, I mean."

Physical attraction. The words slid from her brain, down her throat, and landed like dead weight somewhere near her heart. *There is absolutely nothing about me that would* physically attract *any guy.*

"Sarah?" Jay studied her. "Is something wrong?"

She shook her head. "No. Tell me more about Jane."

"Ah." Jay smiled, a spark of mischief in his eyes. "She's married and has a little girl. And she was never interested in me anyway. No need to feel jealous."

"Did you meet her here or in Seattle?" Sarah asked, her illogical fears still not quite subsiding.

Jay's smile disappeared. "Seattle. Actually, that's a long story. And one I'll share with you, but not now. Tonight, at dinner."

Sarah groaned. "Please don't mention food yet."

"Oh, you'll be hungry by then," Jay promised. "After we've seen Paul Revere's place, we're going to race bikes on Beacon Hill."

Sarah swallowed uneasily. But before she could tell Jay that she'd never really ridden a bike before, he'd launched into a detailed story of the famed midnight ride.

* * *

"I'm going to di—ie," Sarah screamed as she rushed past Jay on her bike.

"Right hand! Rear brake first," Jay shouted. He released his own brakes so he could catch her.

Sarah continued to sail down the south slope of Beacon Hill toward the Boston Common.

She was coming up fast on a parked car.

"Brake!" Jay yelled again.

This time she heard him and grasped both brakes hard enough to bring her bicycle to a halt and send it sliding sideways. Jay came up beside her, reached over, and grabbed her handlebars before she could topple over.

Heart pounding, he helped her from the seat.

"I told you this was a bad idea."

He climbed off his own bike. "You were doing fine until we started downhill."

"Not really," Sarah admitted. "I just didn't want to whine too much."

"Wasn't that a *little bit* fun?" Jay asked. "The whole wind in your hair thing?"

"Almost dying is *not* fun." She walked her bike over to the curb and sat down. "I think you miss your motorcycle more than you let on."

"I do miss it," Jay said. "But you get a much better workout on these." He nudged the front tire of his bike. "And really, we've seen a lot more today than we would have on foot."

Sarah placed her hands beside her on the sidewalk and leaned her head back. "We have seen a lot today." She gave him an appreciative smile. "I'm not even sure what I loved the most. Everything—except the bikes—has been fun."

"No Space Mountain for you when we go to Disneyland," Jay said. "And here I pegged you for the adventurous type."

"So adventurous that I'm going to walk this thing all the way back to the rental shop."

"Not so fast. There's one more place on my list," Jay said. "If you're up for it."

"Can we walk?" she asked.

"Nope." Jay looked at his watch. "Not enough time."

"Is there time for a trip to the hospital if I crash?"

"You won't," he assured her. "And this place is really worth it."

"Hmm." Sarah pulled a water bottle from the cage on her bike and took a long drink.

"Come on." Jay held his hand out. Reluctantly she accepted it, and he pulled her up.

Jay offered a quick refresher course on the brakes, and they climbed on their bikes again. He went slow, and Sarah stayed close behind as they wound their way toward the back bay. When they finally stopped on Boylston Street at Copely Square, Jay felt the late-afternoon chill, even though he was sweating. He noticed that Sarah's cheeks and nose were red with cold.

"You brought me all this way to see a giant teddy bear?" Sarah stared at the sculpture outside of the FAO Schwarz building.

"The bike racks are here," Jay said, "but this isn't our destination."

They parked their bikes and locked them, then headed back down the street to Trinity Church. Jay was sure Sarah had noticed it as they rode past before, though she was still concentrating so much on her riding skills, she likely hadn't been able to appreciate its grandeur.

"Trinity Church," Jay said simply as she looked up in awe. "Shall we?" He held his hand out toward the steps.

"We can go inside?"

"Yep. And not only is it gorgeous, it's *warm.*"

Sarah started up the steps without further invitation. Jay heard her quiet gasp when they entered the chancel.

"We won't have time to see it all *this* visit," he said. "But look at the stained-glass windows. They depict the life of Christ. The carvings on the pulpit are also about Jesus."

Sarah nodded, her gaze fixed on the nearest of the magnificent windows. For the next thirty minutes, they wandered the building. Jay asked an occasional question of the tour guides posted at various locations, while Sarah studied everything with an awestruck expression.

Jay was content to linger behind. He too was usually captivated by the art and reverent beauty of the building, but today it was Sarah who held his attention. Her face was radiant as she studied each piece of art and architecture, appreciating them as only someone who was an artist herself could.

He hated the moment when he had to tap her elbow and tell her it was time to go. They had to get the bikes back before dark. Silently she followed him from the church, out to the busy street. The skyscrapers, cars, and buses seemed a harsh invasion on the peaceful world they'd just left.

She looked back at the church, sighing deeply. "You've studied history. What do you believe?"

"About . . . ?"

"About God, Christ."

"I don't know," Jay said. "I wasn't raised in a particular religion—never went to church growing up. But there's something . . . a feeling I get sometimes that I'm not alone."

"Sometimes when I sing," Sarah began, "I feel it then—a goodness that envelops me. But today, it was . . . *more* . . . I don't know." She wrapped her arms around herself. "Just now it was beautiful. Thank you, Jay."

"It wasn't me."

"But you brought me here. You helped me experience that . . . peace. That's what it was, I think. I haven't felt that peaceful, that *safe,* for as long as I can remember."

* * *

Jay had tried to pack too much into one day, and on the train ride home it became apparent dinner wasn't going to happen. It was all Sarah could do to keep her eyes open—and her hands safely on her lap—as her body swayed with sleep.

Poor girl, Jay thought, amused as he watched her head bob as she struggled to stay awake. She clutched the near-empty bottle of sanitizer in her mittened hand. *I'll have to buy her a case of those. And some good lotion to go with it.* Taking pity—or advantage—of the situation, depending how one looked at it, he scooted closer, wrapping his arm around her.

She didn't stiffen as she sometimes had in the past when he'd touched her, but instead leaned into him, laying her head against his shoulder. "Thank you," she murmured without opening her eyes.

"Anytime." Jay kissed the top of her head, knowing she was too tired to notice. He leaned back against the glass, wishing the subway ride would take a little longer. A year ago, he'd been miserable, lonely. A few months—even weeks—ago, the same. Now, here he was, with a woman he liked—and who seemed to like him back—nestled at his side.

So don't blow it, he warned himself. *You've got a good thing started here.*

They'd made leaps and bounds this week in the progress of their relationship, and the process of extracting Sarah from her shell. She'd been a willing and enthusiastic participant in everything but the bike ride.

Now that she was asleep, he let himself dwell on thoughts that had been plaguing him. It was difficult to comprehend everything she'd missed out on as a child, from really riding a bike, to trick-or-treating, to having friends. He'd thought his own childhood was bizarre, but at least he'd experienced most of the normal milestones. It seemed Sarah's biggest adventures had been her twice-yearly appointments with the dentist.

But why? Jay wondered. Why had her father denied his only child so many of the good things in life? Was he just a control freak? Or was there something else going on? And if so, what? The possibilities—and the way Grant had implored him to watch out for Sarah—nagged at the back of Jay's mind.

Until now he hadn't given much credence to her father's warnings, but riding the T at night, Sarah's head against his shoulder, he suddenly remembered Grant's explicit plea that she never use public transportation. *And here I've given her the very thing she needs to take it whenever she wants.* Jay recalled her excitement at getting her pass this morning.

He glanced at the other passengers. Most, he could tell, were caught up in their own worlds and probably hadn't even noticed Sarah. But a man sitting several seats down, across the aisle from them, was staring openly. When he caught Jay watching him, the man met his gaze a moment, then looked away. The hard look in his eyes unnerved Jay. He guessed the man was probably about the same age he was and at least as tall. He wore a bulky jacket that could easily hide a lot of things—like a weapon.

Unease stirred in Jay's gut, and his arm tightened around Sarah. What if her father wasn't as loony as he'd thought? What if there *was* something to his worry after all? Jay looked down at Sarah, sleeping peacefully, and felt his heart constrict. He cared for her already, and the last thing he wanted was for something, or someone, to hurt her. He wanted to protect her. But to do that he had to know what, if anything, was going on with her dad and cousin. Was there any possibility Grant was right?

Jay looked down the aisle again and met the stranger's eyes once more.

Is there any possibility she's in danger right now?

Chapter Twenty-Seven

Carl withdrew the syringe from the inside pocket of his coat. He held it up in the kitchen's fluorescent light. "What do you think, Chief?"

"One? You just took one?" *Lazy, incompetent fool.* Grant ripped a paper towel from the dispenser and reached for the syringe.

Carl scowled. "Last week you're on my case 'cause I bump a guy's bike with my fender—it's *too* much. And now this ain't enough?" He threw the syringe on the counter, where it skidded out of Grant's reach. "Get it yourself. I'm tired of this. Even following Sarah around was better than listening to you gripe. Least she was something to look at."

"You're going to be looking at the inside of a jail cell if you don't get it right soon." Grant pushed past Carl to retrieve the syringe. Picking it up with the paper towel, he held it up to the light. After examining it for a moment, he wrapped the needle carefully. "This is good. But it isn't enough. You know how lax the laws are. Think of all the times I've gotten you off. This has to be *big*—so much so that no school is ever going to let him finish his degree, and no jury is going to be able to do anything but convict."

Carl yanked open the refrigerator door. He stood there, staring at the empty shelves.

"You did great getting Eddie," Grant said. "You really came through for us, planting *fifteen* bags on him, getting him right where he needed to be." He looked up at the ceiling. "*That's* the kind of big we need this time."

Carl's mouth twitched. "I did do good there, didn't I?" He turned to Grant. "But you had the fun part, watching him die, seeing his expression after he drank—"

"Don't." Grant held up a hand. "I warned you, you're not ever to talk about that—with anyone."

"You brought it up." Carl returned his attention to the empty refrigerator. "I miss Sarah's cooking."

"Me too," Grant said. "The sooner you get this done, the sooner things will be back to normal."

"Yeah." Carl took a jar of jelly from the door. He unscrewed the lid and stuck his finger inside. "Alright. I'll go back. Give it a few days for things to cool off, then I'll take some more."

Chapter Twenty-Eight

"Magnificent Mount Trashmore," Jay announced as they stopped in front of the twelve-foot garbage sculpture on the Science Center lawn. "One of the seven wonders of . . . this twenty-five-foot section of campus."

"I can't believe someone willingly touched all that garbage." Sarah wrinkled her nose. "I feel like I need to spray myself with Lysol just standing this close."

"Go through that latest bottle of sanitizer yet?" Jay asked.

"Almost," Sarah said, not catching the teasing in his voice. "Why would anyone build something out of trash?"

Jay used his foot to point out the sign near the bottom of the sculpture. "They do it every year. It's all about being green. If no one on campus ever recycled, it would be even taller, but if everyone did their part, the pile would only be six feet."

Sarah's mouth twisted. "Does that make my father and me *red?* As in, sound the sirens, these people use disposable everything and contribute much more than their share to the landfills?"

"Nah." Jay reached for her hand as they started walking again. "It isn't your fault he's that way. And now that you're on your own, I'd bet you do things differently."

"Now I'm all about china and silver and at least two forks at every meal. You'd think we were dining with dignitaries every night the way Mrs. Larson sets the table."

"She likes you—a *lot,*" Jay added. "I'm glad you decided to stay with her." *And glad she let me add a deadbolt to the front door.*

"Me too," Sarah said. "She's the sweetest lady, and I feel like I'm helping her with the cleaning and things that are difficult for her to do anymore. Last week she even tried teaching me to drive her car, so she won't have to."

"I hope it went better than the bike lesson."

Sarah bit her lip. "Not really. But we found a place where I can take classes. They offered an extended payment plan, so I'm starting next week."

"That's great," Jay said. "Too bad neither of us *has* a car."

"Mrs. Larson said I can use hers as soon as I have my license. I'll work for her in exchange. If I can learn to drive, it'll be the perfect arrangement."

"I'm sure she feels the same. She told me she's never seen anyone so fastidious about disinfecting," Jay teased.

"Really? That was nice of her."

Jay rolled his eyes. "And what about your *nice,* good-looking, intelligent upstairs neighbor?" He tried once more to pull Sarah from the serious mood he saw underlying her attempts at casual conversation. She'd come so far in the past couple of weeks, but today he could tell something was bothering her.

"Seems to me we have a lot of *noisy* neighbors up there." She glanced at Jay. "That's another good thing about Mrs. Larson. She appreciates classical music."

"There's classical and then there are the *classics,*" Jay said. "And I still say you're lacking formal education in the latter. I'd be happy to show you anytime you want to come up, sit on Tiger, and listen for a while." He opened the door to the Loker Commons.

"*No* thanks." Sarah gave an exaggerated shudder as she walked ahead of him. "Have you forgotten I found a half-eaten hot dog between the cushions last time I was there?"

"And Mike was upset that you threw it away instead of reheating it in the microwave."

"I draw the line at recycling food." Sarah frowned. "Guess there is some of my dad in me."

"Thinking about him today?" Jay guessed.

Sarah nodded. "I do every day. It's still weird, you know. I'm afraid I'll wake up some morning and this whole thing will have been a dream."

Jay squeezed her hand. "No dream. Reality."

"Maybe. But I saw Carl on campus yesterday."

Jay bristled at the mention of her cousin.

"He showed up at the lecture hall where I have biology," Sarah said.

"We can still get that restraining order."

"I know. He didn't do anything, though—other than whispering throughout the whole lecture. He said my dad is sick and that I need to come home."

"He's lying," Jay said, wishing he'd pressed charges after the accident. "It's a trick. That's all, Sarah. Please don't buy into it."

"I know, and I won't." She sighed again. "It was just such a shock to see Carl—and then, well, I do feel sort of bad when I think about my father. It's been almost a month. And I'm wondering what he's going to be doing this weekend . . . this Saturday."

He stopped as they reached their usual table. "What's this Saturday?"

"The nineteenth," Sarah said. "One of the few days that was sometimes kind of good for me—for us." She set her backpack on the floor and slid into the chair Jay held out for her.

Jay took the chair next to hers. "Why?" he asked warily.

Sarah's fingers played a slow melody on the table. "Saturday is my dad's birthday—and mine."

* * *

"Can you believe this?" Trish slapped the latest issue of *The Crimson* on the cafeteria table. "I mean, come on. I'd like to see the girl who wrote this wear pointe shoes."

Jay took a drink of soda to hide his smile. He reached for the paper as Archer put an arm around Trish in a comforting gesture.

"Well, it's not an all-bad review," Jay said, scanning the article. "There are quite a few positive remarks about the second half of the show." He looked up to see Archer shaking his head.

"Trish was only in the first half."

"Oh," Jay mouthed. "Sorry, Trish. I'm sure you were great. You know journalists. Isn't it their job to search out the bad, or, I mean, make things negative? I know Arch revels in it."

"Digging yourself deeper," Charlie warned, looking up from his sandwich.

"Yeah. Shut up already," Mike chimed in, though he had no idea what they were discussing, as he'd just returned from the cafeteria line with his tray.

"Trish was wonderful. All the dancers were," Sarah said, surprising them with her sudden input. In the three weeks she'd been eating with them, she'd hardly said two words.

"Thank you," Trish said. "I didn't realize you'd come."

Sarah nodded. "I wanted to watch—I never get to when I'm playing at rehearsal. And Madame Trenchard gave me free tickets so I could hear the orchestra play my composition."

Trish looked at Jay. "Did you go too?"

"I had to work, but Mrs. Larson had a wonderful time. Didn't she, Sarah?" Jay turned to her, but she had reverted back to her shell and sat eating a banana, head bent slightly so she didn't have to make eye contact with anyone.

"Yes," she answered.

"Look at this," Charlie said. He pointed to an article on page two. "Over the weekend five syringes valued at one thousand dollars were taken from a secure facility in Armensie Building One."

"That's the third time," Archer said. "I know the guy who wrote that story, and he's been following it for almost a month. Campus police are completely baffled. Syringes are cheap, so who'd go to the trouble of breaking into a research lab and stealing expensive ones?"

"Stuff's always getting stolen," Mike said. "Like the other day I ordered this thing of nachos. I went to get an extra cup of cheese, and I get back and the whole thing is gone."

"Strange," Jay said. He brought his hand to his mouth so Mike wouldn't see his smile. Everyone else at the table seemed to be in the same predicament. Even Sarah had her lips pressed together. *Poor Mike,* Jay thought. He'd probably never realize that Archer took his nachos—all in the name of revenge over his carton of rocky road.

"Weird." Archer shrugged. "Who's in for the road trip this weekend? We're taking the Olds to the Yale game, so I need gas money."

"It'll cost more," Trish said. "But it has way more room than Archer's bug."

"Can't," Charlie said. "I've got a term paper I've put off too long."

"Me neither," Mike said. "I've got a date with Liz, and she's cooking me dinner."

"You're going to choose a *date* over the Yale game? Have you lost your mind?" Archer asked. "Since when do you date, anyway? You're too cheap."

"I met Liz in cooking class," Mike said. "She's making me Chinese." He leaned back in his chair, licking his lips. "Mmm."

"Fine," Archer said, sounding annoyed. "Choose Chinese and homework over the best game of the year. I'll scalp both your tickets. Give 'em to me, and I'll put them on eBay."

"Wait a minute," Jay cut in. "Maybe I want them."

"Yeah, right. Mr. Serious Law Student at a football game." Archer rolled his eyes.

Mike laughed. "You're funny, Jay."

"If you can get a date, I can go to a game." Jay leaned forward, holding his hand out. "Give me the tickets. Heaven knows how much you guys owe me for groceries."

"A double date. It will be so fun," Trish exclaimed. She scooted her chair closer to Sarah's. "If you'll come over before Saturday, I can help you put an outfit together."

"This Saturday?" Sarah bit her lip.

Jay nodded. He caught her eye. "We'll have fun. You'll get to go to Connecticut—see another state." He felt just a little guilt at playing the travel card.

"Oh, please come," Trish begged. "It's more fun when there's another girl."

"All the hot chocolate you can drink," Jay tempted.

Sarah's eyes darted around the table at everyone watching her. She swallowed, looked down at her lap, then finally looked up at Jay.

"With extra whipped cream?"

Inwardly Jay let out a huge sigh of relief. "As much as you want."

Chapter Twenty-Nine

Jay finished changing from his shorts and running shoes to his swim trunks. Shoving his dirty clothes in a plastic bag, he put them in the locker with his backpack and street clothes, then shut the door and spun the lock, making sure it was secure. He hurried from the room toward the pool where Sarah was waiting.

A few minutes earlier he'd seen her through the glass windows from the cardio room upstairs. She'd been pacing back and forth in front of the pool—a safe distance from the edge—arms folded across her chest, shoulders rigid. He had hoped this would be fun for her, but he could tell she was stressed. Though she'd had a few sessions of swimming lessons when she was a little girl, her father had never taken her to a public pool or the beach where she could swim and keep up her skills.

"Ready for your brush-up swimming lesson?" He placed two towels on the chair next to hers.

Sarah's eyes traveled past him to the Olympic-sized pool. "It's awfully big. Maybe we ought to start with one of those little plastic things they have outside the grocery stores every summer."

"Oh no, you don't." Jay walked around behind her chair, tipping it forward so she had no choice but to stand up. "Remember, today we're only going in the shallow end where you can always touch the bottom."

"What if I don't want to touch the bottom?" She folded her arms across her middle, keeping her coverup tightly wrapped.

"Is that what has you worried—germs?"

She nodded. "How many people would you say swim in there every day?"

"Sar-ah." Jay groaned. He smiled at her as he shook his head. "Can't you smell the chlorine? Believe me—they put enough in there that no bacteria has a fighting chance. You'll be lucky if your hair doesn't turn green. Come on."

"My hair isn't getting wet," Sarah called to him as he took off across the deck.

"Suit yourself," Jay said. After the bike incident, he had no intention of forcing her to do anything. He hurried down the steps into the water. Pushing off the bottom, he dove in, gliding for several feet. He surfaced for a breath and swam to the steps, where Sarah waded hesitantly.

Jay let out a low whistle. "Nice," he said, trying not to stare at the stunning picture she made in the clingy red and white floral bathing suit.

"Trish," Sarah said, as if that supplied all he needed to know.

It did. He imagined Sarah would have chosen something simpler, and with a little less color, but she looked great in red. Jay took off under the water again. After several long, slow laps, he returned to the steps.

"Show off." Sarah flicked water at him with her foot. Jay managed to grab her big toe and held on. She waved her hands in the air, trying to keep her balance. "Jay!"

He let go. "Come on. Get in up to your knees at least. Besides—" He floated closer, bracing himself with his hands on the bottom stair. He tilted his head back to look at her. "All the guys in here are checking you out. They can't do that as well if you're down in the water."

Sarah cast an appalled, furtive glance around the pool, then bit her lip and hurried down the last few steps. Her breath caught as the water reached her waist. She raised her arms above the surface. "It's cold."

"Not if you're moving," Jay said. "They keep the water right around eighty."

She hopped up and down. "I'm moving, and it doesn't feel eighty."

"Over here it does." Jay took a few strokes then floated on his back to the other edge of the pool.

"Where?" Keeping her arms above the water, Sarah moved in slow motion toward him.

"Right here," Jay coaxed, pointing to the spot beside him.

She reached the wall. "It doesn't feel any warmer."

Jay took her hand and pulled her closer. He put his arm around her waist in a casual, yet possessive gesture. The other guys at the pool *were* checking her out. "Any better?"

"Yes, actually." She sounded surprised.

"Good." Jay moved away.

"Where are you going?" Sarah rubbed her arms.

"We both have class in an hour," Jay said. "And as long as it took you to make it over to this side . . ."

"But I *did* make it—almost all the way across the shallow end." She sounded pleased and started to follow him as he swam across the pool again.

Jay waited for her to catch up. He reached behind her and lifted her braid. "And Sarah, your hair *is* wet."

* * *

Swimming today, football tomorrow. Jay mulled over the progress of his and Sarah's relationship over the past few weeks. Already it was difficult to imagine life before Sarah. His concern over her father and *his* worries were gradually fading as the days had passed without incident. Jay's fears on the subway now seemed irrational and unfounded, and it was only Sarah's cousin who gave him any cause for concern.

But Sarah didn't seem overly concerned about Carl anymore, so Jay dismissed that worry as well. He and Sarah spent every possible minute together, and each day it was starting to feel more like a relationship that went beyond friends.

Like today, he remembered—when she'd splashed water on him and joked with him in the pool. *You're killing me, Sarah.* He grinned, enjoying the torture.

Reaching the dressing room, Jay tossed his towel in the laundry chute and walked down the aisle toward his locker, third from the end. He stopped in front of it and reached up to turn the lock. Halfway there, his hand froze in midair. The door was slightly ajar, the handle bent.

With a sinking feeling, Jay grabbed the door and pulled it open. He stared in shock at the shelves inside.

Empty.

Chapter Thirty

"Here it is." Trish cleared her throat and read loudly from the paper so Jay and Sarah, sitting in the back seat of her Oldsmobile, could hear. "2:50 P.M. Friday—a graduate student had credit cards, assorted IDs, keys, clothing, and a backpack stolen from a secured locker in the Malkin Athletic Center." She paused, then leaned over, giving Archer a quick peck on the cheek. "Nice work, Arch."

"It was nice work, all right," Jay muttered. Thanks to whoever it was that had stolen his wallet, he was practically penniless for this trip to the Yale game. His bank and credit card companies were issuing him new account numbers, but the new cards wouldn't arrive until next week. And without his ID, he couldn't even withdraw from his local account.

"I don't know about 'assorted' IDs," Archer said. "I think I should've used 'various.'"

"It means the same thing," Trish pointed out.

"*Various* would've sounded better, though. And a reporter has so few words to get the whole story in, so it's important he choose each one carefully."

"At least you got the story." Trish scanned the rest of the brief article, then passed the paper back to Sarah.

"Yeah." Archer glanced in the rearview mirror. "Thanks, Jay. For once it was nice to cover something before Morris got to it."

"Glad to help." *Happy that getting my locker broken into worked out well for someone.* Jay frowned as he looked out the window. He wished he had at least some idea of who might have stolen his things. *Is there any possibility . . .*

"Just for that, I'm going to cover the toll." Archer followed traffic onto the ramp toward I-90 and Worcester.

"How come you were at Malkin anyway?" Trish asked. "Didn't they just finish that big, fancy remodel on the gym over at the law school?"

"Yeah," Jay said. "And I usually work out at Hemenway. But I was meeting Sarah at the pool, and I thought it would be easier if I used the weight room there."

"Dumb luck," Archer said. He switched on the radio. "What do you want to hear, Trish?"

"Why don't we let Sarah choose?"

Sarah looked up from the paper. "Oh, whatever will be fine."

"No, really. You choose," Trish insisted. "Who's your favorite band?"

Sarah sent Jay a pleading glance.

"Enya," he said, picking something mellow. It was time he remembered this trip was about having fun with Sarah. He needed to get over having his locker broken into. If he wasn't careful, it would ruin their weekend. He passed the CD forward, grateful he hadn't had his music collection stolen. There was something to be said for not being able to afford an iPod.

Archer passed the CD back. "We can listen to that later. We need some good, get-in-the-mood-for-the-game tunes. Find something else."

Jay flipped through the case and handed another CD to Trish. *"Queen.* Number sixteen."

She popped the disc in the player and turned up the volume. A few seconds later the steady beat of "We Will Rock You" shook the car.

Sarah cast a concerned look at Jay as she took in Trish and Archer, heads bobbing, in the front seat.

"Sometimes they play this at games," Jay said. "It's a *classic.*"

"And if all goes well," Archer put in. "On the way home we'll be listening to 'We Are the Champions.'"

* * *

On the ride home that night, Jay brushed Sarah's hair back from her face and marveled—as he had on their first subway ride home from Boston—that this beautiful woman was sitting next to him with her head against his shoulder. Friday's theft still bugged him, but the miracle of having Sarah at his side put everything in perspective. His wallet was replaceable. Sarah was not.

You're my best friend. His thoughts echoed the sentiments of the song playing on his *Queen* CD. They'd popped it back in for the victory ride home.

In the front seat, Trish slept, her head on a pillow against the passenger window. Archer drove, yawning frequently, munching and spitting out sunflower seeds to keep himself awake.

The four-hour-plus, triple-overtime game had been intense—even Sarah had been on her feet and shouting in that last quarter. And after the game they'd gone out to eat, celebrating Harvard's 30–24 victory. Over milkshakes, fries, and burgers, they'd talked and laughed like four friends who regularly hung out together. Even Sarah had opened up at dinner.

But she'd been shy again when, at the end of their meal, the waitress brought her an ice cream sundae with a candle in it, and the whole restaurant chimed in to sing a twisted version of "Happy Birthday." Jay had never seen her face so red, and the ice cream was well on its way to melting before she could look up enough to eat it. Still, he hoped she had as much fun as he had.

The trip couldn't have gone better. Though he hadn't been able to buy her that crimson blanket as he'd imagined, she'd enjoyed her hot chocolate. It seemed that was quickly becoming her favorite treat.

She had already become his. Jay felt content as they entered Cambridge and neared home. He realized that these past few weeks were the happiest he'd ever lived. No longer was he the guy wondering what it would be like to have someone waiting for him at lunch, someone to walk across campus holding hands with. He had those experiences every day now, and he loved it—was starting to love her. Life was very, very good.

He dozed for a while, enjoying the feeling of doing so with Sarah snuggled against him. He woke up when they were almost home, as Archer turned onto Banks Street.

"What—there's a fire!" Archer braked quickly. The street was filled with emergency vehicles.

Jay rolled down his window and stuck his head outside. "That's our house!"

Sarah and Trish were wide awake now too.

"Stay here," Jay said. "I'll be right back."

Archer parked the car behind a fire truck, and he and Jay jumped out.

"Lock the doors and roll up the windows," Jay instructed. He took off running after Archer.

Within a few seconds his nose burned from the smoke. He could see flames shooting out of Mrs. Larson's kitchen window.

Please let her be okay. Two houses away the policeman stationed at the barricade stopped them.

"We live there," Archer said, straining to see around the officer.

"Sorry," he said. "Until the fire's out, it isn't safe."

"Our landlady—" Jay began.

"And roommates," Archer added.

"I'll see what I can find out." The officer took a two-way radio from his belt.

"Where's Mrs. Larson? Is she all right?" Breathless from running, Sarah stopped next to Jay. She placed her hands on the barricade and stood up on her tiptoes, trying to see farther down the street.

Jay could hear the voice coming through the radio. The officer caught his eye and turned away. Jay's heart sank. He reached for Sarah, just as the officer turned around again. To Jay it seemed he took an extra long time returning his walkie-talkie to its clip on his belt.

He looked at Archer first. "Four male students were evacuated from the building." He cleared his throat. "Are you the two who were out of town?"

Jay and Archer both nodded.

"I live there too," Sarah said. "On the ground floor with Mrs. Larson. She's elderly and doesn't get around much."

The policeman looked over his shoulder.

Jay's arm tightened around Sarah's waist as the officer looked at her and spoke.

"The fire started with an explosion on the ground floor. Crews still haven't been able to get inside all the rooms, and . . . I'm afraid she isn't accounted for."

Chapter Thirty-One

"'A predawn November 20th fire resulted in the tragic death of 78-year-old Marjorie Larson, longtime resident of Cambridge. Four tenants of the other two units in the building escaped unharmed, climbing out windows and down an adjacent tree. Mrs. Larson was asleep at the time of the blaze, which gutted the three-story home . . .'" Trish's voice trailed off, and she let the newspaper drop to her lap. "What if you *had* been home?" She scooted closer to Archer, sitting on the sofa beside her.

We should *have been home.* Sarah's head rested in her hands as she leaned forward over the kitchen table in Trish's apartment Monday morning.

Jay took the paper from Trish and continued reading. "'Lt. Brad Huggins of the Cambridge Fire Department said the fire's official cause has not been determined, though it does not appear to be related to recent gas work in the area near the home or to the nearby construction on campus. The investigation will be ongoing. As a safety precaution, the Banks Street home will be razed later this week.'" Jay ran his fingers through his hair. "And to think a couple of days ago I was complaining about my backpack getting stolen."

"Let me see that," Archer said, reaching over Trish to grab the paper. He scanned the article. "Ha! Morris used the word 'home' three times. What an idiot. Should've been my story."

"Archer." Trish and Jay spoke at the same time. Even Sarah lifted her head to stare at him with red-rimmed eyes.

"How can you even think about the stupid article at a time like this?" Trish demanded.

"The news isn't stupid," Archer said. "It's important that it be done right. All I'm saying is that I do a better job than Morris, and he's vying for editor next year, and it's bugging me."

You're bugging me, Sarah felt like saying, but she didn't. She stared dismally at the Formica table. *What now?* The only thing she could do was go home, but she wasn't sure her father would even take her back. And if he did, he certainly wouldn't let her continue school. *I'm as bad as Archer. Poor Mrs. Larson is dead, and I'm worried about where I'm going to live.* Sarah leaned back in her chair, wrapping her arms around herself.

Across the room, Jay rose from the couch and came over to her. "Walk you to class?"

She tilted her head back to look up at him. "Are you serious?"

He nodded. "Let's not make things worse by getting behind in everything."

"But my books—my notes and assignments . . ."

"Talk to your professors," Jay encouraged. He took Sarah's coat from the back of the chair. "Tell them what happened. They'll understand. This afternoon, we'll figure out where to go from here. I'll stop by the bank to see if they can rush my new card." He gave her a hopeful smile. "We can go shopping."

"I can't spend your money, Jay." Sarah stood and let him help her into the coat. They walked past Archer, still perusing the article, red pen in hand, crossing out words, and Trish, curled up on the opposite end of the couch.

"Thanks," Sarah called.

Trish lifted her hand in response.

I mean really *thanks,* Sarah thought as she left the apartment. The future was suddenly very uncertain, and she wasn't sure when or if she'd see Trish again. Her throat constricted.

Jay took her hand as he did every time they walked. Today she gently squeezed *his* fingers. He looked over at her, an eyebrow raised.

"Stealing my move?"

Sarah shook her head as fresh tears surfaced. After crying most of the day yesterday and half the night, she'd thought she was through. But these tears were for herself. Before, she'd cried about sweet Mrs. Larson. But now, the reality of her own life and dire circumstances sent her into deeper despair. She'd been lonely before, but now it would be a million times worse. She studied Jay's profile, memorizing it, though it was the face in all her dreams. *How will I survive without seeing you, talking with you, touching you each day?*

"I don't know why I'm bothering to go to class," she managed to say. "I don't see how I'll be able to keep going to school now. I'll have to go home. There's no way I can support—"

Jay stopped walking and pressed a finger to her lips. He led her over to a bench outside the sorority house and sat down beside her. "I have a better idea."

"Mooching off of you is not better." She folded her arms across her chest.

"I think it would be, but . . . that's not what I had in mind." Jay turned sideways so he could face her. He touched her arm. "Please listen to me before you make any decisions."

She eased back onto the bench, arms still folded as she waited.

"Here's the deal—or what I think might be the deal, anyway." Jay paused, a pained look on his face. Sarah could tell he didn't want to tell her what he was thinking. "What if someone set that fire on purpose?"

"What makes you suggest that?"

"A hunch. A feeling. I get them sometimes. It's kind of a hereditary thing. Long story."

"You say that a lot, you know."

Jay nodded. "Yeah. And there's a lot about me I need to tell you—but now's not the time."

"So, anything else, aside from a feeling?"

"The obvious one," Jay said. "My backpack. Wallet. Keys. Whoever took them on Friday would've had everything he needed to know about me—including where I live and the key to the main house."

"Oh, no." Sarah's hand covered her mouth and she began rocking back and forth. "You think—"

Jay put his arm around her. "I don't know for sure, but yes, I think it might've been Carl. My locker was the only one broken into. It wasn't a random act."

Sarah turned her face into his shoulder as the tears came more freely. "This could be my fault. Mrs. Larson is dead because of me."

"Shh." Jay wrapped his other arm around her. "It's *not* your fault. We don't know anything for sure yet, and even if I'm right, you aren't the one who started that fire."

"What am I going to do? If you're right—and Carl's finally snapped—then he won't stop. He'll hurt you next."

"Hey." Jay lifted her chin and smiled. "You told me yourself I could hold my own against Carl. Have some confidence that this is a fair fight."

"But it isn't," Sarah argued. "Carl doesn't fight fair. He'll do something like set your house on fire while you're asleep. He's a criminal, Jay. He's got a record."

Jay's mouth twisted in a wry smile. "Well, if that's all it takes to convince you I can handle him . . . I've got one too."

* * *

"Jay's right," Kirk said. He finished scooping the ice cream and put the lid back on the five-quart tub. "You shouldn't go home right now, at least until we have more information about the fire and the break-in at school."

"We'd love to have you here." Christa put spoons in everyone's bowl. "Jay tells me you love disinfecting things, and I could use some help cleaning up our basement."

"I couldn't impose like that," Sarah said.

"And I could use a babysitter—especially during those times I'm giving haircuts. Maybe you could even teach those rambunctious boys of ours to do something with the piano besides beat on it."

"They beat it?" Sarah said, aghast, the spoon stopped halfway to her mouth.

Christa nodded. "Stay with us for a while. We can take it day by day or week by week, but for now, I think we'd all feel much better if you're here."

"Please stay, Sarah," two little voices chorused from the other side of the kitchen door.

"Back to bed," Kirk shouted. "Or I won't save you any ice cream for tomorrow."

The four adults exchanged smiles as they listened to the sounds of two pairs of feet scampering across the living room floor.

"I appreciate the offer," Sarah said. "But you've both done too much already." She looked at Kirk. "If my father found out your part in this . . ."

"He won't," Jay said.

"You can't know that," Sarah said. "Did you have any idea that Carl would follow you and break into your locker and then your home? How do we know he isn't watching us right now?"

"We don't know for sure it *was* Carl," Kirk reminded her. "But we're watching *him*."

"What?" Sarah and Christa asked at the same time.

"It's a weird . . . coincidence," Kirk said. "I've been watching this park on O'Brian."

Sarah swallowed uneasily. She knew that park well.

"The amount of drug activity there has escalated since Rossi's release, so another officer and I are taking turns watching it. Anyway, your cousin's been there a lot lately. He has some new wheels now."

Carl at the park? Is he taking my place? Confused and guilty thoughts tumbled around in her mind. "You're watching him?" she asked, still trying to figure out what was going on with her father, Carl, and the undercover narcotics team.

"Not all the time," Kirk said. "But right now, we know he isn't here. And there are some things we can do to ensure he doesn't find out where you're staying."

"No," Sarah said again. "If Jay's right and Carl started the fire, you'll be in danger too. I won't do that to you or your little boys."

Christa reached across the table and placed her hand over Sarah's. "If you're worried about our house burning down, don't. If those two—" She looked at the kitchen door where two sets of eyes were peeking through the crack. Suddenly it swung shut. "They think we don't know they're listening." Christa rolled her eyes. "Anyway, if those two haven't burned it down yet, I think we're good."

"You don't know my cousin, don't know what you're dealing with," Sarah argued.

"No?" Christa raised an eyebrow. "Maybe I need to get out some photos of the kids we took in when we lived in LA, children who stayed with us while their parents were trying to kick their meth habit. More often than not they kicked their kids instead—and occasionally our front door or window."

Sarah sat quietly, unable to come up with another rebuttal.

Christa caught her eye. "We know it's dangerous. We're going to be very careful. And you're going to be safe."

Sarah finally nodded in defeat. She looked over at Jay, who'd been uncharacteristically silent this afternoon—all day, really, since his startling comment about having a criminal record. She still wasn't sure how she felt about that. He'd refused to elaborate, other than to tell her it was long ago, that he was very sorry about what he'd done, and that he had no current legal issues. He *had* promised to tell her everything in detail soon—if they ever managed to spend an evening alone. "Where are *you* going to stay?"

"We've found another apartment," Jay said. "Archer, Mike, Charlie, and I."

"Is it very far?" Sarah asked. *Maybe I do know how I feel about it. I trust Jay. I want to be with him.*

"No," Jay said. "I'll still walk you to classes each day. Though we'll meet on campus. Some other students will be with you until then."

"I see." It was all planned out, and she didn't really have much say. Though what *were* her choices? She could go home to her father, never see

Jay again, likely never go to school again or even sing in the church choir, or
. . . *Let these good people help me.*

It wasn't much of a decision.

* * *

"Can I help with anything else?" Sarah finished polishing the last of Christa's
silver and tried not to think about Mrs. Larson doing the same task just a
few days earlier. Sarah set the piece on the crowded table, next to the paper
turkey Jeffrey had made at kindergarten.

"I think we're good now." Christa stirred the gravy while using her other
hand to open the microwave to remove a bowl of vegetables.

Sarah lingered by the door, feeling out of place in the cramped kitchen.
The table was set for nine—three other students would be joining them for
Thanksgiving dinner. She wasn't looking forward to making conversation
with so many people, though compared to the group that had been here
earlier, nine was a small crowd.

This morning, Kirk and Christa's young adult group had shown up,
laden with bags and boxes—all full of clothing and other items to replace
those lost in the fire. Overwhelmed by so many people as well as their
generosity, Sarah had hardly been able to put two words together to thank
them. She owned more clothing now than she had when living with her
dad.

With a pang of guilt she thought of her father, all alone today. *What has
he been eating? It's not like he or Carl can cook anything.* Then Sarah thought
back to those awful moments in her father's office when he had made it
painstakingly clear that he viewed her more as a servant than a daughter.
The guilt from a moment before dissipated.

"I think I'll go see what Jay's up to," she told Christa and went to the
living room, where Jay, Kirk, Jeffrey, and James were sprawled across the
floor creating a Lego city.

Sarah knelt next to James. "That's a great little building you have going
there."

"Jeffrey taked all the blocks."

"They're Legos, not blocks." Jeffrey stood up. "Let's play cowboys now.
Let's watch—"

"Let's not," Kirk said, grabbing his oldest by the seat of his pants before
he could reach the DVDs. "Sarah, maybe you could play something on the
piano for us. *Please?*"

A mischievous look in his eyes, Jay leaned over and whispered in her ear. She looked skeptical. He winked.

"What are you two up to?" Kirk asked suspiciously.

"Nothing," Jay said, whistling.

Sarah sat down at the piano. For a few seconds she placed her fingers on various keys as she tried to remember the tune Jay had requested. Raising her fingers, she began an energetic arrangement of the *William Tell Overture*.

"Oh, no." Kirk lay back on the carpet.

"Come on, boys," Jay said. He stood, poised to run. "To your horses. It's the Lone Ranger."

"Hi ho, *Sliver*," Jeffrey exclaimed, slapping his sides. He scurried to get behind Jay before his brother could. The threesome began to gallop around Kirk, still lying on the floor, hands to his face.

"No. Not the horses," he moaned.

"Yes, Daddy. Horses," James said as he jumped over his dad. Barely making it, he fell backward.

"Umph," Kirk said. "Careful. Unless you don't want any younger brothers or sisters."

Sarah continued to play, the notes resonating around the room.

Christa came in, drying her hands on a dishtowel as she observed the chaos. Jay swooped in close to Sarah and sat beside her on the bench.

"This," he said, with a smile that reached his eyes, "is what the holidays should be like."

Chapter Thirty-Two

Carl pulled a burger from the fast-food bag on the coffee table. "Nope. I still ain't figured out where she lives."

"It shouldn't be that difficult," Grant said. His nose wrinkled in distaste as he opened the bag Carl had set in front of him. "You know when and where her classes are. Follow her."

"It's not that easy anymore. She goes all these different places on campus—places I can't get into—and disappears from there." Carl opened a ketchup packet and squirted it on the paper next to his fries. "It's not like I've had a lot of time." He nodded toward a package on the counter. "You want syringes, I get 'em. You want that guy's wallet, I steal it. You don't want her to have a place to stay no more, I even took care of that."

"I never told you to set her house on fire," Grant said. "If they trace it back to you, you're looking at arson and manslaughter."

"They won't be able to trace nothing. The building's gone. What're they gonna do?"

"Plenty," Grant said. He left his sandwich untouched and went to the kitchen for a drink.

"I found out where her boyfriend works," Carl said. "Little hole-in-the-wall nightclub near campus. Plays there nights."

"That's useful," Grant said, his tone sarcastic.

"It is," Carl insisted. "He and Sarah are getting tight. You don't think she's gonna show up there to watch him some night?"

"*Which* night?" Grant asked. "Are *you* going to hang out there every time he works?"

"Nope." Carl finished his burger and leaned back on the sofa, one leg propped on his knee, a smug look on his face. "But *Diedre* works most every night at the bar. And she'd be more 'n happy to get Jay's girlfriend out of her way. I left her my number. She's gonna give me a ring as soon as Sarah comes by."

"That might work," Grant admitted grudgingly. Though the thought of Sarah out at night caused him no small amount of panic. If Carl could get to her, so could anyone else.

"No appreciation." Carl shook his head. "No matter what I do, I don't get no thanks. No wonder she took off," he mumbled.

"What'd you say?" Grant asked.

Carl matched his threatening tone. "You heard right. I said it's no wonder Sarah left."

"I do what I have to to keep her alive," Grant said. "And you'd better remember that it keeps you alive too."

* * *

"I can't figure it out." Kirk looked at the reports spread across the kitchen table. "Why would the chief have someone with a criminal record acting as a bodyguard for his daughter?"

"In my mind the bigger question is why he thinks she *needs* a bodyguard," Jay said.

Kirk nodded in agreement. "Yeah, but look at this guy's rap sheet." His fingers roamed the pages faxed to him from a friend in another precinct. "Armed robbery, grand theft auto, assault. He's no prince. What's to keep him from using his unsavory talents on Sarah?"

"He got off all those times, didn't he?" Jay asked. "That can't be a coincidence. Maybe Sarah's dad is holding that over his head. Maybe he's told Carl that he'll do time if he doesn't behave himself—at least around Sarah."

"Maybe," Kirk said. "But I think it's got to be more than that. This guy's greedy. He wasn't stealing to put bread on the table. His type wants the high life—without working for it."

"I doubt he has that now," Jay said. "You saw that beater truck he drove."

"You're right," Kirk agreed. "And the car he drives now isn't much nicer. But I'd still bet Chief Morgan is paying Carl to keep an eye on Sarah—and now you."

"I haven't seen him at all this week," Jay said. "And I've been watching my back."

"He's been busy," Kirk said. "Since Sarah left, he's developed a sudden drug habit."

Jay stiffened, and Kirk sent him an apologetic look. He was one of the few who knew a little about Jay's less-than-perfect past.

"He's been seen at 'the office' in O'Brian park twice, buying some pretty hefty quantities of cocaine and meth. Too much for one guy, so he's sharing or something."

Cocaine. My old enemy. Jay still remembered the taste, the deceptive feelings of euphoria after shooting up. It would haunt him the rest of his life. "Why don't you bring Carl in?"

"Can't," Kirk said. "Since half the park is in Cambridge, Chief feels like it's their problem. And you know how lax this city is about drugs."

Jay rolled his eyes. "Let's not dare bust any of the rich and privileged youth."

"Especially if they've got parents who contribute to the university coffers," Kirk added. "It annoys the heck out of the chief. But we're supposed to concentrate on the areas closer to the city center. Problem is, half the stuff that's coming from that park eventually makes its way to the city center—the neighborhoods, the schools."

"You're watching off the clock?" Jay guessed.

"Sort of. I get over there during my shift as much as possible, and I'm starting to put names and faces together. It's become kind of an obsession with me—stopping it, I mean." Kirk looked at Jay. "You know what drugs do to people—families. I've seen firsthand that meth is the worst. I keep hoping that if I come to the chief with enough evidence, he'll take some action."

"Except now it's his pet nephew who's buying."

"Yeah." Kirk looked at the papers again. "And I wish I knew why."

Chapter Thirty-Three

"*Now* will you tell me where we're going?" Sarah asked, hurrying to keep up with Jay as he towed her across campus.

"Nope. Top secret."

"So secret Archer wrote about it in the school paper?" she guessed as they neared the Science Center.

Jay frowned. "You're taking all the fun out of it. I wanted to surprise you."

"I think it's going to be the other way around tonight," she said. "That is, if you're planning to take me to the grand opening of the Putnam Gallery."

"I was." Jay sounded disappointed.

Sarah tried to hide a guilty smile. "I came this afternoon, between classes." She shrugged. "But that's okay. Isn't it about time *you* had a first with *me* for a change?"

"It opened *today*. And already—" He shook his head. "What's a guy have to do to surprise you anymore?"

"You surprise me every day," Sarah said. "You're still hanging out with me."

They went in the Science Center's east entrance, and Sarah led the way to the newly completed first-floor gallery.

"Mind if I show you my favorite things?" she asked, excited to have switched roles for the evening. She loved all the new experiences Jay had shared with her, but sometimes their relationship felt unbalanced, as if she had nothing to contribute. There were so many things she felt naive about, so many jokes told at the lunch table she missed, so many references to pop culture she didn't understand.

But tonight would be different. *This* she understood. The sun, the moon, the stars had always been there for her, reminding her of something much bigger than the narrow world she'd been confined to.

Her music teacher Miss Amelia had once told her to "reach for the stars," encouraging her to use her talents to get everything she wanted from life. Sarah had never forgotten that sentiment. There had been times of discouragement certainly, but a glimpse of the night sky sprinkled with stars or of the full moon was all it took to remind her to stay on course. After all, if man could walk on the moon, so far away, she could someday walk away from the life she hated.

But she had never expected to have someone to walk with, someone who encouraged her instead of holding her back. This new combination of freedom and friendship became more exhilarating each day—much more than she'd ever hoped for or dreamt of.

Sarah stopped in front of an exhibit about Galileo, pointing to a geometrical compass. "There are only three of these in existence."

Jay gave a low whistle. "And Harvard has one."

"They have a lot of great things," Sarah said. "Wait until you see the astrolabe. It dates back to 1400."

She took Jay's hand, guiding him through the exhibit, showing him vintage telescopes from the 1700s up through the more modern and complex equipment used to study the stars today.

"How do you know about all this?" he asked when they were about three-fourths of the way through the displays. "You'd have to have a photographic memory to have learned all this in a few hours this afternoon."

"I've been fascinated by the stars, the sky, forever," Sarah said. "It's so immense, and it's always seemed so full of promise."

"How so?" Jay asked.

"Well . . ." She considered, trying to put into words the feelings she had when standing beneath a starry sky or looking up at a crescent moon. "For one thing, it's always there. Dependable. Constant. The moon cycle is exact; its timing precise. The constellations are the same. Always there. Always accessible if you can get somewhere dark enough to see them. When I was younger, my dad took me to the country a couple of times. And out there where you *can* see them . . . Well, there are so many. They represent so much possibility."

"I've never thought of it like that," Jay said. He leaned over a large globe, his finger hovering over the West Coast.

"Are you thinking about home?" Sarah asked, suddenly seeing less promise in her world than she had a moment before. She knew Jay planned to return to Seattle after he graduated next spring. *What will happen when we're separated by 3000 miles?* She was surprised at how much pain accompanied that thought.

"I don't think about home as much as I used to," he said, turning away from the globe. "Seattle's a great place, and I do miss it." He bent his head close to hers. "But all the years I spent there can't compare to the past few weeks with you."

Chapter Thirty-Four

"Joe Sent Me"? Sarah shot Jay a quizzical look as she read the sign hanging outside the redbrick building. "Sent me what? Kind of a strange name for a restaurant, isn't it?"

"It's from the 1920s," he explained. "Back then 'Joe sent me' was often the password to get into a speakeasy."

Sarah walked ahead of him into the pub-style establishment. "I should have known you'd choose a place that has something to do with history." She looked curiously at the bottle cap art on the wall.

"Not history. Pickles," Jay said. "Deep-fried ones, to be exact. That's why we're here. One taste and you'll think you've died and gone to heaven."

A college-aged woman wearing jeans, a white shirt, and a black apron met them inside the door.

"Two, please," Jay said. "And preferably away from the bar and the darts."

"No problem." She led them to a table near the front windows. "This okay?"

"Great," Jay said.

She placed two menus on the table. "Your waitress will be here shortly."

"Thanks." Jay held Sarah's chair out for her, then shrugged out of his jacket before sitting down himself.

"Are you sure we should sit right here in plain sight of the street?" she asked. "What if Carl—"

"Kirk's following him tonight." Jay leaned forward over the table. "And I really don't want to talk about Carl while we're here."

"Agreed," Sarah said. "This evening is all about you. You're finally going to reveal your deep, dark, mysterious past."

She has no idea. The dread he'd felt all week as this evening grew closer settled in his chest.

"I'm glad we're here," Sarah said. "I miss seeing you all the time, miss living downstairs with Mrs. Larson."

"Her funeral was nice," Jay said. "Bringing flowers was thoughtful."

"I'd like to keep it up—her grave I mean. She doesn't have anyone else to do it for her, and . . ." Sarah's voice trailed off as she looked outside at the passing traffic.

"What?" Jay asked after a minute.

"I never visit my mother's grave." She faced him again. "I don't even know where she's buried."

"It wouldn't be too hard to find out," Jay suggested. "Counties have records, and—"

"No." Sarah shook her head. "I think it's easier this way. Sometimes I feel bad, but my mother—there are things you don't know."

"Now who has the deep, dark, mysterious past?" Jay asked.

"Apparently both of us." Sarah opened her menu. "But let's not think about that right now. I'm hungry, and I can't wait to see what you feed me this time. I still haven't forgotten that delicious lunch in Boston."

"This is completely different fare," Jay said. "But also a necessary part of your cultural rounding." He tilted his head toward the speakers on the wall, listening as the song changed. "Classic Journey. 1983 *Frontier* album, 'Separate Ways.'" *Hopefully not a bad omen.* "They also play great music here."

"Another necessary part of my *cultural rounding*," Sarah said.

"Absolutely." Jay grinned. "Though I think you'll appreciate *this* music a little more. Turning in his chair, he reached inside his coat pocket and removed one of two packages. He held a flat, simply wrapped gift out to her. "Happy late birthday."

"Thank you." She took it from him, untied the string, and folded back the brown paper, revealing a packet of yellowed pages.

"I figured it was highly unlikely you'd get any of your sheet music from your dad, and since what little you did have burned in the fire . . ." He shrugged, suddenly uncertain whether his inexpensive gift was acceptable. Her continued silence as she turned the pages seemed to confirm his fears. "I got them at an antique shop. There's a waltz, some ragtime, and a Christmas collection."

Sarah's slender fingers traced the notes in front of her, pausing once in a while to play them on an imaginary keyboard. She turned each page slowly until she reached the end. At last she looked up at Jay. "This is the most thoughtful gift I've ever received. It's even better than the Gilbert Stuart prints." Behind her new, stylish frames, her eyes glistened. She picked up the papers and clutched them to her chest. "I can't wait to play them all."

Jay leaned back in his chair and sighed with relief. "Let me know a couple of minutes sooner next time, okay? I've been having a heart attack over here, thinking I did something awful." He gave her a wry smile. "A lot of fingers have probably touched those. Germs, you know."

"I don't care." She continued holding the papers as she looked around the crowded room.

Jay followed her gaze as she took in the brick walls, cluttered bar, and low lights hanging over the tables.

"I like this place," she announced. "It's cozy."

"And kind of slow with the service," Jay said, noting their waiter still hadn't come. He flipped open the menu, though he already knew what he wanted. "I'm going to get an order of fried pickles to go with my burger. Get whatever you like, but I'm telling you, you haven't lived until you've tried those pickles."

Sarah wrinkled her nose. "I'm not sure I like fried pickles."

"Your loss." He shrugged. "More for me."

"Oh, I'll try them. After the meal you fed me in Boston, I'll try anything you recommend." She studied her own menu. "Do they have hot chocolate?"

"We do," a woman said as she came to their table. "I'm Katrina, and I'll be your server this evening. Can I start you with some drinks?"

"Appetizers," Jay said as his stomach grumbled. "We'll take a couple baskets of fried pickles, and she'll have a large hot chocolate."

"Is it okay if we share the pickles?" Sarah asked. "In case I don't like them. I wouldn't want to waste a whole order."

"They wouldn't be wasted," Jay said. "But we can start with one."

As Sarah questioned the waitress about the different types of burgers, Jay internalized what she'd just said to him. *Is it okay if we share? It's more than okay,* he thought, watching her. *Anytime. Anything. Just ask. I've waited a lot of years to find a woman who wanted to share with me.* He hoped, after tonight, that he wouldn't have to wait several more. He wished he hadn't let things go so long before telling Sarah about his past. He should have told her everything during the day they spent in Boston, but it had been their first real date, and he hadn't wanted to ruin it. And at the time, he'd had no idea of the events that would complicate life in the following weeks.

They both ordered, then handed the menus to Katrina as she left. Sarah dug in her purse for her bottle of hand sanitizer.

"Want some?" she asked Jay.

"No. I've used that stuff so much lately I hardly have any skin left. I'll take my chances that I won't get salmonella from the menu."

"More pickles for me if you do," she teased as she rubbed her hands together.

"Funny," Jay said. His eyebrows rose. "Do you realize you just had a voluntary conversation with a stranger?"

"I did?" Sarah wore an astonished expression as she dropped the bottle into her purse. "You're right. I didn't even think about it—wow."

"To normalcy," Jay said, raising his water glass.

"To normal *me*," Sarah said, clinking hers against his. She inspected the rim before taking a drink.

Getting closer anyway, Jay thought. "Speaking of which—me and abnormal, I mean—we might as well get started." *Might as well get it over with.* He held his hands out. "Ask away. Anything you want to know." He preferred putting it off indefinitely, or at least until they'd eaten, but Sarah had been more than patient, accepting his explanation that he'd tell her later, waiting to learn about his past—especially after he'd dropped the bomb about having a criminal record.

"Oh, I intend to." Sarah re-wrapped the music and set it on the windowsill. She picked up her purse, took out a small notepad, and laid it on the table.

She's taking notes?

"All right." Flipping it open she read, "I know you're twenty-eight, and you're birthday is September fifth, but I don't know anything about your parents."

"You made a *list?*" Jay leaned forward, trying to see how long it was.

She snatched it off the table. "Yes, I made a list. There's a lot I want to know. And I don't want to get sidetracked."

"Women," Jay muttered, though part of him was secretly pleased that this particular woman was so interested in knowing who he was. The other part felt like he was about to collide head-on with a train. One glance at Sarah's paper, and he knew it was going to be a long evening.

"My mom and dad weren't married," he began. "Dad was a professor, my mom a protestor. How they ever got together is beyond me."

"So did you live together as a family for a while?" Sarah asked. "Did they try to make it work—for your sake?"

"Not that I'm aware of." Jay realized he sounded casual and matter-of-fact about the whole business. *What other way is there to be? You can't change the past—even if it hurts.* "I lived with my dad. He was a good guy."

"*Was?*" Sarah asked. "At the museum you told me your mom had passed away, but you never mentioned you'd lost your father, too."

"He had a stroke halfway through my senior year of high school."

"I'm so sorry." Sarah pushed the notepad aside. "And you don't have any brothers or sisters or cousins or anything?"

"None that I know of," Jay said. *None I'd want to know, if they're related to my mom.*

"What did you do after your father died? Who did you live with?"

Jay's mouth twisted in a grimace. "This is where it gets kind of ugly. You sure you want to hear it so soon? Maybe I should tell you about elementary school and summer camp. And don't forget junior high." He raised his hand in the air, pretending to dunk a basketball. "Eighth-grade state champs. It's my one claim to fame. You really should hear it."

"Maybe later. Right now I want to know what happened after your father died." She scooted her chair closer and sat on her hands.

Her nervous habit, Jay observed. He placed his own hands behind his head, trying to look relaxed for a man who felt he was about to face the guillotine.

"I went to live with my mom. Turns out she'd been in nearby Tacoma my whole life. She'd never come to visit—either because she wasn't sober enough *to* visit, or maybe because my dad wouldn't let her. Either way, I didn't really care."

"Go on," Sarah coaxed.

"Her boyfriend at the time was beating her. I found out and beat him up. She told the police I'd started it. I got arrested."

"She stuck up for *him?*" Sarah said, outraged.

"Yep." Jay's head bobbed. "I was lucky, really, since I could've been tried as an adult. Instead I spent two months in a detention facility. And all because I'd tried to protect her. I swore when I got out that I'd never see her again."

"Oh, Jay." Sarah's eyes were filled with sympathy. "That's awful—what she did, I mean. But what you did isn't so bad, wasn't even wrong. I wish you would've told me sooner. I'm so relieved."

He closed his eyes briefly and expelled a long, slow breath. "Don't be. You haven't heard the worst." *Haven't heard any of it, really.*

"Oh." She looked down at the table, but not before Jay caught the disappointment on her face. "Did something else happen while you were in jail?"

"After I got out," Jay said. "I never wanted to see my mom again, but . . ."

"What else could you do? Where would you go?" Sarah guessed. "I know what it's like to feel stuck."

"Yeah." Jay paused, remembering that time, the precise turning point that started him down the wrong path. "I was eighteen, so I could've left, but I didn't have any money or a job—and I still needed to finish high school. My mom pointed all of that out to me when she came to pick me up."

"But it sounds like she didn't want you, so why would she come?" Sarah frowned, a contemplative look on her face as she tried to make sense of his story.

"She didn't *want* me," Jay said. "She *needed* me. The bruiser had moved on, and with him her access to crack. She needed someone—preferably male—to get her drugs. I needed a place to live so I could finish school."

"*Drugs?* That's what this is about?" Sarah raised her head again, absolute shock etched into her delicate features.

"Yeah. It is." Jay's voice was filled with regret. He lowered his arms, placing his elbows on the table. "You want me to stop?"

"Yes. No." Sarah started to rock back and forth on her hands. "I don't know what I want."

"Then I'll keep talking. Tell me to shut up when you've heard enough." He waited until she gave a slight nod.

"I decided to stay with my mom until I graduated. Then I planned to go to the University of Washington, where I'd already been accepted. I figured I'd apply for financial aid, live at the dorms, and everything would be great."

"It wasn't?" Sarah freed one of her hands and reached for her water glass. She raised it to her lips, taking long, gulping swallows.

"It wasn't," Jay echoed.

Katrina returned with their drinks and appetizers. When she left again he took a bite of hot, battered pickle and closed his eyes in bliss. *At least the food will be good tonight.* "Maybe we should've gotten two orders."

"I'm not very hungry anymore." Sarah nibbled the end of a pickle. After a minute she added, "But these are tasty."

Jay brought his straw to his lips and took a drink of his soda. "I'm glad you like them. Are they good enough that I'm off the hook with at least some of those questions?" He glanced at her notebook, pushed to the far side of the table to make room for their plates.

She stopped with a bite halfway to her mouth. "Do you want to be off the hook?"

He considered. "Yes and no. On the one hand, I hope you'll still like me by the end of the evening. The more I tell you, the less likely that is. The flip side is that—other than in a therapy session—I've never told anyone a lot about my past. If you did know and still wanted to be with me . . ." He let the unfinished sentence hang in the air.

Sarah put down her pickle and used her napkin to wipe her mouth. "I . . ." She wrapped her hands around her glass, fingers entwined as she took a deep breath. Jay got the feeling she was trying to shore up her courage.

"I can't imagine losing your friendship." Her grip on the glass loosened, and her eyes softened. "Especially over a mistake you made in the past."

"Mistakes," Jay corrected. "Lots of them."

Sarah folded her arms across the table in front of her. "Tell me."

Chapter Thirty-Five

Jay finished the last of his burger and knew that his respite was almost over. Their meal had arrived just minutes after their appetizers, and Sarah had kept up the cheerful front until they'd both relaxed into casual conversation again. He'd told her about eighth-grade basketball. She'd told him about getting the lead part in the school musical and not being allowed to take it.

But now, seeing her sitting on the edge of her seat, he could tell she was very much on edge once more, waiting for the rest of the story.

He took another drink then jumped back in. "For a while things with my mom were all right—our little arrangement tolerable. I'd get her a stash every couple of weeks. She'd leave me alone to do my thing—which was going to school, working a minimum-wage job, sleeping on her couch, and trying to keep the place clean and the fridge stocked. I thought I was going to be okay, thought I'd make it out of there." Jay's hands clenched into fists on the table. "But I didn't."

He glanced at Sarah and was disheartened by the increasing worry in her eyes. He looked at her burger, only half-eaten, and worried he'd been right about her not being able to accept his past. He'd hoped, but . . . *No stopping now,* he thought and plunged on.

"School was rough. Transferring in as a senior had made me a loner, and now I had a bad reputation too. Home was worse. My mom was either high or wishing she was. Life was awful, and one day I caved." He tried to meet Sarah's gaze, but she was looking away. "Once I got started on cocaine, it was next to impossible to stop. I used on and off for three years. Somehow, during that time, I managed to graduate from high school and even attend the university a couple of semesters. I held down a few different jobs during my more sober months, took care of my mom . . ."

He looked out the window at the snowflakes beginning to fall. The *Frontier* soundtrack still played overhead, but the song was now "Rubicon."

The point of no return. How ironic. He'd arrived there himself. In a quiet voice he told Sarah more than he'd ever told anyone—except Jane.

"Then one day I *really* took care of my mother."

He pushed his plate aside and took his last drink of soda. He waited, filled with self-loathing as he watched snowflakes drift to the pavement and melt away. If Sarah wanted to know more, she was going to have to ask.

"What do you mean you 'took care of her'?"

The dread in her voice told him she'd already guessed.

"I killed her." He couldn't look at Sarah as he spoke the words. "It was Friday. I picked up our usual stash, brought it home just like I picked up the groceries each week. I'd fix dinner, watch the late show with Mom, and we'd both get wasted. Saturdays were the best for me. I could stay in bed—high, then hung over, of course—wallowing in the self-pity that was my life."

He paused, half-expecting Sarah to get up and run away. She didn't, though the color had drained from her face, and she looked like she might throw up. He waited a minute, then continued, speaking quietly as he had before. Most of the patrons were on the other side of the restaurant near the bar, but there was no need to advertise his vile past to anyone else.

"I ate by myself that night. I assumed Mom was asleep because she'd worked the graveyard shift the night before. But I sat down to watch TV, and pretty soon she joined me. After a while she asked me to fix her up with the usual hit."

Sarah grimaced and turned away. "I feel sick."

"I'll stop," Jay said.

"No." She shook her head, blond hair partially covering her face. "Go on. Finish."

Jay's regrets multiplied as he saw the distress he was causing.

"I gave my mom her share, and she went back to bed. After a while I took mine too—a smaller dose. I hadn't been using as long or as much as she had, so a little still went a long way." Jay pulled his gaze from the street and looked directly at Sarah. "When I got up the next morning, I found her dead—overdosed."

"But if it was the same amount she always took—"

"It wasn't," Jay said. "When I thought she'd been sleeping earlier, she'd been in her room freebasing." At Sarah's confused look, he explained. "Smoking a very dangerous, pure form of cocaine. She'd cooked it up when I wasn't home. That she had any to cook up was my fault too. I'd been trying to wean myself off again, taking less and less each week so I could get out. I hadn't told her, but I'd hidden what I didn't use in my closet—an addict can hardly ever do it on his own or make a clean break, so I had some around 'just in case.'" He ran his fingers through his hair and sighed. "I didn't know it, but she'd found some and used it. The dose I gave her doubled what she already had in her bloodstream."

Face ashen, Sarah pushed away from the table. Jay could see that her mind was reeling.

"Want me to take you home?"

"I don't know." She folded her arms across her middle and bent over, close to her knees. "I want to know how you got from there to here. Why aren't you in jail? How are you a *law student* at Harvard?"

"The grace of God," Jay said, quite serious. "When I found my mom, I was scared. Called the cops right away. They came. Took her body. Arrested me. I spent some time in jail awaiting trial, but I wasn't convicted of anything more serious than possession. I was sentenced to a lockdown rehab facility—best thing that ever happened to me." *Next to you, possibly . . .*

"And they cured you and you went to college. Everything was done and fine?" Sarah asked, her tone angry.

"Nothing was done and fine. My body went through withdrawal. I spent months in counseling and therapy. I had to fight off depression over and over again. I performed hundreds of hours of community service." He paused. "Each and every day I have to live with the knowledge that I'm at least partially responsible for my own mother's death."

Sarah lifted her face to look at him, something changing as he spoke those last words. Along with anger and hurt, he thought—hoped—he glimpsed compassion and understanding. He held his hand out, but she didn't take it.

"She killed herself, Jay—and perhaps almost her son."

"Don't make excuses for me." He spoke with conviction. "I was old enough to make a better choice. I should have left, and I knew it." He studied her face. "The real issue now is what I have to live with—what you'd have to live with if you chose to be with me. Once an addict, always an addict. It's something that will be with me the rest of my life. You have no idea how careful I have to be. I can't even drink a beer—won't chance taking anything that might replicate that feeling of being high and make me start to crave it again."

"How long has it been since you were . . ." She couldn't seem to say the words.

He didn't want to either. "Six years. Never long enough."

"Tell me about those years," Sarah coaxed. "What you did, how you survived."

A smile—the first in nearly an hour—crossed Jay's face. "The center—as I came to affectionately call the rehab facility—was my lifeline. One counselor in particular, a young woman named Jane, reached me in a way no one else had been able to."

"Jane," Sarah repeated. "Brown-haired, brown-eyed Jane?"

He nodded. "I ate up her sessions, drank in every word she said. But it wasn't enough, and she became my new addiction."

"What do you mean?" Alarm had crept into Sarah's voice.

"I stole her wallet so I had her phone number and address. I'd call her just to listen to her say hello. Then I'd hang up. I wrote her letters, followed her around when she was at work. Then one day I cornered her in the hall and kissed her. She wasn't expecting it. *I* wasn't expecting the feelings that exploded between us." He looked out the window again, realizing for the first time that the memory wasn't as painful as it used to be. "Her boss *really* wasn't expecting it. She got fired."

"Good." Sarah sat up straight in her chair. "Therapists are supposed to behave better than their patients."

"She did," Jay said. "And technically she wasn't a therapist yet. She was an intern about to graduate. But that kiss was entirely my fault. She was a good girl—wholesome, like you," he added. "For a long time I felt worse about Jane losing her job than I did about my mother's death."

"So *then* you got your act together?" Sarah asked.

"Not right away," Jay said. "I almost got kicked out of the program— would've gone straight to jail, too. But Jane spoke in my defense, and I was allowed to stay." He watched Sarah's expression change as the significance of this sunk in.

"Your own mother betrayed you, but . . ."

"But this woman whose career I'd just ruined stood up for me so I could get my life back."

"No wonder you loved her."

"No wonder," Jay agreed. "But there's love." He reached across the table to lift Sarah's chin so he could look into her eyes. "And then there's *love*."

She turned aside. "I'd love it if you'd finish."

"Almost there," Jay promised. "When I found out what Jane had done, I did get my act together and completed the program. I didn't want to do anything to let her down. After I was done, I tried to contact her quite a few times, but she got a restraining order and put an end to that. Then, a couple of years later, I saw her again. I thought if I'd changed, was drug free, going to school, that sort of thing, she might be interested. I did everything from polishing my new shoes to getting a haircut in the hope of winning her affection."

Sarah was neither smiling or frowning. "Did you?"

"It was too late. She got married during my first year of law school. But I was glad to see her again, and I was able to help her during a crisis. Afterward she told me something I've never forgotten. She said I was like the hero from her favorite movie, *Casablanca,* that I was brave and chivalrous. It was enough that she saw me that way instead of the junkie I used to be."

Sarah clasped her hands together in front of her. "So Jane turned you around."

"*I* turned me around," Jay said. "But she helped. Last time I saw her was at her graduation. After my first year of law school, I went back to the center and spoke with both the director and the dean of psychology at the University of Washington. *I* defended *her,* told them what a difference she'd made in my life, convinced them to let her back into the program. Now she lives in Seattle with her husband and daughter."

"And you live in Cambridge and are about to graduate with a law degree."

"*About* meaning another six months," Jay said.

Sarah held her hands up. "I don't know what to think or say."

That you haven't left yet says a lot.

"Let it digest awhile," he suggested. "I've shared some ugly stuff. I imagine it will take some time to go down." He picked up the three-dimensional menu standing by the salt and pepper, twirling it around with his fingers, willing to sit here all night and the next. He'd give her whatever time she needed.

"When you told me you had a record, I never imagined . . ." Sarah said.

"I'm sorry I didn't tell you sooner." He stared out the window at the snowflakes falling fast and furious now. He thought of the other package in his coat pocket and wondered if he'd ever get the opportunity to give it to her.

Not tonight, that's for sure.

He returned the menu to the table, looking at the side featuring desserts. "Why don't we order something sweet? Maybe it will help wash down all that bitter." *Lame attempt at levity, Kendrich.* He pointed to the Oreo pie. "How about chocolate? And since you're overloaded now with information about me, is it all right if I ask the questions for a while?"

* * *

"You already know everything about me," Sarah said. *And I wish—oh, how I wish—you hadn't told me everything about you.*

"I know about you and your dad and cousin," Jay said. "But you've never told me anything about your mother. What was your family like before she died?"

"I don't remember much." Sarah watched as a busboy cleared a nearby table. When the dishes were moved, one quick swipe with his filthy rag seemed his best effort. She looked down at their own table, remembering that the silverware had been resting directly on it when they first arrived. She'd put a fork in her mouth that had touched a table that probably wasn't clean. What little of the hamburger she'd eaten earlier churned in her stomach. And a fork was nothing compared to—compared to the nauseating thought of Jay sticking a syringe full of cocaine into his arm.

Sarah watched as he caught the waitress's attention and ordered a dessert for them to share.

"Could we have two new spoons to go with that?" Sarah asked as their server left to fill their order.

"Something wrong with these?" Jay asked, picking up his own spoon.

"Maybe." Sarah glanced at the busboy still making his rounds.

Jay followed her gaze. "Maybe you get this germ thing from your mom?"

"No. I'm nothing like her—nothing at all." Her voice was adamant. *Nothing like her or you or anyone else messed up by drugs.*

"Sorry." Jay held his hands up. "Want to tell me why the sudden animosity? I know you're upset with me, and you have every right to be. But why transfer that to your mom?"

"I'm disappointed," Sarah said, meeting his gaze.

"I didn't want to disappoint you, but I also wanted to tell you the truth," Jay said. Genuine regret reflected in his eyes.

"I know."

"It was a long time ago. And I can't change the past. No matter how much I want to." He started to reach for her hands, then stopped as she grabbed her purse from the windowsill, holding the handle in a white-knuckled grip.

"I don't get the whole thing," she said. "It seems like everyone I know has been messed up with drugs in some way. It destroys people and lives, ruins families and friendships."

Jay rubbed the back of his neck. "I agree. But I *don't* agree that it has to destroy this friendship. Drugs are part of my past—not my present or future. I'm not going to do anything to hurt you, to hurt myself. I wish you could bel—"

"Believe you?" Sarah finished, her voice wavering. "Well, I can't. Everyone I want to trust, I *should be able* to trust, lets me down." She brought a hand to her face, covering her eyes. "It's been that way my whole life—since I was a little girl and my mom killed herself overdosing."

* * *

Jay watched as the ice-cream filling in their Oreo pie slowly melted. He hadn't taken a bite—had lost his appetite after Sarah's startling revelation just before she fled to the restroom. At least he hoped that was where she'd fled. Her coat still hung on the back of her chair. He took it as a hopeful sign that she hadn't snuck out the back entrance, eager to be away from him forever.

He was the one digesting now, internalizing the fact that Sarah's mother had died the same way his mother had. *What are the odds?* he wondered as a chill swept through him. He glanced toward the door, but it was shut tight. The feeling seeping through him had nothing to do with the temperature.

And everything to do with fate.

Sarah had once asked him what his religious beliefs were. He honestly didn't know. But he did believe there was some higher power directing all things. He'd always believed in destiny. Somehow it was fated that he, Jay Kendrich, was to do certain things and meet certain people during his life.

Sarah Morgan was one of them.

In his mind Jay traveled across the country to his storage unit in Seattle, where he had centuries of Kendrich records stored. Those records were filled with stories he sometimes had difficulty comprehending—weird twists of fate that brought people together, coincidences too rare to really be such. He'd found those stories fascinating. He'd believed in them, but never more so than at this very minute when he found himself living one, looking at the woman he knew he was destined to be with, as she walked toward him.

Sarah's eyes were red-rimmed, her face blotchy. Wordlessly, she slid into her seat.

You came back. "New spoons." Jay held up the silverware he'd kept tight in his grasp since the waitress delivered it.

"I'm not hungry."

"Me either." Jay stuck the spoons in the pie and pushed it aside. He reached across the table and took Sarah's hands. "Look at me," he begged.

She raised tear-filled eyes. "Jay, I'm scared. I want to trust you, but . . ."

"You don't have to trust yet. Just listen—please."

She nodded. "Five minutes. I called Christa."

He sucked in his breath and started. "When I first heard you play the piano, I wanted to meet you. I knew—just from listening to you play—that we'd have a lot in common, that you felt as passionately about music as I do."

"I like classical. You like rock," Sarah countered.

"We were both raised by single fathers."

"But I'm from the East Coast," she said. "You were born and raised in the West."

Jay ignored her argument. "What really makes us who we are, the things that really matter, are the same."

"I don't see how."

"I do." Jay looked into her eyes. "Doesn't it strike you as odd that *both* our mothers died of an overdose?"

"It strikes me as sad." She pressed her lips together, and he could tell she was trying not to cry. "But I've *never* used drugs. And I *never* will."

"Neither will I, again," Jay promised.

"My mother died alone," Sarah said. "What she did, she did to herself. I know it's the same with your mother, but knowing you were there—that you were the one who gave it to her, and then you took it yourself . . ."

She isn't going to be able to get past this. "I regret that every day of my life," he whispered. *I shouldn't have told her. I had to.* "I live with it every day. That in itself is enough that I'd never do it again." *Believe me—please.* "I'll never hurt you, Sarah."

She broke their gaze, looking away. "You already have."

Her words cut to his heart, and he felt her loss already as if she were gone. *But she's not gone yet.*

"Dance with me," he said, nodding toward the floor where several couples swayed to the music. "Just once. Then you can go with Christa, and I won't bother you again." *You'll never have to see me again.* What seemed like a lifetime ago, he'd said that to Jane. It was a painful reminder of what he stood to lose.

"I don't dance."

Of course not. Jay got up and walked around to her side of the table. "Then let me share one more first with you." He held out his hand.

Lips pressed together again, her gaze went past him to the dance floor. Seconds ticked by. He felt her slipping further away, and there was nothing he could do to pull her back. He was about to sit down again when she placed her hand in his.

His heart, nearly crushed with the weight of his sorrow and regret, beat a little stronger.

Jay led her to the floor, turned to face her, put his arms around her waist, and pulled her close. He couldn't have been more surprised when she wrapped her arms around his neck and laid her head against his shoulder. Feet alternating side by side, they began to sway as the music faded away. He kept his embrace. He could have sworn hers tightened.

The song ended. A new one started. Familiar guitar strums drifted from overhead speakers as Tom Petty's "Free Falling" began. Jay closed his eyes, cherishing every second of this, his lips close to her skin, her head near his heart.

The lyrics were poignantly appropriate. Sarah probably had loved her mother, had probably yearned for her over the years. *How must she feel,* Jay tried to imagine, *knowing the part I played in my mother's death?*

As the song said, he was the bad boy, breaking her heart. He'd never felt worse, never regretted his actions so much. It was going to cost him not only his mother's life, but Sarah's love as well.

Free falling . . .

He was beyond falling, knew he had already fallen hard for this woman in his arms. He adored everything about her—from the way the hair fell across her face to her passion about music to her convictions about life. Her heart, so bruised and tender from past abuses. Their strangely parallel pasts. Even her obsession with germs. He wanted it all, every part of her.

And she couldn't trust him.

Part Two

Holding Tight

Chapter Thirty-Six

Sarah's back was rigid, her hands clasped tight around the single flower in her lap as she sat in her seat on the T. Remembering her last trip to Boston—when she'd come to the city with Jay—was a painful reminder of the happiness she'd felt that day and in the days that followed, and the friendship she'd lost. But she thought of it, of *him,* anyway. Almost constantly it seemed. And she wondered how she'd ever survived almost twenty-four years without him—how she was going to survive now. Her heart physically hurt, as if a piece had been ripped out and she was no longer whole.

But today's quest was an attempt to repair at least a part of her. It had been Jay's suggestion—there he was in her thoughts again—that she find and visit her mother's grave. He'd been right, of course, and a little research had given her a location. Sarah wasn't sure what she was going to accomplish with this visit but knew she had to make peace with her past before she could hope to find happiness in her future. She would never understand what her mother had done, but she needed to be able to forgive her.

Arriving at her stop, Sarah left the train and walked up cobbled streets through the unfamiliar neighborhood. Older apartment complexes towered above the sidewalk, and Sarah wondered if she had ever lived in any of them. She had no recollection of the apartment she'd shared with her mother beyond the bedroom that had been hers—filled with pale yellow sunshine in the mornings and the lights of the city at night.

After several blocks she reached the cemetery and entered its tall, iron gates. She followed the drive as it curved around toward the first row of headstones. Fishing a paper from her pocket, she studied the cemetery layout and read the plot number of her mother's grave. The paper shook in her hands as she turned down the third row and began walking past dozens of headstones. She scanned the names on every one, and, midway across, she found her mother's.

The narrow stone pressed flat into the earth was barely visible. Sarah dropped to the ground—the paper and flowers forgotten as she reached to push the frozen blades of grass aside.

Rachel Sarah Phillips Morgan
June 11, 1958–December 6, 1986
Beloved Daughter, Wife, and Mother

Sarah's breath caught as she read the words a second time. *Sarah? I have her middle name?* She reached for the cemetery map and looked at it closely. The record was for Rachel Phillips Morgan. *Sarah* wasn't included. *Why? Why didn't Dad ever tell me?*

She pushed back the grass again and started ripping it away. She worked at it for several minutes until her fingers were raw with cold but the stone was clear.

Beloved. Daughter and mother, yes. But beloved *wife?* Sarah knew her parents had been separated at the time of her mother's death. She'd always assumed it was her mother's drug problem that drove them apart, yet that didn't entirely make sense. If one parent was a police officer and the other a drug addict, why would the addict be given custody of their child? Sarah searched her memory for any detail about life with her mother but could find none other than an intangible sense that she'd been happy.

And her mother . . . Had *she* been happy? *Or did she feel as alone as I do?*

Beloved daughter . . . Her father had said all of her grandparents were dead. But what if that wasn't true?

Sudden doubt filled her mind, and with a sense of urgency, Sarah rose from her knees and hurried to the grave beside her mother's, searching for another stone with the Phillips name.

Instead, she found another Morgan. The stone was even smaller than her mother's.

Emily Anne Morgan
May 17–May 20, 1984
Precious and Dearly Loved
Daughter of Grant and Rachel Morgan

I had a little sister? Sarah's hands went to her chest, where her heart beat erratically. She knelt again, fingers tracing the name as tears stung and blurred her eyes. *What happened? Why didn't you ever tell me?* She calculated the months between her own birthday and the dates on the stone and realized she would have been just two and a half when Emily was born—and died. *Just four days . . .* Sarah imagined a tiny infant laid out in a miniature casket and felt a new hurt, a longing for something lost she hadn't even known she had.

She reached across the grave for her discarded purse. After pulling a pen out, she copied the name and dates from her sister's stone onto the back of her mother's burial record. Questions and possibilities filled her mind. She wished she could talk to her father and ask him what had happened, but she knew that even if she did, he probably wouldn't tell her. Never once had he mentioned a sister, and only rarely did he say anything about her mother— other than to bring up her terrible and tragic mistake.

Sarah wished Jay were here with her. He'd know what to do next, where to search for answers. He'd listen and share her joy and sorrow at having discovered she'd had a sibling. He would understand why she both loved and hated her mother. She realized Jay was right—they *were* alike in the ways that really mattered, their lives and losses similar.

But the revelation that her mother had suffered the devastating loss of a child was already changing the feelings of anger Sarah had felt for so long.

Oblivious to the cold, she sat between the two stones, trying to imagine the people they represented. She didn't know what it was like to have a child die, but she knew what it was like to grow up motherless. There were times her own pain and loneliness had been so great that she *might* have chosen to turn to something for escape—had her father not been there to keep her away from such paths.

It was suddenly difficult to be angry with either of her parents. Their child had died, and so had the love they felt for each other. It must have been a terrible time. *But they still had me.* The thought—that she hadn't been enough—cut deeply. One person to love and be loved by was more than she'd ever had, and somehow she'd survived all these years.

Sarah hugged her knees to her chest. "Why did you kill yourself, Mom? How could you abandon me?" She squeezed her eyes shut as tears tracked down the sides of her face. How different her life would have been with a mother and a sister. Maybe even her father would have been different—been the kind and good man she'd seen glimpses of throughout the years. But she was never going to know, and imagining *what if* would only make her crazy.

Sarah leaned her head back, looking up at the late afternoon sky. A few rays of the setting sun shone through a break in the thick clouds, bathing the city in orange light. If she left now, she might make it back to the station before dark. But instead of getting up, she sat unmoving, willing the warmth of those feeble rays to reach her and dry the tears on her cheeks. As if in answer to her unspoken prayer, a whisper of a breeze—unnaturally warm—whisked by, touching not only her skin but filling her soul and heart with peace.

You don't know the whole story, the wind seemed to say. *Then who am I to judge?* she thought, and felt some strange measure of relief. She *didn't* have to judge her mother, didn't have to be angry anymore. It wasn't up to her to decide what was right and wrong when a person's world fell apart.

And what about Jay? Some of her newly discovered peace ebbed away. That question she couldn't answer yet. It was a hurt too new, a wound too fresh.

She looked at Emily's stone again, reading the words *precious and dearly loved.* Sarah wanted to believe that she had been dearly loved as well. But if that love hadn't been enough to keep her mother from leaving her—from giving in to the demons of addiction—then how could she ever trust that Jay would be strong enough to win his battle?

When he'd held her in his arms it felt *so* good. She felt love, even if neither of them had dared express the word out loud yet. But how could she ever believe that would be enough to enable him to keep his promise? And if he didn't, could she live through losing him?

Sarah picked up the rose and pulled a few of the vibrant petals from it. These she sprinkled across her sister's grave.

"Emily," she whispered as a smile formed on her lips. She *had* a sister. Once upon a time, she hadn't been all alone.

Turning, she placed the rose across her mother's newly cleaned stone. A lump formed in Sarah's throat as she pulled her hand away, wondering if that was the first flower ever laid there. Once this woman had held her close and loved her—Sarah was sure of it. And she felt only regret that she hadn't thanked her mother before.

"I'm sorry," Sarah whispered. "I'm so sorry I was angry with you for so long." She sat there another minute then stood, brushing dirt from her jeans, and looked up at the sky again.

Her life was still cloudy; in fact, not much had changed at all. But somehow, like the rays of light illuminating the city, her world seemed a little brighter. On her own, she would find a better future. It was time for the past to stop holding her back.

Chapter Thirty-Seven

"How was Relief Society?" Kirk asked as Christa and Sarah came through the front door.

"Fun," Christa said. Her smile faded as she took in the messy living room, blaring television, and her husband sprawled across the couch. "Though something tells me I'm going to pay for those two hours away."

"Make any new recipes tonight?" Kirk asked.

Christa shook her head. "Gingerbread houses. Show him our masterpiece, Sarah."

Sarah turned from the coat rack where she'd been awkwardly trying to remove and hang up her scarf with one hand while balancing the "masterpiece" in the other. "This is my first gingerbread house, so it isn't perfect." Holding it out for inspection, she walked to the couch.

Kirk sat up for a closer look. "Are those wafer cookies on the roof? Yum—my favorite. And Rolos lining the walk? Looks perfectly good to me."

"Uh-uh." Christa shook a finger at him. "It's a centerpiece, not your midnight snack. Quick, Sarah, put it on the table."

"It's gonna *be in pieces* when the boys see it," Kirk grumbled. "Ought to at least let your husband have first pick."

"Sorry." Sarah smiled apologetically and started toward the kitchen, pausing to step around a Lego creation. An image on the television caught her attention as she walked past.

She gasped at the picture on the screen in front of her. "Jay!" The gingerbread house slipped from her fingers, falling to the floor, shattering both the confection and the Lego building beneath it. Neither Sarah, Christa, or Kirk paid any attention to the mess. Their eyes were riveted to the TV and the mug shot of Jay in the top right corner.

"After a month of baffling thefts on the Harvard campus, police now have a suspect in custody," the news anchor said. "They believe third-year law student Jay Kendrich is responsible for stealing more than three thousand dollars worth of hypodermic needles and other equipment used for administering and cooking various forms of cocaine and methamphetamine. Large quantities of both drugs were found in Kendrich's apartment earlier today, along with several of the items stolen from the Armensie Building on campus."

The camera panned to Jay's picture, and it filled the screen.

"An anonymous phone call led police to Kendrich, who they say has a history of drug abuse."

Sarah stared at Jay's face—looking solemn—until it was replaced by the news anchors sitting at the desk. Feeling both nauseated and faint, she staggered back, collapsing on the couch.

"Are you all right?" Kirk and Christa asked at the same time. Christa sat beside Sarah, placing an arm around her.

Sarah clutched her stomach. It felt like she'd just been punched, like the day she'd had the wind knocked out of her when she fell backward trying to save Jay from Carl and his truck. *Oh, Jay.* She closed her eyes, feeling her heart break into a hundred pieces. *You promised.*

"I don't believe it," Kirk said. "He's got everything going for him. He's about to graduate—why would he do something so stupid?"

"I don't know," Christa said.

"I don't believe it," Kirk repeated.

Still trying to catch her breath, Sarah leaned forward, squeezing her eyes shut against the memories assaulting her. Jay at lunch, joking with his friends, talking casually about the thefts on campus. *He would have been lying.* Jay's head bent close to hers over the globe at the Science Center, telling her that the past month had been the best of his life. *Was it because you were doing drugs?* Jay's clear blue eyes, filled with concern as he stared down at her after they were nearly hit by Carl's truck. *He wasn't high that day. I'm sure of it.* Jay standing with her in the Trinity Church, his face reverent and peaceful—the kind of peace she longed for. *Was it an act?*

Sarah opened her eyes and wished she could scream. This couldn't be happening.

Kirk and Christa both stared at her, their expressions worried.

"I'm okay," she said. "Guess it's a good thing I broke up with him, right?" She attempted a weak smile but knew it wasn't very convincing.

"You go on to bed," Christa said. "We'll take care of the mess."

Sarah looked at the ruined gingerbread house. "I'm sorry."

"Don't be," Christa said. "Kirk's right. The boys would have eaten it anyway. The important thing is that we had fun making it."

Sarah rose slowly from the couch. Christa held her hand out to steady her.

"I'm going to look into this," Kirk said. "I'll find out what I can."

She thanked him and went down the hall to her room. Once there she closed the door, then fell back on her bed without bothering to take off her shoes or undress. She stared at the ceiling, wishing for the numbness that often followed pain. Whenever her father yelled at her, when angry words were exchanged, it hurt deeply. But after a while the pain was somehow absorbed, and she became stronger from it, numb to his criticism and cutting remarks. Her ability to feel anything would disappear for weeks or even months at a time. She prayed for that now but somehow knew this was different, that the hurt encompassing her wasn't going to disappear so easily.

She rolled to her side, curling up around her pillow, part of her wishing she'd never met Jay, the other part wishing he were here with her right now. He had awoken all of her feelings, and she was afraid they weren't going away anytime soon.

Chapter Thirty-Eight

"I've got your steak and potatoes," Carl said, depositing a couple of bags of groceries on the kitchen table. "How long, you think, until the cook shows up?"

"I don't know," Grant said. He sat in his chair near the door, the cordless phone in his hand, doubts about the success of their plan filling his mind. Sarah's belongings had been destroyed, her housing burned down, her boyfriend arrested on drug charges. She had no financial support that he knew of, but what if all that wasn't enough to send her fleeing home?

A wistful look crossed his face as he remembered a little girl with a torn dress and bloodied knees climbing into his car long ago, demanding he take her home. Even at a young age, even after facing her mother's death, Sarah had been so resilient. Grant had a feeling that two months of freedom had only strengthened her determination. *If there were any way . . .* He liked to think she could make it on her own, that she could take care of herself and anyone who got in her way, but the past had taught him otherwise. He'd once believed those things of his wife.

"We'd better hope she comes soon," Grant said. "Rossi says he knows where she lives."

"Want me to go pick her up?" Carl asked. "I can be the shoulder she cries on." He sniffed loudly, pushed out his lower lip, and laughed.

Grant didn't laugh with him. "You're to be *nothing* except her protection. You're to *do* nothing to her—got it?" Grant's head pounded, and the thought of Sarah at his nephew's mercy made him ill. *If there were any other way to keep her safe . . .*

"I know, I know," Carl said, dismissing Grant's concerns with a wave of his hand. "So where's she been staying? I bet I got close. I followed that guy who walks with her a few times."

"I'm not sure where she is," Grant said, massaging his temples. A full-blown migraine was coming on. He felt his ulcer acting up too. "Rossi wouldn't exactly tell me. But he said if we don't have her by tomorrow night, he'll take care of it."

"He's bluffing," Carl said. "He'd take her right now if he knew where she was."

Grant slowly shook his head. "Not if she's living with a cop."

* * *

After her classes were over for the day, Sarah thanked and dismissed Austen—the college student from Kirk and Christa's church who usually walked her home—turning, instead, toward the Science Center. She needed some time by herself to think. She knew Kirk would be waiting for her with news about Jay's charges and arrest, but she wasn't ready to hear any more right now. Whether Kirk believed Jay innocent or guilty couldn't help her sort out her own feelings—feelings she'd wrestled with all night.

She entered the Putnam Gallery, hoping to forget about everything for a while. Looking at the telescope display, she marveled at man's earliest attempts to understand the universe. She read about Galileo, persecuted by the Catholic church because of his belief that the Earth and other planets rotated around the sun. Like so many others who came before and after him, Galileo suffered for his convictions. Yet all these years later, those convictions had been proven true.

Sarah thought of the great courage it must have taken to stand by his beliefs when everyone thought him a fool or the devil or both. But through the telescope Galileo had glimpsed much more of the universe than seen by man's eye. He'd discovered truth, and that had become understanding and knowledge—undeniable no matter what the circumstances.

She pondered this as she walked through the rest of the exhibit and found herself at the globe where she and Jay had talked in hushed whispers. Over the past couple of months, he had shown her truths about herself she never would have known. And in return, he'd laid bare his own soul, sharing all that was good and bad in his past. He had trusted her completely, and she'd thrown that trust back in his face.

Feeling the same crushing weight as when she'd seen his mug shot on television, Sarah grasped the arm of a nearby chair and sank into it for support. *She,* more than anyone else, had seen glimpses into Jay's soul, and there were truths there she couldn't deny. Like the Founding Fathers he admired so much, he wasn't perfect, but he *was* a good man—an honest one. When he'd told her he would never use drugs again, he hadn't been lying. She was sure of it. So what was she supposed to think—to do—now?

Buttoning her coat, she left the museum and walked toward Kirk's house. Darkness had fallen, and scattered snowflakes drifted from the sky. Sarah knew she should hurry, but her conflicted thoughts slowed her steps and she found herself wandering the longer, out-of-the-way campus paths she didn't normally take. The night was quiet and clouded, the only glow coming from street lamps and distant Christmas lights twinkling in the falling snow. Bare tree limbs bowed under a fresh coat of white. Words of a Christmas carol . . . *peace on earth, good will to men . . .* trailed through her mind. The world did seem peaceful tonight, and she felt grateful to be out in it, free to wander alone as she pleased.

An image of Jay, sitting alone in a jail cell, flashed into her mind, shattering the brief serenity of a moment before. It hurt to think of him like that. Hopefully someone had posted bail by now. *But who?* She felt suddenly ill. Maybe no one had. And even if Jay *were* out, she wasn't certain his landlord would let him return to his apartment. Where would he go? Would there be someone to help him the way he'd helped her?

Sarah stopped at the 1870 gate leading to the Old Yard and glanced down at the sundial at its base, reading the words inscribed there.

On this moment hangs eternity.

The simple thought went straight to her heart. Whatever she did tonight, right now, was going to determine everything about her future. The time for wavering had passed. The time for standing up for her convictions—what she knew in her heart to be true—had come.

Her decision should have been simple. As a police officer, her father was the icon of everything good and true. While Jay, with his record of drug abuse and his current legal troubles, represented everything she'd spent her life avoiding. But appearances were often deceiving, and people weren't always as they seemed on the surface. If she based her judgment on the obvious, she'd be lying to herself.

"I know he's innocent," Sarah said, needing to hear the words aloud. "I believe him—I believe *in* him." Having acknowledged what she felt, she suddenly wanted to shout Jay's innocence to the world. But the feeling of euphoria was short-lived, followed quickly by shame and distress that she'd judged him so harshly, that she *hadn't* trusted him. That she'd doubted his word when he'd given her no reason to, when he'd been nothing but good and kind.

Jay *was* innocent. No matter what the evidence, she knew he hadn't stolen or used drugs. She couldn't explain why, but she knew he'd kept his promise.

With hurried, purposeful steps she left campus, heading for Jay's apartment. The feelings of comfort she'd had at her mother's grave returned, enveloping her, giving her the courage she needed to act on her newly discovered convictions.

Chapter Thirty-Nine

Kirk paced back and forth in front of the television, his eyes straying to the front door with every turn. In the other room he heard Christa hurrying through the bedtime routine with Jeffrey and James, and he knew she was as worried about Sarah as he was.

It was after eight, and she still wasn't home. That was cause enough for concern; however, Sarah's absence was made infinitely more alarming by the news that Austen, the young man who usually escorted her, had been found beaten to within an inch of his life and left to bleed to death in the snow.

Kirk thought about calling the hospital again to see if Austen was out of surgery and conscious enough to talk yet but decided against it. The Cambridge police knew how concerned he was, and they'd call as soon as there was any news.

Christa joined him in the living room, her eyes following his to the front door. "Are you going to call her father?"

"I don't know," Kirk said. "If it's her cousin who's done this—and taken her—then it's probably at her father's request. And if that *is* what happened and I play my hand now, then I lose the chance to help her later."

Christa wrapped her arms around him. "What about Jay? Have you decided—"

"No." Kirk sighed with frustration. "He had his hearing today, and I could have gone in and posted bail this afternoon, but I'm not sure that's the right thing to do either. Again, if the chief hears about it, he'll put two and two together and figure out we've been helping Sarah."

"Have you prayed about it?" Christa asked gently.

Kirk nodded. "I keep getting the feeling I shouldn't do anything, that I should wait, though the police officer in me—who knows missing person stats—doesn't want to do that."

The sound of a car door slamming sent both of them to the front window. A young woman stood on the sidewalk, directing the driver of an Oldsmobile into a tight space along the curb.

"Does that car belong to anyone in our young adult group?" Christa asked.

"I don't think so." Kirk walked to the front door and opened it, stepping onto the porch. He and Christa watched as the Olds backed in with jerky, halting movements. After several attempts the car was finally in place, and the driver stepped out.

"It's Sarah!" Christa exclaimed, watching as Sarah hugged the woman who'd been guiding her in. Together they started toward the house.

Kirk rushed down the walk. "Where have you been?"

Sarah stopped short, a fearful look in her eyes.

"Kirk," Christa admonished, coming up beside him, placing a hand on his sleeve.

He expelled a long breath. "Sorry, Sarah. Come inside, please—quickly."

Sarah and her friend exchanged confused looks but walked ahead of Kirk and Christa into the house. Once inside, Sarah began her explanation.

"I'm sorry if I worried you. I had some things to take care of." She smiled. "I'm going to post bail for Jay tomorrow, but the bondsman said I have to have a valid driver's license, so Trish has been helping me brush up on my . . ." Her smile faded. "What?" she asked. "What's wrong? Has something else happened to Jay?"

"No," Christa hurried to assure her. "It's Austen."

"I asked him to tell you—" Sarah began.

"He's in the hospital," Kirk said. "Hurt too badly to tell us much of anything right now."

Chapter Forty

Sarah sat in the back of Kirk's cruiser, parked across the street from the jail. She watched out the window as Trish and Archer went inside the building. *It ought to be me,* she thought, frustrated that once again she was confined because of Carl.

Last night Austen had regained consciousness after his surgery. Sarah had been there when he'd talked to the Cambridge police and given a sketch artist an almost exact description of Carl. She'd been only too happy to tell police where her cousin lived, and Kirk had informed her this morning that Carl was now behind bars in this very jail.

She hoped his bail was a million dollars and that her dad couldn't post it. In spite of Kirk's worries—and his insistence she wait in the car with him—she seriously doubted Carl would be out of jail anytime soon, and certainly not tonight. Heaven knew she'd learned that getting a bail bond was a difficult enough process. In the last twenty-four hours she'd emptied what little she had from the bank account Mrs. Larson had insisted she set up, passed a driver's test and obtained her license, convinced Trish to put her car up as collateral, and all but signed her life away as the indemnitor for the bail bond to get Jay out.

If she was lucky, her father would be too worried about his reputation as chief of police to go through the same hoops and expense to free Carl. And with Carl behind bars, she might have a chance at a normal life.

"There they are," Sarah said, face pressed to the window as she watched Archer, Trish, and Jay coming down the steps.

"I still don't like this," Kirk said. "I don't see why you can't wait until—"

"I *can't,*" Sarah insisted. "Please, Kirk. I waited all day for you to be off work. And Carl's not going to get out tonight. I'm perfectly safe. I have to see Jay."

"All right." He raised his hands in defeat and got out of the cruiser to open the back door.

"Thanks." She grinned at him, then made her way across the slushy street to the parking lot. Arms wrapped around her middle to ward of both the freezing temperature and nerves, she waited several cars away from Archer's bug. If Jay left with Trish and Archer, she would know he didn't want to talk to her.

And I'll die a slow death right here. She lifted her face to the sky and caught her breath at the glittering array of stars overhead. *Galileo couldn't deny the truth. Neither can I.* The North Star stood out from the others, sparkling brightly in the clear, cold night. Sarah took it as a sign that she'd made a good decision, that trusting Jay was the right thing.

Archer said something to Jay as they neared the Volkswagen. He looked over at her.

Please. Please forgive me. Her heart sank as Jay turned away and leaned into the bug. A few seconds later he stood up, backpack in hand, and started walking toward her.

"Thank you," Sarah whispered, feeling her heart begin to beat again. She hurried forward, meeting him halfway. They stopped a few feet apart, staring at one another.

"Thanks for bailing me out," Jay said.

He looked tired and defeated, and she wished she'd acted sooner. "I'm sorry it took so long."

Jay shrugged. "I'm surprised you came at all." He put his hands in his pockets and looked away. "What do you want from me, Sarah?"

She took a step closer to him. "I want you to tell me you didn't do it, that you're keeping your promise."

His eyes sought hers again. "I didn't do it. And I always keep my promises."

She crossed the space between them as a huge grin broke out across her face.

"I know."

* * *

Jay looked down at his fingers, intertwined with Sarah's, as they sat side by side on the sofa in Kirk's living room. "I don't have much of a choice," he said, trying to convince both Sarah and Kirk that, though he'd been out of jail less than an hour, he had to work tonight. "I'm going to need all the money I can get. Attorneys aren't cheap, you know." He gave Kirk a wry smile.

"Want me to give you a list of the ones I'm *sure* could get you off?" Kirk opened a drawer in the table beside his chair and took out a pen and paper.

Jay shook his head. "I'd rather represent myself than have someone like Nicholsine defend me."

"Why *don't* you represent yourself?" Sarah asked. "You've almost got your law degree."

"Bad idea," Jay and Kirk said at the same time.

"I don't want to come off as cocky," Jay said. "And a *real* attorney is going to have a lot more access to the documents and information that I'll need to prove I'm innocent."

"It's going to take a lot of investigating," Kirk added. "*Someone* put that stuff in Jay's room. We have to figure out who." He looked at Jay. "Any thoughts?"

"I might have said Archer, but since he came to get me out . . ."

"Your roommate?" Kirk asked.

"Yeah. He's been acting kind of strange, and he's been upset with me." Jay looked sideways at Sarah. "He thinks there's something going on between Trish and me."

"Hasn't he noticed *us*?" Sarah asked, implying they were a couple again—which Jay wasn't really sure was true. They'd come straight to Kirk's house, so they hadn't had a chance to talk privately yet. But he couldn't have been more surprised to see Sarah's name on the papers posting bail, or to find her waiting outside in the parking lot. And when she'd told him she knew he was innocent and reached up to give him a tentative hug, he'd nearly fallen backward. After all, the last time he'd seen her—just before she walked off the dance floor and left him standing there—she'd said she couldn't trust him. Jay wasn't sure what had happened in the last few weeks to change that, or if it was a change that was permanent. *But,* he admitted to himself, *it did feel good to hold her again. Really good.*

"*Us* hasn't been happening for a few weeks," he reminded her. Sarah squirmed uncomfortably under his gaze, looking chagrined. Jay continued. "Trish felt bad for me, so whenever she was over we'd talk, and Archer assumed more was going on."

"Were his assumptions correct?"

"No." Jay heard the uncertainty in Sarah's voice and recognized the same flash of insecurity he'd seen in her eyes when he'd talked about Jane. He needed to remember Sarah was new at the dating game—that it wasn't a game to her at all. She said what she meant and acted and *re*acted according to her feelings. Right now he could tell her feelings were hurt and anxious.

"At the restaurant you said it might take some time for me to come to terms with everything you told me." She had a pleading look in her eyes. "It did."

"I was waiting—and hoping." He brushed a strand of hair from her face, his hand lingering against her cheek a second longer than necessary.

"Ah-hem." Kirk cleared his throat, reminding them he was still in the room.

"As I was saying," Jay began. "I've got to get to work."

Sarah bit her lip. "You don't think you've lost your job?"

"Not this one. My employer will probably advertise it. 'Guitarist arrested. Come see the show.' Unfortunately, it's that kind of place. But my status as a law clerk intern is definitely in question." *What goes around comes around.* He thought of Jane and how she must have felt when she'd lost her internship and couldn't graduate, through no fault of her own. He only hoped he'd be as lucky, and that when this was all over someone would speak up for him, so he could finish school.

"Before you leave, is there anyone else you can think of that would do this to you?" Kirk asked, the pen in his hand, tapping on his leg.

"The obvious," Jay said. He cast a concerned glance Sarah's way.

"Carl?" she asked, as if she were already thinking the same thing.

"That'd be my guess." Kirk leaned back in his chair, resting one foot on the opposite knee. "He's been buying drugs. We know that much."

"And if my father wanted to get rid of Jay—or at least get even with him for helping me . . ." Sarah's voice trailed off. She sounded sad when she spoke again. "I can't believe he's that evil."

Jay let go of her hand and put his arm around her.

"We have to at least look at that possibility," Kirk said. "Difficult though that may be. *Something* is going on with your cousin, and I'd wager your dad knows what it is."

Chapter Forty-One

Carl shuffled down the hall, the baggy legs of his jumpsuit brushing against each other as he moved, the cuffs on his hands in front of him grating. One-size-fits-all wasn't working too well—they ought to have made bigger sizes for guys like him with thick wrists and arms bulky from working out.

He grunted, and a half smile curved his lips as he thought of the guy he'd taken down. It had been a relief—after so many months of controlling his temper—to finally pulverize someone's face. He would've done it even if the guy *had* told him where Sarah was. But when he wouldn't say a word, it had been that much more satisfying to use him as a punching bag. Too bad he'd lived. *Next time,* Carl thought, *I'll make sure there's nothing left of his mouth to blab—nothing left of him at all.*

Moving ahead of the guard, he turned the corner and went through the metal door into the visiting room. *About time,* Carl thought. The chief had never taken so long to get him out before. But after rotting in this jail four lousy days, Carl felt ready to kill someone. It might be the chief himself if he wasn't careful. *Then I could get my hands on Sarah*—all over *Sarah.* The princess had caused him enough grief. She owed him, and—cousin or not—it was about time she paid up.

He walked through another set of doors and was led past the bank of chairs, separated from the visitors on the other side by a glass partition. Carl looked up, scanning the faces on the other side of the windows. The chief's wasn't among them. Confused, he started to turn back toward the guard, who pointed him to yet another door at the end of the room. It buzzed open and Carl walked forward, entering a six-foot cubicle. A single table and two chairs were the only furnishings in the small space. A man he didn't know sat in the chair closest to the door. A folder lay on the table.

Carl looked at the guard. "Who's this?"

"Your attorney. Ten minutes." He pulled the door shut behind him as he left.

Feeling uneasy, Carl sat in the opposite chair. This wasn't a good sign. The chief had never sent a lawyer to the jail before. He'd always bailed him out and then taken care of the legalities.

"Hello, Carl." The attorney's gaze was piercing. "We've been watching your work, and we're most impressed." He spoke slowly, emphasizing each syllable.

"I don't know what you're talking about." Was this some kind of trick? Carl felt sweat breaking out on his forehead. Stupid jumpsuits were hotter than—

"I'm sure you do." The lawyer's mouth twisted in a sinister grin that matched the look in his eyes. He opened the folder and pushed it toward Carl.

Carl looked down at an 8 x 10 photo of him and Sarah at the park—the night he'd been drunk and Grant chewed him out.

"I think you'll find we'll mutually benefit from working together."

"You got a name?" Carl asked, shoving the folder back across the table.

"Rossi," the man said. "But you already knew that."

Chapter Forty-Two

"You're in a good mood tonight," Diedre said, casting an appreciative glance toward Jay, whistling as he walked by the bar.

"Yes, I am," he said. "Don't we have some RESERVED signs around here somewhere?" He ran his hand beneath the bar where the signs used to be.

"Depends," Diedre said. She took one from a basket just out of his reach. Dangling it from her fingers, she held it near his face. "What do you want it for?"

"Front table with three chairs," Jay said. He took it from her and walked to the table, pulling it closer to the stage, a little apart from the others.

Diedre untied the apron from around her waist, tossed it on the counter, and followed him. Frowning, she put her hands on her hips. "It's not for—what's her name? I thought you two weren't an item anymore."

"Things are better," Jay said.

Diedre rolled her eyes. "For how long?" She leaned in close, placing a hand on the front of his jacket. "I don't know what's wrong with these college women you meet, but don't you think it's time you were with someone who would really appreciate you—*all* of you?"

Jay set his guitar case upright on the floor between them. "My feelings haven't changed. I'm dating someone else."

"We don't have to call it a date." She placed her hand over his on the guitar case. "I'm only offering to help with your aching heart."

"Thanks for the offer, but I don't have an aching heart." He pulled his hand free. "Things were a bit rough between Sarah and me, but they're better now." He grabbed a chair and pushed it up to the table. "You'll see when she comes here tonight."

* * *

Diedre watched the door from the corner of her eye as she mixed another drink. It was ten minutes to eight, and Jay's girlfriend still hadn't arrived.

"Hurry up, chick," Diedre muttered under her breath. Jay would be onstage soon, and then she'd have no chance to get Sarah out of here. And after the amount of cash that guy had offered, Diedre wanted to make sure it happened.

"Here you go." She slapped the drink down in front of a newcomer at the bar. With wavy dark hair and a muscled body, he wasn't too hard on the eyes—normally she would've been pleased with such company to look forward to for the evening. But flirting was the furthest thing from her mind as the door opened and a petite blond entered the room.

Diedre watched as she stopped, standing just inside the doorway, face unsure as her eyes took in the surroundings.

Kind of a dump your boyfriend works at, isn't it? Diedre imagined the girl's thoughts. She pulled her purse from beneath the cash register and looked at the picture one more time. A thrill of adrenalin shot through her. *It's her all right. That five hundred bucks is practically in my pocket.*

Ignoring another customer's request for a refill, Diedre left the bar and walked over to the woman.

"Sarah?" she asked, pasting a false smile on her face. *What does he see in you? You're as plain as they come.*

The woman nodded.

"Jay's expecting you. He asked me to bring you backstage. Come on." Diedre started walking toward the rear exit.

"Thanks." Sarah followed, wending her way through the crowded room to a narrow hall on the side of the stage.

"Right through that door," Diedre said. "He's sure excited you're here tonight." *Not as excited as I am.* "I've got to get back to the bar. See ya."

She pretended to leave as Sarah put her hand on the doorknob.

Diedre noiselessly flipped the light switch off, then turned back, nudging Sarah's shoulder as she stood there in the pitch black.

"Oh, these lights," Diedre said. "Let me help you." She reached around Sarah to push the door open. A blast of frigid night air swept into the narrow space.

"I can't see—" Sarah began.

Diedre pushed her hard, sending her out the door into the dark alley. "That's the whole point."

Chapter Forty-Three

Sarah's scream became lost in the swirling snow as she fell from the doorway to the concrete stoop outside. The metal door slammed shut. For several seconds she knelt there, stunned and hurting. A flashlight clicked on somewhere in front of her and shone directly at her face. She held up a hand, shielding her eyes.

A low chuckle came from the light's owner. "Good to see you, Sarah."

"Who's there?" Reaching for the wall to steady herself, she scrambled to her feet. Her knees throbbed and threatened to buckle.

"This was almost too easy. We should have enlisted your cousin to help us a long time ago."

Carl? Sarah's heart beat frantically as she squinted, trying to see the flashlight's owner. Carl couldn't have helped this man; he was still in jail. Kirk had called an hour ago to verify. He and Jay would never have let her come tonight if it were otherwise.

Her fingers groped along the building, searching for the door. She found it and grasped the knob.

"Don't bother. I'm sure it's locked." Heavy footsteps crunched over the gravel, coming closer. "She's not going to let you back in."

"Leave me alone." Sarah jiggled the doorknob, confirming the man's prediction.

"I don't think so," he said. "You've caused enough worry lately—running away from your father, refusing to do your job."

"My job?" *What does that have to do with anything?* Turning away from the flashlight, her eyes darted up and down the alley, searching for her best chance of escape. Her *only* chance was to get past him—next to impossible in the narrow space between buildings. *The longer you wait to make your move, the worse your chances.* Her father's voice rang in her head. She jumped suddenly from the step, screaming at the top of her lungs as she launched herself at her attacker.

She caught him off guard, and he staggered backward but didn't go down. The flashlight fell from his hand, skittering across the alley. Sarah stumbled, then took off running in the direction of the street, but he grabbed her coat, jerking her back.

She screamed again and whirled to face him, clawing his eyes with her nails. He swore at her and twisted an arm behind her back. Sarah yelped with pain and felt tears sting her eyes as he grabbed a fistful of her hair and pulled.

"Shut up and move."

She obeyed, shuffling forward on legs that felt like Jell-O. He pushed her toward the street.

"If you open your mouth again or try to get anyone's attention, you're dead." The barrel of a gun poked at her ribs, confirming the threat. She took a halting step as the back door of the club crashed open, banging against the brick wall.

"Sarah!"

Jay—no. Her captor loosened his grip and turned from her. In the dim light she saw his pistol raised, pointed at Jay.

"No!" She swung her free hand around, batting the gun just as the trigger was pulled. For one horrifying second, time seemed suspended while the bullet traveled toward its target and struck. Sarah screamed as she watched Jay fall back against the wall.

The man jerked her arm behind her once more, but this time she refused to go, falling to her knees. She wasn't going to leave Jay.

"Get up." He bent her arm until she was sure it would break. With her free hand she swiped at the ground as she stood, throwing a fistful of snow and gravel in her attacker's face.

He reached for her hair again, but a hit from the side sent him plowing into her. Sarah fell to the ground, crushed beneath his weight. A second later he rolled off, and in the dim light she saw Jay standing over them.

"Run!" he yelled, his hand stretched out, trying to grab the gun.

Sarah reached for the flashlight lying in the snow beside her. She scrambled to her feet, bringing the light across the man's face while he and Jay wrestled for the gun.

In the distance she heard Kirk's voice. "Stop. Police!"

The man wrenched free, pointing the pistol at Jay's heart. Jay froze, his hands out in front of him.

Sarah threw herself between the gun and Jay. "Don't," she begged.

Their attacker grabbed her coat sleeve, jerking her toward him. Footsteps pounded on the pavement, drawing nearer. His grip tightened around her arm as he glanced toward the sound, then released her suddenly and fled.

Sarah turned to Jay. He stood bent over, panting heavily. Drops of bright red blood dripped on the thin blanket of snow covering the ground.

"Someone help us," she called. Jay tried to stand. Sarah wrapped her arms around his waist, holding him tight.

"Sarah!" Kirk came around the side of the building and skidded to a halt as their attacker scaled a fence at the end of the alley.

"Go!" Jay shouted. "Don't let him get away."

It was all the encouragement Kirk needed to run after him, gun already drawn.

Chapter Forty-Four

Jay and Sarah reached Kirk's cruiser, parked on the street a block from the club, just as Kirk ran up.

"Did you—?" Sarah began.

He shook his head. "Got away. Had a car waiting." He glanced at Jay, breathing as heavily as he was and leaning on the back of the car. "You guys okay?"

"Jay's been shot," Sarah said.

"I'm fine," Jay insisted. "Just a superficial flesh wound."

"You're *bleeding*," Sarah said.

"Get in." Kirk unlocked the car and jerked the back door open. "You two ride here on the way to the hospital. Keep an eye on him, Sarah. He doesn't look so good."

Jay ducked inside, and Sarah followed. Kirk shut the door, climbed in front, and started the engine. "Tell me what happened," he said, pulling out into traffic.

"Jay saved my life," Sarah said. "There was a guy waiting for me in the alley."

"What were you doing out there?" Kirk asked.

"The bartender told me it was backstage, then pushed me outside."

"I heard Sarah screaming," Jay said. "The girl has lungs. All those voice lessons really paid off." His attempted grin more closely resembled a grimace.

"I heard her too." Kirk glanced at Sarah in the rearview mirror. "The guy was *waiting* for *you* specifically?"

"Yes." Sarah met Kirk's gaze, then returned her attention to Jay. He shivered suddenly, and even in the dark she could see the blood seeping through his sweater. "Hurry, please."

Kirk stopped at a red light and twisted around in his seat. "Don't go into shock on me," he ordered, staring at Jay.

"I'm not." But his voice wasn't convincing.

Sarah reached for Jay's hand and was alarmed at how cold he felt.

"Cold is good. Helps the blood congeal," Jay said, as if he'd read her mind.

As they neared the hospital, Kirk's phone rang, and, after glancing at caller ID, he answered the call on speakerphone.

"What's up, Christa?" Kirk said. "I've got Jay and Sarah here, and we kind of need to stop at the hospital."

"Who's hurt? Is it life-threatening?" Christa asked.

"Nah." Kirk glanced toward the back seat. "Though if I were Jay, I'd milk it for all it's worth."

"You all need to come home right now," Christa insisted, startling them. "Jay's picture was just on the news. The Cambridge police are looking for him. They think he shot his roommate."

* * *

Sarah took Jay's hand as they sat on the couch, wedged close together while Kirk worked on Jay's shoulder.

"You are one lucky dude. In and out with only a chunk of flesh to show for it." Kirk poured antiseptic on a gauze pad and pressed it into the wound.

"Geez!" Jay half rose, gritting his teeth.

Sarah's eyes brimmed with tears, and she bit her lip as she watched, making him feel even worse.

Better me than Sarah, he thought, vowing to keep his mouth shut—even if Kirk decided he needed stitches.

"It's me or take your chances at the hospital," Kirk reminded him. "And there's a good chance that if you show up there, you won't be leaving—to go home, anyway."

"I found it," Christa called from the bedroom.

Kirk got up, then held a hand out to help Jay. Sarah followed as the three made their way down the hall to Kirk and Christa's room, where the computer was.

"Ready?" Christa asked, when they stood in a half-circle behind her.

"Go ahead," Kirk said.

Christa started the video, and they watched a rerun of the top story on Channel Three's nightly news.

"Out on bail just four days, Harvard Law student Jay Kendrich is believed to have continued his crime spree, escalating with the shooting of his roommate, a student who lives in this apartment behind me." The camera panned to Jay's apartment, number eleven, on the ground floor, cordoned off by police tape.

Jay gripped the back of Christa's chair. "Which student? What—"

"About an hour ago, police and ambulance units responded to a 911 call from a woman, believed to be the victim's girlfriend."

"*Trish—Archer?*" Jay and Sarah said at the same time. They turned to each other, faces reflecting equally stunned and horrified expressions.

There has to be some mistake, Jay thought. *Archer's fine.*

"The woman told police that Kendrich and the victim were fighting when Kendrich lost his temper and pulled out a gun."

"Trish would never lie about Jay like that," Sarah said. "They've got the wrong apartment. They're talking about someone else."

"Shh." Kirk put a finger to his lips.

The reporter continued. "Kendrich is believed to have fled on foot, and as we speak, police are searching the surrounding area. And while an earlier search turned up nothing, just a few minutes ago we were told a gun was retrieved from a dumpster behind the apartment complex. The victim remains in critical condition at Mount Auburn Hospital."

"Good thing we didn't go *there* tonight," Kirk said under his breath.

"We have to." Sarah's eyes filled with tears. "We have to see Archer—and Trish."

"Yes," Jay agreed.

"No," Kirk said, looking at them both like they'd lost their minds.

Jay's mug shot filled the screen. He felt his stomach churn and was grateful it was empty.

The video ended. Silence filled the room.

Stunned and disbelieving, Jay took a step backward and sat on the end of the bed. He leaned forward, head in his hands. "Archer." They certainly hadn't been best friends, but he never would have wished this on him.

"We have to talk to Trish," Sarah said.

Jay nodded.

"Neither of you can go anywhere. Didn't you hear any of that?" Kirk looked at Jay. You're wanted for attempted homicide—murder, if he dies. And you—" Kirk turned to Sarah. "Bailed him out."

"You know as well as I do that he's innocent," Sarah said, color rushing to her face.

"Of course," Christa said.

"Yes," Kirk agreed. "But there's a witness who saw him."

"She's lying," Sarah argued. "And I can't believe Trish would do something so awful."

"If she was scared enough she might," Christa said.

"Or if she saw someone who she thought was me," Jay added.

"Though I'd say the first is more likely." Kirk began pacing. "And if they take that gun and match it to you—"

"How?" Sarah asked.

"If they're working with Carl, and it was Carl who broke into Jay's locker and took his stuff, then they can lift the prints."

"They don't even have to be that sophisticated," Jay said. "I had my hands all over a gun tonight—the one that shot me."

"And they just barely found a weapon," Kirk said, his face grave. "There would have been time for someone to plant it."

"What about the guy who shot you?" Christa asked. "Wouldn't his prints show up too?"

"He was wearing gloves." Sarah held her arm gingerly as if remembering the damage that the hands in those gloves had inflicted. "But we're both witnesses that Jay couldn't possibly have done it. He was with us."

"Us and who else?" Kirk asked. He pivoted by the bedroom door and came back toward them. "Jay didn't play at the club tonight, and the barkeep who pushed Sarah isn't going to vouch for his whereabouts. Other patrons might have seen him, but we can't count on them—or their sobriety—to get this straightened out. And our testimony—as his friends— would have a hard time standing up against an eyewitness and prints on a weapon."

"You're right," Jay agreed, sounding as hopeless as he felt.

Kirk continued pacing, and Jay could see the detective wheels spinning behind his eyes.

"But *why* would Carl—or whoever—attempt murder and pin it on Jay? Truthfully, we have our work cut out for us getting you off the drug charges. Whoever's responsible had to know there was a good chance you'd be going to jail. So why add murder to the ticket? Why risk it?" Kirk stopped in front of Sarah. "Is there *anything* you haven't told us? Do you have any idea why Carl—or your dad—would go to such great lengths to frame Jay and get you back?"

Sarah's blue eyes were troubled. "I don't know, but the man in the alley did mention something."

"What?" Kirk prodded.

"Something about me not doing my job."

"What job?" Jay asked. Sarah had never mentioned anything to him, and he was surprised her dad would have let her out of the house to work.

She expelled a breath before answering. "Until I left my dad's house, I was a member of the Summerfield PD undercover narcotics team."

Chapter Forty-Five

Kirk held a thick piece of gauze to Jay's shoulder. "The best thing you two can do is lay low for a while. And it's your lucky day, 'cause I'm offering first-class basement accommodations."

"Great," Jay said unenthusiastically as he leaned his head back. Some of the tension drained from his face as Kirk pulled the blood-soaked pad away.

"I was thinking," Kirk said. "Any chance either of you think you might recognize a mug shot of the guy from the alley?"

"I would," Jay said. "And I'm pretty sure I've seen him before, too."

"You have?" Sarah asked. "Where?"

"On the train home from Boston." Thinking about it now, he mentally kicked himself for not doing anything then—but what could he have done? Staring at someone wasn't a crime. Jay turned to her. "He was looking at you. You were asleep."

"Why didn't you say anything?" Sarah asked.

Jay started to shrug, then winced. "He stayed on the train when we got off, and I didn't think any more of it—just another guy enthralled by your pretty face like I am. I thought Carl was the real threat."

"He is, but now we know he's not the *only* threat." Kirk bandaged the wound, wrapping several layers of tape around it to hold the packing tight. "Whoever the guy is that went after you tonight, he was working with Carl. Isn't that right, Sarah?"

"That's what the man in the alley implied."

"And if we can figure out who he is, we might have someplace to start. Because I'd bet money that what happened to you tonight and what happened to Archer are connected." Kirk cut the end of the tape and pressed it carefully against Jay's shoulder. "I wish we could take you to a doctor. Stitches would be a good idea, and at the very least you'll need antibiotics. A tetanus shot probably wouldn't hurt, either."

"Would too," Jay said. "I had one in October, and it hurt a lot. No more needles for me." He lifted the hair from his forehead, revealing the scar from his recent stitches.

"I forgot about those," Kirk said. He shook his head and attempted a smile. "I've never known anyone who finds dating so hazardous."

Sarah leaned around Jay, placing a finger to his scar. "When did you get those?"

Uh-oh. He looked chagrined. "I forgot you didn't know about that. It was no big deal." He flattened his hair again so she couldn't see his forehead.

Her mouth twisted and she narrowed her eyes. "Was it when Carl punched you or when he tried to run us over?"

"Um—the truck thing," Jay said, clearing his throat.

"You told me you weren't hurt," she said.

"I'm not. They don't hurt at all right now."

She continued to frown.

"If it makes you feel better, you can kiss them for me." For Sarah's sake he tried to joke about his own pain, all the while trying to ignore the worry and fear they both felt.

"Not right here you won't." Kirk pushed his chair back. "Get your shirt on, Jay. This is a G-rated house."

"Yeah, I bet." Jay rolled his eyes, but he allowed Sarah to help him get his arm through his sleeve. "I've seen the way you look at your wife."

"Keep my wife out of this," Kirk warned, grinning. "Behave yourself and you can stay here so we can keep an eye on you. Come on. Follow me. Sarah, will you ask Christa for some blankets? It's pretty chilly downstairs."

"Sure." Sarah left the kitchen, and Jay followed Kirk down the narrow stairs to the basement.

"What is all this stuff?" Jay asked, looking at the boxes, jars, cans, and bottles crammed into the only downstairs bedroom.

"Food storage. Between the under-construction salon and the water leak we had, this was the only place left to put everything." Kirk picked up an air mattress from a stack of what appeared to be camping supplies. "Wish we hadn't lost the foot pump."

"I'll blow it up," Jay offered, holding out his good arm.

"Yeah, right. You're in a lot worse shape than you let on up there." Kirk brought his lips to the plastic seal and started blowing air into the opening.

Jay sat in a space between rows of boxes. He leaned against a case of tuna and propped his feet up on a flat of canned vegetables. Food—in any form—sounded awful right now, but *canned peas . . . the worst.* "I'm going to have nightmares down here. The Jolly Green Giant attacking on one side, and Charlie the Tuna on the other."

Kirk took a break, wiping the back of his hand across his mouth. "I swear this thing tastes like the dirt in Yosemite where we used it last."

"No need to eat dirt around here," Jay observed. He moved his finger in the air, counting twelve containers of Morton salt. "You guys planning on a truckers' strike or something?"

"Something like that," Kirk said. "Our church is big into emergency preparedness and having a year's supply of food. Christa takes it very seriously—especially lately because she's afraid I'm going to get fired."

"Me too," Jay agreed. "I shouldn't be here."

"Where else can you go?" Kirk asked.

Jay didn't answer. There was no answer. Only more questions as the evening had worn on and Sarah had told them about working for her dad.

"We're going to have to tell Sarah tomorrow," Kirk said, uncannily following Jay's train of thought. "I don't know what her dad has been up to all this time, but there *is no* underground task force or whatever she called it. I should know. I've been pestering the chief about starting something like that for months."

"But what if there is?" Jay argued. "Maybe you don't know because it *is* undercover and the regular staff isn't part of it."

"And the chief's untrained daughter and derelict cousin *are?*" Kirk shook his head. "No way. Something is out of whack here, and it's not me. Nothing she said makes any sense. She was told to buy from some people but always ignore others? If the chief was serious about cleaning up the park, why not go after those guys, too? And only once in two years did she come to the station to view a lineup? She's never been to court? It's the craziest thing I've ever heard." Kirk went back to work on the air mattress, blowing out his frustrations.

Jay pulled a twenty-four pack of toilet paper from a low shelf and placed it beneath his head as he lay back. "So tomorrow you break the news to her that her dad's a fraud and she's been illegally purchasing drugs for him the past however many years. Then what?" But he knew what would happen then. It was likely the final straw that would put Sarah over the edge. Her emotional reaction to his own drug-filled past was still fresh in his mind.

"I'm going to talk to my buddy at the DEA," Kirk said. "I'd like him to meet with Sarah. Whatever is going on is way out of my league, and I'm going to have to proceed carefully if I want to keep showing up at work *and* get to the bottom of this."

Jay tapped his fingers on the outside of a bucket that was labeled, *Wheat, Hard Red*. "And in the meantime I hang out in the dietary dungeon."

"Unless you've got a better idea." Kirk finished inflating the mattress and tossed it on the floor beside Jay. "You're in for a rough night with that shoulder. I'm sorry we can't have you upstairs. Christa is concerned the boys would see you and say something to someone."

"No problem." Jay grimaced as he tried to settle in on the mattress. "I doubt I'll sleep much anyway. Being wanted for attempted murder and all." *And worrying about Archer.* The agony was back, and Jay knew as soon as he was alone, he wouldn't be able to keep those troubling thoughts at bay.

"Add kidnapping to the list," Sarah said.

Both men turned to the doorway where she stood, arms full of pillows and blankets.

"Christa checked the Internet again. In addition to being the main suspect in Archer's attack, you're now believed to have left town and forced me to go with you."

Chapter Forty-Six

Jay lifted a hand to his face, rubbing the sleep from his eyes.

"How are you feeling?" Sarah asked.

"Awful." His back ached like crazy, and his shoulder throbbed. He had a headache that wrapped around his head and down to his neck. But all of that didn't matter quite so much when Sarah, sitting two feet away from him, came into focus. She had her knees drawn up to her chest, hair tousled as she leaned against a twenty-pound bag of pinto beans.

"Were you here all night?" Jay asked. Somewhere in the cobwebs of his mind he seemed to remember holding her hand and feeling her next to him. But that would've been impossible; the narrow air mattress was barely wide enough for him and kept him a scant inch above the concrete floor.

"I slept on the Charmin." She inclined her head toward several packages of toilet paper spread across the floor a few feet away. "Now that I'm as famous as you, Kirk and Christa don't want the boys to know I'm here either. There's some kind of alert out." She attempted to smile. "My picture was on the *Today Show*. Mrs. Larson would've been so proud."

Jay groaned. "Any news?"

She met his eyes, her own tearing up. "We were right. They released Archer's name this morning. He's in a coma."

Jay brought his hands to his face, the pain of last night and the reality of Archer's condition hitting hard. "Arch is just a kid. He hasn't even grown up yet."

"I know." Sarah reached out, gently rubbing Jay's good arm.

He lay there, wishing the news away, wishing the last twenty-four hours were nothing but a bad dream.

"Is your shoulder hurting?" She leaned over him, forehead wrinkled in concern. "You look like you're in a lot of pain."

"I'm fine," he lied. *My pain is nothing compared to what Archer must be going through.* Jay's eyes burned as he imagined the scene, how terrifying it must have been for Trish and Archer. *I've got to do everything I can to help Kirk figure this out; I've got to keep Sarah safe.*

"I'm going to get Kirk. You don't look fine," Sarah said.

"Don't do that. I'm okay." Jay sat up to prove his point. "I come from tough Scottish stock. One of my ancestors was once stuffed down a well and shot in the shoulder—*twice.* He not only lived to tell about it, but the very next day he walked across the prairie to the nearest town, *carrying* his future bride. She'd been bitten by a rattlesnake."

"And we think we've got big problems," Sarah said.

"That's the attitude." Jay carefully rotated his shoulder. "How are *you* feeling?"

"Awful too." She met his gaze then looked away, staring at the cans of mandarin oranges stacked in front of her. "I keep thinking of Trish . . . and after you fell asleep last night—"

"You mean after someone forced that Tylenol PM down my throat?"

"It was for your own good," Sarah said.

"Hmmph." Jay tried to lighten their somber mood. He could tell Sarah was on the verge of crying, and he felt the same. "Go on. After I was forcibly subdued—"

"Kirk talked to me. He told me how real undercover units work, the training I'd have to have, the procedures we'd go through."

"And?"

"I feel like a complete idiot." She drew her knees up closer, resting her chin on them.

Jay reached out, stroking her arm. "You didn't know."

"But I should have. It seems so . . . obvious."

"Not to someone who has never watched *Law and Order* or even *Charlie's Angels.*"

"It's not just that I feel stupid about that—though believe me I feel bad enough for not knowing anything." She turned her head to face him. "I feel like an idiot for the way I ran out on you at the restaurant. I was so upset that you'd used drugs. And here I've been buying them myself for *two years*—getting them for my father *just like* you were getting them for your mom."

"It's a little different," Jay said. "But I did tell you we're a lot alike. Our pasts are eerily similar."

"The only thing eerie now is whatever's going on with my dad and Carl."

"And Archer."

"Yes," Sarah agreed. "And Trish."

"She really loves him," Jay said. "And you know, he drove me crazy a lot, but he wasn't that bad of a guy. I never would have—"

"I know that." Sarah reached over and took his hand. "Even if I hadn't been with you last night, I'd still know."

"Was that just last night?" Jay asked. "It feels like a couple of years ago at least." He sighed heavily. "But it helps a little, knowing you believe me." He ran his hand across his stubbled chin. "Though I probably *look* like a criminal right now."

"I wouldn't worry about that for too long." Sarah rose from the floor and brushed off her jeans. "Enjoy your rest today, because I overheard Kirk and Christa talking this morning. Christa has big plans for you—for us—tomorrow."

Chapter Forty-Seven

Christa breezed into the kitchen. "Now that Kirk's taken Jeffrey Christmas shopping, and James is at the neighbor's party, we can get down to business." She walked to the sink and turned on the water.

Jay took another bite of Christmas Crunch cereal and grimaced. *Too sweet.* He could see sugar crystals floating in his milk. Still, it was better than the oatmeal he'd eaten yesterday morning, noon, *and* night. Jay had started to suspect that Christa hoped he'd turn himself in to the police, on the basis of wanting a better meal plan. But last night Kirk had assured him that wasn't the case at all. She was more concerned with the possibility that Jay would upset his system after the trauma of being shot. As for Kirk—despite his tenuous position as a police officer harboring a suspect—he insisted Jay shouldn't take the risk of turning himself in. Privately, when the women weren't around, Kirk had been honest enough to say he thought Jay's life might be in danger if he were in jail.

So here Jay stayed, worrying that his presence put everyone else at risk.

"Who wants to go first?" Christa asked. She pulled a sponge from beneath the counter, dumped some cleanser in the sink, and began scrubbing. "I figure hair is a good place to start with making you less recognizable. We can do a cut, color—just about anything you can imagine. If you'd like, Sarah, I have some magazines you could look through for different styles."

"Uh-oh," Jay mouthed to Sarah. He brought a hand to the back of his head, wondering if there was any possibility he could avoid Christa's scissors.

"I don't know much about hairstyles," Sarah confessed. She lifted the mug of hot chocolate to her lips again, a haunted look on her face as she sipped.

Christa continued scrubbing. "No problem. I do. Any idea how short you'd like to go?"

"Not really." Sarah pulled her braid over her shoulder and looked at it. "But I don't really want to color it."

"You have beautiful hair," Jay said. "You shouldn't color it or cut it short."

"Just like a man to say that." Christa tossed her own short hairstyle freely as she turned to face them. She pointed the sponge at Jay. "Have you ever taken care of long hair? It can be a real pain."

"As a matter a fact, I have." He leaned back in his chair. "It's not too difficult when you wear a ponytail."

"But it's cold in the winter," Sarah pointed out.

"Don't you mean hot in the summer?" Jay asked. "I always enjoyed having my hair longer during the winter months. It covered the back of my neck and kept my ears warm."

"It's not warmer when it's wet," she argued. "Whether I wash it in the morning or at night, it takes hours to dry and my head is always cold."

Christa asked the obvious question. "Why don't you blow it dry?"

"I've never had a blow-dryer."

"*Never?*" Christa's mouth hung open with the last syllable. "I know owning four like I do is a little excessive, but . . .Why didn't you say something? I assumed you liked wearing your hair the way you did, or I would have offered one of mine."

"My dad always insisted that all I needed was a brush." Sarah held the end of her braid up. "And rubber bands. I've never owned a hair dryer or a curling iron. He was very particular about that." She pulled out the elastic and began unraveling the braid.

Silence descended on the kitchen. Jay could see Christa trying to digest the awful reality of Sarah's life the way he had when they'd first started dating. It was unfathomable to think of all the basic things she had missed. Things like getting new clothes and glasses more than once every five years, learning how to drive, going out to movies, having friends. Owning a blow-dryer. Each time he was with her he discovered something new she'd missed. With each discovery, he became more determined and excited, thinking about all the experiences he could share with her for the first time—if he was ever free to do *anything* again.

He pushed back his chair and stood. "Where are those magazines?"

Christa pointed to a cart beneath the covered window on the opposite side of the room.

He took the entire stack, returned to the table, and set the magazines in front of Sarah. He couldn't do anything to help Archer right now, but maybe this would help Sarah. "You should do anything you want with your hair. You'll be beautiful however you wear it."

"I want it short enough that I *can't* braid it," she blurted, surprising them both. She looked apologetically at Jay. "What I mean is that I've worn it this way my whole life. I'd like something different—maybe like yours, Christa, or maybe curly?"

"We can do that." Christa walked over to the cart and pulled a black cape and a pair of scissors from the middle drawer. "Unfortunately, we don't have a ton of time. My guys aren't great shoppers, and that party is only supposed to go two hours. Besides, Kirk is leery of being gone too long. Though I say it's best if we act normal—go ahead with our regular plans."

"I agree," Jay said. "Is there anywhere else he can take Jeffrey when they're done shopping?" He sensed how important this was for Sarah, and he didn't want her to feel rushed. Most kids got their first haircuts by the time they were five, and it was a big deal then. Being close to twenty-five made it a momentous occasion.

"I suppose they could visit Santa again," Christa said. "Jeffrey *has* changed his list a half dozen times."

"Perfect," Jay said. "You want to call Kirk?"

"He'll be thrilled." Christa rolled her eyes. "Do you have any idea what the line is going to be like today?"

"A little." Jay flashed her a conspiratorial grin. "A little *long*."

"Your hair is what's long," Christa shot back as she crossed the kitchen to the phone.

"I'll go first," Jay offered, suddenly not caring what Christa did to his hair. "That way Sarah can take her time looking through the magazines."

"All right." Christa called Kirk and explained that she needed him to be gone another couple of hours. Jay could tell from her one-sided conversation that Kirk wasn't thrilled with the idea of revisiting Jolly Old Saint Nick.

"Done." Christa placed the phone back on the counter. "You. At the sink." She pointed her scissors at Jay. "Let's wash that mess and see what can be done with it."

"It's not a mess." Jay ran his fingers over the top of his head, wondering what Christa had in mind. "This is nothing compared to how I used to wear it."

"It *looks* messy," Christa said, sounding like a mom twice her age.

"Sarah doesn't think so, do you?" Jay glanced her direction.

She pulled her gaze from the open magazine in front of her. "Well, it's . . ." She pressed her lips together and squirmed in her chair. "A bit scruffy."

"*Scruffy?*" Jay tried to sound hurt. "This whole time you've thought I'm scruffy?"

"Not the whole time," she said, concern in her eyes. "When you comb it for your internship it looks better—not that it was bad to begin with. What I mean is—"

"He needs a haircut," Christa summarized. She turned the water on and pulled out the spray nozzle.

Jay stuck his head in the sink. "Watch the shoulder. Hey! That's cold."

"Don't be a baby," Christa scolded but moved the handle toward hot. "Better? If this hurts your shoulder you can wash your hair in the shower instead."

"I'll shower when you're through." Jay closed his eyes as she squirted the shampoo.

"I didn't dislike it." Sarah continued trying to explain away her scruffy comment. Jay smiled in spite of his discomfort. She still hadn't quite figured out when he was teasing her.

He turned his head toward her. "And this from the girl who can't remember when she had *her* last haircut." He winked.

She caught on, an embarrassed smile warming her face. "On second thought, I think a buzz would be perfect."

"Just what I was thinking," Christa said. "About a quarter inch from his scalp."

Jay closed his eyes as she turned on the water again. A haircut might change his appearance a little, but it wasn't going to change anything else. Archer was still in the hospital. Sarah was in danger. *I'm a mess.*

Jay waited for Christa to finish applying some other goo in his hair and to rinse that out as well. Finally she handed him a towel. Using one hand, Jay scrubbed his head for a few seconds then straightened, a wry grin on his face as he looked over at Sarah, who was absorbed once again in the style magazines.

"All I know is that this is the second time in my life I've cut my hair for a girl. And I hope—" He caught her eye as she looked up at him. "Things turn out better this time."

* * *

His haircut—slightly more generous than a buzz—and the highlights Christa had insisted on adding—were finished by ten-thirty. When Jay returned from checking his new look in the bathroom mirror, he found the two women huddled over a page in one of Christa's magazines. It was quickly shut as he entered the room.

"What do you think?" Christa asked.

She didn't sound like it really mattered to her one way or another. "It's not quite even. The right side curves more above my ear."

"It does not. Come here," Christa ordered.

"Don't listen to him. He's teasing," Sarah said.

"It's great." Jay ducked as Christa's scissors snipped the air around him.

"Then get out of here," Christa said. "Go watch TV or read Charles Dickens or something."

"What? I can't stay? Sarah got to when it was my turn."

"That was different." Christa pushed him toward the living room. "Do *not* come back in this kitchen until you're invited."

"Can't I at least see—"

"No!" they shouted.

"Women," Jay huffed. He slunk off toward the couch. "Don't worry about me. I'll just watch *It's a Wonderful Life* all day."

And he did—for an hour, at least. But it was difficult to absorb the feel-good message of the movie, thinking about Archer fighting for his life in the intensive care unit. At eleven-thirty, Christa stood in the kitchen doorway and tossed him a sandwich.

"What's the funny smell?" Jay wrinkled his nose at the odor coming from the kitchen.

She ignored his question. "Do you mind going downstairs? I'm going across the street to get James. It'll be hard enough to keep him from seeing Sarah."

"No problem." Jay was halfway out of his chair when the doorbell rang.

"The neighbor must have walked James home." Christa pointed him toward the kitchen, which he'd have to walk through to get to the stairs. "Don't peek. Sarah wants to surprise you."

Jay put his hands over his eyes and made an exaggerated show of bumping into things as he made his way through the stinky kitchen.

"This isn't fair, you know," he whispered, walking past the table where Sarah was sitting.

Though his eyes were covered, they started to water and burn. Whatever they were doing in here was bad, and he was starting to fear the outcome. He opened the door to the basement, only too happy to head downstairs. He'd just made it to the bottom when Christa called him.

"Jay, come quick."

Startled by her abrupt order, his heart hammered in his chest. *Something's happened to Archer,* he thought as he retraced his steps. *Or the police are here.*

"What is it?" Jay asked as he entered the kitchen.

Sarah had towels draped across her shoulders and curlers in her hair. Christa leaned over the table, looking pale and terrified. "James . . ." she said. "This was on the porch." A crumpled sheet of paper shook in her hands.

Jay took it, exchanging a confused look with Sarah, who stood and put her arm around Christa. He flattened the paper and read the handwritten note aloud.

> *We'll trade. Sarah for the boy. You have five minutes. Make sure she comes alone.*

He glanced at Sarah and saw his own shock reflected on her face. He ran through the living room, parting the blinds to look out front. A dark sedan was parked across the street. A man squatted beside it, talking with James.

"My baby," Christa whispered. "What do I do?"

"Just what he asked," Sarah said, coming into the room, removing the towels. She pulled her sneakers from the basket. "Is Kirk's gun here?"

Christa nodded. "He has several. They're all locked up."

"Can you get to them?" Sarah asked.

Christa nodded.

"I need something small enough to fit in my coat pocket. A nine millimeter would be good. Make sure it's loaded." Sarah bent over, curlers clicking as she pushed her foot in to the sneaker.

"You can't go out there," Jay said. "They'll—"

"Take James if I don't," Sarah finished. "Go," she ordered Christa, who hesitated in the hallway. Christa ran toward the bedroom. Sarah shoved her foot in to the other shoe, tied the laces, and stood to face Jay. "I don't have a choice. Mrs. Larson is *dead.* Archer was shot. You were almost killed. None of this ever would have happened if I hadn't left home." Her voice caught. She turned away, taking her coat from the rack. "He's a helpless little boy."

Jay helped her into the coat. He turned her to face him and pulled her close. "It's not your fault. None of it." He held her tight.

She buried her face in his shoulder. "I'm sorry, Jay."

Christa returned, a gun in her hand. "This is the smallest."

Sarah stepped back from Jay's embrace, wiped at her eyes, and reached for the pistol. "A Ruger P90; that'll work."

"You—uh—know guns?" Jay said.

"A little." Sarah chambered a round and flipped off the safety. She put the gun in the right pocket of her coat, and a tremulous smile formed on her lips.

"Trust me."

Chapter Forty-Eight

"Christa, call the police," Jay said.

"I already have."

"Then I *really* have to get out there." Feeling a heightened sense of urgency, Sarah reached for the door. "If the police show up before I cross the street, he'll take James."

Jay put his hand over hers. "I'm coming too."

"You'd only be a liability. It's me they want." She opened the door and stepped outside.

Jay followed. "There's no way I'm letting you go over there by yourself."

She turned around to face him. "You don't have a choice." She looked over his shoulder at Christa, who hovered in the doorway, tears streaking down her face. "Keep him here. Or James won't be safe."

Christa put her hand on Jay's arm. "Please let her get him," she begged. "Then you can go."

"*Then* may be too late," Jay said, but he allowed Christa to pull him back into the house.

"Thank you," Christa called just before closing the door.

Don't thank me yet. Head held high and wobbly from all the curlers, Sarah walked across the street, zipping up her coat.

The man next to James straightened, and his eyes zeroed in on hers. At the house behind him, another child was being picked up from the party. Sarah slowed her walk, angling herself toward James. When she was halfway across the street and the mother and child had safely pulled away from the curb, she called out, "Send him home now."

The man snickered. "You think I'm stupid?"

Sarah kept walking while at least part of her brain acknowledged that her sudden courage was being fueled by anger. That *was* stupid—and dangerous.

With hurried steps she reached James's side. She knelt, pulling him forward in a hug. "It's all right. You go home now—*run.*"

James tried to move, but the man still held his coat tight.

"I'm here," Sarah said. "Let him go."

The man's gaze flickered behind her for half a second before releasing James, who took off as fast as his trembling three-year-old legs would go.

"Stand up and get in the car."

Sarah started to rise, then fell backward, pretending to slip in the icy street. The man swore under his breath and reached for her.

Sarah recoiled. "Don't touch me," she hissed, looking up at him with hatred in her eyes. "I can get up myself." She twisted to the side, crossing her legs, bracing her right hand on the street as she got up. There was no need to exaggerate her slow, awkward movements. Her arm was still badly bruised.

Rising sideways to the man, she put her left hand on the car hood when she was about three-fourths of the way up and her footing was sure. Her right hand slid into her pocket. It rested on the gun for a fraction of a second, then curled around the smaller object beside it. Pulling her pepper spray out, she turned on him, pushing the canister down with all her might.

He yelped, one hand going to his eyes, the other reaching out for the spray. Before he could grab it, Sarah whirled around—and ran straight into the barrel of a mini UZI. The same guy who'd accosted her in the alley stared down at her. She shuddered and stepped back, trying not to look at his face, which was covered with deep scratches—marks no doubt made by her fingernails.

Always watch your back. Good advice. Too bad she hadn't followed it.

"Clever, aren't you, beauty queen?" His mouth curved upward as he appraised her.

Sarah couldn't tell whether he was more amused by her curlers or her attempt with the spray. Behind her, his partner was still holding his eyes and cursing.

"Get in the car, Sid," the machine-gun guy ordered. To Sarah he said, "We can do this easy, or I can go across the street and get the kid again. Or, there's plenty of kids in that house right there." He nodded toward the home where the party had been.

Sarah glanced at it and saw the trio of snowmen built in the front yard.

She shook her head. "I don't want company." *Any time now,* she thought, wondering what was taking the police so long. And she'd been worried they'd get here *too* fast.

"Hand over the pepper spray."

Sarah dropped it, then kicked it under the car. *Never give your weapon to your enemy. If you're forced to surrender it, drop it or throw it away. Don't give them one more thing to use against you.* Her dad was starting to make a lot of sense. Sid would, no doubt, have loved the chance to get her back. She forced her lips into a thin line as she looked at machine-gun guy's scratched face again.

"Get in back behind the driver's seat," he ordered.

"Where are you taking me?"

"Boss wants to chat with you. Otherwise I'd take care of things right here. You've been enough trouble."

They call him Boss? Her anger flared again. "My dad needs to learn to use the phone if he wants to talk to me."

The man snickered. "Your dad's as much the boss as I'm the president of the United States." He nudged her with the gun.

Sarah moved carefully in front of him, internalizing what he'd said. If her dad wasn't in charge of Carl and these thugs, who was? A ripple of fear went down her spine. She reached the car door and hesitated. *Never, ever get in a car with a stranger.*

"Open the door," he ordered.

Unless he has a machine gun at your back and there are kids around? Does that count? She pulled on the handle, plan B forming in her mind as she set one foot inside the car.

"Sarah!"

Jay. Oh, no.

Her abductor pushed down on her head, trying to shove her into the back seat. Her scalp tingled as the hundreds of hairs wound in the perm rods pulled. She kept one foot outside the car.

"Hey, wait!" Through the tinted glass she saw Jay charging down the walk, waving his hands. Her abductor turned away, gun trained on Jay.

No—not again. Sarah threw her strength into pushing the door open. Her abductor lurched forward, and she jumped from the car. His gun was still aimed at Jay, who had reached the far curb.

"Get in or I kill him," he said.

The wail of a siren pierced the air, distracting the man for the half second Sarah needed to get her finger around the pistol in her pocket and pull the trigger.

Chapter Forty-Nine

Sarah dropped to the ground and rolled behind the car. She wasn't sure if she'd hit anything but knew it wasn't wise to hang around to find out. The sirens grew closer. The engine started suddenly, releasing a puff of exhaust. Coughing, she crawled up on the sidewalk to avoid being backed over. Looking up, she saw Sid's face in the passenger mirror. His bloodshot eyes met hers for a second before the car took off. A cruiser screamed around the corner, on its heels.

Sarah jumped up. "Go!" she shouted to Jay, shooing him toward the house. The cruiser slammed on the brakes, stopping at her side of the road. Sarah looked over and saw Kirk's face, as wild and anxious as Christa's had been. She pulled open the passenger door.

"James?"

"Safe," Sarah gasped. "In the house."

Kirk whipped his head around to the back seat. "Get Jeffrey out."

Sarah closed the front door, opened the back, and pulled Jeffrey from the car. She'd barely closed the door when Kirk sped off. A few neighbors had come outside to see what the commotion was. Keeping her head down, Sarah carried Jeffrey across the street, into the house.

Christa sat in the rocker holding James, tears streaming down both their cheeks. "Thank you," she said to Sarah. "Thank you for saving my baby."

Sarah turned away. Thanks was the last thing she deserved when all of this was her fault. Leaving them, she went through the kitchen and downstairs, carefully locking the door behind her so the boys couldn't come in.

Jay was waiting for her. He pulled her into his arms, holding her close. "Nice shot."

"Did I hit something?" Sarah asked.

"His hand, I think, and the side mirror. Ought to make driving interesting."

"When he got in the car, I was going to—shoot him from behind." Sarah felt her stomach roil and a cold sweat break out across her forehead. The terrible realization of what she might have done—what she wasn't sure she could do at all—hit hard.

Jay's eyebrows rose. "You've got a bit of a violent streak I wasn't aware of."

She forced a weak laugh. "Desperate times."

"Desperate measures," he finished.

"Speaking of which," Sarah said, "making yourself a target wasn't exactly smart."

"Bulletproof vest." He leaned over, picking it up off the floor.

"Okay, not *quite* as stupid as I thought. But you could have been shot in the head or—"

"Why do you think I was running around?" Jay asked. "Moving targets are harder to hit."

"He had an UZI," Sarah said.

"Oh." Their banter ceased suddenly, and Jay pulled her to him, crushing her against his chest. "Don't *ever* do anything like that again."

"I didn't have a choice."

"I know," Jay said. "Just the same. Don't ever do that again."

"I won't." She adjusted her head to a more comfortable position, and they stayed in their embrace, waiting as they listened to more sirens outside and footsteps on the floor above.

* * *

Twenty minutes later, a knock on the door startled them both. Jay was the first to get up off the floor where he and Sarah had been sitting. He held his good hand out, helping Sarah up.

"The timer went off." It was Christa's voice. "We've got to rinse your hair."

Sarah opened the door. Christa stood on the bottom step, her red, puffy face beaming with gratitude. "Thank you," she said in a hoarse voice.

"Is James all right?" Sarah asked.

Christa nodded. "He's napping now, and Jeffrey is watching a movie in my room. They're fine. Kirk's outside talking to some Cambridge officers. They didn't catch the car."

"How about you?" Jay asked, coming up behind Sarah. "How is Mom doing?"

"Don't ask." Christa attempted a smile. "You should stay down here a while longer. The officers will want to talk with Sarah and me." She started up the stairs. "Come on. We need to hurry. I have an idea how we can hide your face."

"I'll be in the food storage suite if you need me," Jay said, closing the door behind them.

Sarah followed Christa to the sink and leaned her head over, grimacing as the rods pulled at her scalp.

"Sorry," Christa apologized. "This is the worst part."

"You said that when you put the solution on," Sarah reminded her.

"That's usually true, but when the police come in I'm going to have you stay here. We'll keep a towel over your face—to protect your eyes—and I'll remove the curlers very slowly. You'll be able to talk and answer questions, but the officers won't see your face."

"What do I tell them?" Sarah asked.

"Stick as close to the truth as possible; tell them you were trying to prevent a kidnapping," Christa advised. "But don't use your real name."

"What about the note?" Sarah asked.

"If we show that to them, it will give you away." Christa handed Sarah a towel and unrolled the first rod.

"Jay and I can't stay here anymore," Sarah said. "We're too big a risk for your family."

"It's too big a risk for all of us." Christa sighed as she glanced out to the living room where the Christmas tree stood. "We all have to leave."

Chapter Fifty

Jay stretched out on the air mattress, his attempt at a nap cut short by the consistent thuds coming from the floor above—the cowboys were back in action. Jay wondered why it was that children seemed to have inexhaustible sources of energy as well as the ability to rebound quickly after a crisis. When he thought of James and then Sarah outside with those men this morning, he felt helpless, terrified, and angry all over again. But James, at least, sounded like he was well on his way to recovering from the ordeal.

Jay rolled to his good side and glanced at the travel clock on the floor. 2:36. *What in the world is she still doing up there?* He'd heard the police come and go, but no one had come downstairs to tell him what happened. He worried about that and about Sarah's hair. What could possibly be taking so long? She was under a lot of stress right now, and he didn't think doing something extreme would help. He tried not to think of her pretty blond hair falling to the floor in foot-long pieces. Jay rolled to his back again. *It's her hair, her life,* he reminded himself. Trouble was, he wanted it to be *their* life. *Maybe someday . . .*

A quiet knock sounded at the bedroom door. Jay tensed, then listened as the rhythmic pounding upstairs continued. Thump, thump. Thump, thump—*Jeffrey.* Thump, thump. Thud—*James tripping and falling to the floor in his too-large cowboy boots. Yep. They're both still up there.*

"Jay?" The door opened a crack. "Are you awake?"

He sat up too fast, wincing as the pain in his back reminded him that he'd not only been shot but had spent the better part of the past two days on an air mattress with at least a couple of leaks.

"I'm up. Come in."

The door opened and Sarah stood in the doorway, a shy, uncertain smile on her face.

"Wow," Jay said, his eyes goggling as he struggled to get up off the floor. "Come here."

She stepped into the room.

He braced himself on the buckets of wheat and stood, heart thumping loudly as he took in her appearance. All thoughts of kidnappers and police fled as he gazed at the soft blond curls that framed her face and fell just above her shoulders. Her eyes, free of glasses now that she had her new contacts, seemed bigger and bluer than usual—and after a second Jay realized it was because she was wearing makeup for the first time that he could remember. It wasn't a lot. But a natural pink tinged her cheeks, matching the inviting shimmer on her lips.

Her lips. Man, I want to kiss her.

She'd changed clothes too, and wore a plain, white t-shirt with a pair of form-fitting jeans. Bare feet with painted toenails peeked out from beneath the denim.

"You look—great." *Great* was an understatement for the transformation. There had to be a better word. He wracked his brain for it. *Beautiful—obviously. Gorgeous—that too. Come-here-before-I-die-just-looking-at-you. Closer. Let-me-run-my-fingers-through-those-curls-and-taste-that-flavor-on-your-lips—yeah, that's it.*

"Jay?" Sarah's brow wrinkled with concern. "I did wake you. I'm sorry." She started to back out of the room.

He caught her hand, pulling her closer and pushing the door shut behind them. "I'm plenty awake." He lifted his free hand to her hair. "May I?"

She nodded.

He wrapped a curl around his finger. "Soft." He leaned forward. "Smells good, too."

"Surprised?" Sarah asked.

"Kind of. The smell upstairs worried me. What were you doing up there so long?"

"Christa gave me a permanent. I showed her a picture with curls and asked if she could teach me how to do my hair like that. She thought a perm might be easier than styling it every day."

"You mean these are going to last?"

"You don't like them?" Worry reflected in the deepest blue of her eyes.

"I *love* them," he said. "You look sensational. Your hair, your eyes—your lips." He let his gaze linger there. "You look hot in those jeans, too."

She giggled. "No one ever told me I look *hot* before."

"Well, you do." He let go of her hand and wrapped his arms around her waist, pulling her close. "There hasn't been a day I didn't think you were beautiful. But right now you look—amazing. You're gonna turn heads, I'm afraid." He frowned, worried she would do exactly that.

"There's only one head that interests me."

"Oh?" Jay raised his eyebrows.

"May *I* . . ." Hesitant, she reached up and ran her fingers through his hair, then rested both her hands at the back of his neck.

"Are you intending to kiss me, Sarah Morgan?"

She shook her head slightly. "I don't know how." She broke their gaze, her eyes cast down toward her bright toes, which were scrunching and unscrunching against the carpet. "Another thing I've never done before."

"That's a problem, isn't it?"

She nodded but didn't look up.

"But then, there used to be quite a few things you weren't certain you could do. We've had success with all of them—taking the subway, riding a bike, dancing . . . Of course, kissing is a bit . . . different."

Jay knew the pink creeping up Sarah's cheeks had nothing to do with her makeup. He grinned, thoroughly enjoying the moment. "I'm thinking we should start with a very basic kiss. Maybe lip to cheek."

She shrugged and continued to blush.

He lifted her chin and looked into her eyes. "I'll show you," he whispered, all teasing gone from his voice. He leaned in, placing a chaste kiss on her left cheek. *Her skin feels incredible.* Reluctantly he leaned back. "Well?"

She looked up at him, a smile playing at the corners of her mouth. "That was nice."

Nice? Jay thought. *I'm barely controlling myself here, and she thinks it's* nice. "Your turn."

She took a deep breath, fixed her gaze on a spot on his cheek, and leaned in. The tiniest whisper brushed his face.

"That's it?" he asked, disappointed.

"That's all you did."

"Hmm." Jay's mouth twisted as if he were considering some great dilemma. "Guess this means you're ready for a more advanced lesson."

"I suppose."

He looked down. Her toes were still curling, and her hands trembled where they rested on his shoulders. He wrapped his arms more tightly around her waist. "Think you're up for it?"

"Ja-ay, please." Sarah's eyelids fluttered shut. "No more teasing. Just kiss me."

"My, my. This new haircut is making you bold."

"*You* make me bold." Sarah sighed. "Now please give me my first kiss."

"If that's what you want."

"I've wanted it for a very long time. I've dreamed about it. I've—"

"You've dreamed about kissing me?"

"Yes." She didn't even blush as she admitted it.

"Tell me," Jay whispered, leaning closer so their foreheads touched. "Tell me what you dreamed." He reveled in the heady feeling of knowing she wanted him.

"I will . . . later. But first I want to know if what I imagined was right."

"If you're sure." His breath touched her lips as he spoke. Her eyes closed again, and he angled his head to the side, his lips reaching out to hers, warm and inviting.

"Jay. Sarah." Sharp knocking followed Kirk's voice.

They jumped apart, Sarah blushing once again, Jay leaning his head back with a sigh of frustration. He glanced at her before opening the door. There was no mistaking the keen disappointment written on her face, and it buoyed his spirits.

"Later," he whispered. "And that's a promise."

Chapter Fifty-One

Kirk sat on a bucket of sugar across from Jay and Sarah in the bedroom. "I have some good news."

"You caught them?" Jay asked.

"Not that. Sorry." Kirk shook his head. "Though, miraculously, the police—other than myself, of course—still have no idea you're here."

"How did you manage that?" Jay asked. "I'm sure *someone* saw me dancing around on the lawn.

"The only neighbors who witnessed anything aren't sure *what* they saw, other than *two* men and a woman outside. Two men escaped in the car, so we're covered there. And Sarah"—Kirk turned to her—"pulled off an amazing interview with a Cambridge detective."

"And you're still here?" Jay asked, turning to her.

She nodded, then rubbed the back of her neck. "It was a bit uncomfortable, but we managed." She cast a conspiratorial grin Kirk's direction.

"What?" Jay asked, wanting to be in on the joke—as if there were anything remotely humorous about their situation.

"My hair," Sarah said, "was finally good for something."

"While Christa removed the perm rods, she had Sarah positioned so that the top half of her face was covered by a towel—to protect her from the chemicals," Kirk explained. "Christa informed the officer that the perm was already on the verge of ruin due to the morning's activities—and that Sarah might very well go bald if the chemical didn't come out of her hair soon. The cop never saw her face. And the chemicals smelled so terrible that he could barely stand being close enough to hear her talk."

"But I'm sure he asked your name," Jay said.

"And I gave it to him—Sarah Phillips. That *is* my name—just not the whole thing. I told him Christa is my cousin, and I'm visiting for the holidays. When she saw the man outside with her little boy, she panicked. Instinct kicked in, and I ran across the street to get him. End of story."

"Liar, liar," Jay said, tsk-tsking.

"Pants on fire," Kirk agreed. "I'm going to have a lot of explaining to do as soon as all this comes to light." He sighed heavily. "But we're in it this far; there's no stopping now."

"I can't stay here anymore," Jay said. "You've got a family to support, and—"

"*None* of us are going to stay here," Kirk said. "It's too dangerous. Tonight Christa and I are going to Worcester for a Christmas party at my great-aunt's house. I'm going to leave Christa and the boys there when I come back for work tomorrow."

"You have to work on Christmas?" Sarah asked.

Kirk nodded. "I'm one of the new guys, remember? But half the department has shifts tomorrow. Crime knows no time, or something like that; so the saying goes." Kirk reached in his shirt pocket for a key. "You guys are going to stay at our friends' house a few blocks away. A couple from our single adult group at church got married recently, and they're in Hawaii on their honeymoon. The house they live in belongs to her grandparents, who are out of the country on a mission."

"So no one is going to come home and surprise us in the middle of the night," Jay said.

"Right." Kirk handed him the key. "I wouldn't dance on the lawn while you're there, but you should be safe until tomorrow."

"What's tomorrow?" Sarah asked warily.

"Protective custody, I hope," Kirk said. "I've found someone who can help us. My friend in the DEA, Detective Doyle, has agreed to drive down and meet with you tomorrow afternoon."

"That's great." Jay squeezed Sarah's hand.

"On Christmas?" she asked.

"This is *big*," Kirk's face was serious as he looked at both of them. "The meth problem in this area has grown exponentially, and things are starting to point to your dad having something to do with it. You'll need to tell Detective Doyle everything you can remember. He needs to know about the jobs your dad sent you on, the contacts you met, your cousin."

"I'll try," she said.

"Good. The more you remember, the faster we can put the pieces together, and the sooner you can have a life again. Plan on several hours of questioning. It's going to be hard."

"Can Jay come too?"

"Yes. And after Detective Doyle has talked with you both, he'll be able to make a determination as to what type of protective custody you should be put in."

"Custody?" Sarah flashed a worried glance at Jay.

"Not like you're thinking," Kirk said. "You won't be behind bars or anything like that, though you both need to plan on being cooped up for some time while we sort this out. We could be looking at several months."

"*Months?*" Sarah exclaimed, clearly dismayed. "But winter semester starts after the new year."

"Archer is still in critical condition, Jay is wanted for a host of other crimes, and someone tried to kill you both—twice." Kirk's expression was grave. "I'm sorry, but there's no way either of you will be returning to Harvard in January." He stood. "At any rate, your accommodations will be a lot better than this."

Sarah rested her elbows on her knees and leaned forward, face in her hands. Her crestfallen look reminded Jay of how desperately she hadn't wanted to lose what she saw as her one chance at freedom—her education.

"I have one favor to ask," Kirk said.

"Sure," Jay said, curious since there wasn't much they could do right now—what with the warrants, stalkers, and all.

"I have a couple of Christmas presents for the boys that I haven't had time to assemble." Kirk spoke in a whisper, as if the galloping gang upstairs might hear. "A couple of bikes and a toy castle. They need to be put together tonight, so I can bring them to Worcester tomorrow after I get off work. Think you two can handle it?"

"We get to play Santa?" Jay asked, starting to feel better about everything. Tonight he and Sarah would be safe, and they'd be spending Christmas Eve together—alone. "I'm in." He glanced at Sarah.

"Sure," she said without much enthusiasm.

"Thanks," Kirk said. "I'd better go. We've got to get the boys bathed before we go, and you have no idea what kind of adventure that is." He pushed up his sleeves as he left the room, closing the door behind him.

Jay let go of Sarah's hand and put his arm around her, pulling her close. "Everything is going to be all right."

She leaned her head against his shoulder. "*Nothing* is all right. Archer's in the ICU. My dad is a drug lord or something. We're in hiding for who knows how long. You're not going to be able to graduate this spring. Doesn't any of that upset you?"

"You know I'm worried about Archer," Jay said. "But the only thing I can do is make sure that whoever shot him is caught. As for graduating . . . right now I'm more concerned with keeping you safe. School will work itself out later."

"You're right," Sarah said. "And I'm awful and selfish to even think about such a thing. But I'm worried that when I don't show up at church to sing tonight, the Ladies' Aid may decide to take away my scholarship. There's no way I can pay tuition myself. Then, when we *can* finally go back to school, I'll have to work for a few years to pay for it, and I'm already old for a freshman."

"You're getting way ahead of yourself," Jay said. "I'm sorry you can't sing tonight—*really* sorry—but that doesn't mean you'll lose your scholarship. I'm sure they'll hold it for you, and waiting one semester isn't the end of the world. I'm old too, you know."

"But law school is different," Sarah said. "If I go weeks—or months—without practicing—"

"We'll make sure that wherever they keep us, they've got a piano. And you can sing to me every day."

"Not the same," she insisted.

"I know," Jay said. "But it's a whole lot better than the alternative. We've got to look at the positive side of things. We're likely going to have a lot of time on our hands. We can read books together, play games, watch all the movies you've missed, and then there's *my* music education 101."

"I don't know if I can handle *that,*" Sarah said with just a hint of a smile.

"And of course, there will be ample time for me to teach you the finer points of kissing."

"Must I wait for everything?"

Jay dropped his hand to her waist and tickled her. "Those curls have made you shameless. Or is it the jeans?"

Sarah giggled and tried to squirm out of his reach. "Neither. I told you earlier. It's all your fault." She tilted her face to his.

"Shh." Jay placed a finger over her lips. "We don't want the boys to hear us."

Her smile faded, and she swallowed slowly. Jay's finger left her lips and traced the curve of her face. He still couldn't quite believe that this beautiful woman was the same shy girl from the library only a couple of months ago. Her transformation—both inside and out—was miraculous. How privileged he felt to be a part of it, to have shared so many of her first experiences. *And a first kiss I need to make extra special.*

Reluctantly he let his hand fall from her face. "A first kiss should be something extraordinary," Jay said. "It shouldn't be in a crowded little room in a cold basement."

"It doesn't matter where—"

"Oh, yes it does," Jay countered. "It matters a lot to me that we do this right. I want it to be a moment you never forget."

"I won't."

"I know," Jay said. "For the rest of your life, on Christmas Eve, when you stand by the tree with the lights glimmering, you'll always remember that was where and when I first took your face in my hands and kissed you."

"Tonight is Christmas Eve," Sarah whispered.

"Exactly."

Chapter Fifty-Two

Jay crossed the living room and set a box beside the lopsided, artificial Christmas tree. "That's everything."

"Okay." Sarah pushed the plug into the wall socket, and the soft glow of tiny colored lights filled the room.

"Wish we could turn on the overhead light." Jay pried open the first box. "I have a feeling I'm going to need to read the fine print on the instructions to assemble these babies."

"But the tree lights are nice—*romantic*."

"*Romantic?*" He rolled his eyes. "That's about the saddest-looking tree I've ever seen in my life, and this house smells like old people. We're going to have to postpone the whole kissing thing until we've got a better location."

Her face fell. "*I'm* here. Isn't that the important part?"

Jay chuckled. "Of course. Though I had hoped for a really nice home with a Jacuzzi or something. You're tempting me, though." *You have no idea how much.* "But I'm afraid it's bicycles first, romance later." He leaned over and kissed her on the cheek. "We don't want James and Jeffrey to be disappointed."

"You're taking this Santa stuff pretty seriously." She ran her fingers wistfully over the piano.

Jay pulled a bike frame out of his box. "Santa *is* serious. Take it from a guy who grew up hearing about Santa from his friends, but never actually got a visit himself."

"You didn't celebrate Christmas?" Sarah looked bewildered. "Even my dad believed in Christmas."

"Not in the traditional sense. My father would ask me what I wanted, then he'd go out and buy it—sometimes when I was with him. I could look at it all I wanted, but I couldn't actually open the new toy or game or whatever until Christmas day."

"That's really sad."

Jay placed the last box beside the first two. He shrugged. "Look who's talking. I can't imagine that Christmas at your house exactly resembled a Norman Rockwell portrait."

"It didn't," Sarah admitted. "But my father did take me to see Santa once. And there were always surprises under the tree. The year I was eleven, he bought me a piano—even though he'd told me over and over that we couldn't afford one. He tried to make things good." Her voice had turned melancholy. She knelt beside the square box and began taking plastic parts from inside. "I'll work on the castle while you do the bikes."

He leaned forward, prying a long flap of cardboard free. "I have *two* bikes to assemble. That's hardly fair."

"Whine, whine." Sarah rolled her eyes. "You'd better get busy. I've got the drawbridge together already. She reached inside the box again. "Cool—I get to use stickers."

"Hmmph," Jay grunted as he dangled a chain from his hand. "I get chains, tires, and pedals."

"It can't be that difficult. It's just a little kid's bike."

"And I hope a little kid can safely ride it when I'm finished. This isn't quite the same as working on my motorcycle."

He attached the back tire and monitored Sarah's progress from the corner of his eye. She sat cross-legged on the floor by the tree, busily snapping pieces together. He stuck the handlebars on the front and attached the seat, but the front wheel was giving him problems.

Sarah picked up one of the miniature cannon balls, placed it in the launcher on top of the castle, and sent it flying in his direction. It hit him in the arm.

"Hey." He scowled at her. "Have you forgotten I was near death a couple of days ago? If you're done already, then quit playing and come hold this for me."

Sarah held up the sheet of stickers. "Sorry. I've got some interior decorating to do. A good castle needs banners and swords."

"And Jeffrey needs his front tire to stay on when he's riding. Besides, you don't want my shoulder to get too sore. That could affect my ability to put my arms around you later."

"Since you put it that way . . ." She crawled across the floor and sat on the opposite side of the bike. "You set it in, and I'll attach the bolts."

"You sound like you know what you're doing."

"Every Christmas the Summerfield Police Department has a bike drive for kids who are underprivileged. Who do you think assembles those things—on-duty police officers?" She didn't wait for Jay to answer. "Nope. My dad always brought home about ten of them each year, and I'm the one who got stuck putting them together."

"Your dad had you assemble other kids' bikes but never bought you one?" Jay asked, incredulous.

"You're doing it again," Sarah warned. "I know I'm different."

"Sorry." Jay set the tire aside and reached for her. She leaned against him, looking up at the tree.

"I did ride them around the living room when he wasn't home. One year I even took a bike out in the backyard."

"Ah," Jay said. He rubbed her arm, wishing he could rub away the hurt in her voice. "So you weren't being entirely truthful when you said you didn't know how to ride."

"I didn't think wobbling around on the grass counted," Sarah said.

Jay considered. "I guess you're right. Help me finish this thing, and your deception is forgiven."

He reached for the tire and pressed it into Sarah's free hand. "Tell you what. Now that the odds are fair, we'll race." He pulled the other box closer and ripped it open. "To experiencing our first kiss by . . ." He glanced at the clock. "Nine P.M. On your mark, get set—"

"No." Sarah practically dropped her bike. "Get down," she whispered, eyes fixed on the window beside the tree.

"Crying uncle already?"

She leaned close, pressing a finger to his lips just as the doorbell rang. "I saw a shadow through the blinds. Someone was at the window," she whispered, pointing.

Jay eased his bike to the floor behind the tree. He pushed the castle back there too and moved the tools aside. Sarah unplugged the tree lights and followed him toward the hall. Someone lifted the knocker and rapped it three times.

"Hello," a jolly voice called.

"Who'd be visiting at this hour on Christmas Eve?" Sarah whispered. "Especially when no one is supposed to be here?"

Jay shrugged. "Everyone might not know they're out of town. Maybe it's someone from their church. Haven't you noticed it's a thing with Mormons? They seem to believe in bringing casseroles and banana bread to everyone, kind of like the Wise Men bringing gifts. They'll probably leave it on the porch."

The doorbell rang again.

"Or not." *Kirk said we'd be safe here, but . . .*

Jay stepped into a bedroom, tugging Sarah behind him. He shut the door and locked it. "We can hang out here until they leave."

"Jay?" She felt for him in the dark then wrapped her arms around him, fingers tickling the back of his neck, causing his heart to race. With one hand he traced her jawline. She tilted her face up to his.

He squinted in the darkness, trying to read her expression.

The knocker sounded a second time.

"Go away, we're busy," Jay growled.

Sarah giggled, then they both froze at the sound of a key turning in the lock and the front door opening. She tensed in Jay's arms, and his heart began racing for an entirely different reason.

"The police?" she whispered.

Or worse. "I don't know." He pried Sarah's fingers away and turned in a slow circle, looking for a place to hide her. "In there." He eased the closet doors open and tried to clear a space inside—an impossibility, he realized after only a few seconds. The closet was jammed full of number-ten cans. "What is it with these people?"

Voices came from the living room, and he could hear at least two pairs of feet walking around on the squeaky floor.

"Over here," Sarah whispered.

Jay squinted through the dark and saw Sarah slide the window open. When the screen wouldn't budge, she took a pen from the nightstand and punctured it. He hurried forward to help her rip the hole wide enough for each of them to crawl through.

Sarah climbed up, and he helped her squeeze through the window. Jay followed, then reached inside, sliding the glass closed behind them. He took Sarah's hand and they ran toward the front yard, stopping short at the sound of voices coming from the front of the garage.

They shrank back into the closest bushes. Jay looked at the footprints they'd left in the snow and knew anyone who walked this way would notice too. But there was no time to do anything about it. A man and a woman had rounded the corner of the house and were headed straight for them.

"I know I saw a light inside," the woman said.

"Probably a timer," the man said. "I told you they were still out of town. They asked us to keep bringing in the mail through next week." He stopped in front of the motor home parked in the side yard. "Now let's see about the key."

Jay watched as the man reached under the step. A second later he held up a key and inserted it into the lock. Both he and the woman went inside.

Good thing we didn't hide in there. Jay was tempted to try to sneak out of the yard, but he worried the man or woman might see him and Sarah from the front windshield—literally feet from their hiding spot.

A few minutes passed and the couple came out of the RV. Each wheeled a kid's bike in front, which they took out to the street, presumably to put in their car. They both returned to the motor home again, this time carrying out several large packages. The man balanced his pile against the door while he locked it and replaced the key in its hiding place. He followed his wife to their van parked on the street.

Jay felt his tension release as he heard them drive off.

"Neighbors," he said, turning to Sarah. "Hiding their Christmas presents." He tried to chuckle, but his throat was too dry.

Sarah was crouched beside him, one knee on the ground, the other leg up, poised to spring. A pointy stick was clutched in her fist.

"Nice weapon." He stood, then reached down to help her.

"Jab their eyes out. Immediate results." Both her voice and hands shook.

"I'll remember that." He recalled how well she'd defended herself against her attackers in the alley and at the car today. She wasn't strong, but screaming her head off, throwing gravel, and spraying pepper spray had worked pretty well. Not to mention, she *did* know how to handle a gun. Noticing she still held the stick in a death grip, he said, "That violent streak of yours is rearing its head again."

"Survivor's instinct is more like it." She opened her fist, and the stick fell to the ground. He helped her through the window. She sat on the bed, watching as he climbed through behind her.

"I'd say your instincts are pretty good," Jay said.

"I had a good coach."

"Your dad?" Jay closed the window and sat beside her. He'd have to let Kirk know the screen needed to be replaced before the honeymooners returned. "Have you ever wondered why?"

She looked at him, the moonlight casting shadows across her worried face.

"Just recently."

Chapter Fifty-Three

The grandfather clock chimed as Jay wedged Spiderman handle grips onto the bike. His eyes locked with Sarah's as they listened to nine peals.

"I don't suppose you're still in the mood to . . ."

Her face, much calmer than it had been half an hour earlier, was puzzled. "You mean it goes away for you?"

Jay laughed and grabbed for her, but she jumped up, moving out of his reach. They stood facing each other in front of the Christmas tree.

"As a matter of fact, no," Jay said. "The feeling of wanting you does not go away for me. It keeps intensifying."

A smile of relief lit her face. "Me too. I'm glad I'm normal."

"Want to find out just how normal?" he asked.

She licked her lips then looked at both the clock and the remaining bike parts strewn across the floor. "What about the bikes, Santa?"

"Let the elves finish." Walking to the media cabinet, Jay searched through the CDs until he found one of Christmas classics. He put it in and turned the volume down low. Returning to the tree, he beckoned her closer with the crook of his finger. She stepped into his embrace.

"I'm about to kiss you for the first time, and you're not blushing," he whispered.

She met his gaze. "I'm not embarrassed, just impatient."

Taking her face in his hands, he tilted his head and bent to kiss her. Her eyes were wide open, looking into his. A millimeter away, he paused. "You're not supposed to look, you know."

"Why can't I watch the best moment of my life?"

He had no answer except to crush his lips against hers in a kiss that felt nothing like the first light touch he'd imagined.

She didn't seem to mind. Her hands tightened around his neck, pulling him closer while the Carpenters crooned in the background.

At last they broke apart, Sarah's eyes swimming with tears, Jay sucking in a big lungful of air.

"Wow, that was—" he began, then stopped, noticing her expression. "You're crying?"

"Happy," she managed, freeing one hand to wipe at her eyes. "Twenty-four years is a long time to wait for a first kiss." She smiled through her tears. "But oh, was that worth it. That was the best gift I've ever had. Merry Christmas, Jay."

* * *

Sarah snuggled closer to Jay as they leaned against the sofa on the floor beside the Christmas tree. Their first kiss had been followed by half a dozen more already. It was tempting to add to that number, but she also relished the simple joy of being beside Jay, looking up at the lights twinkling overhead. In the background "The Christmas Song" played softly. For the first time, she felt the magic of the season, the spellbinding miracle of being in love and loved in return. She wished they could stay like this forever.

Jay turned to face her, propping an elbow on the sofa cushion. "Want your Christmas present early?"

"Present?" She sat up quickly, dismay rushing in to drown out the warmth in her heart. "I can't give you yours yet."

"You haven't already?" he teased.

"I thought the kiss was *your* gift for *me*," she said. "I wrote a song for you. But with the neighbors out and about, I don't dare play it."

"You wrote a song for *me?*" he asked, sounding awed. "No one's ever done anything like that. It must have taken a lot of time."

"It helped me not miss you so much these past few weeks."

"You wrote it while you weren't speaking to me?" Jay asked.

"I finished it then. I couldn't stand to think that our friendship was over. Doing something for you helped me while I was sorting things out."

"Friendship, huh?" He sat up, facing her, and reached into his pocket, pulling out a small, brown envelope. "For the record, I don't kiss friends the way I just kissed you. I'd like to think we're a little more—serious." He placed the envelope in her hand. "This used to be in a nice, white box, but I left it upstairs the night Kirk fixed my shoulder. Jeffrey got a hold of it yesterday. He thought it looked like a sugar cube, so he tried to feed it to his horse."

"What horse?" Sarah asked.

"James," Jay said, grinning. "I was just happy Christa caught them before Jeffrey made him chew and swallow the whole thing."

Sarah laughed as she pulled back the flap and took out a pearl ring set in a silver band. She held it up beside a light on the tree, turning it slowly. "Oh, Jay. It's beautiful."

She pulled her gaze from the ring to his face, which was taut with uncertainty. "You're so thoughtful. I've never had a ring—or any jewelry." She ran her finger over the polished stone.

"I got it at the antique store where I bought your music. I wasn't intending to get a ring that day, but I saw it, and I imagined it on your finger." He paused. "Imagined us . . ."

Imagined us what? Sarah felt half-dazed, half-agitated, like she did when realizing she'd just missed a joke in the lunch conversation.

Jay was still talking, his words rushed together as if he were afraid he wouldn't be able to get them all out. "Then, when you told me about your mother, I *knew*. So many of my ancestors have this great story of some fateful meeting with the person they were destined to be with. And I never really believed it, but then at the restaurant that night—" He stopped abruptly.

Her fist closed over the ring, and she held it close to her heart as she looked at him. His brow was furrowed with worry. He reached for her left hand, taking it in his.

"You're like that pearl, Sarah, exquisite and rare, emerging from the shell you've been trapped in your whole life." Jay paused, swallowing. "I was hoping you would do me the honor of wearing the ring and—of someday being my wife."

"You want to marry me?" She felt her mouth hang open on the last syllable and forced it shut. Never in a million years would she have guessed he would ask her such a thing tonight.

He nodded. "I know it probably seems too fast, too soon, but I love you, Sarah. I want us to spend the rest of our lives together."

And if one of those lives is cut short? Sarah opened her fist and looked down at the ring resting on her palm as she grappled with her conflicting feelings. She felt overwhelmed—ecstatic. She'd never imagined *anyone* would want to marry her. And to have Jay—whom she loved with her whole heart . . .

"I love you, Jay." She voiced the emotions she'd felt for weeks but had been too afraid to examine or express. "I'm *in* love with you, but—"

"A convicted felon isn't what you had in mind?" She heard his doubt and hurt.

"*No.*" She brought his hand to her face and held it there. "This has nothing to do with your past and everything to do with right now." She read the uncertainty in his expression just as she had that night at the restaurant when he'd laid bare his soul, his feelings exposed for her to stomp on or cherish. Seeing this side of him, this vulnerability hovering beneath the surface of the confident man, Sarah's heart melted. *How many other things don't I know about you, don't* you *know about* me? *A ton,* she imagined. They'd covered a lot of territory in the past few months, but there was a lot more to cross. More than anything she wanted to be around to do that, to be with him.

"How can we even think about getting married when our lives are so upside down? When we don't even know if I'll be around to meet you at the altar."

"Don't talk like that," Jay said, the confident man back in place. "We're going to figure out what your dad and cousin are up to. It's all going to work out."

"It isn't just my dad and Carl that I'm worried about," Sarah said.

"What then?"

She looked down at her lap. "This morning—those men—they weren't working for my father. When I suggested as much, the one with the UZI laughed. He also told me that if it were up to him, he would have taken care of me right there." She shuddered, thinking of the scratches on his face and the bullet wound in his hand. "If I run into him again, I have no doubt he'll do just that."

Jay's worried look returned. "Why didn't you tell Kirk this?"

Sarah shrugged. "I don't know. He was so busy telling *us* things, and my brain was befuddled from being so close to you." She tilted her head, looking up at him with a half smile.

"You're befuddled now." Jay's free hand tousled her curls. "*Nothing* is going to happen to you. Tomorrow we'll be in protective custody. That's big time. And Kirk knows what he's doing. He's not your average small-town deputy."

"Nor are you the average guy," Sarah said.

"Nor you the average girl." His eyes followed hers, staring at the hand holding the ring.

"I'm scared," Sarah admitted, a catch in her voice. "I'm afraid if I say yes—and I *want* to—something else will happen. We went to the Yale game, and Mrs. Larson died in the fire. I convinced Trish and Archer to help me bail you out, and Archer was shot. I stayed with Kirk and Christa, and James was almost kidnapped. What's going to happen if I agree to marry you?"

"We're both going to be incredibly happy, that's what," Jay said. "We're not talking about cause and effect here. No matter what we do next, the bad guys are still going to be bad—until they're caught and brought to justice. And we're going to help with that."

"I don't know," Sarah said. "We're both lucky to still be alive, but how much longer can that luck hold out?"

"It wasn't luck that brought us together. It was fate." Jay pulled her hands from her face to his and leaned forward, his lips brushing her knuckles. "Destiny, Sarah Morgan. I'm sure of it. But"—he sighed—"if you're not, we'll wait. I don't want to force you into anything you don't want. Heaven knows you've had enough of that your whole life."

"I *know* what I want," she said adamantly. "I want you, and I want to know we'll both be safe—that I'm not going to lose one more person I love, that I'm not going to cause you any more pain."

"I'll give you anything you want, Sarah. I'd get the moon and stars for you if I thought it were possible."

"I don't need the moon and stars," Sarah said. "Just you. Safe."

"I'm right here."

She studied the ring in her palm—a *different* ring, *unusual,* like everything about their relationship. *Everything.* Could that include an engagement that involved police warrants, hiding out, protective custody, and the DEA? *If it involves Jay, what else matters?*

Sarah took a deep breath and expelled it, letting go of as much of her fear as she could. Her mouth bloomed in a smile as she held the ring out to Jay. "Will you put it on for me?"

"Is that a yes?"

Her eyes sparkled then filled with tears. She nodded and tried to speak, but the lump in her throat reduced her voice to a mere whisper. "Yes, Jay. I'll marry you. I don't know when—" She tried to laugh, but instead the tears started spilling down her face. "Or where or how, but I'll do my best to be around to keep my promise."

"I'll hold you to that." He took her left hand and slipped the ring on her finger. "We'll wait until this is all over. You'll have a beautiful gown, and we'll get married in an ivy-covered church with bells pealing. You'll get to walk down the aisle on your father's—" Jay stopped abruptly. "I'm sorry. I didn't mean—"

"It's okay." She placed her finger over his lips. "I don't need all that, don't even want it really. I *am* different, and I never imagined that I'd get married." She tilted her head, smiling at him. "But now that we are, I think

I'd like our wedding to be outside. We could stand beneath a canopy of stars on a beach looking out to the ocean." A wistful, faraway look came to her eyes. "Endless possibilities in every direction."

"Then we'll wait for your ocean and stars," Jay said. "I love you, Sarah."

"I know." She leaned forward, reaching out to him first, kissing him beneath the twinkling lights of the Christmas tree.

Chapter Fifty-Four

Detective Brandt unwrapped another chocolate Santa and stuffed it in his mouth. He let it melt, enjoying the flavor as long as possible—it was the sixth and last one in the pack. Resting his hands on top of his protruding stomach, he leaned back in his chair and thought about Christmas dinner at his parents' house. His mom would fix a turkey and a ham, potatoes, gravy, rolls . . . and her pies. *Oh, her pies.* The chocolate was all but forgotten as his mouth watered in anticipation of the first bite of his mother's pecan tart. In less than an hour he'd be out of here and on his way.

The phone rang, jarring him from his pleasant vision of a table laden with food.

"Can't leave us alone for even one day." Grumbling, Brandt pulled himself out of his chair, went to the front counter, and reached for the central line, only to realize it was Detective Anderson's phone ringing off the hook. *Not my problem. Not gonna answer it,* he thought, returning to his desk to toss the empty candy package in the trash.

The phone stopped ringing. Brandt sat down and took out a crossword puzzle.

Anderson's phone rang again. Swearing under his breath, Brandt swiveled his chair around and used his feet to roll himself over to his colleague's desk. He snagged the receiver on the fourth ring. "Summerfield Police Department."

"Detective Anderson, please."

"He won't be in until noon," Brandt said, remembering how he'd been only too happy to swap shifts with Kirk, who wanted to be with his kids Christmas morning. "Would you like to leave a message?"

There was a pause, then, "Is there another number I can reach him at?"

"He's got a cell," Brandt offered.

"I've tried that already. He's not answering, and his home number isn't listed."

"Then you'll have to leave a message," Brandt suggested, irritated with the demanding voice on the other end. *It's Christmas, buddy,* he wanted to say. *Whatever has your knickers in a wad can wait a day or two.*

"With whom am I speaking?"

"Detective Brandt. Anderson's my partner most days."

Another pause. "It's imperative he get this message. Tell him his appointment is bumped up an hour. I'll be at the Hancock Building at three o'clock instead of four."

"Got it," Brandt said, hanging up before the guy could breathe down his neck anymore. Rolling his chair back to his desk, he remembered the tin of cookies that had been delivered yesterday. He went to the front counter, searching until he found it hidden behind a stack of traffic school forms.

Shoving a pretzel-shaped cookie in his mouth, Brandt scrawled the message across the top of a legal pad, realizing he hadn't even gotten the guy's name or a return phone number. He glanced at the caller ID, but it was an unlisted number.

Oh, well. I'm sure Anderson knows what it's about. He tore off the paper and set it down as the front bell jingled and Simmons came in, stamping snow off his shoes.

"Man, nobody got any time off today," Brandt said.

"I'm covering for Anderson," Simmons said. "Some family emergency came up. He promised to take my shift on New Year's Eve." He pulled the hat from his head, brushing snow from it. "It's really coming down out there."

"Great," Brandt grumbled. "I've got a two-hour drive." The image of his mom's pie was starting to fade. He had no doubt his brothers would be more than happy to take his share if he was late.

"Why don't you get out of here now?" Simmons suggested. "I'm a little early, and I think the chief's even coming in today. I'm sure we can handle the turkey that explodes or the fight that breaks out between Aunt Millie and Cousin Ed."

"Thanks." Brandt didn't need any more urging. Chief Morgan might be a little peeved when he came in, but with his daughter missing he'd been in a constant state of agitation anyway. Grabbing his coat from the back of his chair, Brandt held up a hand in farewell as he left.

Simmons peeled his coat off, poured a cup of stale coffee, and riffled through the cookie tin to see if there was anything good left. He picked up a ginger snap and bit into it, sprinkling crumbs across the counter. He brushed them away, noticing a piece of paper in the process. He glanced at the note in Brandt's handwriting.

Hancock bld. 3:00, not 4

"Must be for the boss," Simmons mused as he stuck the paper in Chief Morgan's inbox.

* * *

Kirk turned in a slow circle, taking in his wrecked living room. The Christmas tree was overturned, the bookshelves emptied, papers and toys everywhere. *Christa is going to freak out.* He bent down, picking up a large piece of glass from a broken lamp. Foolish, he knew, when he ought to call in a team to collect evidence for fingerprints. But he wasn't sure if that was a wise thing to do. Returning to the kitchen—the least damaged room, he'd discovered on his initial search—he poured himself a glass of milk from an unopened jug and sat down to think.

Christa and the boys were safe—for now—with his aunt in Worcester.

Jay and Sarah were on their way to meet DEA agent Judd Doyle, and then they would be safe.

But someone had come here for them, and that someone was likely associated with Chief Morgan. And if he knew . . . Kirk sighed, wondering if he'd already worked his last day for the Summerfield Police Department. *For* any *police department.* He was going to have to be very careful. But, as he'd told Jay and Sarah, there was no turning back now. A lot more than his career was at stake. The only thing to do was see this through.

Kirk got up and opened the cabinet beneath the sink. He pulled a pair of disposable gloves from a box by the dish drainer and took a plastic grocery bag from the recycle bin. He'd be his own evidence team. He'd send whatever he collected to Doyle. If the Summerfield police chief was corrupt, who was to say the chief in Cambridge wasn't as well?

Starting in the bedroom Kirk cataloged everything he could think of that was missing, though surprisingly, it wasn't much. He'd had the foresight to take his laptop and guns with him last night, and Jay and Sarah hadn't left any evidence of their stay downstairs. It seemed the intruders' motive had been to threaten instead of steal.

Kirk worked his way to the living room, filling the bag with broken things that had obviously been handled. Satisfied that he had about as much as he was going to get, he picked up the bag and turned to go out the front door.

As he touched the knob he paused, thinking something else was amiss. Turning back, he looked at the wall over the couch. A chill swept over him as he took in the collage of pictures.

The middle one of his family was gone.

Chapter Fifty-Five

Jay parked Kirk and Christa's Jetta in front of a convenience store with a pay phone—the first they'd been able to find after driving around the city for close to an hour. He looked over at Sarah. "Kirk will shoot us himself if he finds out about this."

"*You* understand why I have to at least talk to Trish," Sarah said. "She's the only girlfriend I've ever had. She encouraged me to go out with you, helped me get you out of jail, and now *she* needs a friend." *And she's hurting because of me.*

"She would understand if you didn't call," Jay said.

"I have to try," Sarah insisted. "Because there won't be any more chances after we're in protective custody." She leaned close and gave him a quick kiss on the cheek. "I'll just be outside for a few minutes, and I look nothing like that awful picture they keep showing on the news, so don't worry." She opened the door.

Jay grabbed her hand. "Be careful."

"I will. I'll be right over there." She inclined her head toward the phone a few feet away, then got out of the car and walked to it. Shivering, she stared at the grimy receiver for several seconds before gathering the courage to pick it up and dial the number from the address book on Jay's cell phone, which they hadn't dared use.

Trish answered right away. Sarah suddenly found herself at a loss for words.

"How are you?" she asked. "How is Archer? We've been so worried."

"Sarah? Where are you?" Trish asked. "If you're with Jay, you've got to get away from him. You've got to go to the police."

"That's the *last* place I can go."

"Please," Trish insisted. "I'm worried for you."

"Don't be. I'm fine. And—"

"You're with a dangerous addict," Trish said. "Jay's not the person we all thought he was. Who knows what he'll do. Tell me where you are, and I'll call the police."

"No," Sarah said forcefully. "You're wrong about him. Jay didn't shoot Archer. He was with me that night. Someone attacked us, and *he* was shot. We're in the city on our way to meet with a DEA agent who's going to help us."

"I know what I saw," Trish said. "Get out of there. Please," she begged.

Sarah turned, half facing Jay, who was waiting in the car. She could read the anxiety on what little of his face—most was covered by a scarf and hat—she could see. "And I know Jay," she said. "You're wrong, Trish. We'll prove it. We'll find out who really hurt Archer." Trusting her heart once more, Sarah hung up the phone and returned to the car.

* * *

Jay and Sarah looked up as they approached the Hancock Tower, a 790-foot architectural wonder. Behind them, Trinity Church reflected in the mirrored glass. Sarah stared at the image longingly, wishing they were headed that direction instead. What little peace she'd felt had been shattered since her phone call to Trish an hour earlier.

If Trish really believed it was Jay who shot Archer, and she testified in court, there was no way Jay wouldn't be found guilty, with both evidence—his prints had been matched to those on the discarded weapon—and testimony against him. Sarah hoped Kirk's friend from the DEA would work on clearing Jay's name as well as keeping them safe.

They stopped at the front of the building and gained entrance with the access card Kirk had given them this afternoon. He'd slipped away from his aunt's Christmas party in Worcester last night long enough to meet with his friend and get detailed instructions and the codes to get into the building.

Walking through the spacious and strangely empty lobby, Jay and Sarah headed for the elevators. While waiting, Sarah glanced at the pots overflowing with poinsettias and the lavish Christmas garlands strung everywhere. Feeling a swell of sadness in her throat, she swallowed, trying not to think of her father alone today, the piano in their home silent, the space beneath the tree bare. *Did he get a tree? Will he be at home next year, or will he be in jail? Could he really be involved in something so awful?*

Jay looked at her with concern, but she pasted a brave smile on her face and stepped onto the elevator. A minute later they stepped off on the fourth floor, heading to an office used occasionally by the area's DEA Mobile Enforcement Teams.

Sarah felt herself becoming numb as they walked down the hall. She knew that what she said to Detective Doyle today might someday lead to her testifying against her father in court. She wasn't sure she could do that—wasn't sure she could do *this*.

They stopped in front of suite 411, but it was locked, a note taped to the door. Jay opened it and read aloud.

"Change of plans. Please go to the 60th floor. Suite 6017. D. Doyle."

Jay shrugged. "At least we'll get to enjoy the view."

"Sure," Sarah said, certain there was no part of this she'd enjoy. As magical as Christmas Eve had been, today felt nothing like Christmas. She and Jay had eaten cold cereal in a stranger's kitchen. They'd watched television and tried to talk about wedding plans, but it was evident that both their minds were on today's meeting and what would follow.

Sarah grabbed Jay's arm as they stepped off the elevator a second time. "I feel queasy." She lifted a hand to her head while the room spun.

Jay put his arm around her. "Make sure you don't look outside then." He waited a minute, giving her time to regain her equilibrium before they started toward suite 6017. This time the door was ajar and they walked right in. Jay helped Sarah to a chair then went to stand at the floor-to-ceiling windows.

"Wow." He gave a low whistle. "Who would've guessed the DEA had such nice digs? No wonder taxes are so high."

Still feeling ill, Sarah lifted her head, taking in the rich, wood walls, the plush carpet, and expensive furniture.

"I've always wanted to come here," Jay said. "I think there's an observation deck on this floor, too. But it's been closed to the public since September 11th. Too bad it takes having a meeting with a DEA agent to get in."

"I don't suppose he'll give us the tour when we're finished," Sarah said. She still couldn't quite believe he was meeting with them at all. This thing with her dad had to be pretty serious—*pretty bad*—for the agent to want to meet on Christmas day.

Jay left the windows and sat beside her. He took her hand in his, looking down at their intertwined fingers. She followed his gaze to the pearl ring. It shone in the light from the window behind them. Remembering the magic of last night, she couldn't help but smile. She bent her head close to his.

"I feel so weird about this," she confessed. "Part of me is deliriously happy, but—"

"The part that has to do with that ring, right?" Jay asked.

She nodded and squeezed his hand reassuringly. "Yes. But how can I feel so happy when, any minute now, I'm probably going to find out my dad has been a drug trafficker for years—and that he used me to do his dirty work?"

"You don't know anything for sure yet," Jay reminded her. "There may be a really good explanation."

"Maybe," she said, doubtful.

"Be happy," he whispered as the door at the end of the room opened. "Grab onto it, and don't let go." He stood, pulling Sarah up behind him.

"Detective Doyle?" Jay asked the older, bearded man approaching them.

Sarah felt her uneasiness return. What she was going to tell him, and what he might tell her, had the potential to change her life irrevocably.

"Thank you for coming," he said, pumping Jay's hand up and down. He turned to Sarah. "Miss Morgan."

His steel-gray eyes sent an involuntary shiver down her spine. *He's the good guy,* she reminded herself. *There's nothing to worry about if I tell the truth.*

"Won't you come into the office?" He held his hand out, indicating the room he'd just come from.

Jay and Sarah preceded him into the simple but well-appointed suite. They sat in the two chairs opposite the desk as he shut the door behind them.

He pulled out a tape recorder. "You don't mind, do you?" he asked, showing it to Sarah.

"Of course not." She slipped her hands under her legs.

He turned the recorder on and set it at the edge of the desk. "I heard from Detective—" He hesitated, shuffling through the papers in front of him.

"Anderson," Sarah supplied.

"Yes. Thanks. Detective Anderson tells me you have information you'd like to share."

I thought you had some questions you wanted to ask. And why didn't you remember Kirk's last name? I thought he said you were friends. "Yes." She glanced at Jay, who was looking as uncomfortable as she was starting to feel. "We're hoping you can help us."

"That's what I'm here for." Elbows on the desk, he laced his fingers together, waiting.

Not going to make this easy, are you? Sarah thought. She'd hoped that working with the DEA would be like working with Kirk. But already she could tell her hope had been in vain. Something about Detective Doyle set her immediately on edge. And it wasn't just that he came off as cold and unfeeling. She wasn't going to get any sympathy for having been duped by her father. In fact, if Kirk's suspicions proved correct, she'd probably be lucky to keep herself out of jail. But still, Detective Doyle represented the law. He shouldn't seem so . . . scary.

"My father is Grant Morgan, the chief of police for Summerfield."

"How long?" Detective Doyle asked.

"We've been in Summerfield as long as I can remember," Sarah said. "We moved there when I was five—shortly after my mother's death. Though he hasn't always been chief."

"Your mother died?"

"When I was five," Sarah repeated. Jay scooted his chair closer and draped his arm across the back of Sarah's chair in a supportive gesture. "She committed suicide."

"That's too bad," the detective said without a trace of emotion in his voice.

Sarah liked him less by the minute. She decided to plunge ahead and tell him everything as fast as she could so they could get out of here and get to wherever they were being sent.

"My mother overdosed, and since then my father has always been fanatical about fighting the war against drugs. Two years ago, he insisted I join him. Nearly every week since then I've been involved in the Summerfield undercover drug task force."

"So that's what he told you." A slight smile curved Detective Doyle's lips but vanished quickly. "Except that there is *no* drug task force. Both Summerfield and Cambridge have always seemed content to let the drug problems slide."

"My father has *never* been content," Sarah said. "He's worked his whole life to get drugs off the street. He's never been satisfied ignoring the problem or busting little dealers."

"Perhaps he should have been." Detective Doyle leaned back in his chair, drumming his fingers on the table as he studied Sarah. "What else do you know?"

"That's all," she said, meeting his gaze. She pulled her hands out from beneath her legs, wrapping her arms around her middle, feeling like she had when she stepped off the elevator—sick and cold all at the same time. *Maybe I'm catching the flu Jeffrey had.*

"Sarah's father has always been very controlling," Jay said. "And very paranoid about her safety. She's even had a bodyguard."

"Really?" Detective Doyle's eyebrows rose. "Tell me about that, Sarah."

"He's my cousin." The room was starting to spin. *Something isn't right.* She told herself that it was informing on her father that had her feeling so awful, *so uneasy. So frightened.*

"Did he go with you on these undercover raids, these busts at the park?"

She nodded. *When did I tell him about the park?*

I didn't. Those eyes . . . Recognition hit with startling force. *He knows because he was* there. The beard was new, but she'd never forget those eyes. Sarah felt the blood draining from her face.

A sharp pain in her stomach was followed by a sudden burning in her esophagus. She stood quickly, tipping the chair backward. "Jay—I'm going to be sick—" Covering her face with her hand she ran from the room.

Jay stood and started after her.

Detective Doyle pulled a gun from the desk drawer and pointed it at Jay. "Sit down, Mr. Kendrich."

Chapter Fifty-Six

Sarah tore down the hall, hand over her mouth as she looked for a restroom. The first one she spotted was men's, but she didn't care. She ran inside, hovering over the sink not a second too soon.

Her stomach heaved as she lost her breakfast, lunch, and what felt like everything she'd eaten in the past week.

Finished at last, she dragged herself to the next sink, turned on the faucet, and rinsed out her mouth.

Stay calm, she told herself, though alarm bells rang in her head. Detective Doyle was the man she'd bought from in the park the night Eddie Martin's man didn't show up—the night her father became so angry, and later worried.

Was it because Dad really was doing something illegal and guessed I'd bought from a DEA agent? She couldn't convince herself that was the truth. Detective Doyle had scared her that night, and he made her uneasy now.

Sarah sagged against the sink, feeling worse by the minute. No matter how important this meeting was, it was going to have to wait. She needed to go somewhere to lie down, and she needed to do it quick—before she passed out. Lifting her head, she checked in the mirror to make sure her face was clean. Her mouth opened, and she stifled a scream, staring in horror at a pair of legs sticking out from beneath a stall, blood pooling around them.

* * *

"Up there," the detective—or whoever he was—ordered, gun thrust in Jay's back.

Jay climbed the concrete stairs as slowly as he dared. When he reached the rooftop, he stepped outside, eyes scanning each direction for any sign of Sarah.

Did she realize something was wrong? Did she go for help? He listened, waiting for the door to shut behind them. When it didn't, he risked turning a little to see why.

His captor had propped it open, the rubber stopper keeping the door ajar, a sure invitation for someone to come up here. *For Sarah to come up.*

Following his gaze, the man confirmed Jay's worry. "Now she'll know right where to find us. Especially with the nice clues I left along the way."

"She won't come," Jay said. "She's long gone by now."

"We'll see." The man held up a blood-soaked washcloth. He squeezed it, sending bright red drops to the pavement. "If I were a betting man—which I am"—he grinned—"I'd say you're wrong. She's more like her father than she realizes, and she'll want to do the right thing."

Jay didn't bother responding, but instead spent his energies scanning the area for possible escape routes. It was windy on top of the building, and with a sinking heart, he saw that the guard rails were nothing more than two bars of metal running horizontally around the roof. It wouldn't take much to push someone over the edge.

Carl doesn't fight fair. He remembered Sarah's warning. It clearly applied to a few others besides her cousin. Not much was fair when you had the barrel of a gun inches from your heart.

"So, you, uh, obviously don't work for the DEA," Jay ventured, deciding conversation was perhaps his only chance of distracting the man.

"Not now I don't. Maybe someday."

"You don't think this kind of thing will be a problem on your résumé?"

"Anything that's a problem, I take care of. Like you," the man said. "Walk over there. All the way to the far side."

Jay did as he was told. He looked around as he walked, unable, even in such dire circumstances, to ignore the view. The sun was low in the sky, casting an orange haze over the city. A few boats bobbed on the Charles River, and the red seats of Fenway Park glistened in the distance. Sixty stories below, all across the city, people were celebrating Christmas, the season of brotherhood.

Jay stopped about five feet from the edge. "I'm afraid of heights." *Actually, right now, that's true.*

His abductor chuckled. "Then maybe I'll have to shoot you first, to make it a believable lover's spat. You think about it though. Personally, I'd rather jump. At least you get a thrill before you go."

* * *

Sarah wrapped her fingers around the top of the bathroom stall, germs the farthest thing from her mind. Stepping up onto the toilet, she peered over the divider into the unmoving eyes of the man lying prone on the floor. His face was frozen in shock, and his suit coat lay partially open, revealing a red stain on the front of his shirt. Another stain, lower, seemed to be the source of the blood near his legs.

Sarah let go of her death grip on the wall and dropped her foot down to the floor. Feeling faint again, she sat on the edge of the toilet, careful to keep her feet away from the blood that was seeping closer.

Who are you? She squeezed her eyes shut, wishing all of this away, wondering how she'd gone from getting engaged to sitting in a bathroom stall next to a dead man in less than twenty-four hours. *What if he's* not *dead?* The thought terrified her even more, because she knew she had to find out.

Taking a deep breath of the stale, copper air, she pushed open the door to his stall. Her fingers shook and bile rose in her throat as she stepped around his legs, reaching down to check for a pulse. His skin was cold, already starting to stiffen. She pressed her fingers against his wrist, waiting, praying.

Nothing.

She stood up and backed away, hands clasped to control her shaking. *What do I do? What—*

A lanyard around his neck caught her eye. It slid off to the side of his chest, disappearing beneath his lapel. Shaking even more violently than before, she leaned forward, reached out, and flipped the lanyard to the center of his body so she could read the attached identification.

Drug Enforcement Administration
Worcester Mobile Task Force
Judd Doyle

Chapter Fifty-Seven

Jay was tired of standing but didn't dare sit down or complain. A quick glance at his watch told him they'd been on the roof for almost fifteen minutes. During that time the sun had dipped below the horizon so that it was almost dark. The wind had picked up. Jay was starting to feel uncomfortable in more ways than one. Thanks to Christa and her scissors, his ears were exposed and freezing. His fingers were numbing as well, but he didn't risk putting them in his pockets; he needed his hands free. Every fraction of a second would count in defending himself. He had to do something soon—before the guy decided he'd waited long enough and carried through with his threat to shoot.

Except that Sarah wasn't here. Jay had extracted enough monosyllables from the guy to understand that she was the bigger concern, while he was an unfortunate bystander, the bait. Sarah was the one with the information—information that couldn't leave this building.

Unless it already had. *Please let her be gone.* Jay uttered the same prayer over and over.

"All right. I've wasted enough time." The man leveled the gun at Jay's heart. "What's it going to be? A tragic fall, or did your girlfriend kill you?"

"Be a bit difficult to pull that one off, since she isn't here," Jay said. Beneath his jacket, his heart thumped wildly. *I'm going to have to rush him. It's the only chance I've got.*

"She's hiding somewhere. My partner and I will find her. Now jump or take the bullet."

Jay raised his hands in the air. "I think I'll reconsider my position on heights."

"Wise choice," the man nodded. "Less messy for me."

"Glad to help." Jay glanced over his shoulder as he stepped backward, judging how much farther until he reached the rail.

"Hurry up." The gunman followed him closely, the Beretta never wavering from Jay's heart.

Grab the rail. Raise my leg to climb up. Kick him instead . . . Lame plan. Think of something else—quick.

He did. He thought of Sarah, alone and hunted down. If she were the one standing by the rail, he'd already be in motion. He couldn't wait any longer, could *not* leave her by herself. He turned, grabbed the rail, bent over, and raised his leg.

A gunshot echoed across the rooftop.

"Jay!" Sarah's voice pierced the air. *No, Sarah*. His foot came up as he looked over his shoulder, kicking as hard as he could, feeling contact. Pushing off from the rail, he whirled around, fist already in motion. It caught air.

The gunman pitched to the side, surprise on his face as he fell. Jay dove on top of him, jerking the gun from his hand, flinging it across the roof. He raised his fist, pummeling it into the side of the guy's face again and again.

"Jay. Stop. I think he's—dead." Sarah touched his shoulder. "We've got to get out of here. There's another man inside. I sent an elevator down empty, and I think he believes I'm on it, but that won't buy us much time."

Jay froze mid-punch, realizing that the guy wasn't fighting back, wasn't even moving. Jay climbed off, staring in shock at the blood starting to ooze through the fabric of the man's shirt.

Jay looked over at Sarah and saw the gun gripped in her hand. She was pale and shaking all over. He wrapped his arm around her and pulled her away from the body.

"You saved my life." Awed, he looked into her eyes. "You can't remember how to use the brakes on a ten-speed, but you can shoot with accuracy from across a roof, fifty feet away?"

Tears slid down her face. "My father taught me how to shoot to kill."

Chapter Fifty-Eight

Sarah met Jay outside of the women's restroom in Boston's South Station. They'd separated for a few minutes so she could attempt to clean herself up and so Jay could purchase tickets to somewhere—far away preferably. "Where are we going?"

"We're not," he said. "Police are all over the place. Probably because of holiday travel, but still . . . We get on a train, we're stuck. I bought two tickets to D.C. at the machine, but we aren't going to use them."

"Oh." Sarah lengthened her stride, trying to keep up with Jay's brisk pace. What she really wanted to do was lie down—on the nearest bench, the floor—anywhere. "The car again?" He nodded. "If we're lucky, they'll track that purchase and think we have something big and important to tell someone in Washington. In the meantime, Kirk's Jetta has almost a full tank. That will get us across the state line and then some. We'll figure out what to do from there."

Sarah shivered as they stepped outside the station. The wind blew hard against them, raining wet snow across her line of vision.

"Keep your head down and walk fast," Jay said. "Stay behind me. I'll act as a shield."

She pulled the jacket tighter and lowered her head as they crossed the street, grateful the blinding snow gave her a real excuse to do so.

By the time they made it to the car, her toes were frozen and her body was shaking with chills. Jay hurried to the driver's side, clicking open the automatic locks. He had the engine started before she was inside. He cranked on the defrost and grabbed the scraper.

"See if there's any kind of map in the glove box, will you?" he asked as he got out.

With difficulty she used her numb fingers to pop the latch while he scraped the windows. The box yielded nothing except an owner's manual and a couple of gas receipts.

"No luck," she said when Jay was seated again.

"Thanks for trying." He hit the automatic locks and backed the car out. "Where do you want to go?"

"I don't know. Connecticut was nice," she said, remembering the Yale game that seemed about a hundred years ago. She sat on her hands while they drove, willing the heater to warm up faster.

"That's the same direction as Washington. I'd rather go north, or west."

"West," Sarah said.

At a stoplight Jay dug through his pocket. He held out a somewhat smashed package of Fig Newtons. "I got these in the vending machine. It was the closest thing they had to a decent meal."

She took the flattened cookies. "Thanks. Did you get some too?"

Jay shook his head. "No. I'm too stressed to eat right now. You have them."

She would have protested, but it had been a long time since lunch, and she'd thrown that up, along with everything else she'd eaten in the last twenty-four hours. Her stomach ached with hunger, though she was more than a little leery of eating again. After ripping open the package, she nibbled the edge of a cookie.

"These wipers are terrible," Jay complained. He rolled down his window, reached out, and tried to catch one as it swished to the side. A clump of icy snow came off and stayed in a perfect diagonal across the windshield. "Great."

"Anything I can do?" Sarah asked.

"Yeah. Take my phone and call Kirk."

She tensed, the bite of cookie sticking in her throat. "Anything else?"

"No."

Sarah turned away, staring out the passenger window. Traffic was thinning now as they neared the interstate. She wasn't sure whether it was good or bad that there weren't a lot of cars. She wasn't sure running away, heading west, was the right thing to do.

She was pretty sure that right about now Jay was rethinking their engagement.

She leaned her head against the cool glass. The heater was finally working. She was starting to get warm. Too warm. *Maybe I have a fever. Maybe I have the flu.* Her eyelids felt heavy. But she didn't want to fall asleep with things as they were now. They'd been tense and stressed in the past hour and a half since fleeing the Hancock Building and the two dead bodies. She'd been frantic and demanding.

Before they'd left the roof, Jay had retrieved the tape recorder and his cell phone from the phony Detective Doyle. Jay wanted to call Kirk, tell him what had happened, and decide what to do next.

Now Sarah cringed, remembering her reaction, her hysteria and outright insistence that he *not* call Kirk or anyone else. After all, it was Kirk who'd sent them to the Hancock Building. Kirk who knew the detective who lay dead.

"That's exactly why we need to talk to him," Jay had argued. "Kirk didn't set us up. Someone found out about our meeting. Don't you think that same person is going to find out Kirk is helping us? Do you want Christa and the boys to be in danger?"

"No." Sarah had pushed the hair back from her face and struggled to see him through her tears. "But the man who found out is dead." She kept her gaze averted from his body. "Let's just go away somewhere—disappear."

"We can't," Jay had said. "Kirk's risked everything to help us, and we have to help him in return. You know that. What happened to the girl who risked her life for James yesterday?"

"She just killed someone." Sarah glanced over her shoulder once more as Jay led her away. "Don't call him," she'd begged. "If you love me at all, *do not* call him."

Jay hadn't called. And now Sarah still didn't give in. It was a critical time to be having their first fight—when they literally needed each other just to stay alive. But they'd made it out of the building and this far safely without calling Kirk. Why couldn't they make it even farther, somewhere so far away no one would ever bother them again?

Her gaze shifted down to the red stains on the knees of her jeans. She'd had to kneel on the bathroom floor to get the real Detective Doyle's gun free. She squeezed her eyes shut, trying to block out the gruesome images parading through her mind—the detective's eyes staring blankly, his cool skin . . . and then Jay against the railing, the pistol held firm in her hands as she took aim. The second she knew that aim was true . . .

Her stomach lurched, and she leaned forward, dry heaving.

I killed a man.

Chapter Fifty-Nine

The rest-stop sign seemed like a godsend to Jay. He concentrated on keeping his eyelids open, as well as the windshield clean, the last mile to the pull-off on I-90 West through New York. It was only one A.M.—ridiculous how tired he felt. He'd worked this late before, and he'd certainly stayed up later than this finishing papers or cramming for exams, but somehow driving in the storm, constantly checking the mirrors to see if anyone was following, had worn him out.

It didn't help matters that they hadn't dared to stop anywhere to eat all evening, and he was starving. Between hunger and sleep deprivation and arguing with and worrying about Sarah all afternoon, he had one heck of a tension headache. It burned behind his eyes, up over his scalp, and around to the muscles in the back of his neck.

Right about now he would have given his whole paycheck for a bottle of aspirin.

And a warm bed. A roof over our heads. A hamburger. A normal life again.

Instead, he tried to be grateful for getting off the road, for making it safely this far.

Sarah, at least, seemed to be sleeping peacefully now. Earlier she'd tossed and turned in her seat, making whimpering sounds every time he thought she was finally in a deep sleep.

Jay had wondered *which* nightmare she was having. The one where Carl nearly ran them down, the one where a man attacked her in a dark alley, or the one where she shot and killed a man who was trying to kill them. *And dozens of others I can't even imagine.* He felt bad he'd pressured her to let him call Kirk. Who could blame her for shutting down this afternoon?

The exit came into view, and he felt overwhelming relief. Slowing the Jetta to twenty-five, he drove down the off-ramp to the roadside rest stop—a tiny brick building, a historical marker about the Seneca Indians, a rectangle of grass and some trees. A parking lot—heaven.

Pulling into the stall farthest from the single light, Jay killed the engine, checked the door locks, and reclined his seat. Aside from a truck parked near the on-ramp, the rest stop was vacant. He hoped it would stay that way for a couple more hours, though tomorrow the roads would likely be heavy with holiday traffic.

A bit of sleep could only help him think through their dilemma with more clarity. That they were on the run from Sarah's father and some drug ring, both the Summerfield and Cambridge police departments, and now possibly the DEA, was a reality he couldn't quite process. That the gas tank was low, they needed to eat, and the car was quickly dropping to a temperature below freezing were the more immediate concerns.

Turning his head, Jay studied Sarah, curled in a ball on her side. It was difficult to reconcile the woman who'd wielded a semiautomatic this afternoon with the girl asleep beside him. With her halo of blond hair spread across the seat, he could only envision her as the angel he'd heard singing in church not so many weeks ago. And though he'd witnessed her kill a man, already he wondered if he'd imagined it. The Sarah he knew didn't shoot to kill. The Sarah he knew didn't shoot at all—or did she? He knew the loaded gun was still beneath her seat.

Sarah shivered in her sleep, instinctively tucking her arms closer to her body. Jay looked in back, hoping to find a blanket or something to cover her with. The only thing he found was an old newspaper on the floor of the car. He reached for it, then hesitated, thinking of Sarah's germ phobia. Being covered with newspaper would only add to her misery, but the jacket she'd brought this morning wasn't warm enough for spending the night in a car without heat.

Feeling helpless and frustrated and totally inadequate as a protector, Jay removed his own coat. This he placed carefully over Sarah, flipping the collar up over her neck and draping the sleeves down her back. He took the old paper, opened it wide, and laid it over him. He leaned back in his seat, eyes closed a second later. Sleep came almost at once.

* * *

Two hours, he'd told himself before drifting off. *Just let me rest for two hours and I'll be able to figure out what to do.* Now the dashboard clock read 5:27. "Shortest four and a half hours of my life," Jay muttered as he raised the seat and the newspaper slid to his lap. If anything he felt more tired than when he'd laid down a little after one. He doubted he would have woken up so soon if not for the fact that he was freezing.

Choosing to ignore the near-empty gas tank, Jay turned the key in the ignition. Cold air whooshed from the vents. He closed them, glancing at Sarah to see if she'd awakened, but it didn't appear she'd moved at all.

"Must be nice," he whispered, "to be able to sleep through all this."

Sarah didn't respond, and Jay returned his attention to rubbing his hands together briskly in front of the heater. He glanced at the gas needle, hovering slightly above the E. He knew he should start driving—using what little gas they had left to put as much distance between them and the dead man they'd left behind, but Jay couldn't force himself to move just yet. There really was no point in running until he knew where they were running to.

Leaning the seat back again, he looked up through the window at the stars overhead. Out here, away from the lights of the city, they were much clearer. *If Sarah were awake, she'd be thrilled with the view.*

The North Star shone brightly, and farther west Orion mocked him. A strong guy like that, with his sword raised, would certainly never get himself, and the girl he loved, in a situation like this. And if for some reason he did, he'd have a plan to get them out of it—even if it was through simple brute strength.

Some chivalrous hero I turned out to be, Jay thought. Old Humphrey would've had a plane waiting to whisk his true love to safety. *I can't even keep the car going much longer.* Jay closed his eyes, wishing all of it—the cold, his hunger, this situation, everything but Sarah—away.

He fell asleep again, this time waking at 6:03. The car was warm, the red warning light on the fuel gauge lit. He switched the ignition off as the faintest hint of dawn began coloring the sky. While he'd slept, an RV had pulled into the lot and parked next to them.

Would the DEA use a motor home? He shook off the sleep-deluded thought and sighed with relief when the door opened and an elderly couple emerged. Each held a poodle on a leash.

From the corner of his eye he watched as they walked the perimeter of the narrow lawn. The man held his arm out for the woman, who leaned on him for support.

Acute longing cut straight to Jay's heart. *I want to be that couple,* he thought. *I want to grow old with Sarah, have children, travel a little. But a simple life. Nothing spectacular, no complications. The kind where you appreciate each sunrise and sunset together.*

The elderly couple was doing just that. They stood at the edge of the lawn, enjoying the first rays of sunlight filtering through the leafless trees.

Jay watched, mesmerized with yearning. On the seat beside him, Sarah stirred. Her lips parted in a worrisome frown. The temperature in the car was already dropping.

Do something. I've got to do something.

The couple returned to their motor home. He thought of the heater they probably had going, the bed they'd slept on, the hot cereal they might eat for breakfast. *We could use a motor home right about now, but I can't even fill up the car . . .* He sat up so quickly the top of his short hair brushed the roof. RVs required a lot of gasoline. Maybe this couple would have a spare container. But if they left before he asked, he and Sarah might be stranded here for hours.

Taking care not to make any more noise than necessary, Jay unlocked his door and got out. The cold took his breath away, and goose bumps sprang up on his skin. He hurried to the RV and knocked, hoping for a small miracle.

* * *

"These are fantastic," Sarah exclaimed after holding the heat packs in her hands for a couple of minutes. "They're actually warm."

"Too bad we didn't know about them last night." Jay bit into a granola bar. It was cold and stale and about the best thing he'd ever tasted. Unscrewing the top of his second water bottle, he took another long drink.

Sarah set the heat pack on her lap and unwrapped a shiny Mylar emergency blanket. Jay finished off the water bottle, opened a pack of Life Savers, and popped three in his mouth. He felt like he'd discovered a gold mine. And it had been with them all along—in the trunk.

He felt like an idiot for not looking there sooner. Most people just had a spare tire—and maybe a set of jumper cables. But Christa and Kirk weren't most people. They were Mormons, and, like Boy Scouts, Mormons believed in being really prepared.

Bless you, Jay thought. *If we get out of this, I promise to listen when you talk about your church. I'll come to the activities. Those guys who wear suits and ride bikes can even talk to me.*

"Look at this!" Sarah exclaimed. She held up a sweatshirt that was probably Christa's, then dug through the bag again. "They even have diapers in here."

"Don't need those," Jay said. "You have to admit, running out of gas where there's a bathroom was pretty good."

"That old couple sharing some of their fuel was pretty good." Sarah pulled a Snickers bar from the bag and looked at it reverently. "Chocolate. *This* is great."

"Peanuts—protein. I can almost hear Christa's logical thought process as she packed."

"I love you, Christa," Sarah mumbled through a mouthful of candy bar.

"And Kirk?" Jay asked warily. "Do you still feel like we shouldn't call him?"

"No." She sounded ashamed. "I know we can't run away. I'm sorry I was so stubborn."

"It's okay." Jay took her free hand. "Yesterday was awful. But you trusted your gut, and it saved our lives. Let me have a turn at it today."

"A turn killing someone?" Her voice cracked, and despair swept across her face. She swallowed hard and shrank against the door as tears filled her eyes. "I killed a man, Jay." The candy bar fell to her lap, forgotten, as she buried her face in her hands and wept.

He leaned forward over the console, pulling her into his arms as best he could in the awkward space. "Don't do this, sweetheart."

"You don't understand," Sarah said in a choked voice between bouts of crying. "I keep seeing his body jerk when the bullet hit, the shock frozen in his eyes, the look in *your* eyes when you realized what I'd done."

Jay held her away from him. "Look at me. What do you see on my face now?"

"I don't know."

"Gratitude," Jay said. "You see profound gratitude that you saved my life and yours. And you see regret, because I sensed something was wrong too, and I didn't act on my instincts. I *wish* it had been me who pointed that gun and pulled the trigger. I wish with all my heart, Sarah, that I could spare you this." His throat constricted. "Because even though the circumstances were different, I *know* what a burden it is to feel responsible for ending someone's life."

Sarah's eyes widened as more tears spilled from them. "Oh, Jay." She leaned forward, throwing her arms around him as her body jerked with a heartwrenching sob. "I'm sorry. I didn't even think of that—of your mother—that you'd understand how it feels."

He held her tightly, one hand stroking her hair as he whispered words of comfort—words he wished he'd heard himself after his mother's death.

After several minutes, he brushed a wet strand of hair from her face. "We should go. There's still a chance our benefactors might have recognized us and call the police."

Sarah smiled through her tears. "I'm more worried about their abilities to recognize the road. They were *so* old."

"We're going to be that couple one day," Jay said. "Tooling around in our motor home with a couple of little dogs, maybe a grandkid or two." He returned Sarah's smile, but then his face grew serious again. "We can't call Kirk right away. My phone's dead. And we've got enough gas to get us to a town to fill up, but the question is, which direction are we going?"

Sarah sat up in her seat and wiped her eyes. "East," she said with conviction. "We're going back. We can't"—she took a deep breath—"run away from our troubles."

"Running away and staying safe aren't necessarily the same," Jay argued.

"But 'safe' is only going happen when these guys are caught. Instead of running, we need to turn the tables and go after them. We still need to meet with the DEA," Sarah said. "I'll tell them everything, and maybe something I say will be the *right* thing, what they need to figure out who is after us and why."

"We'll get Kirk to go with us," Jay said.

Sarah nodded her agreement.

"And maybe," Jay said, a faraway look in his eye, "this time we'll have something to show them."

Chapter Sixty

"We need to meet." The voice on the phone was neither angry nor demanding, but Grant's fingers shook nonetheless. Rossi had always been cool, calculating, and very persuasive.

Grant hesitated before responding. "You have my daughter?"

"She got away again. Perhaps if you'd given us the information about her meeting with the DEA agent sooner—"

They don't have Sarah! "I didn't know," Grant lied. Silently, he celebrated, feeling like he'd been given another chance at life. "And I still don't know how Detective Anderson's message made it to my inbox."

"Don't let on that it did. I've got a man following him, and he may lead us to Sarah. We've already found his family in Worcester."

"Don't do anything to them," Grant warned. "I can't cover up something that far away."

"It *is* far away, so you don't have to." A low chuckle sounded through the phone. "It's good to know you still have a soft spot when it comes to a wife and kids. We'll be sure to keep that in mind."

Grant closed his eyes, fighting off panic as he sat in the nearest chair.

"There's going to be a funeral in three days. We'll talk there."

"A funeral?" Sweat broke out along Grant's forehead.

"There was a casualty yesterday. Someone shot and killed Rick. We think it was the boyfriend. Since it's your fault Sarah's with him, the least you can do is pay your last respects."

Good riddance, Grant thought. "There's no way I can get anywhere near you right now. With that federal agent dead and a record on his cell phone that he'd called the station yesterday morning, I'm in enough trouble already. So say what you have to say right now." Grant felt emboldened, realizing Sarah and her boyfriend had outsmarted—and outshot—one of Rossi's best men.

"All right." There was a long pause. "You lied to me, Grant, told me Sarah didn't know anything about our operation, and I really wanted to believe you. We've had a good thing all these years, and I hate to see it end badly."

It began badly, Grant thought.

"You want to tell me why—if she knew nothing—she went blabbing to the DEA?"

"I told you, I don't know."

"But you did," Rossi said. "You knew about it and didn't tell us. Which means I can't feel good about trusting you anymore. And I *really* don't feel good about your daughter out there, where she might get to the right authorities." Rossi chuckled again. "You know, the ones who try to uphold the law."

Grant was silent. Nothing he said would appease the man. Only one thing would satisfy Rossi now, and Grant couldn't—wouldn't—give it to him.

"I believe in second chances," Rossi said. "Sometimes even third, but I'd say you've about run out."

"You think a new police chief is going to look the other way and ignore your little operation?" Grant asked.

"You were easy enough to persuade. Or you used to be." There was a pause on the line. "Guess it's like they say, all good things must come to an end."

Grant's hand went to the gun on his hip as he rose slowly from his chair. He looked toward the open blinds.

"Yes," Rossi said, confirming Grant's suspicions. "You'd be dead already if I wanted it."

"Go ahead," Grant said. He raised the blinds, staring at the car parked across the street. Sarah would be better off without him. He'd failed her in every way possible, and maybe, just maybe, she'd gone far enough away that they'd leave her alone.

"In spite of my better judgment, I'm going to give you one more opportunity to get your daughter back."

"I have no way—"

"There are plenty of ways," Rossi insisted. "And it's time you found them. Sarah called her friend yesterday. We found out about the DEA. We followed her to the cop's house. We found out where her boyfriend works. Those are all things you should have done, Grant. This is your mistake, not ours. And it's your lucky day, 'cause I'm giving you another seventy-two hours to fix it."

Grant opened his mouth to protest, to tell Rossi he'd be waiting for him on the other side, where they were both going to pay.

"It's not just about you anymore," Rossi said as if he'd read Grant's mind. "You don't deliver this time, Detective Anderson is out a wife and kids."

* * *

"You're sure your dad won't be home?" Jay asked as he parked Kirk's car a couple of blocks from Sarah's house.

"He's had the same schedule for years," Sarah said. "He's the boss, works the best shift, and is always home by five. The only problem we might have is Carl, if he's not in jail." They got out of the car and started walking. "I'm still not sure what it is you think we'll find. I've been cleaning that house for years, and I've never found anything that links my father to any sort of criminal activity."

"Maybe you weren't looking in the right places—or at the right things," Jay said. "We need to go through bank statements, cell phone bills, credit card receipts . . ." A car approached, and he crouched down, pretending to tie his shoe.

Sarah kept her face turned away from the street. "Sounds like a needle in a haystack."

"It is—sort of. But there's got to be something there. And if it's there, we'll find it."

They were silent the remaining block and a half to the house. Jay worried about Kirk and debated over the wisdom of calling him from Sarah's house. Sarah appeared deep in thought too, and Jay could tell from the look on her face she was reliving yesterday—something she wasn't going to get over anytime soon.

They reached the house, and Sarah took the spare key from a broken piece of rain gutter hanging off the side of the garage.

"I can't believe your dad would be so careless," Jay said. "He's got bars on all the windows, and he leaves a key lying around?"

"He didn't," Sarah said. "I hid it there a long time ago. So in case I ran away I could sneak back when my dad wasn't home—to eat and do laundry." Her mouth twisted and she looked down at the dried blood on her jeans. "While we're here, I'll definitely pick up some clean clothes and grab some food."

Jay unlocked the front door and stepped inside. Behind him, Sarah had Detective Doyle's gun drawn. Jay glanced around the living room, remembering the last time he was here and how Sarah's father had implored him to look out for her. *I'm trying,* he thought. *No thanks to you.* Quietly they made their way around the small home, making sure they were alone.

"Where do you want to start?" Sarah asked when they'd finished checking the last closet and she'd taken a few minutes to change into clean clothes.

"How about that filing cabinet?" Jay asked, pointing to one beneath the window in her dad's room. "We should also check his dresser and closet, under his mattress—any place we can think of."

"Okay." She sighed. "This isn't going to be a lot of fun."

"At least we're together." He pulled her close and kissed her. "We just need to find *something* linking your dad to Carl and the drug activity at the park. Then Kirk can take it to the DEA, and we're on the right track."

"I wish I knew what that something was." Sarah started on the dresser.

Jay sat on the floor and began sorting through each boring paper—electric bills, mortgage payments, dental records. Nothing seemed out of the ordinary. An hour ticked by. Sarah moved on to the closet. He neared the back of the second drawer and discovered a file marked, "SARAH." Pulling it out, he leaned against the wall and opened it.

A picture of a little girl with long blond hair and her two front teeth missing looked up at him. Her smile was too wide—the kind forced by the photographer no doubt—and didn't reach her deep blue, sad eyes. Jay turned the picture over and saw it had been taken when Sarah was six years old and in the first grade. He looked at the paper behind it—a report card—and the one behind that, a Father's Day card she'd made for her dad.

The file was thick, packed with construction paper and yarn projects, glowing reports from her teachers, programs from piano recitals. It was the sort of file a loving parent kept for a cherished child. Thinking of Sarah's father and the way he'd looked when he asked Jay to keep her safe, Jay could almost imagine Grant saving these things, tucking them away after he'd tucked his little girl into bed each night. Except that image clashed with the father Sarah told him about—the one who made her assemble other kids' bikes but never bought her one of her own.

The same father who surprised her with a piano. The one who lied about paying her tuition. Jay felt more confused than ever. He wondered if Sarah had ever seen this file, then decided now wasn't the time to show it to her. Her feelings about her dad were conflicted enough. And, whether Grant loved her or not, Jay was certain he was involved in something illegal. Above all else, that was what they needed to focus on.

Sarah backed out of the closet. "The only things that might be considered suspicious are his guns. And since he's a police chief, I doubt those qualify."

"Probably not," Jay agreed. He stuck the file in the drawer and closed it. "Let's lift the mattress." He stood and walked over to the bed, holding up the mattress and then box spring while Sarah peered beneath.

"Nothing," she said. "I'm afraid we're wasting our time."

Jay followed her out to the hall. He still felt certain there had to be *something* here. Her dad had lived here how long? "Is there a crawl space beneath the house—or an attic?"

"No crawl space, but the attic access is right here." Sarah pointed to a rectangle in the ceiling. "To my knowledge, no one's ever been up there."

"It's worth checking," Jay said.

Sarah headed for her room. "I'll get a chair." She returned a moment later, and Jay stood on the chair, reaching up to move the panel.

Sarah wrinkled her nose. "Dust."

"I'll go up, so you don't have to." Jay put his hands on either side of the opening, tried to pull himself up and let out a yelp of pain.

"Your shoulder!" Sarah exclaimed.

"My shoulder," Jay said, moaning. "I think I'm going to have to use a ladder."

"We don't have one," Sarah said. "My dad isn't much for home improvement projects—you probably noticed."

He had. The outside of the house was a mess, with sagging rain gutters, peeling shingles, and faded paint. Inside wasn't much better.

"Just a minute." Sarah disappeared, returning a few minutes later with a flashlight. "I'll go up if you'll help me."

"What about the dust?"

She shrugged. "I'll change later. I have a feeling we should check this out." She smiled. "Maybe your Scottish intuition is starting to kick in."

"Step on the chair and then my shoulder—the good one."

Sarah followed his instructions and climbed up easily.

"See anything?" Jay asked.

"Boxes and baby furniture," she said, sounding surprised. "I had no idea any of this was here."

Pay dirt, Jay thought—or hoped. "Can you hand me a box?"

Sarah leaned forward, reaching across the dusty floor. She pulled the closest stack of boxes to the edge, handing one at a time to Jay. As soon as the last one was down, she lowered herself to the chair and sat on the floor, eagerly prying the first open.

* * *

"It's three o'clock. We ought to get going." Jay raised his arms overhead, carefully stretching his aching muscles. Driving so long, plus moving the boxes up and down, had his shoulder hurting again. "We need to clean up this mess, and I want to be long gone before your dad gets home."

"We will be." Sarah didn't look up, but continued turning pages of the scrapbook in her lap. "Look at this." She turned the book so Jay could see. "My mom must have been pregnant with me."

Jay looked at the faded picture and the woman who looked much like Sarah. Remembering how he'd felt when his mother first showed up in his life, he understood Sarah's feelings. Everyone needed a mother. He hurt for Sarah, knowing hers had let her down.

"We need to go," Jay said gently, closing the book. "Someday we'll come back and get all this."

"I wish we could take it now."

He shook his head. "Too risky."

Sighing, Sarah put the book back into the box it came from. "Did we look through them all?"

"I think so," Jay said.

"One last look," Sarah said. "I'll be fast, I promise."

Jay followed her into the hall, standing beside the chair so she could climb up again. When she sat in the opening, he handed the boxes up to her.

"I'll be right back." She turned on the flashlight and crawled away.

Jay walked through the bedrooms again, making sure nothing looked disturbed. They'd been careful to put things back as they were, and, not wanting to alert Grant that someone had been in the house, they'd decided against eating here too—not that there was much in the way of food in the kitchen anyway.

Sarah still had the spare key in her pocket, and Jay planned to have her keep it when they left. Though they'd decided to call Kirk and then head to Worcester for the night, he knew it was a possibility they'd need to sneak back in the house another time.

"Sarah." He called a reminder for her to hurry, and walked into the living room. Outside a car door slammed. Rushing to the front window Jay peered through one of the bent blinds. A police cruiser was parked out front. Sarah's father walked toward the mailbox at the curb.

"He's home!" Jay raced back to the hall. "Your dad's here." He climbed up on the chair. Sarah scooted over to the edge of the opening, a manila envelope clutched in her hand, panic on her face.

"He's early. I'm sorry." She leaned forward. "Move, and I'll jump down."

"There's no time," Jay said. The only two outside doors—in the living room and kitchen—were at the front of the house, and all the windows had bars. There was no way they could leave without her father seeing them.

"I'll distract him," Sarah said. "You hide in my room and—"

Jay reached up, pulling her face to his and kissing her. "No. If your dad finds you . . ." He didn't want to say it, didn't need to. How many attempts had already been made on her life?

"But if he finds *you,* you'll be back in jail." Sarah held his hand tight.

"Then that's where I'll be waiting." Jay pulled away and jumped down. He moved the chair out of her reach. "Hide up there as long as you have to," he said, tossing her jacket up. "Whatever you do, *don't* come down until you know he's gone."

"I told you I'd never leave you again." She leaned forward, reaching for him. "I—"

A key turned in the front door.

"You're not leaving," Jay said. "I am." He sprinted off to a bedroom, hoping he could pull this off.

Chapter Sixty-One

There was a reason, Jay decided, that *Casablanca* ended before the Gestapo discovered Bogart. He'd made a point of renting that movie a year or so ago, after Jane compared him to the hero. And he'd liked the film, thought old Humphrey acted bold and looked pretty good when the movie was over. But in reality the ending would have been a little different.

Reality felt bad. Reality was the heart-pounding moment he'd spent ransacking Sarah's room while he waited for her father to find him. Reality was a gun at his temple, a punch to the gut, and his shoulder screaming with pain as his arms were jerked behind him and handcuffs snapped roughly around his wrists.

Jay didn't fight back, didn't dare, knowing Sarah heard every sound they made. He feigned being high and hung over, hoping Grant would get him out of the house and into the cruiser as fast as possible, and Sarah would have a chance to escape. He played his part right, and Grant did just that, but the worst part of reality was leaving Sarah behind, knowing she was alone in the cold attic, wondering if she was going to be all right.

Jay stumbled down the front steps as Sarah's father swore at him and shoved him from behind.

"You don't want to tell me where she is," he said. "Then I'll take you to someone who's a little more persuasive."

For the first time since they'd met in the hall, Jay resisted. What if that *someone* wasn't the police? Before now he hadn't considered that Grant *wouldn't* arrest him. He shoved his shoulder into Grant, turning to face him. "Why do you think I came here?" he asked in a belligerent tone. "Yesterday some guy pulled a gun on us, and we got separated."

"You're lying," Grant said. But he sounded unsure.

"I'm not." Jay's eyes were wild. "She's out there somewhere, and some lunatic with a machine gun is after her."

A police car raced up the street, sirens blaring as it braked to a stop in front of the house. Kirk jumped out. Grant swore.

Jay followed suit, continuing to act his part. "Another one. I hate cops." He flinched when Kirk pointed his gun at him.

"I didn't do anything," Jay said. "I'm just here looking for Sarah."

"Nice act, but I don't buy it," Grant said as he and Kirk faced each other, guns drawn, on either side of Jay. "I know Officer Anderson's been helping you—and Sarah." Neighbors were starting to come out to see what the sirens were for.

"Let him go," Kirk said.

Looking trapped, Grant put his gun away and spoke to Kirk. "Arrest him and book him into jail. If you do anything else, that little vacation your wife and kids are taking in Worcester ends early."

"Are you threatening me?" Kirk asked, his tone belying the emotion Jay was certain he felt.

"Not you, *them*," Grant said under his breath as he pushed past Kirk to the sidewalk. "Just an intruder, folks," he called to the small crowd gathered in the street. "My officer's taking care of it."

Kirk grabbed Jay's uninjured arm and hauled him toward the car. He opened the back door, and Jay climbed inside, watching out the window as Grant returned to the house—and Sarah.

Chapter Sixty-Two

Sarah peered through the slats of the attic window, watching until the car with Jay in it disappeared down the street. She hadn't been able to hear the words exchanged outside, but seeing two guns pointed at Jay was enough that she understood what had just happened.

The front door slammed, and she jumped, steadying herself on the crossbeams as the tears fell. She wrapped her jacket around her and shivered, more from worry than cold. Jay was going back to jail and, worse, Kirk was the one taking him. Had she been right to doubt Kirk's loyalties? Judging by the scene she'd just witnessed, it appeared he might be working with her father after all.

Clutching the flashlight in her hand, Sarah listened to the sounds coming from below. Her father was in the kitchen, making a considerable amount of noise, banging pots and pans and the occasional cupboard door. This lasted a few minutes, then all was silent until the front door crashed shut, rattling the house.

Sarah leaned forward, peeking out the round window again. She watched as her dad got in his car and drove off. For a second, she was too relieved to move, then she sprang into action, scooting along the beams toward the hall access. One hand held the flashlight, guiding her so she didn't step wrong and crash through the ceiling below. Her other hand held the manila envelope she'd found taped inside a cradle. She'd yet to open the envelope, but her name—written in her father's handwriting—was scrawled across the front.

Reaching the opening, Sarah slid the cover aside and looked down, half-expecting to see Jay there, his arms held out. She wished she could rewind time, wished with all her heart she'd listened and hurried when he suggested they go. A quiet sob escaped her throat, and she jumped to the floor, the gun in her pocket banging against her hip as she landed.

Wiping her eyes, she grabbed the chair from her room and carried it to the hall so she could close the attic access. Once she'd covered her tracks, she took the flashlight and envelope and left through the kitchen, noting the mess her father had left behind. She guessed the earlier commotion had to do with the lack of food in the house and the necessity of grocery shopping. If so, that meant he'd be gone long enough for her to get out of the neighborhood before he returned. She was walking now—Jay had the key to Kirk's car, and even if he hadn't, she wouldn't dare drive it for fear of being recognized.

More than ever before, it was imperative she not be found. Jay needed her.

* * *

The ride to the station took less than ten minutes, but it was enough time for Jay to remember how much he hadn't enjoyed being locked up the last time.

He wanted to talk to Kirk, but as they pulled away from the curb, the look and slight shake of the head Kirk gave him in the rearview mirror kept Jay silent. For whatever reason, Kirk didn't want him talking right now. But he would when they got out of the car, before they took him away for yet another mug shot and fingerprinting. He had to let Kirk know where Sarah was. He was her best chance at getting away safely.

All too soon Kirk parked in front of the station and came around to let Jay out. When they were a few feet from the car, Kirk spoke.

"We were being followed, and I think my car might be bugged. Where's Sarah?"

"In the attic at her dad's," Jay said. "We were searching for something to connect him or Carl with the drug activity at the park. We didn't expect him home so soon."

Kirk shook his head and frowned. "That was stupid. How am I supposed to get her out of there now?" He turned to Jay. "You heard what her father said about Christa and the boys?"

"Yeah."

"Night before last, our house was broken into, then when you and Sarah went missing yesterday, and Doyle didn't call—"

"You knew the chief was onto you," Jay guessed. They started up the steps of the station.

Kirk nodded. "Doyle's murder made the news this morning."

"Did they find the guy on the roof?" Jay said. "The phony detective who tried to kill us?"

"Yeah. They didn't give a name though. I don't know how Chief Morgan—and whoever he's working with—found out about your meeting. I'm sorry. I never would have sent you."

"It's not your fault," Jay said. "And we got away, didn't we?"

"I'll have to hear all about it sometime." They reached the door, and Kirk pulled it open. "You know I don't want to do this. If there were any other way—"

"Don't worry about me," Jay said. "Just get Sarah and keep her safe."

"I will," Kirk said. "I'm worried about Christa and the boys too. The chief sounded like he knew where they were, and I don't dare trust that he's bluffing. I feel like we're two animals circling each other right now, waiting for the other to make his move."

"You're gutsy for sticking around," Jay said. "But are you sure that's wise?"

"Not at all," Kirk said. "But I haven't gone to work. I've been following the chief, watching his house when he's there."

Jay sensed Kirk's frustration. "I know you want to figure this out, and believe me, I really want you to, but it's not worth risking your family or Sarah. I'll be okay here no matter how long it takes." Jay lowered his voice as they approached the desk. "Take Christa and the boys and Sarah—and get out of town. Keep her safe for me."

Chapter Sixty-Three

It had taken Sarah more than three hours to walk a circumspect route from her house in Summerfield to the home in Cambridge she and Jay had stayed at two nights before. As Kirk had instructed, they'd left their belongings there to be stored or brought to them later, once their federal protection had been arranged—or so Kirk had told them.

Believing the couple who lived in the house was still on their honeymoon, and hoping Kirk wouldn't think to look for her there, Sarah had the idea to stay at the house again. She and Jay had locked the key inside when they left, so she hoped to get in through the bedroom window with the newly-cut screen. But a car in the driveway and lights shining from the windows put an end to that plan, until she remembered the motor home parked beside the house. It wasn't a great hiding place, but it would do.

Being careful to stay in the shadows, Sarah crept along the side of the house. According to her watch it was almost eleven P.M., and most of the house lights on the street were out.

She crouched in front of the motor home and reached beneath the step, searching for a key as she'd seen the couple do two nights ago, when she and Jay hid in the bushes nearby. Her fingers scraped against the rough, cold metal then stopped, her nails snagging on a piece of duct tape. Sarah tugged it away, and a key fell into her hand. Elated, she stood, quickly inserting it into the lock. The door swung open and she climbed inside, closing and locking it behind her.

She switched on the flashlight again, grateful the beam was low and that the front windshield had a cover. She didn't dare turn on the lights—if they even worked—but seeing the bed in the back, complete with a stack of folded blankets, Sarah felt like she'd arrived at a five-star hotel.

Sarah removed her shoes and sat down, taking a minute to stretch her aching feet. She took the gun from the jacket pocket and set it on the floor beside the bed. Pulling a quilt over her lap, she angled the flashlight so it illuminated the small space. Then she turned the envelope on its side, sliding the papers out.

While walking here she'd given in to curiosity, glancing at a few of the documents. But the need to stay alert and aware of her surroundings kept her from reading anything in detail.

Sarah picked up the paper on top of the pile—a copy of a police report from the early eighties. She scanned the form, noting her dad's signature at the bottom. Subsequent pages, paper clipped together, described the bust of an art counterfeiting operation run by one James Devon Rossi. Sarah paused, rereading the name, certain she'd heard Kirk mention it before.

"You really do have intuition," she mused aloud, thinking of Jay and his suggestion they search the attic. She sensed this report was important and wished Jay were here with her to figure it out.

What does an art counterfeiter from the eighties have to do with Dad and drugs in 2005?

After a few minutes, she set the report aside and went on to the next item—a car repair bill. Behind that were two hospital bills—one for her mother and one for Emily. Instead of feeling sad, Sarah held the papers reverently, grateful for proof of her mother's and sister's existence.

There were other things in the stack, as varied and unusual as those she'd already looked through, and exhausted as she was, she couldn't seem to find a common thread linking them together.

She felt a headache forming and began massaging her temples as she glanced at the last two documents. The first was a petition for divorce filed by her mother, the last a page from the *Boston Globe*, dated December 1986. Red ink circled her mother's obituary, and above that the sentence, *Are we in agreement now?*

Agreement with whom? Goosebumps sprang up on her arms, followed by an involuntary shiver. Sarah flattened the paper, reading both columns of the newsprint for any additional clues. There were none she could see; the obituary gave only the date and place of her mother's death. But the red circle around it, along with the note that *wasn't* in her father's handwriting, indicated it had been significant to someone.

Sarah decided that a trip to the medical examiner's office tomorrow might be a good place to start. But for now her eyes blurred and stung, and she couldn't remember ever being this tired. Giving in to exhaustion, she set the papers aside and lay back against the pillow, pulling the quilt up to her chin.

She had plenty of questions and no answers—nothing that would help Jay. The thought of him in jail made her sick to her stomach. She wondered if he was alone or with other inmates. *Is Carl anywhere near him? Why did I let him go? I'm the one who should have faced Dad.*

Rolling on her side, Sarah curled in a ball, wrapping the quilt around her. *What if I can't get Jay out?* The turmoil continued as her imagination took flight and the worst possibilities filled her mind. Too tired to cry anymore but too worried to sleep, she lay alone in the dark, praying for a miracle.

Chapter Sixty-Four

For the second time in twenty-four hours, Sarah unlocked the front door of her father's house and went inside. Turning the deadbolt behind her, she stood in the living room for a moment, letting her eyes adjust to the light while she battled ghosts of the past and fought off feelings of oppression. Her father's and Carl's voices echoed through the halls of her memory, and the room seemed to shrink, closing in on her—suffocating. Yesterday, with Jay here, it had been different. Today it was all she could do not to turn and run outside.

She thought of Jay, and the very real walls closing around him—indefinitely if she couldn't prove his innocence—and knew that all she *could* do was stay here and face her father. He alone had the answers she needed, the information that might set Jay free.

She didn't bother turning on any lights, but she opened the kitchen curtains enough to see what she needed. Getting right to work, Sarah pulled the phone cord from its jack in the wall and stuffed it in her pocket. She took the knives from the drawer and dropped them, one by one, into the overflowing garbage, making sure to bury them well, without the trash looking like it had been disturbed.

Another glance around the kitchen and she felt satisfied—and depressed. She'd forgotten how dreary the whole house was. A few months away had changed her perspective so that she wasn't sure anymore just how she'd survived here for almost nineteen years.

Her father's room was next. Again, she disabled the phone and collected all the weapons she could find. When she'd finished, a pocket knife, five guns, and a rifle lay across the bed. The knife she zipped into her jacket pocket with the cords. Then she took her time checking each of the guns and searching her father's closet and drawers for additional ammunition. Certain she'd found everything, she traded out Detective Doyle's gun for her father's PP7, the clip and several extra rounds, and the silencer attachment. The remaining weapons and ammo she hauled up to the attic, balancing on her tiptoes on the chair to push them as far as she could from the opening.

Sarah returned the chair and brushed the dust from her jeans. With the loaded pistol in one hand, and the newspaper with her mother's obituary in the other, she sat down in her father's chair to wait for his arrival.

* * *

Grant closed the front door behind him and was reaching for the light switch when instinct kicked in, telling him he wasn't alone.

"Drop your gun belt on the floor."

"Sarah?" He turned toward her familiar voice.

"Do it." She stood on the far side of the room, one of his own pistols in her hand, pointed at his heart. A determined expression on her face, she looked for all the world as she had the day they'd buried her mother and Sarah demanded he take her home.

"You wouldn't really shoot your father," he said, calling her bluff.

"Wouldn't I?" Sarah said in an angry voice that wasn't as familiar. "A *father* is someone who loves his children, but I mean nothing to you except for ironed shirts and a hot meal."

"Rossi was listening in when I said that," Grant tried to explain. "If he'd heard me say I loved you—"

"Throw it over there," Sarah said, cutting him off. She inclined her head toward the sofa.

They locked eyes for a minute before Grant decided to humor her. She wasn't in her right mind; this wasn't the Sarah he knew. He removed his belt, tossing it, along with his gun, baton, and phone, onto the couch. "You've got this all wrong. It isn't me you need protection from. Put the gun down. You don't want to shoot anyone. And anyway, without your glasses on, we both know you're blind as a bat."

"Contacts." Her grip remained steady. "But you're right. I didn't want to shoot that phony DEA agent you sent after us either."

"That was *you?*" Grant's mouth turned up in a smile of admiration. "Well done, then. He was one of Rossi's best, and a thorn in my side for a long time."

"Then you know how I feel about Carl." She stepped in front of the couch, putting herself between him and his weapon—a smart move.

Grant's chest swelled with pride. She would have made a good cop—

even if that wasn't what she wanted. Though just now, in spite of the gun she wielded with authority, she looked more like a movie star playing a part. She'd cut her hair and it curled around her face, showing off blue eyes that stared at him with intensity. Noticing Sarah had attached the silencer, Grant felt a stirring of unease. He backed toward the kitchen, putting more distance between himself and her gun, though he still didn't believe she would really use it.

"Carl's in jail for good. You won't have to worry about him anymore. But we need to leave. I've got enough money for—"

"Run away?" Sarah said in a choked voice. "You think I'm going to leave Jay rotting in prison when you know something that can free him?"

"So that's what this is about?" Grant reached the counter separating the living room from the kitchen.

"It's about *everything.*"

He'd have to lie to her, tell her they'd get her friend out. Otherwise she'd never leave. He could see it in her stubborn countenance. And they had to get out soon. If Rossi discovered she was here, they'd both be in trouble. And while Grant knew his sorry life wasn't worth much these days, Sarah's was. If it was the last thing he did, he'd make sure she was safe. He glanced toward the phone and saw that the cord was missing. *Smart girl.* "Give me the gun." He held out his hand.

She followed him with her eyes but maintained her stance.

"*Now,* Sarah."

"No!" She pointed the pistol down and pulled the trigger, sending a bullet whizzing past his kneecap, into the wall behind him.

Grant jumped back in surprise, then lunged forward, furious. She fired again, this time just missing his arm.

"I *will* shoot you," Sarah screamed as he continued to advance. "Why shouldn't I?" Her hands were steady, but a tear rolled down her cheek. "You killed Mom—and Emily."

Emily. The word stopped him where her weapon had not. Grant froze, the painful image of a tiny infant flashing through his mind. He hadn't heard that name in so long, and he was sure he'd never mentioned it to Sarah. "What do you know about that?" he asked in a gruff voice unrecognizable to his own ears. Hearing *Emily* made him feel as if his air supply had been abruptly cut off.

"I know Mom wasn't an addict," Sarah said. "I went to Boston this morning and read the medical examiner's report. For some reason the examiner ignored a lot of unusual facts." She paused, breathing in deeply.

It seemed he wasn't the only one fighting for oxygen.

"He's retired now," Sarah continued. "But after the current examiner looked at the report, he decided to make some phone calls. There's going to be an investigation." Her lips pressed together as another tear leaked from her eye. "But you already know what happened, don't you, Dad?" Her knuckles were white as she gripped the gun. She took a step toward him. "I want to know *why*. Why did you kill her—and my little sister? And I want to know about this." Sarah opened one hand, and a yellowed newspaper clipping fluttered to the carpet.

Grant didn't need to read the words to know what it was.

He backed into his chair and sat down as the pieces of his life crumbled around him. This was the beginning of the end. He took a deep breath and looked up. Sarah was serious, the anger in her eyes real. At the very least she deserved an explanation. "I didn't kill Emily. At least I didn't mean to."

* * *

"Thought of everything, didn't you?" Grant asked as he opened the knife drawer and found it devoid of anything sharp—including scissors.

"You taught me well," Sarah said. "I'd be dead if you hadn't."

"Glad I did something right." He grunted, then used his teeth to rip off a piece of duct tape. He should have felt humiliated that his own daughter held him at gunpoint, had forced him to tape his legs together, and was now forcing him to tape his arm to the chair. But at the moment worry was the more prominent emotion. "There are other places we could go to talk," Grant said, trying again to convince her they should leave. "If Rossi finds out you're here, we're both dead."

She shrugged. "Talk fast. Tell me about him."

Who are you, and what have you done with my daughter? Grant continued to be astonished, irritated, and ultimately impressed by the confident young woman standing in his kitchen. "I intend to tell you everything," he said, finishing the awkward job.

Sarah pulled out the chair across from him, but instead of sitting in it, she pushed RECORD on the tape recorder she'd hidden there.

She really did *think of everything.* Grant leaned forward, his free elbow propped on the table. "It won't do you any good to take that to the police, you know."

"Don't worry. I wasn't going to bother. Who knows how many of your underlings are just as corrupt as you."

Grant raised his head. "That isn't true. I work alone. No one else in the department is in on this."

"On what? And don't lie to me. I saw Detective Anderson arrest Jay yesterday."

Grant sighed. "You're wrong—*especially* about Anderson. He's a good cop. I hired him hoping—" Grant stopped, realizing he was getting ahead of himself. And since Sarah was recording this, he might as well make it good. "I'm going to start at the beginning. This has been going on a long time—a lifetime. My lifetime." He paused, hating to open the door to such painful memories. "But once, long ago, things were different."

Sarah leaned against the wall. Grant knew her arms had to be getting tired, but she hadn't let her guard down. Not that he could do much if she did. It was over now. The best he could hope for was to confess everything to her as quickly as possible so she could get out of here. She'd managed to stay safe this long; maybe she *could* get the information to the right authorities and end this once and for all. He hadn't heard from J.D. today. There was a chance . . .

"I was a rookie cop when your mom and I married. We didn't have much—not a decent car, not enough money for a movie, but we were happy. A couple of years later, you were born. Life was even better." A wistful smile touched Grant's lips. He thought he saw Sarah's tremble.

"Then one day I broke a case I'd been working on for several months. A man named J.D. Rossi had been smuggling counterfeit art into the country and selling it at quite a profit. He was arrested, tried, and sent to prison pending sentencing. I'd interrogated him during the process, and I went to see him while he was in jail. He'd been offered a plea agreement if he'd testify in another case. Turns out he had an offer for me as well."

"Go on," Sarah said.

"The paintings were not only imitations, but they concealed drugs—a relatively new one called methamphetamine. Rossi told me it was worth a lot of money, and he agreed to testify in the other case if I'd help him get the meth out of the paintings, still held in our evidence room. He said he'd give me half the profit, and he planned to use his portion of the money to bring his family here from Costa Rica."

"You agreed," Sarah guessed.

Grant nodded. "I was naive. I figured it was for the greater good in getting his testimony, and I justified taking the money by reminding myself how little I was paid for my public service. It took weeks, but a little at a time I slipped the paintings out of our evidence room then back in again.

One of Rossi's friends took care of extracting the meth. His name was Eddie Martin."

Sarah gasped. "The same Eddie you had me tracking all those months?"

"The same. Eddie sold the meth and gave me my share of the money. I used it to fix our car and pay off debt. Rossi testified in the other case. Our deal was complete—no harm done, or so I thought." Grant looked up at Sarah. "Water, please?"

She went to the sink and filled two paper cups. One she drank; the other she placed on the far side of the table. With his free hand, Grant reached across, took it, and downed the whole thing.

"Rossi was released about eighteen months later, about the time your mother got pregnant with Emily. He came to see me, said he needed his portion of the money so he could get his family."

"But didn't Eddie have it?"

"He was supposed to, but he insisted he'd given it all to me. I was in a real mess—two criminals angry with me and nowhere to turn."

"Because you'd broken the law yourself," Sarah said.

Grant looked up, wanting her to understand he hadn't started out intending to do wrong, intending to ruin his life and destroy his family. "I didn't want to go to jail. I had a wife, who I loved and adored, a precious daughter, and another child on the way. I felt I had no choice but to agree to work with Rossi again. He was going to smuggle in the meth, and I'd watch his back and make sure the cops stayed away so he could do his thing. When he had enough money for his family, then I'd be done."

Sarah's lips were pinched, her expression anything but understanding. "It didn't work that way?"

"Of course not," Grant said. "I was young and stupid. There was no family waiting. Everyone was already here, working full-time introducing meth to the East Coast. And Eddie *had* split the money with him, but I didn't know until it was too late and I was so far in I knew I'd go to prison for years if what I'd been doing came to light." Grant sighed, wishing as he had so many times that he could go back and make different choices. What had seemed monumental then was nothing compared to what happened afterward.

"Your mother found out what was going on, and she wanted me to come clean. She said she'd wait for me, that she'd rather see me go to prison an honest man than keep living a lie and breaking the law I'd sworn to uphold. We had a terrible fight, and I left. Shortly after this she went into labor and they couldn't stop it. I blamed myself. Maybe if I hadn't been arguing with your mother, maybe if she hadn't been under so much stress . . ." He rubbed his free hand across his forehead. "Emily was born three months early. The doctors and nurses did everything they could, but your sister died a few days later."

Vulnerability replaced the guarded look in Sarah's eyes. "Did I ever see her?"

"No." Grant knew Sarah had always wished for a sibling—and a mother. "They wouldn't let you because you were so little. I'm sorry." *About that. About Emily's death. About everything.*

"Your mom and I split up after that. I wanted to get back together, but she wouldn't have anything to do with me unless I'd break from J.D. and turn myself in. About two years later I missed you both so much I finally decided I'd do what she wanted. I figured it would be better to live a few more years without you instead of a lifetime. But I made the mistake of telling Rossi. I offered him the chance to relocate. I told him I wasn't going to name names, but that I was going to turn myself in. He didn't care for that arrangement, and soon after your mother was dead."

"*He* killed her." For the first time Sarah's gun wavered. "All those years, you let me think . . . you *told* me . . ."

"Forced overdose," Grant said quietly. He looked at Sarah. "You were playing at a friend's house when Rossi followed your mom from the bus station. I thank God for that every day of my life."

"How did he get away with it?" Sarah asked. "How could you not turn in your wife's murderer?"

Grant forged through the facts as quickly as possible. There was no easy way to tell it. He knew he sounded callous, unfeeling—evil. What he'd done was all those things.

"The medical examiner decided to ignore the bruises on her arms and throat—Rossi can be very persuasive," Grant added. "Her death was recorded as a suicide. And suddenly I had a lot bigger problems. I had a child to raise, but I was in over my head with blackmail, deceit, and drug trafficking. For more than two years I'd been leading a double life, working late hours, making sure the meth shipments got delivered without a problem. I was constantly covering my trail at work, stealing files, altering evidence anytime someone got close. It was exhausting, and now I had you to think about. I knew I should send you away, somewhere safe, but I couldn't. I'd already lost your mother, and I couldn't bear to think of losing you as well.

"I moved out of Boston, thinking that if I went to a small town like Summerfield, Rossi would lose interest and leave me alone. Instead, he moved his operation here, blackmailing me once again. And now I knew that if I ended up in jail, you'd be without any parent, and I feared for your life if I didn't do what Rossi asked."

Sarah walked away from the table. She put the gun on the counter, far out of his reach, and leaned forward, arms wrapped around her middle. Her breathing sounded unsteady.

"Are you all right?" Grant asked.

"No, I'm not all right." She straightened, anger flashing in her eyes. "How could you—he murdered your own wife, my mother!"

"I've asked myself that same question for nineteen years," Grant said. "And wondered if your life would have been better if I'd turned myself in and you'd gone to someone else, some other family, another father."

"It's a little late for second-guessing." She ground out the words but couldn't mask the pain on her face.

Grant looked toward the front door again. They needed to get out of here. Rossi had watched the house before, and if he did it again . . . "We should go. I'll take you anywhere you want."

"I *want* Jay. I want to know how he figures into all of this. Who planted those drugs in his apartment?"

"His roommate," Grant said. "Carl learned that there was some tension between them, and he convinced the roommate to help set Jay up."

"Archer?" Sarah asked, clearly shocked.

"I think that was his name. It had something to do with his girlfriend."

"But Archer was almost killed," Sarah said. "He's in ICU, and his girlfriend claims Jay did it."

"How do you know he didn't?" Grant asked. "His past isn't entirely spot-free, you know."

"I know," Sarah said. "And I know he's innocent. He was with me the night Archer was shot. Jay saved my life."

Grant brought his fist to his mouth, considering. "It was Carl who set Jay up. We wanted to get you away from him, and I figured if he was behind bars—for drug use, no less—that might persuade you to come home. But Carl didn't shoot the roommate. He couldn't have, since he was in jail by then."

"One of this other guy's—Rossi's—men?" Sarah guessed.

"I don't know. Maybe the two incidents aren't even related."

Sarah picked up the gun again. "That was a terrible thing to do." Her mouth twisted in a grimace. "Though after what happened to Mom, I suppose I should be grateful you *only* set him up, only ruined a life he's worked hard to rebuild and make something of."

Grant turned his face to her. "I had no idea you cared for him so much."

"But you would have done it anyway," she said. "So you could get me back under your thumb and I could keep your little operation going."

"It's not like that," Grant said. "I needed you to come home so we could protect you from Rossi. The last two years, he's required your help as proof of my loyalty."

"What do you mean?"

"Your *job*," Grant said. "I came up with the idea of a phony drug task force."

"But why?" Sarah asked. "He wanted me to go after his partner?"

"*Ex*-partner," Grant clarified. "Eddie crossed J.D. one too many times. They had a falling out, and Eddie started up his own ring, thought he could put his old friend out of business."

"And he might have if not for us."

Grant nodded.

"I can't believe you sent me out like that—put me in the middle of something so dangerous. You might as well have killed me when you killed my mother."

Grant flinched.

Sarah's voice quieted as she drew the obvious conclusion. "It was only a matter of time before I met the same fate."

"No." Grant shook his head. "You had Carl."

She laughed. "Tell me how that made it better."

"He's smarter than he looks," Grant said. "I figured one criminal mind would be able to keep an eye on another, so I got him out of jail when he had some trouble. I hired him to protect you, which he did more times than you can imagine."

"He hurt and threatened me more times than you can imagine," Sarah said angrily.

"You should have told me," Grant said. "I knew you didn't like Carl, but—"

Another bitter laugh escaped Sarah. "I *loathe* him." She quieted. "I feared him, but you never noticed. And I didn't dare tell you outright because he'd threatened me."

"I'm sorry," Grant said once more, wishing he had something more than an apology to offer.

"Why did you have to mess with Jay's life too?" Sarah asked.

"He got in the way. Carl wasn't to let anyone get close to you. Jay tried and was a little too persistent. I never said I approved of his methods," Grant added. "Just the results."

"What a mess." Sarah sagged against the counter. The hand with the gun hung at her hip.

"We need to leave," Grant reminded her gently.

"I'm not going anywhere. Not with Jay sitting in jail for crimes he didn't commit—or Archer fighting for his life in a coma. And then there was my sweet landlady, Mrs. Larson, who died in a fire *someone* set?"

"It was Carl. He went too far. And you left off Detective Anderson, risking his life and job to help you."

Sarah frowned. "But I saw him hold that gun on Jay and arrest him yesterday."

"Detective Anderson didn't have much of a choice," Grant said. "Unless he wanted to admit he'd been helping you two and investigating me. Not to mention, I threatened his family, letting on that I knew something was up. I was afraid Rossi had someone watching the house. If that were the case and Kirk and Jay didn't leave, things could have gone very badly."

"That's some good news anyway. I like Kirk." She took a deep breath and looked steadily at her dad. "Gets a little hard to trust people, though, when you find out your own parent isn't who you thought him to be."

Grant didn't have a response for her. What could he say? If she never believed in anyone again for the rest of her life, it would be understandable—and his fault. If a daughter couldn't look up to and rely on her father, who else? He tried to explain more about Detective Anderson, wanting Sarah to know she really did have someone to turn to. "I hired him last year, because of the great things he did in California, the way he was able to ferret out the big dealers. I hoped he'd do that here, that he'd figure out what was going on with Rossi before it was too late and something happened to you. Looks like I was right."

"You expect me to believe you wanted to be exposed?" Sarah shook her head. "Why did you send Rossi's man after us, then? Why did you send someone to Jay's nightclub to kidnap me?"

"I didn't," Grant said. "I've been telling Rossi for weeks that I'd had no contact with you and didn't know where you were. I also tried to convince him you knew nothing of his operation. He obviously didn't believe me and took matters into his own hands, tracking you a little more successfully than Carl did."

Sarah crossed the kitchen and moved the tape recorder from the chair. She sank into it, looking exhausted and overwhelmed but not defeated. "What am I going to do?"

"Don't you mean *we?*" Grant asked. If she wasn't willing to leave the house, she certainly wouldn't buy into his idea of leaving for good. *If you can't beat them, join them.* It was about time he did and got on the right side of the law.

Her eyes narrowed. "You've done enough."

"You're right," Grant said. "And I think it's about time I made up for it."

"Can you release Jay? Can you guarantee Archer lives? Can you promise me a normal life?"

"No," Grant said sadly. "But together we can keep things from getting worse."

"Worse?" She gave a choked laugh. "Things are about as bad as they can get."

"Not really," Grant said, wishing he didn't have to tell her any more. He lifted his head, meeting her gaze. "If I don't deliver you to J.D. by tomorrow, Detective Anderson's wife and children will be the ones who pay."

Chapter Sixty-Five

Grant pulled the station door shut behind him and locked it. It was supposed to remain open twenty-four hours a day, but tonight he wasn't taking any chances. If the public needed something, they could call 911.

Grant raised a hand in passing to the two officers on duty. Then, instead of going to his office, he led Sarah farther down the hall, to the employee's lounge. He pushed open the door and flipped on the light, wrinkling his nose at the smell of stale coffee. "This isn't great, but it's about the safest place I can think of, and there's a couch so you can catch a little sleep."

"You know I won't," Sarah said. "Not until we figure out how to get Jay out of jail."

"You've got your priorities wrong," Grant muttered. "What we have to do is figure out how to get Rossi—and his team—*in* jail, so you're safe."

"That's easy enough. I just need to get this tape—" She patted her jacket pocket—"into the right hands. I'd imagine your testimony will have some significant weight."

Grant ran his fingers through his thinning hair. "It will. And make no mistake, Sarah, I meant what I said at the house. I'm through running. I'll turn myself in. But it's going to take more than that. If it comes down to it, I've no doubt Rossi could figure out how to take care of me while I'm in prison."

Sarah turned away and walked over to the couch. "You know that's not what I want."

"It's no more than I deserve," Grant said. "But it won't help you. And that's what *I* want." He followed her across the room and sat beside her, careful not to get too close. It had taken a lot of talking to convince her to free him and go with him to the station. She still had his gun, and though he'd feared the worst when they'd finally left the house, at her insistence he'd walked out unarmed. *Thank goodness we weren't being watched*, he thought again.

"You're saying we need more people to testify," Sarah said.

Grant nodded. "A lot more. And that could take some time. I know enough about J.D.'s operation to bring in the little guys—though we'd have to do it all at once, or he'd be onto us."

"You can't set something like that up overnight." Sarah bit her lip.

"No," Grant agreed. "It will take time—which we haven't got. That's why you should leave, let me send you somewhere far away and safe. Because I *won't* deliver you to Rossi tomorrow. I'll do what I can to protect Detective Anderson's family, but I won't involve you."

"*Can* you protect them?" Sarah asked.

Grant didn't answer immediately but rose from the couch and walked to the counter. He unrolled a strip of paper towel from the dispenser, ripped it off, and beckoned for Sarah to join him at the table. After finding a pencil, he bent over and began sketching. "This is the funeral home where Rossi will be tomorrow. The streets run like this, and the building has three entrances. I think there are some possibilities. If I pull every one of my men—"

"Don't you think he'll expect that? He doesn't know you've found me, after all."

"Maybe, maybe not," Grant said, though privately he agreed. The second Rossi knew where Sarah was, he'd grab her.

"So you're able to get him at the funeral tomorrow. That doesn't necessarily help Christa and the boys. He's probably got someone else watching them, just waiting for the word to—"

"You would have made a good cop." Grant looked up from his drawing to give her a half smile.

"You've taught me quite a bit over the years."

He reached out, almost touching her hand, but pulled away at the last minute. "I wish I'd taught you other things—wish I'd done right by you, Sarah."

"You can do right now," she said, meeting his gaze. "You can make sure Jay goes free and Kirk's family is safe."

"Tell me how," Grant said, skeptical, but interested to hear her ideas.

"Well." She straightened, arms folded across her chest. "If I'm right about Carl somehow being involved with Rossi, then he could provide additional testimony."

"He's not going to—"

"Let me finish." Sarah held up her hand. "You're right. With Carl already locked up, he has no motivation to talk, but I can almost guarantee that he'd love the chance to brag to me about anything he's been involved in."

"What are you suggesting?" Grant asked uneasily.

Sarah looked down at the map he'd drawn. "I'm suggesting—" She took a deep breath. "That you get Carl out of jail and act as if you need him again to help keep me . . . *safe*."

Grant noted the sarcasm in her voice.

"Convince Carl that he's the only one you trust to do this job, to watch out for me. Tell him that he's got to take me to meet Rossi." She put her finger on the building Grant had drawn. "Here."

"Absolutely not," Grant said in the tone he always used when he wanted no arguing from her. But he could tell by her determined look that she was no longer intimidated. *Well, there's something*, he thought, feeling glad, in an odd sort of way, that she had the guts to stand up to him now. Still, he cursed himself for ever mentioning Detective Anderson's family. *Just add it to my list of mistakes.* Back at the house, he'd hoped that would convince her to release him so he could get to the station and put a plan together that might possibly protect them. He hadn't guessed that Sarah would feel an obligation to be part of that plan.

"Why can't I go?" she demanded. "It will accomplish both our goals of protecting Christa and the boys and getting an additional witness. I'm sure I can get Carl to talk, and you were just telling me you thought you could protect Kirk's family."

"You look like you did as a little girl," Grant said, unable to keep a corner of his mouth from turning up as he studied her, arms folded, lips pursed, looking ready for a fight. "Reminds me of the time you told me to go back to your mother's place and get your kitty."

"But you didn't," Sarah said, a pained look cracking through her exterior bravado for a split second. "That cat was real. Mom got it for me for my birthday."

"I know." Grant looked away, unable to bear the hurt he saw in her eyes.

"But if you knew, then why—"

"The kitten was dead, strangled. Rossi and his men don't believe in sparing so much as a fly when they do a job." Grant watched Sarah's sharp intake of breath and noticed the sudden moisture in her eyes. He took a step forward, then stopped. More than anything he wanted to reach out to her, to take his little girl in his arms and make it all better. But his chance to do that was long past. "I never bought you another kitten because I was afraid Rossi would find out. He followed me to Summerfield almost as soon as I'd made the move. And I always knew he was out there watching. If I'd bought you a real cat he might have known how much I loved you. And it was *imperative,* Sarah, that he never found that out, never knew how much you meant to me."

She looked up at him with eyes full of unshed tears. "I never knew it either."

"I know."

Grant pulled out the closest chair and sank into it. The way Sarah was looking at him made the guilt he'd felt at Emily's death pale by comparison. Sarah had lived, and he'd done so very wrong by her.

Sarah patted the pocket that held his taped confession. "I know I can get Carl to talk. And you can protect me long enough for Rossi to see that I'm there and to call off his henchmen with Kirk's family. If you *do* love me, then let me do this, Dad."

He looked up at her. "You can't ask that."

"I'm *not* asking. I'm telling. Either you help me, or I'll do it myself when you're behind bars. I'll go alone."

Chapter Sixty-Six

Sarah gave Carl a withering look as he settled in the driver's seat. She hated being near him again, but along with her father's taped confession, they needed proof that Carl was working with Rossi and that Rossi—or more likely, one of his hit men—was responsible for shooting Archer.

Grant leaned through Sarah's open window and looked over at Carl. "Drop her off a block away from the funeral home. My guys will take over from there."

"Got it, boss," Carl said.

A little too eagerly, Sarah thought. She chalked it up to his being happy he was out of jail. *But not for long.* If they played this right, if she got him talking, Carl would be locked up for years.

And so will Dad. The thought was accompanied by a myriad of feelings, each disturbing. Part of her—the hurt, angry Sarah who'd confronted her father at gunpoint yesterday—was glad. He'd done terrible things and deserved to go to prison, should have been put away years ago. But in a different corner of her heart, she could hardly bear the thought of seeing her dad behind bars. She realized that in his own way he'd also loved and protected her.

Still standing beside the car, Grant turned his attention to Sarah. "Be careful." Their eyes met for the briefest moment, then he leaned in, giving her a quick kiss on the forehead. As he backed away, Carl stepped on the accelerator and the car went speeding down the road, headed toward Boston and the funeral of the man she'd killed. It was the last place she wanted to go, and J.D. Rossi was the last person she wanted to meet, but keeping Christa and the boys safe necessitated doing things this way. Sarah prayed that the bulletproof vest beneath her bulky sweater, and the plainclothes police officers stationed at and around the funeral home, would keep her safe.

Conscious of the tiny microphone hidden beneath her collar, she rolled up the window and glanced at Carl. He seemed uncharacteristically quiet—the one time she *wanted* to get him talking. She shuddered involuntarily. If he'd done the things she suspected he had, then he was even worse than she'd always known him to be. But at the very least he was prone to violence, anger, lechery, and—grinning.

From the corner of her eye Sarah caught Carl's leer as he changed lanes, taking a left from Massachusetts Avenue onto Main.

"I thought we were supposed to take the Harvard Bridge," she said casually.

Carl didn't respond but continued to speed down Main. Sarah moved her right hand slowly, edging toward her pocket with the cell phone.

He drove faster, just making the last traffic light before the Longfellow Bridge.

Sarah's fingers closed around the phone.

"Hey!" Carl swerved, slamming her into the door. "Whatcha got? Show me your hand."

She dropped the phone in her lap where he could see it. She'd already dialed.

He grabbed it, lowered his window a couple of inches, and threw it out. "Any other tricks?"

"No." It wasn't the time to pull out the gun concealed beneath her sweater. She cowered in her seat, but inside she was simmering. *What does Carl think he's doing?* Her earlier confidence began draining away, and she wondered if she'd been completely stupid, getting herself into this situation. Maybe she should have driven herself to the funeral, done what she needed to make sure Christa and the boys were safe, then dealt with the Carl issue later. "Where are we going? Rossi won't like it if we're late."

"We won't be. We've even got time for a little fun before you two meet, and you owe me, princess." Carl reached over, squeezing her knee. "I've been sitting in jail because of you."

She pushed his hand away. "My dad got you out."

"But Rossi pays better," Carl said. "Since I told him where to find you, I've made more than I do in six months working for the chief."

I knew it! Sarah stared straight ahead, careful to mask her excitement. This was exactly what they needed. She hoped the mic was picking everything up. "You're working for *Rossi?*" she asked, doing her best to sound shocked.

"Yep. And let me tell you, even from the inside of a jail cell, it's a lot more exciting than following *you* around." Carl pounded his fist on the wheel. "Rossi makes things happen."

"What do you mean?" Sarah asked, still feigning shocked surprise.

"I mean the way we took care of your boyfriend—or his friend, at least. Either way, your guy doesn't have much in life left to look forward to. We fixed him real good."

Sarah swallowed uneasily. For the first time she felt grateful that Jay was in jail, where he was safe for the time being. She refocused her attention on getting Carl's confession while keeping track of their route and surroundings. *Just a little more information, and I'll jump out at the next light, get away from Carl, find a way to get where I'm supposed to be . . .*

"Jay's roommate?" she asked, returning to one of the last things Carl had said. "The one who was shot on the same night a man attacked me in the alley?"

"All me," Carl said, gloating. "I told them where your boyfriend worked and how to find you there, and in exchange they took care of the kid for me. When you posted bail for your boyfriend, I was afraid the kid might go soft and spill his part of the planted drugs."

"So you *shot* Archer?" Sarah's voice escalated.

"Not me." Carl raised his hands and shook his head. "I was locked up; there's no way anyone can pin that on me."

Sarah's stomach twisted with fear and anger as Carl sped through two more lights, taking them farther and farther from their intended course. "Maybe not, but there's another murder on your head—from the fire you started that killed Mrs. Larson."

"Wasn't my idea," Carl said. "The night after I almost ran your boyfriend over—should have—I followed him and heard him and this other guy arguing. One of them mentioned something about a fire—gave me the idea."

Tears burned behind Sarah's eyes as she thought of Mrs. Larson. Carl sped up again, driving so fast Sarah began to fear they'd get in an accident. She looked out the window, wondering what her chances were if she jumped out while the car was moving. They were on the north end of town now, heading toward the waterfront.

"Not thinking of leaving, are you?" Carl's fist wound through her hair, pulling her toward him. "It's gonna hurt my feelings if you don't give me some of what *he's* been getting."

"I'd rather die." She grabbed Carl's hand, trying to pry his fingers away.

"That's already been arranged, sweetheart. But in the meantime, I like these curls, this new look. It's—"

She threw her head back, smashing into his chin. The car swerved. Carl released her as he fought to get it under control. A van passed them on the right, its horn blaring. Sarah unbuckled her seat belt and reached for the door handle.

"Go ahead," Carl said. "Rossi's got a man tailing us. You leave now, they'll shoot you right on the street."

Sarah hesitated, turning in her seat to look back. Carl made a right turn. A sedan two cars behind them followed. She couldn't be certain, but it looked an awful lot like the one the men who'd tried to kidnap James had been driving. Remembering them—and the way she'd pepper-sprayed one and shot the other in the hand—she suddenly wasn't so sure now was the time to jump. Better to take her chances with Carl a little longer. At least she was positive he was unarmed. *If I can just get my gun out . . .*

Carl took a side street, slamming her into the door again, and headed straight for the wharf. The car stayed with them. He grinned. "Told you. When I heard the chief was gonna spring me this morning, I made a little phone call. And anyway, you don't want to leave and miss the boat ride."

Sarah's gaze swung around to the front and the yacht anchored off the closest dock. "Rossi isn't going to like you interrupting his plans like this."

"I'm not." Carl chuckled. "Whose boat do you think that is? Rossi's taking care of your dad across town, but he wanted you here—says it makes things convenient for getting rid of bodies." Carl pulled up along the curb, cut the engine, and jumped out of the car.

Sarah stayed in her seat, her father's voice ringing in her head again, as insistent as he had been last night when they went over and over their plan.

Rossi is evil. He has no qualms about killing, or making his victims suffer first—especially if they've caused him trouble. You've *caused him trouble. Don't go anywhere with Rossi or one of his men. There will be plenty of people at the funeral to protect you.*

But I'm not at *the funeral!* she wanted to scream.

Carl came around the car and reached for the handle. She pushed the door open, shoving it into him, then pulled it shut, locking it and scrambling to the driver's seat to get out of the car that way.

She had one foot on the pavement when Carl dove over the hood and grabbed for her. Sarah screamed for help. Carl ran around the door and hauled her from the car as she fought him. She was reaching for his face when he spun away and a fist connected with his jaw, barely missing hers. Sarah looked up at her rescuer. "Jay!"

"Move," he shouted, punching Carl again, hard, in the eye. She cringed at the crunching sound and jumped aside as Carl fell back to the pavement.

Jay shook his hand out. "Wanted to do that for a long time. Come on!" His other hand grabbed Sarah's, and they ran toward the car she'd seen following them earlier.

"It was *you?* You were following us? But how—" She stopped suddenly, tugging on Jay to get him to do the same. A man with a drawn gun was coming straight at them.

"It's okay," Jay said as the man sprinted past, heading toward Carl, who was struggling to get up. "He's with me—I'm with him. Hurry." He continued to pull her to the car. A bullet whizzed past them, coming from the direction of the dock.

Instinctively she crouched down, running with Jay to the driver's side. They both dove in—Sarah in back—and pulled the doors shut.

Jay started the engine and put the car in gear.

"What's going on?" Sarah asked. "How are you here? Who is that man?" She leaned forward over the front seat, looking out the windshield, watching as Carl began raising his hands as if to surrender. The man who'd passed them stepped closer, gun trained on Carl one second, his entire body crumpling to the ground the next. Sarah flinched then gasped at the reverberating sound of a gunshot. "Who—Carl doesn't have a weapon."

Jay tossed her a cell phone. "Call 911. And get down." He pulled away from the curb.

Sarah punched in the numbers as the car rolled forward and she continued to stare at Carl.

"Look. He *doesn't* have a gun. Just a phone."

"And now isn't a good time for him to be making a call." Jay pressed down on the accelerator and cranked the wheel to the right, driving straight toward Carl. "Hold on." The car bumped over the sidewalk, chasing him to the edge of the wharf. At the last second Jay swerved, keeping them from following Carl over the side into the bay.

Sarah clung to the seat back with one hand as she spoke into the phone, requesting an ambulance and police. Jay drove off the grass, back onto the street, and away from the wharf.

"What about that man? The one you said you were with?" Sarah turned around in her seat to see if he had moved at all. "We can't just leave him."

"We have to," Jay said. "Carl wasn't the one doing the shooting. Someone else is still out there—someone who wants you dead. Agent Miller would expect us to leave."

"*Agent?*" Sarah said. "As in—"

"DEA, FBI—I'm not really sure," Jay said. "There are so many people involved in this now."

"So many people hurt because of me. Another person has been *shot* because of me." Sarah climbed over the seat to the front.

"*Not* because of you." Jay gave her a rueful look. "Someone might still follow us. You should stay in back. It'd be safer for you to lie down there."

"So you can be the target?" She shook her head. "I don't think so." She reached under her sweater, pulling a pistol from a belt at her waist. "We should go back."

Jay looked in the rearview mirror. "No. Give the police some time to get there."

Sarah turned around in her seat. "It'll be too late then. That man may be dying."

"He's a trained professional," Jay said. "I know how you feel, but I can't just take you back there. It isn't safe."

"Like I've *ever* been safe," Sarah said, but she faced forward in her seat again. "Want to tell me what's going on then? How you're out of jail, how you knew where I'd be?"

"You sprang Carl just as the feds were arriving to chat with him. They'd gotten word of Rossi's vacation plans, and Kirk convinced them it'd be wise to see if Carl knew any details—like where you were." Jay looked over at her, relief evident on his face. "But then you were there, and *appeared* to be going with him willingly. I knew that couldn't be the case, so I got in the car with Agent Miller to follow you."

"But *you* were in jail too," Sarah said. The sound of wailing sirens came from the direction of the wharf.

"I only spent about five hours locked up—long enough for Kirk to make sure a story about my arrest broke that night, and long enough for the DEA to come in and take over."

"So this whole time—these past two days—you've been free?"

"Free and *frantic*." Jay reached over and squeezed her hand. "We tried to find you. An agent searched your dad's house when he wasn't home. Others combed the neighborhood. Kirk and I even spent the night at his friend's house again, hoping you might come back there."

"You mean the house you and I stayed at—the one with the motor home parked beside it?" Hysteria tinged her voice.

"Yes." He glanced at Sarah as she leaned her head against the seat and laughed.

"Oh, Jay."

"What's so funny?" he asked.

"Nothing." She leaned over and kissed him on the cheek. "I'm so happy to see you, so glad you're okay."

"*Okay?* I think I aged about twenty years worrying about you the past couple of days."

"I'm fine. And I think we should go back now. You heard the sirens. The police are probably there."

"Still not a good idea," Jay said, moving into the left turn lane. "Why did you go with Carl in the first place? Did your dad force you? Did he find you in the attic?"

Sarah shook her head. "I was trying to get testimony from Carl. My dad's already given his, and then Carl was supposed to take me—the funeral! Christa and the boys. What time is it?" She pushed back her sleeve and looked at her watch. "If I don't meet my dad there, something bad will happen to Kirk's family."

"Your dad can't meet you anywhere. He was arrested as soon as you and Carl took off—or at least that was the plan last I heard."

"He was leaving to meet Rossi at a funeral as soon as we left," Sarah said. "Most of Dad's officers are *already* there—undercover. We had a big meeting with everyone at the station at six this morning." She placed her hand on Jay's sleeve. "If Dad doesn't show with me, then Christa and the boys are in trouble. Rossi knows where they are."

"Nothing's going to happen to Kirk's family." The light changed and Jay made a left turn. "The night Kirk arrested me, your dad threatened Christa and the boys, alerting Kirk that your dad—and whoever he was working with—might know where they were. Federal agents picked them up that night. I don't think they're even in the state now."

"Really?" Sarah leaned against the headrest, sighing with relief. "Then I *don't* have to meet with Rossi, I don't have to—" She frowned. "But you aren't positive my dad was arrested?"

"Call Kirk. He was there. He'll know." Jay nodded to the phone still in her hand. "And ask *him* if he thinks it's a good idea if I take you back to the wharf."

Sarah found Kirk's number and called, putting him on speakerphone when he answered.

"Hi, Kirk," Sarah said. "I'm with Jay, and he told me my dad had been arrested. I was wondering if you could tell me where they took him."

"Are you two all right?" Kirk asked, his voice sounding odd and strained as it carried through the phone.

"We are," Jay said. "But Detective Miller was hit. Sarah called 911, and an ambulance and police should be there by now. There was only one shooter that I could tell, though possibly more on the boat."

"I doubt it," Kirk said. "Agents combed Rossi's yacht this morning and found absolutely nothing—no one. It was a false lead."

"But that's exactly where Carl took her," Jay said.

"What about my *dad?*" Sarah asked again. She didn't care about Carl or yachts right now, but a sickening feeling of urgency was growing in the pit of her stomach. If her dad had been arrested—fine. They both knew that was going to happen before the day's end, *and* it meant he was safe. *But* if he'd gone to see Rossi alone . . .

"The DEA wasn't able to apprehend him because a car picked him up almost as soon as you and Carl had pulled away from the curb. Unfortunately our tail lost them. Do you have any idea where he might be headed?" Kirk asked. "Almost all the officers from his station are missing too. Do you know anything about that?"

"Yes," Sarah answered, dread settling deep in her heart. "I know exactly where they are."

Chapter Sixty-Seven

An UZI pressed between his shoulder blades, Grant preceded Rossi into the darkened chapel. In the dim light shining from the foyer behind them, Grant squinted, taking in the empty pews, the silence, the casket at the front. His step faltered as instinct kicked in. "Where is everyone?"

"I persuaded the director and his employees to take the day off," Rossi said casually. "Told them we wanted a private viewing."

Grant nodded, pretending that made perfect sense, though J.D. hadn't answered his question at all—not only as to where the mourners were, but where over half of the Summerfield police force had disappeared to. They'd been the ones posing as the director, ushers—

"Don't worry too much about your guys," Rossi said as though he'd read Grant's mind. "I went easy on them. There won't be any murders on the news tonight—none you'll be around to hear about anyway," he added with a chuckle.

"They'd better be okay," Grant said in an equally menacing tone. Worry for the men under him—those who'd trusted him to uphold the law and to keep them safe—made his chest tighten. And on the heels of fear for them came fear for his own life—and especially Sarah's. *Where is she?* he wondered again. She should have been here by now, and he felt relief mingled with fear that she wasn't. It was on the tip of his tongue to demand that J.D. tell him what he'd done with her, but there'd been no mention of Sarah, and if there was any chance she'd never come, that she was safe . . .

"Take a seat." Rossi nudged Grant into the second pew from the front. "We may have to wait a while."

"What are we waiting for?" Grant asked, unsure he wanted to hear the answer but certain he needed to figure out what Rossi had planned—and fast.

"Your daughter, of course."

Grant struggled to hide his unease. Without his men in place to protect Sarah, he didn't want her within five miles of here.

Instead of sitting, Rossi continued to the front of the chapel. "We had a little hiccup, but she's en route now." He reached the casket and ran his fingers over the polished wood. "Cherry," he said. "Nothing but the best for someone who's served us so long."

"Where's his family?" Grant asked. *Where are the rest of your thugs?*

"As I said, *she's* on her way." Rossi flipped open the top half of the casket. It was empty.

"What I can't decide," Rossi said, "Is whether I should kill you before I put you inside, or if I should let you suffocate once you're in there." He turned to Grant. "Which do you think your daughter would prefer?" Without waiting for an answer, he continued. "After all, I still remember the scene at her mother's funeral, the way Sarah threw herself across the casket sobbing. Quite touching. Do you think she'll do that for you?"

"No!" Grant stood, his hands gripping the back of the pew in front of him. "Sarah hates me. She wants nothing more than to see me in jail—or dead. So whatever you hope to achieve by this—"

A shaft of light from the back of the chapel stopped his speech. Grant turned, hoping against hope that he wouldn't see Sarah.

"Everything all right, Mr. Morgan?"

It wasn't Sarah, but that boyfriend of hers—alone. Grant had never felt so relieved in his life.

"Detective Anderson said we should hurry over here," Jay said, glancing at Rossi momentarily. "That you'd been hurt."

We. Grant's fear returned.

"But I told Sarah I wanted to make sure everything was okay first. After all, things didn't go so well with your nephew."

What happened with Carl? Is Sarah all right? Before Grant could ask, Rossi spoke.

"You're a poor liar, Mr. Kendrich." J.D. left the casket, venturing down the aisle toward them. "Sarah would no more allow you to come here by yourself than she'd allow Kirk's family to be in any kind of danger. And Grant—" Rossi threw a glance his direction. "I can't believe you didn't realize we had *every* room in the station wired."

"They *aren't* in danger," Jay said.

"And Detective Anderson isn't really the one who sent you here," Rossi replied calmly. "Amazing what can be done with cell phones these days, isn't it? I'm afraid his number was temporarily forwarded to a colleague of mine."

Grant noted Jay's hesitation. For the first time since he'd entered the chapel, Jay didn't appear as confident. Behind him, the double doors creaked shut, leaving them in almost total darkness, save for the lone skylight at the back of the room. *To our advantage*, Grant thought.

"We were just about to get started," Rossi continued. He swung the UZI in Grant's direction again. "Commemorating the end of the Rossi-Morgan era. Grant's going to take his permanent retirement in that casket, and Sarah's going to take a little cruise with me. You, Mr. Kendrich, will have to join her cousin at the bottom of the ocean, I'm afraid, as I didn't plan for extra guests." Rossi nudged Grant with the gun.

Grant slowly began making his way toward the aisle. *Let her be gone. Please let Sarah really be somewhere else.*

Instead of trying to leave, Jay took a step forward.

"Don't annoy me, Mr. Kendrich," Rossi said. "And I'll see that you have a quick, painless death. Unlike my friend here, who deserves much less."

Grant reached the front.

"Stop here," Rossi said, leveling the gun at Grant's temple.

A gunshot echoed through the chapel at the same moment Grant felt a bullet whiz by. Behind him, Rossi yelled. Grant turned on him, reaching for the gun, taking advantage of the moment. Lights flickered on above them, and he saw the blood oozing from just above Rossi's collarbone. *High and to the right. Sarah.*

"*You* stop." Sarah's voice, full of authority, reverberated through the chapel. Grant turned his head and saw her walking toward them, pistol drawn as if she were a match for Rossi and his machine gun.

Rossi laughed. "You were almost too late," he called, "to say good-bye to dear, old dad."

"Get out of here, Sarah!" Grant shouted.

"No, Dad. He's ruined your life—our entire family. No more."

Rossi's eyes met Grant's for a split second before he pulled away, turning toward Sarah and taking aim.

"No!" Grant shouted, launching himself at Rossi at the same moment he saw Jay knock Sarah to the ground. More shots sounded, and pain blazed through Grant's back. He fell forward, and all was silent.

Chapter Sixty-Eight

April 2006—four months later

Jay lagged behind as Sarah led him toward the entrance of the Casablanca restaurant. Though he'd passed this place several times—thinking of Jane and how she'd compared him to Humphrey Bogart—he'd never eaten here. He didn't need to see the menu to tell it was pricey. "You're kidding—right?" he asked as they reached the door. "'Cause if we have this kind of cash, maybe we should use it for a down payment on a car or something."

"Who needs a car when public transportation is so great?" Sarah said. "Besides, we have a lot to celebrate. Having your name cleared and getting back into Harvard—with a letter of apology, no less—is a pretty big deal."

They stepped inside, and he lingered behind while Sarah spoke to the maître d'.

"We're in luck," she said a minute later. "We can get a table in the lounge right away." She linked her arm through Jay's.

He glanced up, taking in the twenty-five-foot murals. The hostess led them to a cozy table beneath Humphrey and Ingrid.

"This is cool," Jay said after they were seated in two oversized, rattan chairs.

Sarah beamed at him. "This is *you*. I've wanted to take you here for a long time—a little thank-you for saving my life."

"I think the who-saved-whom issue is still in question," Jay said. "You had the gun."

"There's saving, and then there's *saving*," she said as their eyes met. "You opened up the world for me."

He brought her hand to his lips and kissed it. Doing his best to imitate Bogart, he said, "This is just the beginning, sweetheart."

"Hey, you two," Kirk called as he and Christa walked toward the table. "None of that."

"You didn't tell me you invited *these* guys," Jay said, pretending to be upset.

"I asked Trish and Archer to come too," Sarah said. "But they already had plans. Archer had tickets to the theater."

Good for them, Jay thought. He was glad both Archer and Trish were recovering well from their physical and emotional trauma. The Archer that had emerged from a coma eight weeks ago was a kinder, gentler, more considerate boyfriend, and while Trish wished Arch could've gotten there another way, she was happy with the changes. Jay wasn't exactly ready to be Archer's roommate again, but he did think he'd finally forgiven him. He'd certainly forgiven Trish. After witnessing Archer's shooting, and being threatened herself, no one could blame her for doing as she was told and pointing the blame toward Jay.

Christa settled in the chair next to Sarah. "We would have been here sooner, but Jeffrey wanted to show James what a cast feels like, so he wrapped him in three rolls of toilet paper and poured my big bottle of glue on top. We had to give him a bath."

Jay burst out laughing, imagining James, sticky and toilet-papered.

"I hope you got a picture," Sarah said.

Christa nodded. "We document all these things, so when James has mental issues as an adult, we can prove it's his brother's fault."

"Speaking of family . . . Have you seen your dad lately?" Kirk asked Sarah as he walked around the table to his own chair.

"Yesterday," she said. "He's crabby as usual, but doing a little better each time I visit. Going from being chief of police to being behind bars hasn't been easy. But his physical therapist tells me he's a little nicer each day. And he's getting around with a walker now—not something everyone who's been shot in the spine can say."

Being alive after what we went through isn't something everyone can say, Jay thought. All too often the scene at the funeral home replayed in his mind. Rossi with that machine gun, Grant—and Sarah standing in that aisle, facing the man who'd destroyed her family. She'd *twice* wounded one of the most successful drug dealers in America. That she'd survived was truly a miracle, one attributable, Jay admitted somewhat begrudgingly, to her father. Though Grant's quick action had saved her life, Jay still had difficulty feeling any sort of goodwill toward him. After all, it was entirely Grant's fault Sarah had been in danger in the first place.

"Any news on a trial date?" Kirk asked, pulling Jay from the disturbing memory.

"Not yet," Sarah said. "And honestly, the longer it takes, the better. After being under Rossi's thumb for so many years, Dad needs some time to work up the courage to testify against him." She looked at Christa and Kirk. "Not that it will shorten Dad's sentence. Last week he admitted to me that he killed Eddie Martin. Carl was the one who set Martin up, but it was my dad who administered the lethal dose of drugs the morning Martin was brought in."

"Drugs Rossi gave him," Kirk said.

Sarah nodded. "Yes."

Jay rubbed her back, wishing away the hurt in her voice.

"I'm okay." She tried to smile. "Dad was trying to keep me safe. After Rossi's man saw Carl with me at the park, he suspected my dad had someone following me—a bodyguard."

"Some guard," Jay muttered under his breath.

"So Rossi didn't trust your dad anymore and wanted Martin as some kind of proof of his continued loyalty," Kirk guessed.

"He wanted Martin dead." Jay tensed as he realized yet again how much danger Sarah had been in.

"And how are your trial preparations going?" Kirk asked.

"As well as can be expected." Sarah leaned into Jay. "My inside sources tell me I have nothing to worry about."

"Jay's right," Kirk said. "You were doing what you thought was your job—getting drugs off the street."

"She *was* getting drugs off the street," Jay said. "Just because she only went after Rossi's competition . . ."

"So are you looking for a job?" Kirk asked, grabbing a menu from the end of the table. "We have a few openings."

"No," Jay and Sarah answered together. Jay wrapped his arm around her protectively.

"I'm quite happy with my new piano students, thank you," Sarah said.

"Enough of this serious talk," Christa said. "Aren't we supposed to be celebrating tonight?" She turned to Sarah. "Have you given Jay his present yet?"

Sarah brought a finger to her lips. "Shh."

"Present?" Jay asked. He sat up straight. "No one said anything about gifts."

"*Gift*," Kirk corrected. "We don't like you *that* much."

"Still, this is a first—a gift when it's not my birthday or Christmas."

"I know." Sarah's eyes shone, reflecting the light of the lantern hanging overhead. "And first experiences should be something extra special."

"How about some special food? What are we eating?" Kirk opened the menu he'd grabbed a moment before.

"The tapas menu is supposed to be the way to go. Maybe we could all pick a couple of different things to share," Sarah suggested.

Kirk made a face as he looked at the choices. "Ew. Curried squash soup, mixed greens, romaine hearts?" He looked accusingly at his wife. "You didn't tell me this place was all about vegetables."

"It's supposed to be Mediterranean cuisine," Sarah said. "You know, like the movie set in North Africa. And Jay *likes* vegetables. Fresh ones," she added.

"*Love* them," Jay said, looking up from his menu. "I think I'll get the crispy thin eggplant with herbed ricotta, roasted tomatoes, and fresh mozzarella." He closed his menu and leaned back in his chair, a smile of anticipation on his face. *Who cares what this costs? This place is great.* He watched Sarah's hair fall across her face as she studied the menu. *She is great.*

"I want the burger," Kirk said. "With extra fries."

"That's my husband." Christa patted his hand. "Always going out on a tastebud limb."

The waiter came and they placed their orders. Jay noticed a jukebox across the room. Excusing himself, he wandered over to it, his eyes scanning the titles, hoping that maybe . . . *Bingo.* He searched his pocket, found a couple of quarters, and put them in the machine. As he returned to their table, the music changed from cool jazz to a song he knew was familiar to Sarah now. It was the song they'd been dancing to when she'd walked out on him those many months ago.

He watched her chatting with Christa and Kirk and noticed the second she recognized the tune. She looked up, eyes following him. Jay didn't sit down.

"Miss Morgan, I believe you still owe a partial debt—in the form of a dance." He held his hand out.

"No one else is dancing." She leaned to the side, peering around him toward the bar.

"No one else is here with *you.*"

"You guys want to join us?" Sarah sent a hopeful, pleading glance at Kirk and Christa.

"No way." Kirk held his hands up. "I don't do vegetables *or* dancing."

Christa punched him in the arm. "I can see why we don't get out much, either."

"The song is going to be over," Jay said. "And I'm going to start charging interest."

"Go on, Sarah," Christa urged. "Be grateful you have a date who *likes* to dance."

Sarah sighed dramatically, but she put her hand in Jay's. He pulled her away from the table and into his arms as "Free Falling" played overhead. He held her close. "I love you, Sarah."

She wrapped her arms around his neck. "I love you too, Jay." She laid her head against his chest, and his arms tightened at her waist. They swayed in a slow circle near the palm trees.

He wondered if she could hear how loud—and fast—his heart was beating. Dancing this way, holding her close, had to be the best feeling in the world. *Free falling, indeed.* He'd fallen about a million miles and crashed through the floor.

The final chorus started to fade. Gradually he became aware of the sounds around them—conversations, dishes clinking, people laughing together. Sarah lifted her head and looked up at him, eyes moist and shining.

"I'll never leave you again," she promised.

"I know." He pulled her close for another hug. When she stepped out of his embrace, she reached in her back pocket and pulled out a small envelope. "Ready for your surprise?"

Jay took it from her and tore open the flap. He pulled out a single photograph—of a beach.

"Wall art?"

She laughed. "Not exactly. Though I hope you'll keep it up for the next four months." She rocked back on her heels as anticipation lit her face. "It's a beach near your home in Washington."

Jay turned the photo over, but there wasn't anything written on the back. "Where did you get this, and what's happening in four months?"

"Come sit down, and I'll explain." She took his free hand, tugging him back to the table, where she took a second envelope from her purse and handed it to Jay.

He opened it and pulled out two papers—two itineraries for flights to Seattle. "We're taking a vacation?" The same worry he'd felt earlier about finances returned tenfold. Sarah barely covered her rent teaching piano. He was touched she'd planned a trip to his home, but he knew she couldn't afford it.

"Reward money," Kirk said, as if he'd read Jay's mind. "Sarah wouldn't let me tell you. You've got a wad coming your way."

"Don't you mean *her* way?" Jay asked. "Sarah was the one who— "

"When we're *married*"—Sarah placed her left hand over his—"everything that's mine will be yours."

Jay looked from Sarah to Kirk and Christa—all staring at him with slightly goofy expressions. He returned his gaze to Sarah. "*Are* we getting married sometime soon?"

She sighed as if she'd been holding her breath for an hour. "I thought you'd never ask." She pointed to the photo. "Even in the picture this beach looks breathtaking. Look how far you can see the ocean, and I imagine at night, if the sky is clear, we'll be able to see hundreds of stars."

"Endless possibilities as far as the eye can see," Jay said.

"But I'll only be looking in your eyes," Sarah said. "When I promise to love you and always stay by your side."

Epilogue

Holding her daughter's hand, Jane walked across the beach toward Jay. "You're the only guy I know who could pull off getting married in a tuxedo and bare feet."

Jay shrugged as he looked down at his toes and the sand squished between them. "Sarah wanted to get married on a beach, and I can't stand the feeling of sand in my shoes." He grinned. "I was just trying to please my *wife.*" The word rolled off his tongue easily. He'd waited a long time to say it—eight months of being engaged, and a lifetime before that, searching for the perfect girl.

"She seems pleased with your wedding gift," Jane said, inclining her head toward Sarah, several feet away, bouncing up and down on her own bare feet as Jane's husband, Peter, showed her how to use the telescope Jay had given her shortly after the ceremony.

"Tell Pete I really appreciate his help picking that out. And I really appreciate *your* help finding this place and—with everything."

"It's been my pleasure." Jane let go of Maddie, and the little girl squatted down, scooping up two fistfuls of sand and dumping them on top of her sandals.

"She doesn't seem to have a problem with sand in *her* shoes," Jay observed.

"Of course not. I've been encouraging her to play in the dirt since before she could walk." Jane leaned over, her own fingers digging in the sand to retrieve a shell. "Look, Maddie."

"Eat?" the little girl asked.

"No, silly," Jane said. "It's a seashell." She brushed Maddie's fingers over the sea-polished ridges. "Isn't it pretty?"

Jay thought Jane looked especially pretty in that moment, kneeling beside her daughter, head bent close to the little girl who looked nothing like her. Jay could see the love Jane felt for the child who had become hers only through a series of extreme, trying circumstances.

His heart constricted as he indulged in a fantasy that perhaps wasn't so farfetched anymore. In his mind he could see himself and Sarah walking along this beach, a little child between them, her hands nestled in theirs.

Jane stood again, brushing the sand from her dress. "I'm glad everything went so well. It was nice your friends could come. I enjoyed visiting with them."

"Kirk and Christa are great," Jay agreed. That they'd flown all the way out to Seattle so Christa could be Sarah's maid of honor and Kirk could walk her down the "aisle" on the private beach Peter had arranged, was definitely going above and beyond. Though Jay suspected Kirk and Christa were enjoying the trip—the first vacation they'd taken without their boys—almost as much as he and Sarah were.

"I'm so happy for you," Jane said. "If I've done any good in my life . . . today's evidence of it. You're doing so well, and Sarah's perfect—told you you'd end up with a blond," she added, the sparkle in her eyes and her half smile telling Jay she remembered the long-ago moment they'd shared.

It was that day at the airport, her words of praise about his character and chivalry, that had become his catalyst to truly change and had helped make him into the man Sarah loved.

"*Everything* you've ever told me has been right on." Jay felt his heart swell with gratitude. But this time, his feelings toward Jane ended there. He would always be grateful to her, would always feel he owed her a debt, but it was Sarah he loved.

"*Pay It Forward,*" Jane said, as if she'd read his mind about the debt he felt. "I helped you once, and you've gone on to help Sarah—and a lot of other people, it seems."

"You and your movies." Jay laughed. "And I didn't set out to do anything great. It all started when I heard her play the piano."

"Mine started with a phone call." Jane's expression grew tender as she looked Peter's way. "You never know what will happen in life."

"I hope I know exactly what is going to happen in mine and Sarah's. We just want to finish school, find a nice little house somewhere, and settle down into a very *quiet* sort of existence." The only kind of shooting Sarah was interested in had to do with stars, and that was fine by him.

Jane stepped closer. "Will you do me one favor while you're having that nice, quiet life?"

"Okay." Jay stuck his hands in his pockets, wondering what she wanted.

"Keep hanging out with Kirk," Jane said. She leaned her head back, looking at the sky and the stars beginning to appear. "And listen to what he says. Everything he tells you will be right on too."

* * *

Jay picked out a tune on his guitar as he watched Sarah, standing a few feet away, eyes glued to her new telescope. He was beginning to wonder at the wisdom of giving it to her on their wedding day, quickly turning into wedding *night,* when he'd hoped her fascination would lie elsewhere. It had been almost an hour since the last of their small wedding party left, and while stars were great, he found his wife much more interesting. "Sar-ah," he sang. "Stars are shining in your eyes."

"Is that a real song?" She turned from the telescope and the breeze caught both her hair and dress, blowing wisps of blond around her face and pulling the fabric close to her body, outlining her figure.

"Sort of." Jay strummed the melody again. "I changed the words a bit, but the tune is borrowed from an eighties band called Jefferson Starship."

She shook her head as she walked toward him. "You must know a million songs."

"At least," Jay said. "Good thing I have a lifetime to play them for you."

She sat beside him on the blanket and then lay down, staring up at the night sky. Jay put his guitar away and lay beside her, reaching for her hand. She shivered and he reached over, flipping a corner of the blanket up, partially covering her.

"We could go inside." He inclined his head toward the cabin, just up from the beach, that was theirs for the next three nights.

"In a minute." Sarah rolled on her side, wrapping the blanket around her as she faced him. "So much for swimming."

Jay grinned. "The Pacific Northwest isn't known for its warm water and great beaches."

"But it's beautiful just the same," she said.

You're beautiful. "Think you could ever live here?" Jay asked.

"I could live anywhere you are." Sarah scooted closer, placing her hand on his face. "I'll be happy anyplace, so long as we're together."

Jay leaned over, kissing her, feeling his heart swell with love as she reached for him, pulling him close. They held each other tightly as quiet waves lapped the shore and all the stars in heaven shone overhead.

Endless possibilities in every direction.

About the Author

Michele Holmes spent her childhood and youth in northern California and Arizona. After marrying her high school sweetheart in the Oakland Temple they moved to Utah, and she now feels very blessed to enjoy a beautiful mountain view from her Provo home.

Michele graduated from BYU with a degree in elementary education—something that has come in handy with her five children, all of whom require food, transportation, or Band-Aids the moment she sits down at her computer.

In spite of all the interruptions, Michele is busy at work, with more story ideas in her head than she will ever likely have time to write. Michele's first published novel, *Counting Stars,* won the 2007 Whitney Award for best romance. *All the Stars in Heaven* continues the story of one of the characters from that first novel.

To learn more about Michele's writing, please visit her Web site at michelepaigeholmes.com, or the Writers in Heels blog. You may also contact her via Covenant email at info@covenant-lds.com or through snail mail at Covenant Communications, Inc., P.O. Box 416, American Fork, UT 84003–0416.